THE WAR ON ALL FRONTS

KIM OCLON

TRISM BOOKS
Turning Pages. Growing Minds.

The War On All Fronts / Oclon, Kim

ISBN 978-1-7363474-0-9

[1. LGBTQ – Fiction. 2. Vietnam War – Historical Fiction.
3. Friendship – Fiction.] I. Title.

Printed in the United States of America
10 9 8 7 6 5 4 3 2 1

Trism Books, Deerfield, IL, USA
www.trismbooks.com

For Wallace

You amaze me.

I can't wait to see how you leave your mark on the world.

PART I
THE WAR AT HOME

JULY 28, 1967

Thousands of little pins pricked Anthony's hand as he ran it over his freshly buzzed head. He had decided to do it himself so he could get used to what he looked like without the usual shag of black hair hanging over his forehead. After staring in the mirror for a minute, he decided his nose looked bigger, his eyes wider. But it did make him look a little tougher.

Anthony's twelve-year-old sister, Maria, looked at him as she headed upstairs with a glass of milk and the latest Trixie Belden mystery. She didn't read Nancy Drew because *everyone* read Nancy Drew.

"You look weird." A thick curtain of bangs covered her forehead while her hair flipped out, just above her shoulders.

"I'm going to miss you too."

Maria stopped midstep, and turned to Anthony. "You don't think I'm going to miss you?"

Anthony smiled. "You're not going to miss me."

"Yes, I am. I'm going to miss you so much." She continued up the stairs, not spilling a drop from her milk.

Anthony rubbed his head. It felt like low-grade sandpaper.

The screen door thwacked on the side of the house. That couldn't be Anthony's mom. She wasn't supposed to be home for a couple hours at least.

"I gotta see it! Where is he?"

Anthony grinned and turned to see Sam step over the bulging duffle bag sitting in the doorway. Sam stopped suddenly, as if a ferocious dog jumped in front of him. His playful eyes widened. The smile morphed into an "O." The shoulders tensed.

But as quickly as it left, the smile returned, the shoulders relaxed, the eyes glinted. "Well, that's a fuckin' improvement if you ask me."

Anthony punched Sam in the arm. "Asshole."

"I tell it like it is," Sam said, leaning back, hands in his pockets, taking in the yellow walls and matching green furniture.

"Ma's over at St. Francis's making these care packages to send to the guys over there," Anthony said.

"Are you going to deliver them yourself?"

"Come on, Sam. That's how you want to spend our last few hours?"

"We could have a lot more time."

Anthony rubbed his head again. "What's your bag, man? You're leaving in a few weeks."

"That's different. It's college."

"It's not here." Anthony scraped a chair across the vinyl kitchen floor and flopped into it, folding his arms. This was not how the afternoon was supposed to go.

"It's not there."

Anthony lowered his chin. The only thing he knew about *there* was what the TV told him every night. There must not have been any sidewalks in Vietnam, only rice paddies. They always showed the soldiers trudging through shallow water. Whenever an image of a blindfolded Vietcong fighter or injured American soldier came on, Anthony's parents would make Maria get something from the kitchen. His mom always gasped and clutched the medal of the Virgin Mary that hung around her neck when an American soldier on a stretcher was carried across the screen. And now Anthony was going *there*. He couldn't believe the North Vietnamese had held on for this long. They looked weak in the T-shirts they were sometimes captured in. Some of them wore these wide hats that had to be useless when it came to stopping a bullet.

Anthony's dad kicked Nazi ass in World War II, and had a hand in saving the world from evil forces. Just like a real-life Superman, minus the cape. But with a gun. Those VCs didn't look evil, but that didn't mean they weren't.

"I was never going to cut it in college," Anthony said.

"You could have tried," Sam countered, folding his arms. A hint of a smirk twitched at his upper lip.

"No point in trying." Anthony eyed the clock above the stove. His mom had sauce simmering all day and veal thawing out on the counter. The makings of a big feast. There was a lot of cooking to do and she'd have to come home soon to get started. "And no point in trying to change my mind. You want to try again or you want to do something else?"

"Something else." A sly smile passed over Sam's face. "Maria home?"

"She's in her room with a new book. She said she'll miss me."

"She'll stay away?" Sam asked.

"I don't bother her. She doesn't bother me." Anthony darted to the stairs and raced up the short flight, feeling a tingling spread from his chest to his arms as he heard Sam a step behind him. They hurried past Maria's door and the numerous signs taped on it. Big bubble letters in a variety of colors. One said *Keep Out, Girls Only*. Another said *No Boys Allowed*. Anthony's favorite said *Brothers must knock before entering*.

As soon as Sam crossed the threshold into his room, Anthony shut the door and dragged his desk in front of it. He turned to Sam, leaning on the desk and feeling the smile on his face fill his body. Anthony's eyes traveled from Sam's dark brown hair, to his blue eyes and all over his pale skin.

"What are you looking at?" Sam covered himself like a cartoon character who suddenly realized he was naked.

"I bet guys get photographs of their girls back home all the time. Since I can't hang a picture of you next to my bunk or tuck one in my helmet, I'm making sure I remember everything about you."

Sam raised his eyebrows and held his arms out, slowly turning in a circle. "Got everything?"

"I hope." As Anthony's eyes traveled over Sam's parted brown hair and down to his fingernails bitten to the skin, he remembered how he had tried to push away everything he felt when he first saw *The Good, the Bad, and the Ugly.* Clint Eastwood came on screen with those steely eyes and Anthony almost choked on his popcorn. With his dad whacking him on the back, the only thing Anthony could think about was how beautiful the man on screen was. But guys didn't call each other beautiful. Guys didn't look at Clint Eastwood and feel the things Anthony did. But with Sam, he didn't want to push those feelings into his depths and he didn't have to. He learned he wasn't the only one.

Sam took a step forward.

Anthony took a step, inches from Sam.

And before he knew it, Sam's face was directly in front of his and they were kissing. Their lips moved around one another as if they were trying to find a way to perfectly line up. They stopped to take a breath and smile at the floor.

"Should we put on some music?" Anthony asked.

"Sure." Sam sat on the edge of the bed.

Anthony picked up the needle on his record player and set it on the record. The refrain of "Sloop John B" started playing.

"Ugh. The Beach Boys? Really?" Sam flopped back and put a blue and white plaid pillow over his face.

"Yes, really." Anthony grinned as he lay next to Sam. They lay side by side, their arms touching.

"Jimmy says it's hot there. *Really* hot. You need a machete to cut through the heat." Sam picked up Anthony's olive arm and held it next to his own pale one. "You're gonna catch some rays and come back with a righteous tan." He smiled to himself. "Because you're going to come back."

Anthony rolled on his side to face him. He saw his reflection in the pupil of Sam's eyes. His reflection got bigger and bigger as he leaned into him. He closed his eyes and kissed him again.

Sam's mouth broke from Anthony's and he pulled him into his body. Anthony burrowed his head into Sam's hair, reminding him that he no longer had hair hanging over his forehead. He hoped his prickly scalp didn't scratch Sam as he rested his cheek against it. Anthony pulled Sam closer, knowing it was impossible to get any closer. But he tried anyway.

"I'm going to come back," Anthony said into Sam's hair. "I will." After holding each other for a moment, they lay side by side, holding hands. Anthony glanced from the wall of White Sox pennants to the desk with books piled with school supplies from last year. It looked like a bedroom that belonged to a kid. He and Sam spent so many secret moments in this room, whenever they knew the house would be empty. Sam's house was never an option because his mom was *always* home. It wasn't the first time they kissed with Maria hiding out in her room, but it was the first time they ventured to his bed with her so close by.

Sam sighed and grinned at Anthony as the closing notes of "Sloop John B" faded and the intro to "God Only Knows" started up.

"Do you think God hates us?" Anthony asked. It was one of his favorite songs but it also made him ask questions he tried so hard not to think about.

"I ask myself that a hundred times a day."

"Me too," Anthony said to the ceiling.

"I hope he doesn't," Sam said.

"Do you think…" Anthony stammered. "Do you think he'll make sure I die over there?"

"He better not." Sam propped himself up on his elbow. "Because we have big plans."

Anthony smiled and faced Sam. "Oh yeah? Like what?"

"Well, nothing crazy at first. I have a lot of school left, but I bet you can get your job back at the garage so we can save some dough."

"What do I need to save money for?" Anthony asked.

"We'll have to figure that out. I heard New York City is an expensive place to live. California?"

"California is by the ocean." Anthony rested his head on Sam's shoulder. "Let's go there."

"Sounds like we have a plan." Sam leaned his head against Anthony's. "Don't die, Anthony." He held up a hand.

"Wait for me, Sam." Anthony laced his fingers with Sam's and squeezed. With the summer heat wafting into his room, Anthony closed his eyes, thinking about California and ocean breezes. He'd never been there but would make it there one day with Sam. God only knew where he'd be without him.

A pounding came from somewhere. At first it sounded far off but once Anthony shook the daze out of his head, he realized the noise came from the other side of his bedroom door.

"What the—" Anthony rolled and fell out of bed.

"What?" Sam jumped up.

Anthony's eyes darted to the door, double-checking the desk was still in place. His heartbeat throbbed in his head.

Another pound. "Ma says come downstairs." Maria's voice came from the other side.

"Shit," Anthony muttered. He went to rake his hands through his hair, but it wasn't there. "For Christ's sake, Maria. Do you have to sound like the house is being dive bombed?"

"Come on, it's your last dinner with us." Maria whined like a kid with two nickels burning a hole in her pocket, begging her big brother to take her to get an ice cream cone.

"I'll be down in a second," Anthony called to the closed door.

Several squeaks on the stairs told Anthony that Maria was on her way to the kitchen and he and Sam only had a few moments left. He threw Sam his shirt. "Jesus, how can you be so calm?" Anthony turned his shirt inside out even though it was already the right way.

"Practice." Sam slipped his shirt over his head. "Lots of practice." He straightened out his clothes and modeled them for Anthony. "How do I look?"

Despite knowing his mom was downstairs, piling food on plates and waiting to serve them, Anthony had to pause and take in Sam. The ever-present smirk, the eyes he was swimming in minutes before, the arms that were wrapped around him until Maria interrupted them. "Why did we fall asleep? Why did we spend our last few minutes sleeping?"

"I had fun."

Anthony smiled.

"Come on," Sam said. "I'm hungry."

Anthony led the way. His mom gasped upon seeing him and he immediately looked at Sam. Was there something about his hair, his shirt, anything that gave them away? They'd made out before but always made sure they were fully composed way before anyone would be home.

"What?" Anthony stammered.

His mom walked over. "You did it," she said with a sad smile. "You said you were going to." She reached out and touched his head.

"Oh yeah." Anthony rubbed his head with a nervous laugh.

"You'll get used to it," Anthony's dad said from his seat at the head of the small rectangular table. His greasy coveralls lay in a heap by the door and he still wore the T-shirt that was much whiter when he left for work. "I liked it so much, I decided to keep it." Anthony's dad pointed to his own head of closely cropped hair, black with a sprinkling of white and gray.

Maria studied Anthony as he sat down. "I'm not used to it yet." She moved her serving of veal to the edge of her plate, away from the small mound of spaghetti and meatballs.

Anthony's mom picked another full plate up off the counter. "You're joining us again, Sam?" She raised an eyebrow, clearly already knowing the answer.

"I'll never turn down an invitation to a dinner you made, Mrs. Lorenzo." Sam sat and made a show of picking up his knife and fork like someone who hadn't eaten all day. "My mom's specialty has been TV dinners ever since Jimmy left. She says she doesn't know how to cook for three people instead of four."

Anthony's mom sat between Anthony and his dad. She reached to her side and squeezed Anthony's hand. "Tell your brother to keep an eye on my son."

"Come on, Ma." Anthony fought the urge to shake his hand from his mom's grasp. "He's in the Air Force. He doesn't even spend any time on the ground."

"He's not going to need anyone to watch over him," Anthony's dad said.

"Can we say grace?" Anthony's mom cut in.

As everyone joined hands, they recited the prayer they had been saying for as long as Anthony could remember. *Bless us, oh Lord, for these thy gifts...* He didn't even think about the words or what they meant. They just tumbled out of his mouth.

Anthony ran a finger over Sam's knuckles. The best part of having Sam stay for dinner was saying grace beforehand. Anthony could hold his hand, in front of people, in front of his family, and no one would think twice about a boy holding hands with another boy. No one thought it was sick and wrong. As everyone bowed their heads and closed their eyes, Sam turned over Anthony's hand to trace the calluses on his hand that came from working under a car at Politti's Garage for the past year.

What would his parents do if he leaned over to the chair next to him and kissed Sam? Full blown, on the lips, just like he did for over an hour in his room before dinner.

Probably send him away. Some place that would *fix* him. Make him normal by any means necessary. That was what everyone said would happen to the history teacher from Bowen who was fired after rumors started to fly around. Maybe his parents would say he wasn't their son. He wouldn't be going to Vietnam, that was for sure. It was pretty clear the army didn't accept everybody, and not on an account of flat feet. But Anthony had wanted to go ever since he was a boy, when he and his friends would play Americans and Nazis instead of cowboys and Indians. Plus, if he could show his dad he was just as tough and strong and brave as any soldier that killed the enemy and won, then maybe, when he got home, he could feel he was like any other man. The only difference was, he loved another man. Well, he'd never told Sam he loved him, but he was pretty sure he did. How could Anthony not love someone who allowed him to be his true self?

"Amen," the Lorenzo family and Sam chorused at the end of the prayer. They were about to let go of one another's hands when Anthony's mom continued.

She did this sometimes, added an extra request if she felt someone especially needed it.

"Dear heavenly Father, please be with my son." Anthony's mom kept her head bowed and her eyes closed as she gave his hand a long squeeze. "Keep him safe. I know there are so many of our boys over there, and all their mothers are asking you to watch over them and keep them safe, but please. Please bring my son home. Amen."

The "Amen" echoed around the table again.

Anthony held on to his mom's hand. "It's only a year, Ma. I'll be fine."

"I'm sure a lot of those boys tell their mothers that."

"It's what I told my ma," Anthony's dad said. "And here I am."

"Maybe I can fix cars or tanks or something." Anthony cut into a meatball with the side of his fork. "With all the stuff I know, I might not even see any action, just the undercarriage of some jeeps."

"Exactly." Anthony's dad took a pull off a sweaty bottle of beer. "Why stay here and fix cars when you can go over there and do it?"

"Do you think you'll be on TV?" Maria twirled her fork to pick up some spaghetti.

Anthony shrugged with a smile. "I don't know. Maybe." He thought about the soldiers on TV half dragging a blindfolded Charlie past the camera. And of the American soldiers on stretchers.

Sam's laugh broke through some of the heaviness hovering over the dinner table. "You're leaving to fix cars in the jungle and she has you coming back as the next Andy Griffith."

Maria made a face at Sam. Sam made the same face but crossed his eyes.

Anthony's mom pointed at Maria with her eyes, her way of saying *enough*. "Eat up. God knows what they put in those cans they make our boys eat out of. We sent ketchup and mustard over there today because it's what they asked for. Ketchup *and* mustard. That's what they use to make the *food* taste better."

"Nobody ever sent me any ketchup," Anthony's dad said and then shrugged. "I don't like that shit anyway."

Now Anthony's dad got one of his mom's looks. "Antonio. Please."

"Could you get me some ketchup from the fridge, pal?" Sam slapped Anthony on the back. "This stuff could use some." He put a whole meatball in his mouth.

"Samuel," Anthony's mom said with mock shock. "I invite you into my house. Feed you. And this is how you say thank you?"

Sam tried to make up for his request with silly apologies while Anthony scanned the people around the table. His mom and Sam laughing at one another. Maria wiping away a milk mustache. His dad dragging a meatball through some sauce and giving him a proud smile before putting it in his mouth. This was what he wanted to remember. This was what he wanted to take with him. What it felt like to be surrounded by the people that mattered most. It took everything inside of him to not reach under the table and grab Sam's hand. It happened in the movies all the time. Steal a kiss. Sneak a touch. Maybe Sam would smack him on the back again and ask him to find some mustard, but the joke must have run its course and everyone was busy eating. His dad's plate was almost empty.

"You can come over any time you want," Anthony's mom was saying to Sam. "I'll always have a plate waiting for you."

"Great," Maria rolled her eyes.

"As much as Maria loves my company," Sam shot her a smile, "I'm not sure I'll be able to commute home for dinner from Madison."

"That's right," Anthony's mom said. "Both of my boys are leaving."

Sam wiped tomato sauce off his mouth with his hand. "You can send me some ketchup whenever you want. It might be better than those cans Anthony has to eat out of, but dorm food won't be like this."

"No more talk about ketchup," Anthony's mom pointed a fork at Sam. A couple spaghetti noodles fell off of it and onto the table.

Anthony's smile spread from his mouth to his chest. He allowed himself to believe for only a few seconds that if he ever did tell his parents about Sam and him, this was what it would feel like. Even though it would never happen, he could at least pretend. He had so much practice pretending, just like Sam.

SEPTEMBER 5, 1967

Sam shuffled the width of his bedroom to the open suitcase on his bed. His arms began to sweat under the load of sweaters dangling from his elbows. He heaved the sweaters into the suitcase and set about refolding them.

"Sammy, let's go! Traffic!" His dad's voice came into the room through an open window.

Sam stuck his head outside, bracing himself against the windowsill. "It's 9:30, Dad."

"I know. We better get a move on." He leaned against the station wagon, tapping the watch on his wrist. "You were supposed to have all of this done yesterday, Mr. Brainiac."

"I'm almost done," Sam yelled to his dad before ducking his head back inside. His dad had a dozen nicknames for him. The most recent ones were created when Sam was awarded an academic scholarship to the University of Wisconsin to study history. His ultimate goal was to become a professor.

Sam tried to blow his hair out of his eyes but it was too damp with sweat. He pressed the sweaters down as much as possible before closing the suitcase. His dad was right. The plan was for Sam to be packed and ready to go by the morning, but Sam had been working at Kinney's, a local shoe store, almost nonstop since Anthony had left. With not much else to fill his days, Sam decided he'd make as much bread as possible before heading off to school, even if it meant kneeling at the feet of men who wanted to get a good deal on the end-of-season sandals.

"Here." Sam's mom came into his room with a smaller, olive green suitcase. "Take this one too."

"That's Jimmy's." Sam felt stupid for stating something his mom already knew.

"Well, he's not going to need it for a while. Bring it back at Thanksgiving." She scanned the walls, looking at his posters of The Who and The Rolling Stones as if they were paintings in a museum that needed to be pondered and analyzed. Then, she moved on to the bookshelf full of model airplanes and boats. Sam had gotten one each year at his birthday and Christmas for five years, even though what he really wanted all those years was a guitar. Below the shelves of kits was a set of presidential biographies from when he was ten and became interested in the founding fathers.

"I wanted to go to college," Sam's mom said to the shelf of airplanes and boats. She beamed at him as if sharing a secret. "I wanted to study English literature. I loved reading Shakespeare."

Sam folded the sweaters as best he could and placed them in his brother's suitcase. With all this extra room, he scanned what was left in his closet. "Why didn't you?"

Sam's mom shrugged with a smile, her hair brushing the collar of her green checked dress. "Your grandfather heard there were jobs available for telephone operators."

Sam nodded. He didn't know a lot about his mom's life before he was born, but he did know she worked as a telephone operator for a few years before Jimmy came along.

"Come on, College Boy!" his dad yelled again from the driveway.

"He's nervous about the empty house too," Sam's mom said.

"That must be it." His dad was probably nervous his mom's cooking would go from TV dinners to bread and butter with both sons gone.

"Well, finish up in here." Sam's mom had to stand on her tiptoes to kiss his cheek. "You know your father hates to wait." He would bitch about it the whole ride there. The wind whipping through the car along with comments about the lucrative sales career he had that didn't require a college education.

When his mom's footsteps stopped creaking in the hallway, Sam lifted his mattress and pulled out a Snoopy T-shirt he took from Anthony's room the last time he was there. It was the one with the faded red collar and little hole in the right armpit. Anthony had four T-shirts with Snoopy on them. He had no idea Sam had taken it.

Sam's new roommate—Paul Aiken from Green Bay, Wisconsin—would probably cover his cork board with photos of him and his girlfriend. Maybe there would be a prom photo. There would definitely be a senior portrait. Sam didn't have any pictures of Anthony and wouldn't be able to hang them even if he did. He couldn't lie and say it was his brother. No one would believe that. So, he took the shirt. It was the one Anthony had worn the first day of school last year when he walked into Mr. O'Brien's English class. Sam had seen Anthony in the halls before that day but this was the first time he'd gotten a good look at him. He had a little ocean wave of black hair above his forehead, and he was wearing this Snoopy T-shirt. Sam had to dig out a pencil and pretend to write something in his notebook to keep from staring.

Sam folded the shirt as small as it would go and tucked it into the corner of his pillowcase. Then, he went to his desk and opened the thin center drawer. In the back, behind an address book he never opened, were the four letters Anthony sent him from basic training. Well, the first one was actually on the bus on the way *to* basic training. The others came from his new home at Fort Campbell in Kentucky. The last one came in the mail yesterday. He seemed to be getting on okay, maybe even digging the runs that went on for miles, saying it was a lot like phys ed except for the guns strapped to everyone's back. Apparently, they even had to run the five miles to the shooting range and back. Anthony said he was surprised by how good he was with the M-14. Sam carefully unfolded the last letter, already fragile from being unfolded and refolded a dozen times.

I thought I saw Drill Sergeant smile when he saw my score the first time on the shooting range. But I probably didn't. I think he's smiled twice. He's everything you thought a drill sergeant would be. Yelling. Swearing. Making guys scrub the toilet with a toothbrush. I didn't think that stuff really happened. No toothbrush duty so far, but I have done about a million push-ups since being here. You do something wrong, you do push-ups. You do something right, you do push-ups. I think the hardest thing is getting my clothes folded just right for Saturday inspection. Mom will make me do the laundry from now on when I get home. Yep, you read that right. WHEN I get home.

Anthony had underlined *when* twice. Sam read those lines as if they were a promise.

Nights are hard. It's hard to fall asleep in a room with a bunch of other guys. Some of them snore, some of them grind their teeth. I've heard some cry. They make fun of you for a lot of little things here, but no one makes fun of anybody for crying in the middle of the night.

The food's not bad. Not good. Nothing like at home. But you know what it needs.

Sam stared at the signature scrawled in a blue pen and bit his lip at the postscript.

Ketchup. Lots of it.

That was their secret. Something no one would decipher or suspect. Anthony's parents would think it was a joke. His own parents might send a case of it over to the boy who had become their son's best friend over the past year. But only they knew what it meant. How it encompassed everything that couldn't be written.

Sam tucked the letters in the address book and folded the sweater sleeves around it. The suitcase closed easily this time, and so did the other one. His whole life, packed into two suitcases. He heaved them off the bed and looked around his room, not expecting to feel sentimental about not seeing it for a few months.

Another blaring honk came in through the window.

"Sammy, the neighbors are going to have a fit if I have to honk this horn again!"

With another sweep of his bedroom, Sam lugged the suitcases out the door. It wasn't like he was going off to war like his brother and Anthony. It was college. And it wasn't far, although he would have preferred somewhere further away, but not across the ocean in a crazy country.

Sam swung open the door to his dorm room in Sullivan Hall with his back because he was holding both suitcases. He hurled himself around to see his home for the next nine months: a square room that could've been mistaken for a juvenile prison cell if not for the open window that allowed in a slightly cooler breeze than the one he left back home. Two metal frame beds were pushed against opposite walls. One was bare, and a blue-checkered bedspread perfectly covered the other one. Not a wrinkle in sight and the corners tightly tucked in. A pencil cup with five sharpened pencils accompanied a small stack of folders on the desk at the foot of the impeccable bed. And there was the photo: a girl in a yellow dress. Some sort of crown-looking thing was nestled in the bouffant of auburn hair.

Sam heaved his suitcases onto the bed on the empty side of the room. His dad barreled in behind him with a box of sheets and towels with a radio resting on top. "Huh," he grunted, looking at the room and putting the box at the foot of Sam's bed.

"Would you like me to help you make the bed?" Sam's mom asked when she came into the dorm room carrying a bag of groceries. She had insisted on stopping to pick up some snacks on the way to Madison. Sam's dad had waited in the car, grumbling.

"I can do it." Sam opened his suitcase and started to put things in the dresser at the foot of the bed. "I've been making my own bed for a few years now."

"I know." Sam's mom sidestepped through the room to put the bag on the desk. "That doesn't mean I can't give you some help this once."

"I'll get to it after you guys split."

Sam's dad made his way to the door. "We probably shouldn't stay too long, Betty. Traffic."

"I know, James," Sam's mom said. "But this is a big day for Sam. Wouldn't you have loved to drop Jimmy off in Texas for his training instead of just putting him on a bus and waving good-bye? "

Sam glanced at his dad. His mom didn't win many battles, but bringing up Jimmy was a good strategy.

Sam's dad glanced at his watch. "Okay. A few minutes."

"Where would you like me to put your pillow?" Sam's mom lifted it off a box and held it with the open side down.

It happened in slow motion. Sam's mom lifted the pillow. The faded red collar of the Snoopy shirt slipped out of the case. It dangled for a nanosecond as if gravity somehow stopped working, then tumbled out and unfolded itself in midair.

Sam froze. His arms wouldn't move. He couldn't catch it.

His mom bent and picked up the shirt, shook out the wrinkles and studied it for a moment. Sam knew she was putting the pieces together in her head. He winced, as if preparing for a punch.

"Where'd this come from?" his mom asked.

"Uh, it's mine," Sam blurted out.

"Hmm." She put her finger in a hole in the shirt. "I don't remember seeing it before."

"I just got it." Sam silently cursed himself. New shirts don't have holes. Lots of *old* shirts don't have holes.

"It doesn't look new."

Sam's dad sighed loudly. "You want to sit around and talk about a shirt, Betty? Have you seen the way the kids dress today? The clothes? The hair? They all look like they live on the damn street. Coming in, I saw a man with hair down to here." He put the side of his hand against a shoulder and then pointed a finger at Sam. "You're here to study. Not to turn into one of those freaks."

"Got it." Sam took the shirt from his mom and stuffed it in the pillow. "All books. No freaks."

A guy in a plaid shirt and a buzz cut stepped into the room. "You must be Sam." He crossed the small room and held out his hand. "Paul."

Sam smiled, taking the guy's hand. "Paul, yeah. Good to finally meet you." He gestured to Paul as if he were a prize on a game show. "Mom and Dad, this is my roommate, Paul Aiken."

"Hello." Sam's mom nodded at him with a smile while his dad grunted a hello.

"Well, we should probably get going." Sam's dad pushed himself off the doorframe.

"So soon? Maybe we could help Sam unpack a bit more? Perhaps have an early dinner?"

"We'll stop for dinner in Milwaukee." He turned to Sam. "I'm sure he can figure this out on his own. He's a smart one."

"I can handle it, Mom," Sam said.

"I know." She embraced him like she was leaving him in the wilderness with only a flashlight and pocket knife. "I love you, Sam."

"Love you too, Mom. Thanksgiving will be here before you know it."

"Nice to meet you, Paul." She turned to Paul, who had taken a label maker out of one of the desk drawers and set it next to a stack of folders. "There's a bag of snacks over there. Make sure Sam shares with you."

"Thank you, ma'am."

"Ma'am? Sir?" Sam's dad looked impressed. He weaved through the tight space and extended his hand to Sam. "Goodbye, son."

Sam looked at the hand for a second before taking it and feeling his dad's grip tighten around his fingers. Not in a way where he was trying to break his hand, but rather his dad's version of a hug.

"Bye, Dad. Don't worry. I'll spend all my time hitting the books. No booze. No girls." Anthony would have thought that last one was hilarious.

"You better."

Sam's mom gave Sam one last smile as his dad left. "He's not one to get choked up."

"Oh, I know."

"I already miss both my boys." She hugged him again. "Let me know if you read any Shakespeare." Sam's mom dug in her purse and gave Sam a handful of change. "Call home whenever you want."

"Thanks, Mom." After she left, Sam put the change in a little pile on his desk. He turned to see Paul standing at attention with his heels together and chin lifted. "At ease, soldier."

Paul actually stepped to the side with his hands behind his back. "Where's your brother going to school?"

"Somewhere along the shores of the Mekong River." Sam lifted the box off his bed and set it on his desk. "At least that's what he wrote in his last letter."

"You're brother's in 'Nam?" Paul unhooked his hands and leaned forward. "How long has he been there?"

"Almost eight months, I think." Sam flung a fitted sheet out in an attempt to get it to cover the bed, but half of it ended up on the floor.

"Neat." Paul picked up the sheet and stretched it to cover the far corner at the head of the bed. "You ever think about joining up?"

"No. You heard my dad. Professor Sam, in the making."

Paul worked on the other corner. "I wanted to join right after high school. I went through ROTC and everything."

"ROTC?" Sam asked. "I was the towel boy for the basketball team."

"All I want to do is go over there and serve my country but they won't let me." Paul straightened up and extended his arms in front of him. He raised his right arm all the way up but the left stayed level with his shoulder. "I can only raise my arm this high."

"Yeah?" Sam asked, inviting Paul to continue because clearly that was what he wanted to do. At least he was helping him make the bed. Sure, he could have done it himself, but Paul did such a nice job on his.

"I dislocated my shoulder when I was eight and had some tissue damage. My brother told me to jump for a tree branch and I couldn't reach it." The incident might have been ten years ago, but the disgust was fresh. "I would join up in a second, but now it's a career in finance for me."

"Bummer." Sam smoothed out the flat sheet. "Thanks for the help."

Paul knelt to fold the bottom of the sheet so it could be sharply tucked into the bottom corner. "No sweat."

Sam took his pillow from the desk, putting the open end toward the wall so he could reach in and pull out the Snoopy shirt whenever he wanted to, in the dark, after Paul was fast asleep. When Sam put his radio on the desk, he noticed Paul's collection of girlfriend photos went beyond the senior portrait. There was one of her leaning against a boss muscle car, one of her and Paul on a porch swing, and a few others.

Paul followed Sam's gaze. "My girl, Debra. We've been going steady since March."

"She's pretty," Sam put his address book in the bottom desk drawer. "Are you going with anyone?"

Sam had to pause, remembering how he told Anthony he had a lot of practice pretending he *wasn't* going steady with someone. He *didn't* think someone was fine as wine. Paul would never know. "Yeah. I am." Saying it made him feel like a ray of sunshine burst from his chest. Paul must have thought he was a bozo for standing there with a stupid smile on his face. He was going steady with someone and someone else actually knew it.

"There's some welcome event going on at Bascom Hill. I think they're giving away some free stuff. You going?" Paul asked.

"You go," Sam said. "I'm gonna put a couple more things away."

As Paul left, Sam still had on the stupid smile. He just wanted a few minutes to hang on to that feeling.

SEPTEMBER 16, 1967

With only a few minutes before lights out, Anthony tore into the letter from Sam that arrived earlier but he was only now getting a chance to read. He'd already hit the showers, a pro at speed washing and keeping his eyes on the faucet thanks to his time in high school phys ed.

As Anthony unfolded the letter, the noise coming from the bunk beds that lined both walls was drowned out by the black ink and block letters.

Anthony,

I'm hitting the books nonstop over here. Here's my day today: get up, breakfast, Bio chalk talk, Early American History chalk talk, lunch, homework, English 101, dinner, and then more homework. Dorm food isn't bad but of course it's not as good as your mom's. I'm going to need some ketchup. Lots and lots of ketchup.

Something in his deepest depths tingled as Anthony rolled over to lay on his stomach. He had never wanted to hug a piece of paper before.

"Whaddya got there, Capone?" Eddie Capstone peered up from the bottom bunk. Almost everyone in the army got a nickname. Being Italian and from Chicago, Anthony's came pretty quickly. It wasn't as creative, but everyone called Eddie Capstone, from Lexington Kentucky, Capper.

"A letter from my buddy." Anthony hoped Capper would get the hint if he didn't look at him. Any other night, he wouldn't have minded shooting the breeze with his bunkmate.

"Seems like you get one every day. My girl hasn't written me in a week." Capper settled back on his bunk. He had been going steady with Lorraine for almost two years, ever since they graduated high school. "When's your mom sending you another package? I like those."

"Me too," Anthony murmured.

College is bitchin. I love it. It's a different world compared to high school. I'm sure you can dig that. What's weird is, there's all these posters hanging up at the student union or on the quad telling me about how the war is wrong and we have to get out of there. I don't know of anyone who LIKES war but these dudes must not know what upstanding people we have over there fighting in this thing. Maybe you can swing by and enlighten them. I know you're going to do your best once you get there. Only a few more weeks now, huh? Remember what I told you about dying, okay? I hope you're-

"Lights out!"

And with that the bunkhouse went black. A few recruits scrambled to their beds in the dark. The dull bang had to be a shin connecting with a bed rail. A muffled grunt followed it.

Anthony held up the letter, trying to find the angle to catch a few slivers of moonlight. But the shadows dancing along the paper made it impossible to read. Besides, his eyelids were starting to droop. Anthony folded the letter as quietly as he could and put it in the envelope before tucking it in his pillow. In the morning, he'd have to put it in his footlocker along with the other letters from Sam and his mom.

He hugged his pillow and ran his feet along the bottom of the bed, letting the coolness of the sheets massage his feet. Particularly the blister on his big toe. At first, the bed was uncomfortable and almost impossible to sleep in, especially in a room with so many other people. Some of whom snored like plane engines. But after the first couple days of runs, drills, crawls, and whatever else, sleep came easy. Especially on rainy days like today. At least it wasn't as hot as it was when he first arrived.

Tonight, Anthony fell asleep seeing his reflection in Sam's blue eyes. The only difference was, in his dream, Maria didn't interrupt them. But something louder did. A clanging of some kind.

"Rise and shine, ladies!"

Anthony's eyes popped open to find the barracks still dark. The daze vanished from his head. He swung his legs over the side of his bunk and hopped down, almost crushing Capper's hand on the way.

"Let's go, girls. The sun might be taking a break, but we know Charlie doesn't!"

Everyone stood at attention at the foot of their beds in their army-issued white boxers and T-shirts. Drill Sergeant Dalton stalked between the two rows of bunk beds eyeing each recruit as he passed them. At first, Anthony was certain the drill sergeant knew everything about him just by looking at him. He could look inside of Anthony and see Sam and all of their stolen time together. But the first time he saw Dalton without his hat on, Anthony was surprised by how young he looked. He might've been only six or seven years older than Anthony. Maybe less.

Dalton reached the end of the row of bunks and turned on the heel of his boots. "Two minutes. Let's go!"

It took a half second to react, but soon everyone was digging through footlockers, groping for T-shirts and fatigues. Anthony dressed quickly. No more dragging ass in the mornings with his mom calling to him every five minutes to wake up. His dad would be proud to know he'd adjusted to the army life quickly and was one of the first ones out the door. While the drill sergeant inspected the group, making sure every stitch of every shirt was smooth and every belt buckle was perfectly centered, Anthony would keep his eyes forward and focused by imagining his dad grinning at him with an "atta boy" smile. According to Anthony's dad, he was one of the top recruits during his training.

The lights outside the barracks cast criss-cross shadows over the shoulders of the soldier in front of Anthony. He felt a soft drizzle on his arms and head. The soft drops didn't bother him as much as the three hours of steady rain earlier.

"What are the two types of soldiers?" Dalton bellowed.

"The quick and the dead!" Anthony and his fellow privates shouted.

"And which are you?"

"Quick!"

Drill Sergeant Dalton lifted his chest and shoulders. "Prove it to me." Everyone knew the routine. Down the path, past the mess hall, up the hill, around the obstacle course. Adrenaline coursed through Anthony's body. His legs and arms pumped in a steady rhythm. Breaths came in short but effective bursts. He found himself a spot in the middle of the pack. It blocked the crisp air, making it feel warmer than it actually was. Sweaty stripes formed on the back of his shirt. But the night runs were invigorating, reminding Anthony of childhood games of capture the flag played right out in the street during the summer months. They went way past sundown despite all the moms repeatedly calling for their kids to come in.

Better bask in the feeling now. Charlie didn't play capture the flag. And if he did, he played with mines.

As they stood in formation waiting for everyone to finish, Drill Sergeant Dalton kept one eye on his recruits and one on his stopwatch. "I think I misunderstood. What kind of soldiers did you fucking say you were?"

"Quick!"

"What kind?"

"QUICK!"

Dalton held up his stopwatch. "Not according to this. Pick up the pace, Privates!"

Part of Anthony groaned at the command. Another round meant at least another fifteen minutes of lost sleep. The other part of him was grateful for the second go-around. His legs were warmed up. The drizzling had stopped. He wanted to be one of those quick soldiers.

Anthony weaved his way to the front, cruising past Capper in the first two hundred yards. But after another fifty yards, Capper caught up, matching him stride for stride. "You wanna race?" Capper asked.

"You wanna lose?"

"Haven't lost yet."

They both kicked it into high gear at the same time. Capper pulled ahead at the hill but Anthony passed him on the way down as gravity did most of the work. Their legs moved in perfect synchronization as they approached the barracks. Drill Sergeant Dalton stood under a light holding his stopwatch up to his face.

Capper leaned forward, jutting out his chest. Anthony felt like he'd left his legs by the obstacle course. Somehow, he was moving but he couldn't feel his legs pumping him forward.

"There's a quick soldier I heard about," Drill Sergeant Dalton said as Capper and Anthony flew past him. "There's another."

Anthony bent forward, hands on his knees, trying to slow the breaths that made him sound like a panting dog. The other guys from his bunk plodded in and dragged themselves into formation.

"If we're not quick then we're dead." The drill sergeant held up his stopwatch as proof even though no one could make out what it said. "Now that you can outrun Charlie, let's learn how to kill him. Without shooting a gun. Hit the sack. Lesson begins at oh eight hundred hours."

Five minutes later, Anthony heaved himself up on his bed, grateful for the two hours he had before the wake-up call. He knew there was more to killing Charlie than learning how to shoot a gun. They had plenty of practice with the M-14 already and he took to it better than he thought he would, not sure how it would feel to fire a real gun. It was a far cry from the plastic things from the Five & Dime he played with when he was a kid.

Drill Sergeant Dalton had come up to Anthony as he cleaned his gun at the end of the first drill. "Not bad today, Private Lorenzo."

Recruits needed to score at least a thirty on the shooting range to pass Basic. With a max score of 84, Anthony already had a 53. He wrote his dad about it already. But tomorrow, it was on to hand-to-hand combat. Shooting the target from a distance was one thing. Actual fighting was another. Looking the enemy in the eye knowing your job was to kill him and his job was to kill you.

Anthony heard the loud snores of the guys who passed out as soon as their heads hit the pillow. All he could think about was the only fight he had ever gotten into. Well, could it still be considered a fight if it only involved one punch that he didn't throw?

He and Maria were walking home from the ice cream parlor with generous scoops of cookies and cream resting on cake cones. There was no way Maria would finish it, but she was only six and wanted to be like her big brother then. This kid from down the block, George Romano, came running in between them and bumped into Maria, sending her ice cream cone to the ground.

"You better lick that up," Anthony had yelled.

"You gonna make me?" George got in his face.

"Yeah." Anthony stepped forward, his face a few inches from George's.

"Gross, man." George jumped. "He's trying to kiss me!"

"No, I'm not," Anthony yelled.

"Get away from me!" George threw a punch that connected with Anthony's chin, sending him to the sidewalk, right next to Maria's ice cream.

"Every man has to take a punch every now and then," Anthony's dad had said when he heard about the incident. He held a frozen rump roast on his son's face. "And you took one to protect your sister. You're a good man, Anthony."

After breakfast, the recruits stood in straight lines, as they always did. Everything in the army was straight.

At Drill Sergeant Dalton's command, everyone grunted a yell while they raised their guns over their heads and stabbed the air with the bayonet attached to the end of it. First high and then jabbing low, perhaps because the imaginary Charlie fell but didn't surrender.

They repeated the routine at least a dozen more times. Each time, the yells intensified and everyone's movements grew more precise. Almost everyone.

"You're not twirling a fucking baton, Private Lorenzo!" Drill Sergeant Dalton bellowed. "If that's how you're going to take on Charlie when you see him, might as well surrender now."

Anthony's cheeks got warmer. Shooting was easier. Lay on the ground, prop up the gun, hit the target, hit the target, hit the target.

But this felt like the square dancing unit in phys ed.

"Attention!" Drill Sergeant Dalton yelled from the slightly elevated wooden platform.

Everyone stood at attention as Dalton stepped down from his perch and snaked his way through the lines. Every muscle in Anthony's body tensed as Dalton got closer. He felt the tendons sticking out of his neck from his clenched jaw. The sun inched higher in the sky, closer to its noon position. Every single ray struck his forehead.

Drill Sergeant Dalton snapped his heels together, inches from Anthony. He could see the slight stubble sprouting from the drill sergeant's face. "Would you prefer a broomstick, Private Lorenzo?"

A droplet of spit landed on Anthony's cheek. "No, Drill Sergeant!"

"Maybe a fairy princess wand?" Coffee breath blew into Anthony's face.

"No, Drill Sergeant!"

"You're real brave from a distance, hiding behind a gun. But what are you going to do when the VC jump out of the jungle?"

"I'll kill him, Drill Sergeant!"

Drill Sergeant Dalton stood so close to Anthony he could see how uneven his bottom teeth were, like a jagged little mountain range. "Show us how it's done Private, and stop dancing around like a faggot!"

Faggot.

Anthony lunged forward with a loud yell, so loud that the privates next to him jerked their knees at the sound. He raised his gun and stabbed the air in front of him.

"Again!" Drill Sergeant commanded.

Again and again. The bayonet stabbed high at the neck and then low at the gut. This time, he was envisioning the chest of Tommy Maloney when he'd strolled into the 7-11 a few months ago. He and Sam were looking over the movie times in a newspaper. It was the second fight Anthony should have gotten into.

Anthony pierced the air, aiming for Tommy's chest.

"You look like a couple of faggots planning a date," Tommy had snickered on the way to the Slurpee machine.

Anthony wanted to charge at Tommy but Sam held him back before he could even put down the newspaper. He wanted a reaction and they couldn't give it to him. Anthony hated Tommy. He should have kicked Tommy's ass. Kicked his ass in front of the Slurpee machine.

Anthony had to settle for beating the shit out of the air today. He kept stabbing and stabbing, and yelling and yelling, trying to forget the look on Sam's face when Tommy walked by.

Finally he stopped, breathing heavily, holding his weapon at attention. He felt tears forming behind his eyes. He willed himself not to blink so the tears would stay put.

Don't cry.

Drill Sergeant Dalton stepped into view with a half-smile. "Well done, Private. We just needed to get you a little pissed off."

Don't fucking cry.

After Dalton dismissed the group and they began making their way to the mess hall, Anthony dropped his weapon to the ground and allowed the heaves in his chest to escape silently. He leaned over, hands on his knees, pretending he needed to catch his breath. The sun glinted on the bayonet's blade, giving Anthony something to stare at.

Capper walked by Anthony and patted his back. "That was pretty badass, Capone."

It was only noon, but Anthony already felt like all the energy he had for the day had been used up. He didn't get a chance to finish reading Sam's letter last night and there definitely wouldn't be time to write a response tonight.

OCTOBER 17, 1967

Sam hesitated, his fingers clamped on the letter in his slim metal mailbox on the main floor of Sullivan Hall. The envelope was long. His mom's were usually smaller and square.

It was from Anthony.

Sam was up a flight of stairs before the stairwell door even closed. He raced up the four flights of Sullivan Hall and speed-walked to his room. He had a few minutes before Paul would come back from his afternoon class and in that time, he could read Anthony's letter and maybe even get in a song on the radio. Paul wasn't the biggest music fan, especially when it came to rock and roll. It was like he had super hearing powers. Even when Sam had the radio volume so low *he* could barely hear it, Paul would ask him to turn it off. Well, he asked at first anyway. Now it was more like a demand.

When Sam threw his books on his bed, his history book bounced a little and his folder fell to the floor. He ignored them and leaned against his desk, tearing into Anthony's letter.

Sam,

Three weeks into AIT and they say I'm too good to hide under jeeps. It's infantry for me. They need me out there in the action. My pops is going to love that. I got the highest score on the shooting range, even better than Capper. But my hand-to-hand still needs some work. It's hard to think about coming face to face with

Charlie. I'm not telling you all this to scare you, but to let you know I'm learning to defend myself. And I'm getting good at it too. I pretend I'm fighting Tommy Maloney and kicking the shit out of him. Like I should have done that day in the 7-11. When it comes time for me to finally get over there, Charlie and all his friends better watch their asses. Capper is doing the advanced training with me and then we'll head out together. Charlie doesn't stand a chance when the two of us get over there.

Sam hadn't thought about Tommy Maloney in months. They didn't say anything to each other as Tommy sauntered to the counter with his Coca Cola Slurpee and paid for it. He went right past them muttering, "See you around, fairies." Tommy hadn't seen Sam put his hand on Anthony's chest to hold him back. They stared at the paper, no longer seeing the movie options and show times, just doing their best to pretend they were.

They had gotten really good at pretending.

He glanced at the date on top of the letter. It was written three days ago. Anthony didn't say how long this part of the training was or how much time he had left.

I hope I get the chance to prove myself and use all this stuff I'm learning. Aside from all those anti-war chickens who don't have a clue what's going on, I don't know what you hear about the war at school. There's talk we might go home as soon as we get there. Things might be slowing down. Someone in the barracks said something about Hawaii. Maybe I'll just get a righteous vacation out of this whole deal. I don't think my dad will be impressed by my sunbathing skills but my mom might. She sends biscotti every couple weeks and I'm the most popular guy on those days.

Food at AIT is mostly stuff out of a can that we eat in the field while on a drill. It could taste worse. But, it could use some ketchup. It always could.

Write soon.

Sam turned the dial on the radio. Through the static came "Light My Fire" by The Doors, a worthy soundtrack for the second reading of Anthony's letter. He leaned against his desk, half-sitting on it as Paul came barging into the room. He tossed his books on his desk, knocking over his pencil cup. With a huff, he shoved the pencils in the cup and put his books into a straight little tower.

"Having a good day?" Sam asked, keeping one eye on the letter.

"BS Sam! That's what this is, BS!" Paul folded his arms.

"Did you get a B on a test or something?" After a month of living with Paul, Sam had learned that he was an expert at two things: making a bed and being a complete spaz.

"Of course not," Paul huffed and then looked around the room as if trying to figure out where an offensive odor was coming from. He zeroed in on Sam's radio and turned it off.

"No. I wasn't listening to that." Sam also wasn't listening to The Beatles while doing biology homework yesterday when Paul told him to turn it off.

"Those people think they know everything but they have no idea what's going on in this world," Paul went on. "They act all high and mighty like you should be able to win a war by saying 'please.' Dow Chemical is a big reason why we're winning for crying out loud!"

Sam sifted through his memory, trying to remember if his brother's letters said anything about whatever it was Paul was talking about. "Don't they make soap or shampoo?"

Paul rubbed the sprouts of hair on his head. "Jeez, Sam. Don't you pay attention to anything? Dow Chemical makes napalm. They send it to Vietnam. Our guys drop it all over the place and it burns the VC out. We need them."

Sam remembered seeing a bunch of signs all over the student union that had something to do with Dow, only the sentiment wasn't the same as Paul's. "That sounds effective."

"Hell yeah it is," Paul crossed his arms with a firm nod of his head. "It's like they don't want us to win. Like they're actually on the side of the communists. Maybe *they* are communists."

He said *hell*. Harsh words coming from Paul. "I don't think anyone here is a communist. And if they were, I don't think they'd be freaking out and drawing attention to themselves." Sam tucked the letter into the cover of his history book. "I'd love to talk more about this war, but I have to read up on one that happened a few centuries ago."

Paul shook his head. "Doesn't anything bother you?"

Sam was halfway out the door and slowly turned, willing himself not to hurl his textbook at Paul. "A lot of things bother me," Sam said evenly. "But I can't do anything about a lot of them so I shut the fuck up."

Paul winced when Sam cursed.

"You know what bothers me?" Maybe it was the memory of Tommy Maloney. Sam felt everything boil inside of him. "It bothers me when the pay phone is full of dimes and my mom gives me a hard time for not calling more often. It bothers me when they run out of rye bread in the cafeteria. It really bothers me when you turn my music off when you know damn well I'm listening to it."

Paul straightened like a soldier in front of a drill sergeant. "But it doesn't bother you that these hippie freaks want to shut down a company who's helping us win the war."

Sam pressed his lips into a firm line. "You don't know the first thing about what bothers me." He glared at Paul until he looked away.

"Yeah, well," Paul stammered. "You read about history so much, you have no idea when it's happening right in front of you."

That hurt in a way Sam wasn't expecting. "I guess I'll read about it later." He waved his history book at Paul before stalking out the door and to the stairs.

Instead of going into the library, Sam sat on a bench outside of it. He zipped up his windbreaker, mad at Paul for making him leave their room so quickly that he didn't have a chance to think about grabbing something warmer. He held Anthony's letter but needed to calm down before reading it again.

Paul was the one who thought he knew everything. Just because that ROTC reject wanted to be in the Army, he thought that made him an expert on everything about the war. And just because Sam wasn't as hacked off as Paul didn't mean he didn't get mad. He was mad he couldn't listen to The Doors when he wanted to. He was mad Paul could hang up a photo of Debra in her yellow dress while Sam had to settle for a wrinkled Snoopy shirt stuffed into his pillowcase.

Sam wrapped his arms around himself and burrowed his chin into his chest to fight off the brisk breeze that came with dusk.

"Is that a letter from your sweetheart?"

Sam turned to see Suzy standing over him with a warm smile on her face. They had biology together and got set up as lab partners. She was nice enough.

"I already told you," Sam looked at the ground. "No sweetheart." He didn't tell anyone besides Paul on that first day in the dorms that he was going steady with someone. If too many people knew he would have to make up stories and keep the lies straight. It was easier to pretend.

Suzy flipped her stick straight blonde hair over the collar of a fringed vest with a cluster of peace sign buttons over the heart. "Is it from your friend at Basic?"

"Yeah." They got the chance to know a little bit about each other during bio labs. Suzy was from Ithaca, New York and an English Literature major. She loved Emily Brontë and smoking grass. The only person she knew fighting in the war was the son of someone her dad worked with.

She sat next to Sam. "There's this big thing going on tomorrow at the Commerce Building. You should come."

"To do what? Go see a presentation about the stock market? No, thank you."

Suzy laughed. "Yeah. Stock prices. I dig that."

"Are you thinking of changing majors or something?" Sam asked.

"Dow Chemical is doing interviews tomorrow and we're going to tell them to get the hell off our campus and out of Vietnam," Suzy said, showing Sam a different side of the girl who took diligent notes in biology class and read every step of a lab before getting started.

"You too? My roommate just got done giving me a lecture about those guys." He should have gone inside the library. Then he could have read Anthony's letter a million more times *and* be warmer.

"Did he give you the lowdown about napalm and what it does to people? Innocent people?" She pulled a flier out of a textbook. It said *Down with Dow* on it along with a photo of a Vietnamese person with burns on their face. "The stuff they make doesn't just burn up trees and Vietnamese soldiers, Sam. It burns people and melts their skin. And their huts and the land they use to farm."

"Oh." Sam looked away from the photo of the burned person. "I didn't know all that."

"Well, consider this your first lesson." Suzy's expression softened as she put a hand on Sam's knee. "I didn't mean to yell at you."

Sam looked at the hand: short, trimmed nails, two wire rings, one with a turquoise stone, another with a dark blue. "I didn't think you were yelling at me." He picked up his books, forcing Suzy to take her hand off his knee.

"So, are you going to come?" Suzy asked. "You don't have to do anything. We just need people to be there."

"I don't know." The photo of the man from Suzy's flier flashed in Sam's brain. Until a few minutes ago, all he knew about the war was that he had a brother fighting in it and soon his best friend would be too. Maybe he *should* pull his head out of the sand. Sam wondered if his brother ever flew a plane that dropped napalm on a cluster of huts among the rice paddies.

"I don't hate the people who are fighting over there," Suzy explained. "But, I'm against hurting people who have nothing to do with it. Think about Jimmy and Anthony."

It surprised Sam to hear someone say Anthony's name, especially like they knew him. The bio labs gave Suzy and Sam a chance to talk. He guessed he didn't realize how much talking he did. "What about them?"

"Napalm doesn't just burn the Vietnamese, Sam."

Sam turned his head to watch several squirrels chase each other up a tree. Jimmy spent most of his time in a plane and at the base. But Anthony would probably be on the ground.

"It's okay to get mad about this stuff," Suzy said.

Sam scoffed. Here was another person telling him he wasn't mad enough or mad about anything for that matter. "You're a psych major now?"

Suzy looked confused.

"Yep. You've got me figured out," Sam went on. "I'm not mad. I have nothing to be mad about." He swiped up the rest of his books and stood up in one motion.

"Wow. What's your bag?" Suzy called after him. "I thought maybe you also thought those idiot sticks from Dow need to stop killing people." Suzy might have said something else but Sam was too far away to hear.

Sam's textbooks sat on one side of him and a sloppy stack of newspapers sat on the other. The librarian gave him a stern glare as he flipped through the pages, the noise louder than he intended for it to be. Sam had no idea there were so many. Article after article about napalm, Agent orange, firebombs…whatever you wanted to call the jelly substance planes dropped on the land and people of Vietnam. He saw pictures of a napalm cloud as it descended upon rice paddies and jungles. The pictures of what it did to a person were way worse than the one on Suzy's flier. Sam had to quickly turn the page, earning him a pair of raised eyebrows from the librarian.

He read about military personnel justifying its use. He learned about the chemical make-up of the stuff that was almost one thousand degrees hotter than boiling water. Sam couldn't even fathom what that meant. He knew what boiling water felt like. When he was seven, his mom tripped over him as she was transferring a pot of boiling water from the stove to the sink, scalding his left shin. What was a thousand degrees hotter than that?

It was way past sundown when Sam emerged from the library. He hadn't read a word of his history textbook or given a single thought to his English paper due next week. On his way to his dorm, he passed the Commerce Building. There was a pretty big crowd outside of it. Several of them held signs in the air that said *Down with Dow* or *Dow Shall Not Kill*. Sam thought he saw Suzy, but it was hard to tell. It was dark and there were lots of long-haired girls with fringe vests.

"Hey, man. Check this out." A guy with a head of curly hair shoved a flier at Sam. It looked like a one-page newspaper with the headline *Dow-The Predictable Explosion*.

Up until that afternoon Sam had only heard about Dow in the

background of his life. He might have heard a snippet of a news story that mentioned the name and then there were the posters sprinkled across campus that he barely glanced at. Suddenly it was everywhere. Paul thought they weren't getting a fair shake. Suzy thought they were a ruthless killing machine. Sam didn't know what he thought. But he learned enemy bullets weren't the only things that could get Anthony hurt…or killed.

He took the paper with a polite nod at the curly-haired guy.

"Tomorrow. Commerce Building," the guy said as if delivering a message in code.

"I heard." Sam shoved the paper into his windbreaker pocket and kept walking.

The cafeteria in Kronshage Hall would be closing soon but Sam wasn't hungry, especially not for whatever they were serving. Every trip to the cafeteria made him think of his last meal at Anthony's house. He thought about Anthony at least a thousand times a day, but he missed him the most right after he turned out the light to go to sleep. It was stupid to think he and Anthony would ever live together, let alone share a bed every night. They were going to somehow move to California or New York together? Sure. Yeah. Good one.

Sam pushed open the door to Sullivan Hall and headed to the stairs with much less energy than a few hours ago when he had checked his mailbox. He wanted to talk to Anthony about what he had read and the pictures he'd seen. Anthony wouldn't be the one burning those poor people. Sam knew that. Maybe it was what Jimmy was doing in his airplane. Dropping actual firebombs on people below who had nothing to do with the war and why it was being fought.

He half listened to the news when it came on in the evening. He got most of his information from his brother's letters and his dad's praise for the "hell of a job" the boys were doing there. Sam hated to admit he really didn't know a whole lot else.

Dammit. Paul was right.

As Sam walked down the hallway toward his room, Paul stood at the pay phone that hung on the wall a few doors away from theirs. Sam could tell by the way he leaned against the wall with the cord wrapped around a hand that he was talking to Debra. If he were talking to his parents, Paul usually stood at attention.

Maybe Paul had enough dimes to talk to Debra for the next two hours so Sam could finally listen to his music in peace. Maybe there'd be some Beach Boys on the radio. Wouldn't it be nice.

OCTOBER 17, 1967

Darkness engulfed Anthony. He couldn't see where he was going. The bag over his head was rough against his skin. All he could feel was the wet ground under his bare feet, mud seeping between his toes and caking his ankles. His feet sank with every step and it was getting harder and harder to pull his feet out of the mud as they got wetter and heavier.

A heavy mist soaked his shirt and shorts. A cold breeze made him shiver.

Anthony's breaths came fast, filling the bag with hot air. Someone pushed him from behind and he stumbled forward a few steps. Someone else poked him with what had to be the butt of a rifle. There was a chorus of laughs as he tripped forward again before falling. When he went to catch himself, he landed head-first, suffocating for a moment with his face stuck in the mud. He tried to move his hands and found them bound behind his back. He pulled his wrists apart, but they only moved a couple centimeters.

"The little faggot thinks he's going to escape." A deep voice came from somewhere outside the bag.

Anthony's breaths came faster. They knew. How could they know?

"That's fucking hilarious." Another voice came from somewhere.

Anthony jerked his head from side to side inside the mud-caked hood, trying to loosen it somehow.

"You know what else is hilarious?"

"No. What?"

Was that Capper? Anthony tried to say his name but choked instead. He tried to talk, tried to scream, but he couldn't make a sound. He heard a series of clicks, the unmistakable sound of an M14 being loaded.

No no no no.

The smallest noise managed to escape Anthony's lips.

"Say goodbye, soldier."

Before the gun went off, Anthony opened his eyes. His heart pounded in his head, his stomach flipped, and every limb felt like as if it were tied to an invisible weight.

"Shit, Capone, what the fuck is going on?" Capper loudly whispered from the bottom bunk.

It took Anthony another second to comprehend that he was in his bunk, in the barracks, at Fort Polk in Louisiana. There was no bag over his head. No one was trying to kill him. Capper wasn't trying to kill him.

"I, uh," Anthony struggled to talk. "I think I have a Charlie horse." He rubbed his leg for added effect even though Capper wouldn't be able to see anyway.

"A Charlie horse?" Anthony heard Capper turn over. "You gotta be kidding me." In a matter of seconds, his breaths came in slow exhales.

Anthony laid still, afraid to move. Afraid a sudden movement would somehow make the darkness close in on him and send him back to the same nightmare he'd been having ever since arriving at AIT. The only variation was how many times he was pushed and hit. Or how many times he fell. One time he was blindfolded and his mouth was gagged. But it was always dark.

The deep breaths did little to calm his racing heart but the feeling returned to his limbs. Anthony turned over on his side. He squeezed his eyes shut, praying to find sleep. He'd lost many hours over the first few weeks at AIT and they were beginning to add up, especially considering that privates only got three to four hours as it was. For all Anthony knew, Drill Sergeant Evans was going to wake everyone up in a matter of minutes. He needed those minutes.

Instead of finding sleep, Anthony found himself replaying the lecture from POW training. How the drill sergeant informed the recruits of the tactics the VC could use to get him to talk. It wasn't always physical torture. They might know things. They might know everything. Your family's names. Use that information to get you to talk, to get you to break. They might know things you thought were a secret, things no one else knew.

No one else except Sam.

One time, the nightmare was that Charlie had somehow captured Sam. *He* was the one in the hood being dragged through the mud. Anthony could only look on in horror. He couldn't do or say anything.

Anthony had learned to turn himself off when Drill Sergeant Dalton called him or another one of the recruits a "fag". He had to remind himself how Dalton called them girls and ladies, not because he thought they were, but because it was supposed to be an insult - motivation to be better and move faster.

Anthony couldn't lose it again the way he had during hand-to-hand combat training. The drill sergeant at Fort Polk loved the word queer. He said it in almost every command. *Queers, girls, ladies, nancies,* sometimes *fairies.* It all blended together and stopped standing out after a few days.

But the POW lecture haunted Anthony. He feared being captured more than being killed.

He tried to match his breathing to Capper's, thinking that if he could mimic his deep, long breaths then the same sleep would find him. In the middle of the fourth breath, Anthony heard the doorknob to the barracks turn and the door open.

He squeezed his eyes shut even harder. Just ten seconds. Maybe he could get ten more seconds in.

"Rise and shine, ladies." Drill Sergeant Evans stood silhouetted in the doorway, hands locked behind his back.

The quiet and simple command was all it took to get everyone up and standing at the foot of their beds. At the start of Basic, it took a good holler and sometimes a bang on the wall from Dalton to get everyone going. By the end, a whisper would have woken up the recruits. The body adjusted to the Army's demands. They didn't need to be told to get up. The body knew.

Anthony's body knew it was tired and spent. It needed to sleep, not just for another two hours but another two days. As he stood at attention at the foot of his and Capper's bunk, he told himself it was all part of the training. It wasn't like he was going to have a suite at the Drake Hotel out in the jungles when he was in Vietnam hunting Charlie. It wasn't like everyone would return to base at sundown because the war was over for the day.

There would be no letter to Sam tonight. Just like there was no letter last night, or the one before, or even the week before that. As he pulled his shirt over his head and laced up his boots, Anthony allowed himself to leave the army for a second. Long enough to lift a thought into the air and pray it made it to Sam all the way in Madison, Wisconsin.

OCTOBER 18, 1967

Luckily there was a chalk talk in biology. Mitosis. Cells. Something about these miniscule things that multiplied to form a bigger thing and multiplied even more to form an actual living thing. Sam and Suzy passed notes during most of the lecture. Suzy started it by throwing a little piece of paper that landed on his tiny lecture hall desk.

I don't think you're stupid.

Sam smiled. Since Suzy was sitting behind him, he had to stretch and drop the paper on the floor in order to return the note.

We're copasetic. And you're right. I graduated second in my class.

Another piece of paper bounced off Sam's desk and landed next to his dirty white tennis shoe.

Dow is on campus as we speak. Fuzz is blocking the entrance to demonstrators.

There was already a crowd gathered outside the Commerce building when Sam had gotten to his 8:30 class. He'd seen the police officers positioned outside the door. "I heard the cops have permission to pound anyone getting in the way of the interviews," Paul had said before he left for his morning econ class.

"I heard cops don't pound people for standing around," Sam had responded as Paul closed the door behind him.

When he and Suzy got out of biology and walked by the Commerce Building, the sky was a flat gray. It was the kind of sky that didn't predict rain but guaranteed a gloomy day without sun. A cold wind found its way to his neck and down his back. The crowd had grown during Sam's lecture on cells and their reproduction. He couldn't count how many swarmed upon the Commerce Building and Bascom Hall, fanning out in an uneven, huge half circle.

Suzy grabbed Sam's arm, dragging him to the outer edge of the crowd. "Come on. Let's stand over here. We can try to see what's going on inside." Suzy stood on her tiptoes, trying to get a glimpse of the doors leading into Commerce. All they saw was a cop stationed at the entrance, his arms folded.

"We?"

"Yeah. You're staying right?"

"Maybe for a little while." Sam glanced at his watch.

"You have to stay, Sam." Suzy pulled on his arm again. "The more there are of us, the more it sends a message."

The message was written on signs that said, "Dow shall not kill!" "End the war in Vietnam!" "Baby Killers not welcome!" Some had horrifying pictures of the burned bodies of Vietnamese children Sam had seen in the newspapers. The crowd chanted too. "Down with Dow! Down with Dow!" A drumbeat came from somewhere and banged along with each word.

Sam shifted to his other leg, checking his watch. He had just learned about Dow Chemical and their horrific contribution to the war. All these people seemed to have known about it for a long time. He felt like an imposter.

"I don't think I know what their message is." Sam found the source of the drumbeat. It was part of a band of sorts, a group of hippies with long hair and colorful threads playing an assortment of instruments. One had a bugle and another, a set of maracas. Someone dressed up as Uncle Sam walked behind the band on a pair of stilts.

"The band adds to the noise and makes our presence bigger," Suzy explained. "And Uncle Sam…" She looked up at the stilt walker and watched him walk among the crowd. "Maybe it's symbolic. How America feels like they're above everyone else."

Sam couldn't tell if Suzy was being serious or not. "There's a lot of people here."

"And there's going to be a lot more." Suzy joined in the chat of "Dow shall not kill."

The chants and noise surrounded Sam, filling his ears and his brain. He felt an energy pulse in him. It was like being at the Rolling Stones concert last summer. They had ended with "Satisfaction". At the first notes, the crowd started screaming, Sam included. Everyone at the concert sang along to every word. It felt like he belonged there, like he was part of a community of people who felt the same way he did.

Maybe it was the hippie band and the guy banging on the drum. Maybe it was the Dow chant. Maybe it was the crowd itself that surrounded Sam, some in sweaters, some in flower child threads, like Suzy. Some wore letterman jackets. Some were black, some white. But everyone was here for the same reason. It was amazing. Maybe even thrilling. And no, Sam didn't want Dow to continue making Agent Orange. He didn't want his brother to drop bombs of it on the Vietnamese. And he didn't want a single molecule to fall anywhere near Anthony. It was ironic, to join an anti-war protest to protect someone serving in the war.

"Down with Dow," Sam mumbled with a straight face, pumping his fist shoulder high.

Suzy grinned at him. "You're going to have to be louder than that," she cried, standing on her tiptoes to get as high as possible. "Down with Dow!" She waved her fist over her head.

"Down with Dow!" Sam yelled as loud as he could, laughing.

"Well done."

He yelled it again, this time along with everyone else. Sam laughed again, not because it was hilarious, but because it was exhilarating.

Just then, a young man in a suit with perfectly side-parted hair slinked his way between Sam and Suzy. He clutched his briefcase to his chest like it was a shield as he used it to push his way through the crowd.

"Don't let him in!" Suzy yelled.

"Future baby killer!" Someone else yelled.

The guy managed to make it through the crowd and get inside.

When he opened the door, Sam was able to see that the hallway inside Commerce was also filled with people.

"Some people are camped out outside the classrooms where the interviews are," Suzy explained. "That guy might not even get the chance to go in."

Sam looked at his watch. He had to get to history. Part of him wanted to stay to witness history as it happened. The other part of him knew the professor was going to review for a test coming up. But he'd taken good notes all semester and did well on the quiz last week. He couldn't help fidgeting.

"Do you have to go to the bathroom?" Suzy asked him.

"I should probably go to class."

"Seriously?"

"Yeah. There's this test…" Sam knew he sounded like such a square, insisting class was more important than this.

"You know what's happening right now, Sam?" Suzy spread out her arms, gesturing to the spectacle going on around them. "History. History is happening as we speak. Right now."

He remembered what Paul said the night before, about how he only read about history. "I'll stay," Sam finally said, shushing the voice of his dad, who'd probably call his son a dumb hippie for skipping class to attend a demonstration against a war his other son was fighting in. "It's for research, right? Imagine the professor I'll be when I tell my students I was there and this is the side I was on."

Suzy's grin stretched across her face. "The right side."

"Down with Dow! Down with Dow!"

Sam and Suzy yelled along with the crowd and in time with the beating drum. He glanced at his watch one last time. 10:23. Class had already started. No use worrying about it now. College wasn't high school where the principal called your parents for skipping a class. Besides, this was the first one he'd missed all semester.

"Down with Dow! Down with Dow!"

Even though he yelled as loud as he could, as loud as he did at the Stones concert, Sam couldn't hear his own voice. Part of the crowd jeered at another briefcase-carrying student who exited Commerce with

his head down, attempting to escape the scene by going off to the side.
"Down with Dow! Down with Dow!"

Sam wondered what Anthony was doing at the advanced training he'd mentioned in his last letter. Was he running, shooting, fighting, eating? He wanted to know what he was doing at this exact moment. Maybe if he thought about it hard enough, Anthony would be able to feel this energy, this sense of belonging, and it would give him the strength to endure whatever was thrown at him. Sam was doing this for him.

A squeal from Suzy interrupted Sam's thoughts and broke their participation in the chant. A girl in a long dark skirt and woven jacket came up behind Suzy and gave her a hug. "You're finally here," Suzy said to the girl.

"It was pointless to go to class anyway." The girl dug around in her large, patch-covered bag. "You could hear everything going on outside. The professor had to yell so we could hear him." She revealed a woven band of pink and yellow flowers and placed it on Suzy's head.

Suzy raised her eyebrows in an attempt to see how it looked. "I love it."

"You're not going to flip your wig at her for going to class?" Sam asked.

"Academic probation," the girl said, not sounding the least embarrassed about this piece of information. She turned to Suzy. "And this must be Sam."

"Sam's one of us now," Suzy smiled.

"Sam is not sure what that means but he got a necessary lesson about napalm and that's why he's here," Sam clarified.

Suzy shook her head and rolled her eyes. "This is Gloria. I met her at SDS."

"SDS?" Sam asked as Gloria extended her hand.

"Oh yeah, I forgot. You're new at this." Suzy gestured to the crowd. "Students for a Democratic Society."

"Hi, Gloria." Sam shook her hand.

"Nice to meet you, Sam." She smiled at him and kind of winked at Suzy.
The band was on the move, weaving through the crowd. They

whooped in appreciation for the musicians. Gloria did a little sway that caused her skirt to swish and swirl as they banged their drum past the group.

A police officer walked out of Commerce and stood next to another one who was guarding the entrance. They folded their arms, staring out at the crowd.

"How many fuzz do you think are inside?" Sam nodded at the officers.

"Who knows," Gloria said.

"I'm not looking to get arrested."

"Don't be such a square," Gloria scoffed.

"It's for show," Suzy insisted. "There's this agreement or something. They let us protest and they stand there like they're actually doing something. We're fine." She patted Sam's shoulder.

"Okay." No one else seemed bothered by the cops' presence. Sam's stomach churned the scrambled eggs he'd doused with ketchup at breakfast. "Are they here for show too?"

Several police cars and a paddy wagon pulled up at the edge of the crowd. The officers' boots hit the ground and they morphed into something like a machine that moved in perfect synchronization. They parted the crowd by simply marching through it.

Sam, Suzy, and Gloria stood gaping at the officers as they marched past them with nightsticks, handcuffs, and guns secured in their belts. "Shit," Sam muttered.

The cops' presence quieted the group at the edge of the half circle for a moment but energized those closest to Commerce. Sam heard jeers of "fascist" and then shouts of "sieg heil." The chant caught on as some of the students punctuated their words with a Nazi salute.

"Sieg heil, you pigs!" Suzy yelled, bouncing on the soles of her faded brown boots. The flower wreath almost fell off as she craned her neck to see over the crowd. "I have to see what's going on inside." She made a move to lunge through the crowd.

"You probably have a pretty good idea." Sam pulled on her shoulder.

Suzy glanced at his hand and smiled. "I told you, Sam. History is happening. I'll give you a report so you can tell your future students about it." She bent and pushed her way through the crowd by shoving them to the side at the waist. While the cops at the door were yelling in a bullhorn about disorderly conduct, she snuck around them amid the chaos and squeezed her way inside.

"Well, hell." Sam scanned the crowd as if someone would tell him what to do next.

The crowd's attention shifted from Dow to the police officers. "Down with Dow!" was replaced with shouts of "Fucking pigs!"

"What do we do?" Sam asked Gloria, wondering why he thought for a second she would have an answer.

"They asked for it," Gloria shrugged. "We're just here trying to stop some baby killers."

A collective gasp from the front of the crowd made Sam look at the entrance to Commerce. A small group of students lay by the doors, struggling to stand. Sam had to squint to verify what he saw. Yes, it was blood. Blood dripped from the head of one of the students. They were followed by over a dozen police officers, recklessly swinging their nightsticks at anyone who got in their way.

A police officer dragged a student in a denim jacket out of the building. Someone threw a shoe at the officer. Someone else threw a chunk of a brick.

"Fuck you, fucking fascist pigs!"

Sam stood on his toes, trying to stand his ground as everyone in the crowd started going in different directions. He strained for a glimpse of Suzy's flower wreath and long golden hair but a lot of girls had hair like Suzy's. A boy with a sweaty mop of dark hair and a bruised cheek ran past him, clutching a swollen hand. An officer half carried, half dragged a girl who had her face painted white like a mime.

Students poured out of the Commerce building. There had to be over a hundred.

"They're beating the hell out of everyone!"

Something clanked at Sam's feet and landed nearby.

"Run! Run!" Gloria yelled. She turned, her dark purple skirt willowing after her.

Smoke immediately filled the air. It was like a cloud exploded in Sam's face and in a matter of seconds his eyes burned. He choked on the fog and wildly flailed his arms, struggling to feel his way out. When he put his hands on his knees, something struck the base of his spine and pain radiated through each limb. A half second later, firecrackers went off behind his eyes but they were nothing like the ones he'd seen on the Fourth of July. And it hurt. God, did it hurt. Somehow the blow also turned off the sound and Sam could no longer hear the crowd yelling. He wobbled forward a few steps, still clawing his way out of the smoke that gagged him, before falling on the trampled grass under the relentless gray sky.

"Sam! Oh my god, Sam!" Someone was yelling, or maybe they were crying. "I'm sorry. I'm so sorry."

Sam was in a dream. He could hear, but not see. His eyes could not be pried open. He tried to talk but coughed instead. His throat burned.

"Wake up, please!" The person was definitely crying. "Please wake up, Sam."

He felt a tug on his arm and then pain shot through his head. Sam groaned, wanting to clutch the back of his head but the nerves in his brain weren't communicating with his arms.

"He's awake. I think he's awake."

Sam blinked. He blinked again and only saw the flat gray sky directly above him. Then Suzy came into view, her blonde hair in tangles, tears sliding down her cheeks. Sam heaved himself into a sitting position but immediately flopped to the ground.

"Oh my god. Shit." Sam squeezed his eyes shut as if that would somehow ease the throbbing in the back of his head.

"I'm so sorry this happened. Are you okay?" Suzy's face crumpled. "Do you want to go to the hospital?"

"No." No hospital. That was all he needed. His mom to worry about the son *not* in the war and his dad to tell him he got what he deserved. "Let me lay here." He spread out his arms, feeling the cool grass on his hands and neck. "I'm fine."

Popping sounds suddenly filled the air and Sam instinctively pulled Suzy down as he rolled over on his stomach to cover his head.

With her chin to the ground, Suzy looked around, her eyes darting to the roof of Bascom Hall. "Look." She pointed.

Sam angled his head and saw fireworks, real ones this time, exploding over Bascom as the flag that usually waved from the flagpole on the roof hung limply at the bottom. Someone had cut the rope. Sam turned over on his back, looking at a corner of the flag caught on the roof and the small wisps of smoke from the fireworks as they disappeared into the air.

What did he just get himself into?

OCTOBER 25, 1967

Anthony marched into the office and closed the door behind him. He stood at attention.

The commanding officer raised his eyes at Anthony from his seat behind his desk. "At ease, Private Lorenzo." He opened a folder and sifted through the papers inside but didn't look at them. "You've had an impressive run in the Army thus far, Private, and you haven't even seen any action yet."

A muscle in Anthony's arm twitched. He wasn't sure if a smile would be inappropriate or not. "Thank you, sir."

The officer put the folder to the side. "I'd like to recommend you for OCS."

Anthony had to remind himself to remain at ease with his hands behind his back. "Officer Candidate School?"

"Do you know of another one?"

"No, sir."

"Would you like to fill out the paperwork, Private Lorenzo?" The CO reached for a drawer.

Anthony never considered advancing in the military. He didn't think that was something he'd be asked to do. The plan was to enlist, serve, not get killed, and get back to fixing cars in the States. If he went through the officer school it would mean six more years of service, at least. Six years in the Army would mean going wherever they tell you. Living where they tell you to live. Small towns, big cities. He had no idea where all of the bases were.

"Well, Private?" The commanding officer paused with his hand in the desk drawer.

"I don't have an answer right now, sir."

"You don't?"

"I always thought I'd be on the front lines, sir. Like my father in World War II. Like my grandfather in World War I." Anthony decided to omit the fact his grandfather fought for Italy before coming to the United States. "This is unexpected, sir."

The commanding officer closed the drawer and folded his hands on the desk. "We all want to be like those men," the CO finally said. "The soldiers like your dad are considered the best."

Anthony continued standing at ease. Sweat dampened his armpits and back.

"I understand your desire to pursue infantry and that is admirable. However, if you change your mind, you let me know."

"Yes, sir. Thank you, sir." Anthony saluted and sharply turned on his heel before marching out of the office.

That night Anthony lay in his bunk, knowing lights out was only minutes away. His body was dead weight on the bed, fatigued from a day of humping equipment through the thick Louisiana heat. Which was the Arctic compared to the jungles of Vietnam. With his arms like jelly, Anthony could barely hold Sam's letter up to read it. His body might have been completely spent, but his eyes felt like sleep wouldn't be coming for a long time.

Anthony,

Midterms are coming up and that means more studying, more homework, and no time for anything else. These professors make us read so much. My nose is in a book all the time. Maybe even when I'm sleeping, because I have actually woken up on a textbook before.

Thanksgiving is in a couple weeks. Do you get to celebrate with a turkey and all that stuff, or do they just give you turkey-flavored shit out of the can and call it a day? I'm hoping my mom is up for a feast even though it will just be her, Dad, and me. I bet your mom will try to mail you some lasagna in honor of the holiday. Maybe I'll stop by and see if I can bogart a piece before she puts it in the mail.

I guess I better head to the dining hall before it closes. All this talk of Thanksgiving food and lasagna made me hungry, even though nothing like that is going to be served tonight, I'm sure of it. I'm going to have dinner now. If nothing looks good, maybe I'll just have a big bowl of ketchup.

When is this part of the training over? What next? Watch out, Charlie!

Anthony lowered the letter and laid it on his chest. It was the second time he'd read it and he scrutinized every word for something he might have missed. The letter read like how he'd answer his mom when she'd ask how his day at school was. She got the information. The facts. That's it. Nothing special. At least Sam included something about the ketchup. But, what wasn't Sam telling him? What wasn't in the letter? Was he too busy studying and figured no letter was worse than any old letter? What Anthony held in his hands could barely be considered a letter.

"Lights out!"

The barracks went dark, with the exception of the slivers of moonlight that seeped inside. Anthony folded the letter as quietly as he could and shoved it into his pillow. He'd add it to the collection in his footlocker in the morning.

Anthony turned over and hugged his pillow. Maybe Sam had met someone. Maybe a girl. Maybe he realized he was done with what they had been doing for the past year. He was done with Anthony and didn't know how to say it in a letter.

The thought made him want to cry. It took Anthony so long to recognize what he felt. To not push it away and bury it but let it flutter up into his chest. And it took so long for him and Sam to go from being friends to being more than that. Long after the project for English class was over, Sam still spent many afternoons in Anthony's room, listening to music, talking about school and parents. Anthony's thumb still tingled when he remembered Sam reaching for a Byrds record and brushing his hand—purposely or accidentally, he didn't know. But that touch was the beginning of everything.

They weren't the only ones. Anthony knew that. But he had no idea how many more there were.

As Capper made clicking noises with his tongue, signaling he was in a deep sleep, Anthony thought about OCS. Six years. Six years was a long time. Six years of waiting to get his life back. He wished he could talk to his dad about it. Even though he knew his dad would be proud, he'd understand a life devoted to the Army was demanding, right? Anthony's dad had enlisted, fought for eighteen months, and and then got out. He and his mom met almost right after he returned from war.

Anthony squeezed his pillow again, hearing the paper crinkle from inside the pillowcase. He squeezed his eyes shut, willing sleep to find him. He was almost done with AIT. He was so close to shipping out. The army thought he was good enough to be an officer, but he needed to finish his training first.

He'd try to write Sam tomorrow night. Something that had to somehow convey everything he couldn't put in a letter.

OCTOBER 27, 1967

Sam was able to hear the tubas and drums of the pep band even though he was nowhere near the stadium. He had gone to every single football game in high school, thinking it was something he was supposed to do, and that maybe if he did all the things he was supposed to do, he would stop feeling and wanting what he wasn't supposed to. All that football and nothing had changed inside of him. His feelings for Anthony only grew stronger and stronger.

The pay phone was finally usable. Every kid on the floor needed to call their parents in the days following the protests to say they were okay, they were mad, the administration was wrong, the other students were wrong, the police were wrong, the war was wrong, the war was right. Sam did try every day to use the phone and this was the first chance he got. Maybe it was because everyone else was at the football game. Well, almost everyone. Suzy was on a bus making its way back to Madison from some huge protest in Washington, D.C. Of course, she asked Sam to go but one crack in the skull and a dose of tear gas was enough for him to hole up in his room for a few days, only leaving to go to classes, eat, and the library. That letter to Anthony was stupid. Sam knew it. But he had wanted to write and had no idea how to explain the day, what he had witnessed, and what he had felt. Just because he didn't hop on a bus to D.C. with Suzy and all her SDS buddies didn't mean Sam regretted going to the Dow demonstration. In fact, he'd stopped to read some of the notices hanging up all over the quad and student union and a lot of it made sense to Sam.

Sam dropped a few dimes into the coin slot. He had a few more in reserve but maybe it would be a quick call.

After a few rings, his dad answered. "Hello?"

Sam took a deep breath, bracing himself. "Hi, Dad. It's—"

"Sam?"

"Yeah, it's—"

"Why the hell haven't you called?" Sam's dad yelled. "Your mother's been beside herself, worrying about Jimmy *and* you. She wanted to drive up the second we saw that ridiculous spectacle on the news."

"I wanted—"

"I told your mother, 'no'," Sam's dad rushed on. "Our son doesn't need a babysitter."

"Is that Sam?" he heard his mom's muffled voice in the background. "Let me talk to him."

"In a minute, Betty."

"Dad, I wanted to call," Sam said before his dad could start up again. "There's only one phone on the floor and everyone's been using it the past few days."

"All those kids found a way to call their parents," Sam's dad said. "We see these things on the news. Kids bleeding, yelling at cops. Some getting arrested." As he exhaled, Sam knew his dad was shaking his head, cursing the youth of America. "Hold on a second, Betty…"

"Sam? Sam? Are you okay?" his mom came on to the phone.

"I'm fine, Mom." Sam touched the back of his head where the police officer struck him.

"Were you there? Did you see any of it?"

"I'm not hurt. I'm okay." Sam decided to not answer the question directly. The pep band started up again. UW must have scored.

"I was so worried." His mom's voice broke. "I thought maybe you were in the hospital and no one knew how to reach us."

"He wasn't in the hospital because he wasn't even there," Sam's dad piped up in the background.

Sam pressed his lips together so the words in his mouth couldn't get out. Yes, he was there. Yes, he missed his class. But he didn't participate in the class walkout the day after. Like a good boy, he went to his classes and handed in his assignments and reviewed for his upcoming tests. What Sam really wanted was more of that feeling he had yelling along with Suzy, Gloria, and everyone else, but he got caught up in something without fully understanding it. The Stones concert was easier. You sang the songs because you liked them. You didn't have to agree or disagree with them.

"Do you think you should come home, honey?" Sam's mom quietly asked.

"It's fine here, Mom. I swear. It's not like the fuzz is walking around campus looking for people to beat."

"I know." Sam's mom didn't sound convinced.

A beep cut into the conversation. Sam dug into his pocket and put another dime into the coin slot. "I'll be home in a few weeks for Thanksgiving, right? I got my bus ticket already."

"It will be such a small Thanksgiving this year." His mom's voice cracked again.

"Come on, Mom. It's always a small Thanksgiving. It just means more leftovers for us."

"I'll make extra mashed potatoes for you." His mom was trying to smile. He could hear it. "Have you read any Shakespeare yet?"

"Not yet. English 101 is a lot of writing and diagramming sentences. Maybe next semester."

"If you get to read *Twelfth Night*, I'd love to talk to you about it." There was a bounce in Sam's mom's voice.

"Give me the phone, Betty. Let me talk to him." Sam's dad's voice came from the background again.

"All right. Here's your father again," Sam's mom said. "I love you, honey. See you soon."

"I love you, Mom." Sam braced himself for another round of whatever his dad had to say. He was out of dimes, so his dad better be quick.

"I know you got some big tests coming up," he began.

"I took one last week and got an A."

There was a short pause and Sam knew his dad was letting that information sink in. "Heh. Well. That's pretty good. I bet it would be easier to study without all that nonsense going on."

"Maybe," Sam said quickly.

"Those kids don't know what they're talking about," Sam's dad went on. "Just because you don't like something doesn't mean you go around like a jackass. They said on the news someone threw a *brick* at an officer. And another one's in the hospital with a broken nose. He's going to need surgery."

Something started to simmer in Sam's gut. He had another secret he was keeping from his parents and now his dad was going on and on because he thought he knew everything about everyone.

"All those kids should have been in class. They have their parents send them away to college so they can run amok and forget everything their parents taught them. Maybe you *should* come home. I don't need my son around people like that," Sam's dad continued. "You are not—"

"I was there, Dad," Sam said the words before he lost his nerve. There was so much about him his parents didn't know. He couldn't keep secret after secret.

"You what?"

Sam had to take the phone away from his ear. "I was there."

"Trying to talk some sense into those knuckleheads, I hope." The way he said it, Sam knew his dad knew that wasn't the case. "Telling them you have a brother in the war and that what they're doing is a disgrace."

"It was against Dow. Not Jimmy."

"Don't you say his name," Sam's dad seethed. "Don't you say it."

"It burns people alive, Dad, but it doesn't kill them. What if napalm fell on Jimmy? What if he was burning in the middle of the jungle?" An image of his brother screaming in pain, being burned alive, flashed in Sam's head.

Sam heard his mom ask what was going on but his dad said nothing. Then the phone beeped again. He patted his pocket, hoping for an overlooked dime, but no luck. "I'm gonna run out of time soon, Dad."

"Next time you call, it better be to tell me you came to your senses."

Sam heard a click on the other end. He held the receiver in his hand, listening to the dial tone for a few moments before hanging up and heading to the stairwell. The common area was quiet for a Friday night. Sam felt weird knowing he was the only person in his dorm at that moment. It made him feel small and insignificant, like it didn't matter to anyone where he was or what he was doing.

Sam opened his mailbox with a quick prayer but it was empty.

Sam felt his body sink. He dragged himself over to one of the mustard-colored couches in the common area and flopped onto it.

Maybe Anthony was really tired and didn't have time to write at night. He had mentioned how he was lucky to get a few hours of sleep most nights. Maybe at the end of a day of drills and running and pushups and whatever else he did, Anthony passed out as soon as his head hit the pillow. Sam should be able to understand that, right?

Or maybe he saw right through his letter. Sam should have never sent it. There was so much he wanted to put into it, about the protest, about the police, about how it felt to be there. Sam wanted to tell Anthony how he was confused about the war and what he felt while yelling along with everyone at the demonstration. But there was no way he could, so he scribbled out some words and stuffed the letter in the envelope, figuring any letter was better than no letter. He was wrong. No letter was better than the letter he sent.

The door to Sullivan swung open and three guys charged in, all wearing a red and white sweatshirt with Bucky Badger on it. They high-fived one another, all smiles.

Sam narrowed his eyes at them from the couch off to the side of the door.

"Hey, man." One of the guys trotted up to Sam and raised his palm to him. "We lost!"

"And you're celebrating?" Sam ignored the guy's hand.

"It was a close one. 17-13. In a shit season you gotta celebrate the moral victories." The guy thrust his hand forward.

Sam folded his arms. "What counts as a moral victory?"

The guy slowly lowered his hand and glanced at his friends. "In this case, one where you don't get your ass slaughtered."

His friends chuckled. The guy nodded at them with a smile.

"Well, go Badgers then," Sam said with the enthusiasm of someone who was on their way to get their teeth cleaned.

The frog lay on its back, like it was sleeping with its feet pinned out to its sides. Sam poked at it with a scalpel. Part of him thought the frog would ribbit at him to leave him alone. Suzy read the directions, as she always did before a lab. Some students dove right in, but not Suzy. "We cut here to here and then here to here." She pointed to the frog and made a cutting motion in the air. "Do you want to do the honors?"

"Uh, you can do it." Sam shifted on his stool at the lab table.

"If I do the first cut, then you have to find the organs." Suzy pointed her scalpel at him.

"That's something I never thought someone would say to me, but okay." Sam flipped the page of the lab, looking again at the organs labeled on the frog diagram.

"Are you going to ask me how DC was?" Suzy kept her eyes on the incision.

"How was DC?" Sam asked, unsure if he wanted the details. If it was a letdown where nothing happened, like the student march to the capitol building a few days ago, Sam would feel defeated. After the blowup with his dad, he needed to know he didn't get tear gassed for nothing.

"It was super bitchin'." The excitement in Suzy's voice grew as she pinned back the flaps of skin. "There were so many of us. So many. Busses lined the streets. The subway system was packed. You couldn't even get into the station."

"Cool." Sam imagined the swarm of people descending upon the White House. There were a lot of them, more than the crowd gathered outside Commerce, and they were from all over the country.

"And when people found out we went to UW, you would have thought they were talking to a movie star or something."

"Miss Clemmons? Mr. McGuern?" the professor called from the large desk at the front of the room. "The frog is not interested in your conversation. Please stay on task."

Sam and Suzy mumbled apologies and bent their heads together.

"There's an SDS meeting on Thursday," Suzy whispered. "You should come."

"I don't know if I'm game for SDS. Some of those guys are crazy." Sam found out it was one of the SDS guys who cut down the flag on Bascom Hall. "Plus, I found out I don't like being tear gassed."

Suzy sighed. "You're going to let a little tear gas get in your way?"

"A little tear gas and a blow from a nightstick? Yes."

Suzy bent her head so their temples practically touched. "You can't give up now, Sam. We need as many people as possible. If everyone quit because they got a little scared there'd be none of us left. Think about the people in Alabama fighting for civil rights. Did they run away because things got a little dangerous?"

"I wouldn't say what happened in Alabama was 'a little dangerous.'" Sam glanced at the frog's exposed chest.

"Exactly. It got really dangerous, but they didn't give up. And they did it. They won."

"I know what they were fighting for." Sam poked at the frog with a scalpel in a weak attempt to make the professor think he was hard at work. "What are you fighting for? What's this all about for you?"

Suzy straightened, her shiny straight hair falling past her shoulders. "There's people dying, Sam. Getting blown up. Americans. Vietnamese. Kids. Soldiers. Grandmas. And for what?"

Sam shook his head a little.

"Exactly." She took the scalpel from Sam and explored the organs with a light touch. "I don't know either. And I don't know anyone who does."

He didn't go to the SDS meeting, but Suzy did convince Sam to help her hang up some fliers in the student union that demanded peace in Vietnam. Since it wasn't about throwing things at cops or anything against the soldiers fighting over there, Sam figured it was a safe way to get involved, without actually being involved. His dad couldn't get mad at him for encouraging people to be kind to one another. Anthony would dig that Sam wanted the two sides to stop fighting, right?

Sam stapled the last flier to the bulletin board by the mailboxes and figured this would be a good time to check the mail. His box had been empty the past couple weeks.

Of course Anthony had stopped writing. He saw right through Sam's letter and knew he was hiding something. Anthony was also well versed in the art of pretending.

Sam was in the middle of giving himself another list of reasons as to why Anthony would stop writing when his fingers felt something in his mailbox. He felt every muscle in his body tense as he prayed this letter wasn't something from his mom who wrote on occasion to say she missed him, loved him, and hoped he was studying hard.

But there was Anthony's name in the corner of the envelope looking right at him. Sam felt relief but hesitated from immediately tearing into the letter. What if this was Anthony telling him to stop writing, to forget about him. As long as he didn't open it, there was still a chance they were okay. He slowly ran his finger under the flap and took the letter out carefully, as if it might somehow fall apart in his hands.

Sam,

I got my orders for when I ship out. Looks like Capper and I are in this thing together for the long haul. Glad to have a buddy along for the ride. I get some leave in a couple weeks before going over there. It would be cool if I could see you but I know you have school and stuff. Thanksgiving would have been a bitchin' time to see you but I leave right before. But it seems like you're busy. Good job on those tests. I'm doing good on mine too, but they don't really involve pencils and paper. More like lots of running and push-ups with a bunch of gear strapped to your back on a shit night's sleep. But lots of ketchup too. That doesn't have anything to do with the tests.

Sam stared at the letter. He read the few sentences over and over again, questions swirling in his head. When was the leave? How long? Where was he going after that? How could they see each other? For how long? Where?

Sam would have given anything to be able to call Anthony to find out the details of his leave. He had to see him. They had to see each other. Sam had to tell Anthony, in person, everything he'd done this semester that had nothing to do with dissecting frogs and equations.

Sam dropped his books and tore a sheet from his notebook but it came out on an angle like a dog had bit it. On the second try, it was a clean tear. He squatted against the wall, using his notebook as a little table.

Anthony,

Yes. Yes. Yes. When? How? Let me know. Ketchup.

There was more in this letter of ten words than in any other he had sent.

NOVEMBER 10, 1967

As Anthony pushed open the door to his house, he didn't expect to get emotional but he had to swallow something rising in his throat. The smells greeted him first, like lifelong friends. Simmering sauce. Garlic. Onions. Sausage. He had lunch when the bus stopped somewhere in Kentucky but you would have thought Anthony hadn't eaten since that last meal of veal and meatballs before heading to Basic. His stomach made a noise it had never made before.

"He's going to be here soon," Anthony heard his mother say. He couldn't see her yet but could envision her apron decorated with drops of sauce, up to her elbows in whatever she was making at the moment. "It has to be perfect."

She turned, her hands covered in some sort of ground meat. "Oh my goodness. Oh my goodness." She tried to wipe the excess into the massive bowl in front of her but settled for her apron. "My boy. My boy is home." She scurried over and held him in her arms. Even though Anthony probably had six inches on his mom, it always felt like she was the one supporting him whenever they hugged.

Feet clamored down the stairs. Maria bounded into the kitchen still dressed in her uniform from St. Francis, but she had put a pair of pants on under the skirt. Anthony looked at her over his mom's shoulder.

"You cut your hair," Anthony said, still holding his mom.

Maria played with the ends of her chin-length bob. "I like it."

"I like it too." Anthony released his mom and walked over to Maria. He held out his arms and raised his eyebrows.

Maria rolled her eyes at him but went over to Anthony to wrap her arms around his waist. She got taller too. Anthony noticed he didn't have to bend as much.

"You said you were going to miss me." Anthony said into Maria's hair. "Did you?"

Maria squeezed him harder. "A little."

"This coat is so thin." Anthony's mom ran her hand over the sleeve of the army issued jacket. "How can they send you out in the winter wearing only this?"

"It's not winter in Louisiana, Ma. And it's never winter in Vietnam." Anthony tried to keep his tone light.

She went back to the large bowl on the counter. "Well, it's winter here. I don't want to send you back to them with pneumonia." She shook her head. "I don't want to send you back at all."

"We don't have to talk about that right now." Anthony sat at the kitchen table. The green cushion remembered his body, like he'd never missed a day sitting in it. "Let's talk about what we're going to eat tonight."

"I'm mixing the meat for ravioli now." Anthony's mom plunged her hands into the bowl and broke up the mixture of ground meat. "Maria helped me make the dough earlier."

"You're cooking now?" Anthony asked his little sister.

"A little," she shrugged. "It's Dullsville around here with you being gone."

"I had no idea I brought so much excitement to your life."

"Me either." Maria crossed the kitchen and opened the refrigerator. "Do you want a Coke? Dad said when he got back from Europe, all he wanted was a Coke."

"I could buy Coke from the store on base. Ice cold."

"Oh." Maria's shoulders fell as she closed the refrigerator.

"But, I would love one," Anthony said. "I bet they taste better coming out of my fridge at home and not some cooler."

Maria beamed as she popped the top off a bottle and presented it to Anthony. He mimed the cheers motion before taking a long swig. He was right. It did taste better. Anthony's mom pulled a step stool in front of a tall cupboard. "Did you have a good trip home? Do you want to rest before dinner? Are you hungry now? I could make you a sandwich."

Anthony held up his hands to get his mom to stop talking. "The trip was fine. Yeah, maybe I'll go upstairs for a little while. And no, I can wait until dinner."

From the top step of the stool, his mom brought her hand to her heart. "Oh my son, I missed you. I missed you so much."

Anthony stood up and gave his mom another hug. She was way taller than him this time with help from the stool. "I missed you too, Ma. I'll be home again before you know it. And I missed you too," Anthony turned to Maria. "I have no idea what Trixie Belden's been up to this whole time."

Maria smiled at him as Anthony headed to the stairs. He climbed the short flight and stopped for a moment at the top, feeling like a guest in the house he grew up in. Like this was a hotel he had been to many times but wasn't home. Maria's door was closed, as usual, but the "no boys allowed" signs had been replaced with a poster of Rosie the Riveter telling everyone, "We can do it." He felt like he'd become one of those old relatives he only saw at weddings and funerals, usually fat with a head of thick white hair. They would go up at him and grin, "You're getting so big! How old are you now?" He wanted to ask Maria that question. When he left she was thirteen and turned fourteen in October. After just a few months, with her new hair and redecorated door, she seemed much older.

Anthony's room looked exactly the same. Even the clothes his mom set on his bed right before he left were still there. A small pile of undershirts and boxers. He lifted his mattress, ignoring the pile of clothes that fell to the floor and breathed a sigh of relief. A pilfered copy of *Playboy* still hugged a small stack of *GQ* Magazines. With the bed put back together and the clothes moved to his desk chair, Anthony squeezed his pillow, breathing in the scent of his house: spices, finished wood, and something he couldn't place but was always a reminder that this was home. When he closed his eyes, Anthony only saw Sam and remembered their last moments together in this room and the calm way Sam had gathered himself after Maria banged on his door. So good at pretending. It was clear he was pretending in his last letter.

Anthony hadn't heard from Sam in a while. It was hard to write near the end of AIT. So many nights spent in the mock jungles of Louisiana that were supposed to simulate what it would be like to hump through the rice paddies of Vietnam. There were so many letters he composed in his head that never made it to paper, let alone the mail.

Anthony was so close to Sam. Only a few hours away. He had to see him. If his leave would have been a couple weeks from now he would have been home for Thanksgiving. They definitely would have seen each other, maybe even more than once.

Sam was the first person Anthony wanted to tell about being on leave as soon as he found out but so many things got in the way. Even if Sam responded as soon as he opened up the letter, Anthony would have never gotten it. He should have told him to write him at his parents' house. Dammit. Sleepless nights made him forget common sense when it came to civilian life.

There had to be a bus. Anthony would look up the schedule tomorrow. He wished he could go over the weekend but with tomorrow being Saturday, that wasn't going to happen. His mom would never go for it. Anthony didn't even know when Sam had class. Maybe he could-

"Dinner's ready!" Maria interrupted Anthony's thoughts, just like she did on that steamy afternoon a few months ago. He didn't have a plan yet but at least there was a meal waiting for him that put every crumb in the mess hall to shame.

Dinner was delicious, just like Anthony knew it would be. It was what he expected. What he didn't expect was how his dad would sit in front of the TV, getting updated on the latest in Vietnam, with a scowl on his face, loudly exhaling through his nose with his lips pressed together in a thin line.

On screen, a group of American soldiers carrying a stretcher ducked their heads as gunfire came from somewhere. The soldier on the stretcher didn't look injured. He looked like he fell asleep in the middle of battle.

Anthony glanced at the screen and then to his dad. The image didn't bother him. Part of his brain didn't fully comprehend he was headed to where the scene was taking place and the other part of him remembered going through a drill similar to what was being shown on TV. Capper was the one who got a ride on the stretcher.

"Are you okay, Pops?" Anthony asked slowly. Almost three months of training and Anthony came home feeling like the kid who had just graduated high school, instead of a soldier.

Anthony's dad shook his head and grabbed the wicker armrests. "It's the same shit every night. More stories about our boys getting slaughtered."

Anthony glanced at the TV, but luckily Walter Cronkite was on the screen.

"What's the plan? That's what I want to know. Do they even have a plan?" His voice rose.

Anthony's mom came in, drying a large baking dish. "We don't need to watch this tonight, Antonio."

Anthony's dad glanced at her.

She forced a smile. "Why don't we see what the CBS movie is tonight?"

"It's fine, Ma," Anthony said. "It's what we always do, right?"

"Not me," Maria said from her place on the floor. "They still make me leave when something really bad comes on."

Anthony's mom slung the towel over her shoulder. "You don't need to see these bad things."

"You decide." Anthony's dad nodded at him. "The news or whatever CBS has on."

It shouldn't have been that hard of a decision. Anthony didn't want to watch either. "The news is fine," he finally said. "I haven't seen a whole lot of what's going on over there in a while."

"Maria," Anthony's mom said sharply. "Please help me put the dishes away."

Everyone's head snapped to the footage of dozens of soldiers in a makeshift hospital, sprawled out on beds. Miles of gauze had to be used to wrap leg wounds, head wounds, and chest wounds. Cronkite said something about the soldiers storming a hill for days with little success.

"Maria," Anthony's mom said again.

Maria got up with a huff and followed her mom into the kitchen.

"See what I mean?" Anthony's dad threw up his hands. "It's been like this for days. What's the plan?"

Anthony smiled uneasily. "I'll let you know when I find out, Dad. Maybe they'll let me know as soon as I get there."

Anthony's dad was about to say something else when the phone ringing cut him off. Anthony heard his mom answer it in the kitchen. "Hello, Lorenzo residence," she said. "Samuel! Hello!"

Anthony's stomach flipped as he craned his neck toward the kitchen.

"I wish I could send you some of my meatballs, but the mailman would be careless with them. Are you eating well at college? Do they have anything good?"

Anthony's knee bounced up and down. He wanted to yank the phone from his mom's hand.

"That sounds terrible. And you have to eat it?"

Anthony poked his head into the kitchen and raised his eyebrows at his mom and then at the phone, hoping to signal he was pretty sure Sam was calling for him, not to talk about college food.

"Okay, you take care of yourself. Here's Anthony." Anthony's mom handed him the receiver of an olive green phone.

There was noise in the background, making it sound like Sam was in the middle of a passing period in high school. Voices called from somewhere and he heard doors closing. "Hi," Anthony finally said, disappointed he couldn't think of a more special way to greet Sam.

"Hi!" Anthony could hear the thrill and excitement in Sam's voice.

"I wasn't sure if you would be home by now. I mean, I know your letter said today, but I wasn't sure when. And then I didn't know if–"

A warm feeling filled Anthony's chest. "I'm here. It's good. I got in a few hours ago." He caught the eye of Maria who slouched at the kitchen table with the glass of water their mom had asked for. "Hold on a second." He raised his eyebrows at the family room and TV.

"I have to leave here too? Is this even my house anymore?" With a sigh, Maria brought the glass to her mom and headed for the stairs.

"I only have a couple dimes," Sam said. "We gotta make this quick."

Anthony clutched the phone as if the time they had depended on how hard he held it. "Okay. We're good."

"Can we see each other? Do you think you can come up here?"

Anthony could already hear his mom telling him that he was leaving for a whole year, can't she have him for a few days? But if he was old enough to fight in a war, old enough to defend his country, he was old enough to decide how to spend his time on leave. At least some of his time. "Yes, when? Any time."

"I don't want to be swamped with midterm stuff while you're here." There was a pause as Sam muttered about class times. "How about Tuesday? I get out of class in the afternoon. You can catch the last bus back." He sighed. "I wish there was a way for you to stay here. Maybe I can find a way to kick out Paul for twenty-four hours, if not longer. Maybe for the rest of the semester."

Anthony calculated the ratio of time on the bus to the time actually spent with Sam and it was totally lopsided but totally worth it. "Will you meet me at the bus station?"

He could hear the smile in Sam's voice. "Hell yes." Another pause. "I only have a little time left. I'll call you on Monday. Let me know what bus you're coming in on. I'll be there. I promise."

Anthony didn't know why he felt nervous riding a bus to Madison, Wisconsin and navigating the schedule of knowing which one to take. He took a bus to Basic. He took a bus to AIT. He took a bus home. He'll take a bus to the airport that will take him across the ocean into an unknown land. "Okay. I'll let you know. I'll see you soon."

"You know what they had in the dining hall today?" Sam asked.

"What?"

"Ketchup sandwiches."

Anthony smiled at the floor, feeling heat rise in his face. "That sounds delicious."

"It was. I had two. Extra ketchup." A beeping sound interrupted Sam. "Shit. Okay, I gotta go."

"See you soon." Anthony heard a click. He wasn't sure if Sam's time had already run out or if he had heard him.

NOVEMBER 14, 1967

Sam stuffed his hands as far as he could into the pockets of his wool winter coat. He checked his watch for the hundredth time in the last two minutes and looked down the street for any evidence of a Greyhound bus arriving. Even though Anthony's bus wasn't due for another few minutes, Sam still left class twenty minutes early to make sure he would have enough time to walk three quarters of a mile and anxiously wait and wait and wait.

With his books tucked under his arm, Sam walked to the wall of the bus station, determined not to add to the list of the reasons why Anthony's bus might be late or why he might not come at all. As he envisioned a car wreck of monstrous proportions on Interstate 90, a bus pulled into the station. The few people gathered around Sam folded their newspapers as he put his books down at his feet, next to the bus station wall. He needed his hands free for when he finally saw Anthony.

The bus driver opened the door and people began to get out. A man in a hat and dress coat was first, followed by a woman holding a sleeping baby. Sam's stomach twisted as another man got off the bus. He stood on his toes to see into the bus and get a glimpse of disembarking passengers. He could see people standing in the aisle but couldn't make out any faces.

"Hi."

Sam froze. He knew that voice. He felt that voice radiate to each limb, toe, and finger. Sam turned slightly to his right and there he was. Anthony stood right in front of him in a puffy navy blue coat with several stripes going across the chest. His hair was longer than it was when he left for Basic but still shorter than Sam was used to.

Sam could feel the smile on his face stretch across his cheeks. He lunged at Anthony and wrapped him in a hug and Anthony's arms squeezed him back. It was hard to feel his body underneath the jacket. After a few wonderful seconds they knew they had to break apart.

"I am so happy to see you," Sam said.

"Me too." Anthony had the same grin Sam was sure he had on his own face.

They stared at each other for a moment, not blinking or talking, just stupid smiles.

Sam laughed. "God, this is outta sight."

Anthony laughed too. "I know." He shivered a little and lifted the white collar of his coat.

"Let's get going." Sam went to the wall to pick up his books. "It's not a long walk." All Sam could think about on the way to the dorm was that Paul would soon be gone, attending one of his many study groups. That meant he and Anthony would have the room to themselves for a little while, and there was something important he needed to tell Anthony. It was something big and he hoped it didn't make Anthony run back to the station to get the next bus out of town.

"Paul, my roommate is here but he should be leaving in a few minutes. Every second of his life is scheduled and he never goes off course." Sam glanced behind him to see Anthony taking in the walls of the dormitory and glancing at the bulletin boards advertising activities and upcoming events.

When they got to Sam's room, Paul was sitting at his desk, hunched over a textbook. He didn't look up when Sam walked in. "Hey, Paul," Sam said. "Anthony's going to hang out here for a few hours, you dig?"

Something clicked in Paul's eyes as he quickly stood and extended his hand to Anthony. "You're Sam's friend in Basic?"

Anthony glanced at Sam as he shook Paul's hand. "Yeah. I'm on leave for a few days."

"Boss," Paul grinned. "So boss." He stood there, shaking Anthony's hand.

"Uh, thanks."

"Tell me about Basic. I would join up if I could but I can't. I know I can still annihilate a VC with one good arm, right?" Paul looked at Anthony as if he could overturn the decision on his ability to be a soldier.

Anthony shrugged and Sam cut in to rescue him. "Paul, don't you have a study group for econ today?" He made a show of looking at the calendar tacked by Debra's picture. Each date was crossed off with a diagonal line and plans noted in each day.

Paul glanced at the clock. "Not for another five minutes."

"You should probably get there early. I know punctuality is your middle name." Sam picked up an economy textbook off Paul's desk and handed it to him, along with a notebook with *Economy 101* written on it in black block letters.

"They can wait."

"No, I don't think they can."

Anthony chuckled.

"You're right. These econ dudes are serious," Paul sighed. "But it was cool meeting you."

"Yeah," Anthony said. "You too."

"See you later, Paul." Sam opened the door and gestured to the hallway.

"Bye, Anthony. Kill a VC for me, okay?" Paul left with a wave.

For a few seconds, Sam and Anthony stood staring after Paul until he was in the stairwell and the door latched behind him. Sam pushed the door closed and dragged his desk chair over, hooking the top of it under the doorknob, locked it and slid the chain lock into place.

He turned and saw Anthony was still standing there. It wasn't a dream. It wasn't wishful thinking. It was real. As Anthony took off his coat, Sam's eyes explored every inch of Anthony: the jeans, the green sweater that hugged his arms. Everything about Anthony looked stronger, even his face. Sam could see the effects of three months of training and they were beautiful.

"Your hair's a little longer," Sam said.

"So is yours."

Sam shook his head, feeling the weight of two months without a haircut. It flopped into his eyes and he swiped it out of the way. "A lot longer."

"I can't believe you're actually here," Sam breathed, wrapping Anthony in the hug he had wanted to give him at the bus station.

"I'm here." Anthony leaned back in the embrace to rest his forehead against Sam's.

"For how long? A week? A month?" How could he freeze time? How could he make it be four o' clock on this day forever?

"A few hours," Anthony sighed. He kept his forehead glued to Sam's and closed his eyes. "I couldn't believe it when you called. I wasn't sure if you wanted to see me or not."

Sam leaned back. "What?" Anthony thought *he* wouldn't want to see *him*?

"Your last couple letters were weird. I thought maybe you didn't want to do this anymore or—" Anthony started.

"No, nothing like that. At all." Sam took Anthony's hand and they sat on his bed together. He squeezed Anthony's hand for emphasis as his stomach swirled with the thought of being at the demonstration and liking it and how he truly believed he was there for Anthony as much as the poor Vietnamese kids who were being burned alive. He'd also helped Suzy hang up some fliers two more times.

Sam kissed Anthony's hand and pushed up the sleeve of the wool to kiss his wrist and forearm. The sleeve refused to be pushed up any further. Anthony laughed as he took it off, tossing it on the floor. Underneath he wore a white T-shirt. Sam was able to see his chest and biceps beneath the thin cotton.

"Wow," he breathed.

Anthony ducked his head with a smile.

Sam took Anthony's hand again and resumed kissing his elbow, his bicep, his neck. As Sam went for his cheek, Anthony turned his head and caught Sam's lips.

Without his brain telling it to, Sam's mouth responded, pressing into Anthony's, trying to make up for the time they'd spent apart. Anthony lifted Sam's shirt and ran his hands along the back of his jeans.

Sam jerked. "Sorry," he laughed. "Your hands are cold."

They broke apart, smiling. Anthony rubbed his hands together. "I'm away for a few months and my body forgets that it gets cold at home. It was hot at AIT. I think it was 85 when I left."

"Good thing Paul left. Any mention about army stuff and he would have rapped all night about it."

"He's...organized." Anthony glanced at Paul's side of the room.

"Yeah," Sam shoved a few dirty shirts under his bed. "We don't have much in common."

"Yeah. You just share a room the size of a shoebox." Anthony gestured to the dorm room.

"Yeah, I guess it's like Basic except with more guys crammed into a small space." For the first time, Sam realized being at Basic was like living in the locker room in high school, and Anthony had been living it for almost four months.

"Yep. It's exactly the same," Anthony agreed with a smile. "And it looks like he's got a special friend too." He nodded at the picture of Debra.

"Is that what you are? My *special friend?*" Sam laughed. "We're like Lassie and Timmy?"

"Well, their friendship was pretty special, so yeah, I guess Lassie and Timmy." Anthony picked at a fingernail that was already too short. "I was so stoked when you called. Your last couple letters sounded like your mom forced you to write about school to your grandma."

"My grandma doesn't feel the way I do about ketchup," Sam said, trying to stall.

"Come on, Sam. Talk to me. I came all the way here and I don't know if I'll ever see you again." Anthony's dark brown eyes pleaded.

"When," Sam corrected.

"Huh?"

"When. You don't know when you'll see me again, not if."

Anthony stood up and crossed the room, leaning against Paul's desk. "They asked me to be an officer. They think I'm that good, they want me to be an officer."

"Really?" Sam tried to remember if Anthony had written anything about that.

"Yeah and I turned them down."

Sam was about to ask why but Anthony rushed on.

"It would mean six years, at least. Six years. I don't want to give them six years. I want to help my country win this war, but I don't want to give them my entire life. After I'm done, the only thing I want is you."

"That's it? Just me?"

"Just you."

Sam could feel Anthony trying to pull the words out of him, to get him to explain why his letters sounded like something a kid wrote to his parents from sleepaway camp. But, Anthony was here. He had taken a three-hour bus ride to see him for just a few hours, only to take another three hour bus ride back.

"What are you thinking about?" Anthony asked.

"Huh?"

Anthony pushed himself off Paul's desk chair. "Your eyes are moving all over the place. It looks like you have a million things going through your head."

He deserved to know and if he hated Sam after finding out then he'd get on the next bus leaving for Chicago instead of the last one for the night. "I'm thinking about how a month ago I went to a demonstration to protest Dow Chemical," Sam blurted out.

"The Agent Orange guys?" Anthony leaned forward like he hadn't quite heard what Sam had said.

"Yeah."

"Why?"

"Because I learned what that shit does to people. And I didn't want it to fall on any more kids. I didn't want it to fall on you." Sam hugged himself, bracing for Anthony's reaction.

"You did it because you were worried about me?"

"Yep."

"So, I'm not going to OCS because of you and you're protesting a chemical company that supports the war because of me?" Anthony crossed the small room and knelt in front of Sam, taking both of Sam's hands in his. "I think it all makes sense."

But there was more, more than protecting the innocent kids and Anthony. Sam had started it. He needed to get everything out in the open. "I liked being at the protest," Sam quietly said. "I liked being in the middle of a group of people and feeling like they were like me."

"You're against Dow and napalm. I dig that. It's not like you're against the war and against the soldiers. It's not like you're against me."

Sam leaned his forehead against Anthony's. "I could never be against you." He closed his eyes. "Everyone is against us. Everyone thinks we're wrong. We can't be against each other."

They started kissing again, their breathing intensifying, and their hands exploring every inch of each other. With their mouths connected, they stood. Sam reached for Anthony's belt at the same time Anthony reached for his. Every inch of his body immediately reacted to the touch.

A pound on the door. "Hey, Sam!"

Sam and Anthony separated as if an invisible force dragged them to opposite ends of the bed. Sam's heart pounded in his ears and he felt the vibrations throughout his body. He glanced at Anthony who stared at the ground as if ignoring the sound at the door would make it stop.

"Sam?" Another pound. "You in there Sam?"

"It's this guy Mike. He lives on this floor," Sam whispered to Anthony.

Anthony gave Sam a look that said that information meant nothing.

"There's a skirt downstairs looking for you," Mike called from the other side of the door.

"Shit." Sam leapt off the bed and dragged the chair away from the door. He tried to open the door but the chain lock prevented it. "Hold on a sec." He quickly slid the lock out and swung the door open.

"The chain, huh?" Mike stood on the toes of his dirty white socks to peer in the room. "You know the rules, McGuern. The door has to be open." He must have seen Anthony because his grin became crooked.

Sam looked behind him to see Anthony standing next to his bed with the green sweater on. "We're studying. French. Verbs."

Mike thought for a moment. "Well the skirt downstairs said you're supposed to study with her. Are you cheating on her with another study buddy?"

"There's a lot of studying to do." Sam threw up his hands.

Mike stepped back. "I delivered the message. My work here is done." He gave Sam a little salute and walked off.

Sam watched Mike turn into his room and then closed the door to his dorm. He felt like his heartbeat was making the room vibrate. "That's Suzy. She told me about this party going on tonight." He'd meant to tell Anthony on the way back from the bus stop. When Suzy mentioned it, the idea of hanging out with Anthony at a party like the two of them went to UW together sounded like a lot of fun. But now, after being alone with Anthony in his room for a few minutes, Sam thought maybe it was a better idea to keep doing that.

"A party?"

"Yeah. But if you want to stay here, I dig that too. I get if you're not up for it." Sam needed some direction from Anthony. Suzy would understand if he bailed on her.

Anthony put on his coat and began buttoning it. "I haven't had a chance to hang loose in a long time."

Sam smiled, remembering how the two of them had snuck two beers from the cooler at his graduation party over the summer. It *had* been a long time. He zipped his own coat with a smile. "We don't have to stay long. We can hang for a little while and then come back here before Paul's study group is over."

"Cool."

"Cool," Sam grinned. Anthony didn't hate him for going to the

Dow demonstration. In fact, he understood. And now they were going to a party together and afterwards, they could spend some time locked in his dorm room. It was shaping up to be one of the best nights of his life.

NOVEMBER 14, 1967

Anthony followed Sam down the stairs. He was hoping for something a little more solitary, a little more just them. But rarely did his time with Sam ever turn out the way either of them had hoped. Plus, this was a chance to understand Sam's life at college a little more. He'd written about Suzy, and now Anthony would know who he was talking about.

"It'll be fun," Sam turned back to Anthony as he continued down the stairs. "And who knows, maybe you'll have such a gas you'll decide college is for you after all."

Anthony pretended to think. "Probably not."

Sam shrugged. "I had to try." He opened the stairwell door and rushed up to a girl with long, perfectly straight blonde hair. She played with the fringe of her suede coat and absently swayed from side to side, causing her long skirt to swish around her. The girl next to her in a similar skirt had wavy brown hair and looked annoyed.

"I'm sorry. Anthony and I were catching up and I lost track of time," Sam said.

"Well, let's get going. We only have a couple hours." Suzy noticed Anthony standing off to the side of them. He leaned back, hands in pockets, hoping he didn't look as out of place as he felt. There were guys his age hanging out on a couch, some leaning against walls, and a few sitting at a table around an open book. This was not his scene at all. School wasn't hard for Anthony, but it wasn't his thing. Cars made more sense. "Glad you could join us, Anthony. Sam talks about you a lot, so it's good to finally meet you."

Anthony nodded. "I've heard about you too."

"Really?" She grinned. "Well, if it were up to Sam, you'd spend your time here in the library learning about the parts of a cell. We should at least show you a good time before you go over there."

Anthony rubbed his head, feeling the hairs beginning to grow out so he no longer looked like someone who had just boarded the bus to Basic. "I haven't been to a party in a while so now seems like as good a time as any."

The girl next to Suzy cleared her throat loudly.

"Since Sam is bringing a friend, I brought a friend too." Suzy pulled the girl closer into the group. "This is Gloria."

"Always a pleasure, Gloria." Sam looked at Anthony and rolled his eyes. That small moment between the two of them calmed Anthony's nerves. He'd endured almost four months of training. Why was he so nervous about some party?

The four of them headed outside and Anthony had to let everyone else take the lead because he had no idea where he was going. "I have to catch the last bus to Chicago," Anthony said.

"And Gloria and I have to be back to the dorms before they lock the doors on us," Suzy glanced over her shoulder. "That gives us a couple hours to show you a good time because where you're going isn't exactly going to be a party."

"I don't expect it to be," Anthony said. He was pretty sure Suzy wasn't saying anything about the war, but he was extra sensitive to anything sounding like a criticism after spending the last few days with his dad, who had suddenly become an expert in modern-day military strategy.

"Well, it's not going to be much fun. That's for sure." Gloria took Suzy's hand who took Sam's hand.

There was no room for Anthony on the sidewalk and it felt wrong to walk on the grass. Instead, he looked at the buildings they passed and imagined Sam walking along this very sidewalk to get to his classes.

He liked getting this peek into Sam's world. One he knew nothing about and would never be a part of. But now, when he got a letter from Sam about his classes, he would have some idea of the world they existed in. When he talked about his dorm room, Anthony could imagine it, seeing Sam sit on the light blue sheets covering his bed or on the wooden chair at his desk. They passed the library and now Anthony knew how far it was from the dorm.

"Come up by us, Soldier," Gloria called to Anthony and dangled her hand at him.

Anthony took a couple quick steps and walked next to Gloria on the grass. "My name's not Soldier." Sam might have been at that Dow protest to protect him, but Anthony was pretty sure Gloria had other ideas.

"I know." Gloria took Anthony's hand and the four of them walked like this was something they had done many times before.

The dusk air was beginning to bite at Anthony's ears. He was grateful for it so he could let go of Gloria's hand to pull up the collar of his winter coat. His mom had insisted he bring a hat and gloves but Anthony had shrugged her off.

"Where's this party?" Sam asked.

"Mifflin Street." Suzy smiled like she was a kid in class who knew the answer to a tough question.

"How'd you get invited to a party there?"

Suzy shrugged and offered another smile. "I know people."

"Mifflin Street?" Anthony asked, feeling like an outsider again.

"Yep," Suzy said. "It's this place right off campus where the most intelligent and forward minds meet. And we get to hang with them tonight. This doesn't happen all the time, you know."

Anthony stuffed his hands into his pockets. "I didn't know."

Sam chuckled. "Intelligent and forward minds? That has to leave you out, Gloria."

"Shut your face, Sam," Gloria said, clearly unaffected by Sam's comment.

"Do they let people in who are on academic probation?" Sam asked Suzy.

"Just because I'm not a book buster like you doesn't mean I don't know things." Gloria slyly smiled. "Some things aren't learned in a classroom, though. You dig?" She elbowed Suzy, who laughed. The two girls linked arms and walked ahead while Sam and Anthony dropped back a step.

"Am I going to be okay at this party?" Anthony asked, rubbing his head.

"Yeah, fine," Sam said. "Why wouldn't you be?"

"I don't know." Anthony's nerves were on overdrive. He spent several nights in a hole in the ground in the pouring rain at AIT. He'd finally learned how to fight Charlie in hand-to-hand combat. And here he was, about to throw up at the idea of a college party. "It seems like they don't let just anybody in and we only have a few hours. I don't want this to be a bust."

"We'll be fine," Sam assured Anthony. "We will. Suzy wouldn't have said we all could go if we couldn't. As soon as you want to leave, we'll leave."

In the orange glow of the street lights, Suzy and Gloria walked arm in arm, the fringe of their coats swaying and lightly slapping their backs. "I don't like Gloria that much," Anthony admitted.

"Me either."

"And I think Suzy likes you," Anthony continued. It hurt to admit it. A couple more demonstrations and Sam might realize the huge mistake he'd made by being with Anthony.

Sam shrugged, confusion creasing his forehead. "Yeah, I like her too. We're friends."

"That's not what I mean." Anthony wished he could grab Sam's hand and yank him back so they could stop walking. Maybe they could turn around right now but a good excuse wasn't coming to mind.

Instead, it was the girls who stopped. Gloria turned around. "What are you two whispering about? Come on."

Anthony and Sam picked up the pace until the group stopped in front of a small house with a steep triangular roof. From the silhouettes in the windows, it was clear the place was packed. As he climbed the steps of the porch, Anthony felt like he was back on the bus headed to Basic. He had little idea what was in store for him during those few months and the scene going on behind the pale blue door held just as much mystery.

Suzy pounded on the door and it was opened by a girl dressed almost exactly the same as her and Gloria. Long skirt, fringe vest, love beads, long hair down her back, only she had a yellow bandana wrapped around her forehead. "Hey," she said as if it were a lyric in a song. "Come on in." The girl pushed open the screen door and Anthony followed Sam inside. The chorus to "Gloria" by Van Morrison blared from a record player in the corner.

"I love this song!" Gloria immediately started dancing. "G-L-O-R-I-A!"

"Do you know that girl who let us in?" Sam asked Suzy.

"Nope," Suzy said, scanning the room.

Anthony relaxed a little when he saw a few guys dressed in sweaters or button up shirts. He felt a little less out of place, even though everyone's hair was at least a good inch longer than his.

"There's Andy and Mary." Suzy pointed to two people in the room, but Anthony had no idea who she was referring to. "Let's go say hi." She grabbed Gloria's arm and the two of them scurried away.

Anthony and Sam hung by the door. A sweet odor wafted into Anthony's nose and he inhaled deeply. He and Sam had smoked grass a couple times over the summer and he didn't realize until now that he missed it.

Sam elbowed Anthony. "Come on. We have a few hours and we're going to have fun."

The deep breath of the sweet-smelling air helped. He didn't come all this way to hang by the door. He was with Sam. That was why he came and nothing else mattered. Snaking through the people blocking the way to the kitchen, Anthony and Sam found a stash of Pabst Blue Ribbon and each grabbed a can.

They found some space by the record player and leaned against the wall. Gloria was still belting out the song's chorus as Suzy turned to Sam and smiled. Sam raised his can to Suzy and then turned to Anthony. "To you."

"To me?" Anthony laughed.

"Yep," Sam nodded. "To escaping your mom for twelve hours. Bet that wasn't easy."

Anthony clinked cans with Sam. "It wasn't. But it's worth it."

"Hey, change the record. You dig?" A guy who looked like he was trying to do his best John Lennon impression, complete with glasses, called to Sam and Anthony.

"Got it, man." Sam bent over the milk crate of records. "Any special requests?"

"I'm guessing this isn't a Beach Boys crowd," Anthony joked.

Sam pretended to survey the room for a second, taking in the sheepskin collars, denim, and peace sign buttons. "Probably not. Maybe some Beatles?" He held up the record for *Sgt. Pepper's Lonely Hearts Club Band.*

"That's probably a better choice."

As the opening notes to the title track started up, Anthony took a swig from his can at the exact same time as Sam, complete with their elbows in the air. The two of them shared a laugh and Anthony relaxed some more.

"Hey," Suzy wandered over, swaying to the music. "Are you having a good time?"

"Good beer, good music, good friends." Sam snuck a smile at Anthony. "What more could I ask for?"

"Thanks for letting me tag along." Anthony decided Suzy was okay and he was being stupid about her scheming on Sam. This might be his only chance to get to know her, so he might as well be nice. He needed to mellow out if he was going to make the most of these precious hours in Madison.

"A friend of Sam's is a friend of mine." Suzy elbowed Sam. "I want to hear all your stories about little Sammy."

"I don't have any little Sammy stories," Anthony said. "We met last year when he got stuck with me for this English project."

"So, was he a big nerd in high school or a hunk all the girls fell over for?" Suzy slid closer to Sam.

Anthony laughed. "There were a couple girls, but they didn't ex-actly fall over for him." He gave Sam a look that said *it's true.* "Being the towel boy for the basketball team wasn't very impressive to the chicks back home."

Sam firmly shook his head. "Not going to work. She already knows about my towel slinging days."

Anthony shrugged. "I have nothing else. Sam was really smart and funny in high school. And as you can tell, he still is."

"Seriously?" Suzy waved her beer through the air and a few drops fell out. "No good stories? No secrets to share?"

Anthony's smile tightened. "Nope. What you see is what you get."

"I'm an open book," Sam said. With "Sgt. Pepper" coming to an end and "With a Little Help from My Friends" starting, he moved his shoulders to the beat and finished off what was left of his beer.

Gloria bobbed over to the group with a joint. "Anyone wanna get high with a little help from their friends?" She giggled and held it out for any takers.

Sam took a long hit and passed it to Anthony.

Anthony hadn't had a beer or smoked grass since Sam snuck away from his own graduation party and the two of them hid behind a small shed to take a few hits. He held the joint between his fingers, hoping it would take him back to that sweltering summer day, before Sam's dad yelled at him for not appreciating the party his mother had worked so hard to throw for him. Anthony's own mom had sniffed the air when he rejoined the party, wondering if someone was wearing a strong cologne.

"Are you allowed to do that?" Gloria cut in before Anthony could take a hit.

"Do what?" Anthony rushed to inhale before Gloria interrupted him again.

"That." She gestured to the joint. "Doesn't Uncle Sam own your soul now?" She pointed a finger at Anthony in imitation of the poster. "Ask what you can do for your country." Gloria's lazy smile and absent sway to the music told Anthony she was high and probably drunk. Anthony told himself she wasn't trying to be rude. Gloria was just a stupid college girl at a college party.

"I've got a few more days," Anthony said tightly, taking another hit.

He handed the joint to Suzy who handed it to a nearby girl.

"Dance with me." Suzy grabbed Gloria's hands and the two began dancing like two little girls at a wedding as they sang along with Ringo Starr.

Sam tugged on Anthony's sleeve. "Let's get another beer." He nodded to the kitchen where they had found the other ones.

Anthony followed Sam through a thin doorway into a cramped galley kitchen. He had no idea so many people were here. For a few moments, it had felt like him and Sam were at their own private party.

"Over there," Sam nodded his head at a torn-open box of Schlitz on the counter. "I'll get us a couple."

"Cool." Anthony found an open spot on the wall to lean against. He let the music and grass go to work. He wasn't only in the same state as Sam, he was in the same city, the same house.

A guy with hair that fell below his ears gave Anthony a nod. "You just get back?" he said loudly over the chorus of "Lucy in the Sky with Diamonds."

"Huh?" Anthony leaned in and saw Sam snag two beers.

"From over there?" the guy asked. "Vietnam?"

"Uh, no." Anthony rubbed his head, reminding him his hair hadn't grown out as much as he had thought.

Sam finally returned and placed a beer in Anthony's hand. "Hey," Sam said to the guy. "You go here?"

"Yep. I'm Pete. Mechanical engineering."

"Cool. I'm Sam. History."

Suzy wedged her way between Sam and Anthony. "You get one of those for me?"

Sam looked at the open beer in his hand. "Here. I didn't drink out of it yet." He turned to weave his way to the torn beer box. "Be right back."

Pete turned to Anthony. "What about you, man? What are you majoring in?"

Anthony opened his beer. "I'm in the Army."

"Huh?" Pete said.

"He doesn't go here," Suzy said.

A small group of people joined Gloria in shouting the chorus to "Lucy in the Sky with Diamonds." Anthony took a swig. "I just got done with Advanced Infantry Training. AIT. I ship out in a few days."

"Whoa." Pete's eyes went wide. "I'm sorry, man."

Anthony wasn't sure what he expected Pete to say, but that wasn't it. "Sorry for what?"

Pete put a hand on Anthony's shoulder. "My brother's buddy got his notice a few months ago."

"I don't have to go. I want to go."

Suzy turned to Anthony. "I didn't know you volunteered to go. Why would anyone want to go over there?"

"What?" Anthony furrowed his eyebrows.

Sam came back with a beer for himself and opened the can. "Come on, guys, don't be so sad. I was only gone for five seconds." He chuckled but quickly stopped when he realized no one was joining in. "What'd I miss?"

Suzy pointed to Anthony with her beer. "We were telling Anthony he shouldn't *have* to go over there."

Anthony felt heat rush to his face. It reminded him of learning about being a POW. There was no way he was going to survive Charlie and his line of questions if he was going to let a couple hippies get to him. "I said I want to go."

"But it's so messed up-" Suzy began.

"Come on, Suzy," Sam cut in, "I told you how important this is to Anthony."

Suzy waved her beer around. "Yeah, I know. Your dad fought Nazis. This isn't exactly the same thing."

Pete nodded. "Those Nazis were fucked up. We had to go over there to stop them."

Anthony exhaled. "And we need to be in South Vietnam to stop the VC." For being a mechanical engineer, Pete was thicker than a five-dollar malt.

"We're not helping," Suzy insisted. "We're making things worse."

"Have you been there?" Anthony asked. His dad would have cuffed him on the ear for being so disrespectful to a girl but his dad wasn't here.

"She knows some things," Sam quickly cut in.

The hazy air swirled around Anthony as he took a huge gulp of his beer. He focused on how it was warm and how it felt heavy when it settled in his stomach.

"I do know some things. I know about the women and children," Suzy said. "Civilians being killed."

"Yeah," Pete nodded. "I heard on the news about these soldiers—"

"When you volunteer to stand up and fight for your country, you can give me a lesson, but for now you can shut your face." Anthony slammed his beer can on a nearby counter and glared at Sam. "This was a stupid idea." He shoved his way in between Sam and Suzy to make his way to the door.

"Where're you going, Soldier Boy?" Gloria shouted from her place near the record player.

Anthony slammed the door behind him. The lyrics to "It's Getting Better" followed him out onto the porch. He jumped down the three steps and looked down the sidewalk in both directions. Dammit. He was too busy looking at Suzy trying to hold Sam's hand and didn't pay attention to how they'd gotten to the party.

He seethed as he wrapped his arms around himself. His coat was still inside, thrown over a chair by the door. His breath came out of his mouth in small puffy clouds. Anthony inhaled the cold air, willing it to calm the adrenaline coursing through his body. There were a lot of people who questioned what was going on over there and the tactics being used to get closer to victory. He knew that and saw it on the news every night at his parents' house. But he also saw his fellow soldiers doing a job he was proud to do and it was clear not everyone had the balls to do it.

Anthony thought about just leaving, figuring he could somehow find his way to the campus, or the bus stop. The screen door to the house banged against the side of it.

"Good, you're still here." Sam held out Anthony's blue and white puffy coat.

"Where else would I be?" Anthony huffed. "I have no idea where I am and I came here to see you. But instead you drag me to some party."

He yanked the coat from Sam's hand and pulled it on. "I shouldn't have come." He started off again in the direction they had come from.

"Shouldn't have come?" Sam hustled after Anthony. "Are you kidding me? This is the best thing that happened to me all semester."

Anthony whirled around to face Sam. "This is the best thing?"

"By far."

"What about the thing with Dow? You made it seem like that was the best moment of your entire life. Like it made you discover who you really are so you could be with people who felt just like you." That hit Sam in the gut. It took a lot for Sam to tell Anthony not just about being there but also liking it.

"My first day at Bowen was the best day of my life," Sam said. "Actually, no. The best day was when Mr. O'Brien assigned us that research project."

"Yeah?" Anthony said in a gruff voice. A warm feeling crept into his chest when he remembered Sam walking into the school in a pair of jeans and a blue plaid shirt. "That was a good day for me too."

Sam looked a bit relieved.

"And after the project? That was good too," Anthony continued, not altering his tone. He wasn't sure what exactly he was mad at, but he was still mad.

"Every day after that has been good," Sam said.

They stood silently facing each other. Sam shivered, still holding his own coat. Anthony zipped his coat and stuffed his hands in his pockets. "My hands are freezing."

"Mine too." Sam put on his coat and fumbled with the buttons since his hands were close to frozen. "Come on. I can figure out the way."

They walked side by side, silent for about a block. "My bus leaves in about two hours. My mom will kill me if I miss it," Anthony said.

"Then we have two hours." Sam picked up his pace.

Different feelings gnawed at Anthony. Part of him wanted to go back inside the party and kick Pete in the head and give Suzy some more information about what the last few months of his life had been like. What it took to be ready to face whatever was waiting for him at the other side of the world. Anthony took a few quick steps to catch up with Sam. The only certain thing was that time was running out and he had to make the most of the next 120 minutes.

After sliding the chain lock into place, Sam leaned over Paul's desk, scrutinizing the calendar with diagonal lines and block lettering. "He's got another fifteen minutes with his study group and then he'll probably stop to get something to eat before the dining hall closes. He's pretty predictable." Sam stood and turned. "I'm guessing we have a half hour. Maybe a little more."

Anthony couldn't ignore the queasiness he felt in the pit of his stomach that had nothing to do with the beer he had at the party. He had to talk to Sam about it. Who knew when he would get another chance. "I think Suzy *likes* you."

"She's my friend," Sam said. "We cut open frogs together. We eat lunch together sometimes-"

"You go to demonstrations against Dow Chemical together."

"Yeah? Gloria was there too. Maybe I'm scheming on her too."

"Gloria's not the one who hangs on your arm, who goes around a group of people so she can stand right next to you." Anthony didn't know how he was going to make it through the next year if Sam wasn't waiting for him.

"Okay, fine. Suzy likes me," Sam said flatly. "But I don't like her. Not like that."

Something in Anthony relaxed a little. Maybe he just needed to hear it.

"If I did, I'd tell you. I promise." Sam held up three fingers. "Scout's honor."

Anthony shook his head. "You were never a Boy Scout. I don't believe it." He couldn't stop his lip from curling. Sam wasn't even holding his fingers against each other. He looked like a little kid who'd just counted to three.

"True." Sam cocked his head at the ceiling for a second. He took a step toward Anthony and placed a hand over his heart. "I, Samuel Francis McGuern, solemnly swear on every ketchup bottle in the

whole entire world. I am not scheming on Suzy. Not now, nor will
I ever." He put both hands on Anthony's shoulders. "If something
changes, you'll be the first to know."

Anthony put a hand on one of Sam's. "You promise?"

Sam nodded. "I really promise."

"Okay." Anthony tried to forget the image of Suzy leaning on
Sam with her long hair draped over his arm. She looked the way
Maria did whenever Van Morrison's "Brown Eyed Girl" came on the
radio, convinced he had written the song about her.

With his hands still on Anthony's shoulders, Sam bent his head
so his eyes were even with Anthony's. "Anything you want to tell me?
Something going on with that Capper guy?"

Anthony laughed out loud. "Yeah. We're getting pretty close."
Capper had become a friend, a good friend, during Basic and AIT. He
needed someone like him by his side, but there were some secrets
Capper would never know about him and so would no one else in the
Army.

"We're okay?"

"We're okay." Anthony held his hands out and Sam placed his
hands in them. "You keep fighting for me here. Not against me. Or
any other soldier. And I'll do the fighting over there."

"I don't know how to fight."

"I think you're figuring it out." Anthony leaned forward, pressing
his lips as hard as he could against Sam's. As if the size of this kiss
could somehow guarantee everything and everyone would be okay
when he returned home in a year.

They rested their foreheads against one another.

"And no secrets," Sam said.

"No secrets," Anthony agreed. "About anything."

They released one another, staring with silly smiles on their faces
when the door opened a few inches, stopped by the chain locked in
place. Anthony and Sam leapt apart, each backed up to one of the
desks. The door opened and closed again with the same result.

"Sam?" Paul called, his face between the door and the wall. "What gives?"

Anthony kept his eyes on Sam, memorizing his walk. His fingers as they undid the chain lock. His playful tone as he told Paul he had no idea how the chain lock got in place. How weird. Anthony had thought that summer afternoon in his bedroom was the last time he would see Sam before going over there. He was wrong. He got another chance. But there would be no more chances. This was it.

PART II
THE WAR OVER THERE

NOVEMBER 21, 1967

An actual bus drove Anthony and the other new arrivals from the airport to the base where they were supposed to report. It reminded Anthony of riding the city bus in the middle of a record-breaking summer, except this was hotter, wetter, and the ride was a lot bumpier. It started out smooth as they left the airport, cruising along on a paved road, but gradually the buildings faded away and the only things Anthony could see were trees, rice paddies, grass that might have been taller than him, and a dirt road.

A bus driver was taking them to the war, just like a bus driver took him to school. It was weird. There was no evidence of the war outside of the window, except for the wire and bars that crossed it.

Despite the sun directly shining into the useless open window, Anthony's eyes began to droop as his head bobbed in time with the bumps in the road. After traveling for well over a day, he had no idea what time it was.

Someone tapped his shoulder. "I want you to have this, Capone."

Anthony narrowed his eyes in the tap's direction. Capper's square, squat body reached across the aisle and held an envelope in front of Anthony's face.

It said *Mama and Dad.*

Anthony almost had to shout to be heard over the other soldiers and the roar of the bus. "What's this?"

"You know what it is." Capper stretched over the aisle seat and tossed the envelope. Part of it landed on Anthony's leg.

"You're not gonna need that." Anthony turned to the window, scanning the green, wet countryside, looking for signs of civilization and the base they had been driving to for the past hour. It was so hot it was hard to breathe. How was he going to hump through the field if he couldn't even breathe on a bus?

"I know I'm not. But I want you to have it anyway." Capper attempted to wipe the sweat from his flat top.

Anthony took the envelope by the corner. "Where am I supposed to put it?"

"I don't care. But don't stick it in your pants. My mama doesn't need to find out I'm dead *and* smell your sweaty ass." Capper laughed as he settled into his seat, but it was the kind of laugh someone did when they heard a joke they didn't get.

Anthony reached into the pocket of his army-issued rucksack. He pulled out his own envelope and held it out to Capper without saying anything, shaking it for emphasis. Capper took it without a word.

Anthony had scrawled out the letter while they were waiting in an airport in Hawaii so the plane could be refueled. No one was allowed to leave the airport so Anthony had written a letter to Sam that he dropped into a mailbox and another to his parents that he prayed would never be sent. The palm trees swaying in the perfect sky outside the airport had mocked him as he licked the envelope and wrote *FREE* in the corner. You didn't have to pay for stamps when you were fighting in a war. That was a bonus Anthony didn't expect.

It didn't *look* like there was a war going on outside where he was now. Anthony wondered where the war was actually happening and if they would pull right up to it, and be dropped off in the middle of a battle full of bullets and explosions.

He must have dozed off because when the bus lurched to a stop Anthony saw some sort of little town had sprouted up in the middle of nowhere. A cluster of small, long buildings with triangular roofs and tiny windows that had to be the barracks. Lots of jeeps, convoys, and trucks. As Anthony disembarked the bus, a whole new level of heat and humidity hit him. He recalled many summer nights, baking in his room, wondering why he even bothered opening the window. That was an ice box compared to this. Sweat formed on his forehead and forearms as soon as he stepped off the bus.

Capper wiped his wet forehead with a wet arm. "Welcome to Vietnam, huh Capone?"

Home for the next 365 days.

Anthony sat at the edge of his rack and tried to figure out where to put everything the supply sergeant had just given him and all the other new guys. He put the helmet next to his bed, and opened up his backpack. He rolled up the camouflage cover, poncho, and poncho liner as tightly as he could and crammed them into the ruck. A change of clothes went in as well. He left the other set out. The rifle and ammo he left alone for now since no one else looked like they were ready for an attack. The guns would be locked up for the night in a few hours anyway.

Anthony imagined that this is what sleepaway camp must be like during a break from canoeing, swimming, and kickball. Guys lounged on their racks, most of them not wearing shirts. Some read books, some read letters, some slept, almost all of them smoked. No one was concerned about the war.

Anthony picked up the carton of cigarettes and candy that came with his supplies. It was ironic to do all this training, all this running, all these pushups, only to get cigarettes and candy upon arriving for battle. His mom hated that his dad smoked. She would make him go outside in the summer, and in the winter she'd make him open a window in the bathroom. Anthony never knew when his dad started smoking. Maybe he'd been issued a pack when he arrived in France and had been lighting up ever since.

Anthony tucked the cigarette pack into a pocket of his backpack, where he had put Capper's letter. Hopefully he would never have an occasion to use either.

"So, this is it, huh?" Capper scanned the barracks. Cots lined the perimeter with a little footlocker at the foot of each one. "This is war."

"Don't get used to it, FNG." A shirtless guy with a bronze chest and hair that hadn't been buzzed in months spoke from underneath his helmet. The guy had the body of a sculpture chiseled from marble.

"Are you talking to me?" Capper asked.

"Are you a Fucking New Guy?" The guy lifted the helmet off his face to glance at Anthony and Capper.

Capper looked like he was trying to come up with a retort but he half-smiled instead. "Yeah, I guess I am. Only been in town a couple hours."

"Well FNG, and FNG's buddy," he turned to Anthony. "Soak it up. Who knows how long this is going to last and my bet is not long." He repositioned the helmet over his face so he could go back to his nap.

Well, Helmet Guy, who everyone called Jersey because he was from New Jersey, was wrong. Anthony, Capper, and the rest of the crew spent a week hanging out at the base doing nothing that was in any way associated with the war, unless you counted drinking Coke, playing cards, and challenging other squads to games of volleyball as contributions to the war effort. Anthony definitely didn't and was sure his dad would agree.

"Mail call!" Sergeant Avery, short in stature but tall in presence, followed a gust of wind and rain into the barracks. He held a large bag that had dark green spots on it from his journey in the rain.

"Mail's here!" a soldier nicknamed QB called, as if everyone didn't just hear the announcement. He claimed to be a football star at his high school in Newton, Iowa. Despite coming from a family of farmers, QB enlisted at twenty-one years old because he also came from a long line of soldiers and felt the need to join that family business instead of the one involving corn and beans.

Anthony and the other soldiers gathered around Sergeant Avery like he was an ice cream truck who pulled up in front of a playground. He was losing at cards anyway, and mail call was the most exciting thing that had happened the last few days.

"Capper." Avery threw a letter like a Frisbee and it hit Capper in the chest.

Capper glanced at the envelope and grinned. "It's from my girl."

"Give Capper some time alone in the outhouse tonight," Mikey chuckled. At nineteen, he was a little older than Anthony but looked younger. With factories being one of the few employment opportunities in Detroit, he decided to join up. His girlfriend of over a year, Katherine, was not excited about this decision. She reminded Mikey of this in her first couple letters.

"Maybe this time it won't smell so bad when he's done," Tim added. He was from Minnesota and got drafted after graduating college with an English degree.

Several of the guys made farting noises and laughed as Avery continued to pass letters out. "Jersey, Lennox, Picasso…"

Anthony felt like he was in PE in seventh grade, hoping he wouldn't be the last one picked for basketball. He'd gotten two letters since arriving. Both were from his mom, and they both said the same thing: I love you, I miss you, be safe, and some detail about what Maria was doing in school or the tough day his dad had at the garage.

"Capone." The point of a letter hit his chest.

It was from Sam. Finally. All he needed to see was the WI in the return address. His heart did a little flip as he slipped his finger under the flap.

"That's it." Avery shook the bag upside down to prove his point. "I hear we're getting ready to move out so don't get too comfortable." With that, the sergeant swung open the door and went back out into the rain.

"What's your girl have to say, Capper?" Jersey asked. At twenty-three, he might have been one of the older soldiers. And one of the most serious, since he planned to make a career out of the Army. But even Jersey became a kid at story time when it came to the mail.

Capper dramatically unfolded the letter and cleared his throat. "Eddie Bear…"

Chuckles erupted from the group of guys dressed in fatigues, all sporting various stages of a buzz cut growing out.

"What?" Capper lowered the letter. "That's what she calls me." He cleared his throat and began again. "Mom's already talking about Christmas and the family coming over and the ones we'll be visiting. I have to say, my heart's not in it. It was such a wonderful surprise to be able to see you so close to Thanksgiving and it makes me sad to know there'll be no surprise visit at Christmas. I'm doing my best not to worry about you. I try to keep myself busy with my classes so that by the time you get home I can have a good job and you don't have to worry about taking care of me. I'll be able to take care of you."

"She sounds like a keeper," Picasso said. He arrived on the same day as Anthony, only he'd been drafted after failing out of Stony Brook University and losing his student deferment.

"I'd like some chick to take care of me. Does she have any sisters?" QB asked.

"She's got three older brothers. So shut your face if you want to hear the rest," Capper responded.

Anthony already knew all about Lorraine and how she didn't like that Capper enlisted and how she would have much preferred that he stayed in Kentucky to help his dad manage the local supermarket. It was safer, of course, and it was a good job. Good enough for the plans she had for the two of them. Anthony had heard bits and pieces of Lorraine's letters throughout Basic and AIT. As their training came to an end, her letters got more desperate. She'd heard about jobs in the rear, working in some office. Or, could he change his mind? The post office was hiring. Capper got a good laugh out of that and told Anthony he thought camouflage suited him better than mail carrier blue.

So while Capper held center stage, still reading Lorraine's letter, Anthony opened the one from Sam. He knew he would have to share it. That was the unspoken rule of the mail. Anthony had appreciated the rule the last few days when QB didn't bring anything for him and he got to hear about Jersey's mom heading up a bake sale at church, and Mikey's girl getting a job at some soda shop. All the guys shared their letters, allowing everyone to have a small piece of their hometowns and family dinners.

Would they see through Sam's letter? See something more in

the descriptions of his classes and trips to the library and know that *ketchup* had to stand for something else? Would they understand he was just a buddy writing to his buddy overseas? Nobody gave Tim a hard time when a pal wrote him, but that friend was also a soldier going through OCS.

"Forever yours, Lorraine." Capper folded the letter. "Until next time, gents. What about you Capone? You're next."

"Uh," Anthony's eyes swept over the letter for something that might give everything away but only saw the usual words: school, library, work. He also saw Christmas and Jimmy. "It's from my buddy back home. Sam. He goes to school at UW."

"Groovy," QB said. "Tell us all about the life of a college boy."

Dozens of eyes looked at Anthony with anticipation. They might as well already have known who Sam was and been familiar with his snarky smile and sarcasm. It didn't matter it was some guy thousands and thousands of miles away.

Anthony,

Well, Thanksgiving sucks when your dad's all hacked off at you and your mom doesn't make enough mashed potatoes for you to eat on the bus on the way back to school. What a raw deal, huh? I put some ketchup on them at Thanksgiving and that helped. But as you know, ketchup has that effect on me.

"Your friend sounds like a weird cat," Mikey said.

"He's weird, all right," Capper agreed. He'd heard pieces of Sam's letters from his bottom bunk throughout training.

Anthony hoped the smile would mask the nerves he felt.

So I'm back at school now. Suzy keeps asking me if you hate her or hate Gloria. She's sorry Gloria was a ditz when she saw you. I'm sorry Gloria was a ditz too but I already told you that.

"Gloria?" Picasso asked. "Is she your girl?"

"You going steady, Capone?" Capper joined in. "All this time and you never told me?"

Anthony wanted to throw up at the thought of him and Gloria being together, and not because of what he felt for Sam. If the guys knew the slightest thing about Gloria, this would be a completely different conversation.

"No girl," Anthony said. "It's a friend of Sam's friend."

"Maybe I can ask one of Lorraine's friends to write to you," Capper suggested. "Another nursing student?" He raised his eyebrows at Anthony. "A guy needs a girl besides his mama writing to him. And your mama is no good when you gotta keep your hands busy."

"I bet QB thinks about his mom," Mikey grinned.

"Shut up. I think about your mom," QB smiled like that was the cleverest thing ever said.

"I think about both your moms," Lennox said from his seat on his footlocker. "Let him finish."

"You guys gonna behave yourselves?" Anthony glanced between Mikey and QB like a strict teacher. After they both sort of nodded, he held the letter up and kept going.

It's going to be a hairy semester come January. I'm taking six classes because I was thinking about how long I'll have to go to school to get my PHD. You skipped out on officer training. Maybe I should amp up my course load. If I can be done in three years instead of four I can figure out where I want to go for graduate school. NYC? LA? Maybe stick around Chicago and go to UIC for a couple years if you get your old job at the garage after you get back. You got any other ideas?

Jersey snorted. "You gonna live with this dude when you get home?" He glanced at the guys around him. "Something you want to enlighten us about, Capone?" A chuckle ripped through the soldiers.

Jersey thought he was joking, but Anthony still relived the nightmare he had over and over again in AIT. What would happen if anyone found out? He had done his best to try to read the letter out loud and scan a few words ahead so he could prepare himself for what came next but it wasn't like he would be able to rewrite Sam's letter on the fly. A million thoughts flooded his brain as he tried to think of a believable answer for Jersey: they both hated their parents and never want to go back home, their moms converted their bedrooms into sewing rooms and they wouldn't have a place to stay, Sam always had a hard time making any sort of decision and always asked for someone else's opinion before doing anything.

Finally, Anthony shrugged, doing his best to steady his hands and voice. "Maybe I'll sack out at your mom's." He grinned. "Might be the best option. QB talks about her in his sleep."

That got everyone roaring and Anthony slowly let out a long breath to stop his racing heart. It worked. A couple guys punched him in the arm to signal their approval. QB shrugged as if to say *it's true.*

As Lennox opened his letter, getting ready to take the floor, the door to the barracks swung open and bounced off the wall a few times. Sergeant Avery stood at ease in the doorway. According to Jersey, Avery wasn't even thirty, but he looked older with his dark sunglasses on. Avery's mouth moved but Anthony couldn't make out what he was saying as the ribbing moved from mothers to sisters and one another's girlfriends. "I said we're moving out!" he bellowed. "My squad. Saddle up, let's go!"

Everyone stopped moving like they were in a game of freeze dance and determined to win. QB balanced on one foot, not swaying in the slightest. Capper's mouth hung open with his arms bent at the sides as if he was about to thrust his hips back and forth.

"Playtime's over, ladies," Sergeant Avery barked as he walked further into the barracks. "There's a village about thirty clicks away that needs some attention. It looks vacant, but that doesn't mean it is. Search and destroy."

The barracks were the picture of organized chaos as the squad grabbed their packs, ponchos, and helmets, and tied and retied their bootlaces. Adrenaline pumped through Anthony's hands as he reached for his helmet and settled it on his head at a lopsided angle. He quickly adjusted it. A second ago he worried his whole world was about to fall apart, that his secret would be exposed. Now he took a seat in a crammed jeep next to Capper, headed into the war. It was happening. It was really happening. After almost two weeks of being in some weird summer camp, it was finally happening. During Basic and AIT, he had learned how no one could be completely trusted over here. The little old lady with no teeth could be harboring a whole brigade of VC. The boy who begs for food could lead you right into danger.

And abandoned villages were a perfect hiding place for Charlie.

The war Anthony's dad fought in required strategy and planning.

Those same tactics didn't work in the jungles and rice paddies of
Vietnam, where Charlie didn't play by the established game plan.
Anthony's dad wanted to know the strategy. The same strategy
didn't apply.

Now, Anthony could write home and tell his dad how it was done
over here. A thousand soldiers didn't storm a beach. They went out in
small groups to find Charlie and drag him out.

The ride out was bumpy, cramped, and hot. Anthony kept wiping
his forehead with a bandana and his cheeks against the shoulder of his
soaked shirt. He had heard plenty about the soaking rains, but *this* is
how wet he got by sitting in the back of a jeep underneath a perfect
sky. And the heat. Damn. This was a new level of heat that couldn't be
explained. Anthony swatted at a bug trying to make a meal out of his
forearm.

As the jeep rambled along and Anthony held his weapon against
his chest, he scanned the tall grass lining the road. He expected
someone to jump out even though that would have been the stupidest
thing for Charlie to do. Instead, he focused on the ville, wondering if it
would look like the clusters of huts he had only seen in photographs.

Suddenly the jeep let out a slight squeak as Avery pumped the
brakes. "Watch out for mines. No one's losing a foot today, got it?"

Anthony double checked the ground trampled by tire treads. Watch,
he'd step on a mine less than five seconds into his first mission.

"Charlie's got 'em everywhere," Capper whispered as they fell into
formation. "Booby traps in trees, holes with spikes on the bottom.
Fuckin' crazy, right?"

Anthony didn't want to think about the other photographs he
saw of the creative ways the VC had invented to kill, maim, and
destroy him. He focused on Jersey who was leading the way in. In a
matter of moments, the ville materialized out of the thick trees with
long, dangling leaves. Jersey pushed past a branch and there it was.
Huts mostly. Lopsided doors ajar. Thatched roofs. A lone chicken
strutted out of one of the huts and clucked as it crossed Anthony's
path.

Avery had assigned everyone a particular area of the village to sweep. Anthony, Capper, Lennox, and Jersey were given a cluster of huts at the other end. It was strangely quiet considering that a war was supposedly raging on in every direction. A door from one of the huts swayed in the heavy breeze and Anthony's heart began to pound, his neck throbbing with each beat. He held his gun up, unable to control the adrenaline spasm in his arms.

Jersey gave a signal, indicating he was going in first and for Capper and Anthony to follow him. Lennox would stay on the rickety porch. As Jersey sharply turned to point his gun at the doorway, Anthony and Capper also raised their guns at the ready, prepared to shoot.

Empty.

Everyone let out a loud breath at the same time. There was no place to hide among the small table and few chairs scattered about. There were plates on the table with bits of rice stuck to them. But no sign of the enemy.

Jersey picked up one of the plates to study the rice. Anthony scoured the room with his gun on his shoulder. If all missions could be like this, he wouldn't win any medals but he'd make it home alive, that was for sure. Maybe his dad had a point. How do you win a war if all you did was mess around in empty huts?

Capper went out on the porch and told Lennox it was all clear. He kicked off several pots standing next to the doorway. They shattered upon hitting the ground but one made a dull thud before exploding into shards. "What the—"

In less than a second, Anthony and Jersey were outside. They looked to where Capper was pointing. There was something off about the ground where the last pot had landed. The leaves looked off. The grass didn't sway in the wind. It was an arts and crafts project and the teacher's pet took extra care arranging the leaves and grass. Jersey squatted off to the side and ran his hand over the dirt and leaves. He looked up at Capper and Anthony. "Sergeant?" he called. "You're gonna want to see this."

Avery hustled over as Anthony took a step back, his heartbeat returning to his neck. He had learned a lot about Charlie during his training. And he wasn't *like* a rat. He *was* a rat. He dug and burrowed his way through tunnels throughout South Vietnam. He ate in the tunnels, slept in the tunnels, lived in the tunnels. You had no idea where they were or where they would lead but they were everywhere. And Charlie could be in there right now.

"Cover me," Avery ordered as he gripped what must have been the edges of the tunnel cover. In perfect unison, Anthony, Capper, Jersey, and Lennox pointed their weapons at the area between Avery's hands.

Anthony sucked in some air as Avery swept off the cover.

Nothing. Just an entryway to an underground world.

Again, a collective exhale came from everyone.

They waited in silence for a few moments, straining to hear anything. The hole looked like something an extremely large rabbit would have dug in Anthony's backyard. Avery stepped toward the hole and peered inside.

"If there's a VC in there, make sure he won't be for long." Avery strode to the center of the ville where other soldiers were gathering, having come up empty in their search for anything.

Anthony pointed his gun into the hole and fired. Releasing round and after round. Tufts of grass and dirt bounced into the air, covering everyone's boots and dusting their pants. Anthony glanced at Capper and Jersey who were still annihilating the hole so he fired another round inside.

After a few seconds, they stopped and listened. No screams. No yells. Silence.

Jersey swung his gun across his back like he was getting his backpack on after a day at school. He held a freshly lit cigarette in his mouth. "And that's our day, boys."

"That's it?" Capper said.

"For today," Jersey responded, taking a long drag. He headed to the group gathered at the edge of the village.

Anthony's whole body coursed with adrenaline and for what? Wasting a hole in the ground? Almost two weeks in Vietnam and the only thing he can write home to his dad was he'd gotten pretty good at cards and hadn't taken up smoking yet. And oh yeah, that hole in the ground never stood a chance.

On the other hand, only 351 days to go.

DECEMBER 17, 1967

Sam saw his dad's station wagon as the bus pulled into the terminal on Canal Street. He knew his dad would have preferred to pick him up at the one on 95th since it was a lot closer to their house, but that bus didn't work out with Sam's class schedule. The windows were fogged up which means his dad had been waiting in the cold without the engine on in order to save gas. He opened the back of the wagon and threw one of his suitcases in there along with Jimmy's empty one.

"Hey, Dad." Sam slid into the passenger seat and slapped his dad's knee.

Sam's dad sat with his hands on the steering wheel at a perfect ten and two. He exhaled puffs of air that swirled around his head and added to the condensation on the windows. "Your brother came home last week."

The smile on Sam's face faltered. This was old news. Sam's mom had told him all about the pot roast she was making in honor of Jimmy's first meal home. "I know. It's cool his time ended before Christmas. It was weird not having him there last year. Plus, I got one less present." Sam chuckled.

Sam's dad pulled out of the bus station and navigated the frigid streets of Chicago's Loop. Snow piled up against every curb and sidewalk. "He looks good. A little skinny. A little tired. But good."

"I'm glad to hear that," Sam said. "Really glad." Hopefully he could say the same thing about Anthony when he came home in the fall. His mom would take care of the skinny thing during his first meal at home.

Sam's dad stopped at a red light and turned, looking him right in the eye. "Not one word about that hippie crap in front of your brother."

Sam had to stop himself from rolling his eyes. His dad was bringing this up again? "Okay," he said to the dashboard.

Sam's dad's eyes went to the road. "Not one word."

"Got it." Sam leaned on the armrest on the door. He wasn't planning on recounting every detail of his extracurricular activities with Jimmy or give him a transcript of all the shit that came out of Gloria's mouth. He didn't need to know that the best friend he'd made at school was a proud SDS member who'd gotten him to hang up fliers all over the student union.

"You're not going to ruin his first Christmas home," Sam's dad pressed.

"I said okay," Sam said with more force than he meant. If he had been about five years younger, that tone would have earned him a cuff on the back of the head. Now, his dad grunted as he waited in a long line of cars wanting to go south of Lake Shore Drive.

Sam's mom had left up the baseball pennants and the model air-planes still stood ready for takeoff on top of the bookshelf. But there was a table in the corner with her sewing machine on it, and bins of fabric and supplies underneath. A lopsided pile of pillows had toppled over, all of them embroidered with candy canes, wreaths, or Christ-mas trees. Sam's mom never missed a chance to participate in the St. Francis Holiday Bazaar. The old ladies *loved* her special holiday pillows. They made such *lovely* gifts. It looked like Sam would be bunking up with them for most of his holiday break. He heaved his suitcase on top of the bed.

"Hey, Pint-size."

No question who that was. Sam turned with a cocky grin. "Hey, Half-gallon."

Jimmy stood in the doorframe. Usually his form filled it, but he did look a bit skinny. His dad was right. Before he'd left, he had a little extra baggage around his middle. But he'd kept his hair in the flat top he'd given himself about two years ago. Jimmy flopped onto the beige bedspread and put his hands behind his head as if they were hanging out on a typical afternoon. "How's college life?"

Sam thought about the semester thus far and shrugged. "Busy. Different. It's nice to be away sometimes."

Jimmy nodded. "I think that's a pretty good description of the Air Force too."

"So you're home?" Sam shoved his suitcase under the bed. He didn't see the point in using the dresser. "For good?"

"For the next few weeks," Jimmy said. "They lined up a job for me at Whiteman Air Force Base."

"Where?" Sam asked.

"It's in Missouri," Jimmy explained. "Closer than Vietnam, right?"

"But probably not close enough for Mom."

"You got that right. She cried and cried when I told her I wasn't here to stay."

"She's probably sick of living with Dad all by herself." The car ride from the bus stop was enough for Sam, and he was only going to be home for a few weeks.

Jimmy laughed a little. "Probably."

Sam sat at the edge of the bed since Jimmy took up the entire length of the twin. He always towered over Sam, and not because he was the older brother. Jimmy was the tallest one in the family. No one else was over six feet. "What was it like over there?" Sam asked.

Jimmy shrugged a shoulder. "Hot. Wet. Hot and wet. I think it rained the entire month of June."

"I know that already. What else?" Sam wanted something that would assure him Anthony would come home too, just like Jimmy did.

Jimmy pulled himself up and swung his legs over the side of the bed. He slapped Sam on the knee hard with a grin. "You don't want to hear about that shit, little brother." He stood up.

"Yes, I do." Sam's eyes followed his brother to the door.

OCLON

"It was a war, Sammy." Jimmy shrugged, as if that was what needed to be said. "A lot of shit happens in a war."

Sam tried to think of another angle to get Jimmy to talk. He needed more.

"So, what's it like where you are, huh? I heard it can get pretty crazy there too." Jimmy sat up with a grin, his eyebrows going up and down.

"What?"

"There's quite a crowd up in Madison, huh?" Jimmy leaned against the doorframe. "Hippies. Blacks. Fairies."

Jimmy's effort to change the subject was noticeable. "Yep. Quite a crowd."

"You ever meet one?" Jimmy asked, as if Sam had been on some expedition looking for the abominable snowman.

"Meet what? A hippie? You can go to Grant Park and see a couple for yourself in their natural habitat."

"That's not what I mean," Jimmy said. "A fairy."

"I don't know." It was true. Maybe he'd met hundreds of guys like him and Anthony. He had no idea.

"You be careful up there, Pint-size."

"You ever meet any where you were? In the Air Force?" Sam had been so busy worrying about Anthony being hurt or injured or captured, he had forgotten to worry about what would happen if someone found out about him.

"We had some ideas about a couple guys in Basic. But they weren't there for too long."

"Maybe they made their way to Madison and are now walking among us," Sam said. A joke was usually a good distraction.

"All the places to go to college and you chose there, huh?"

"I guess so."

"Well, it's good to have you home, Sammy." Jimmy tapped on the door frame twice, about to leave, but he stopped with one foot still in the bedroom. "I'm going out with Sandy tonight. You want to come along?"

"It's been a long day, Jimmy, and I don't feel like being the little brother who tags along."

116

"Her cousin, Patty, is in town for the holidays," Jimmy explained.

Sam narrowed his eyes at Jimmy. "Are you asking me to come or did you already tell them I was?"

"Come on, Sammy. Humor a pretty out-of-town girl for a night. She's a college girl at U of I and going to be a teacher, like you. But she wants to teach the ankle biters, not the smart asses." Jimmy nodded at Sam with a grin. "When was the last time you went on a date anyway?"

Sam knew the answer to that. It was Homecoming senior year, a couple weeks before that English project changed his life. He'd asked Sherry, this cheerleader, because he thought a night dancing with a pretty girl like her would make him not feel all the things he wasn't supposed to and make him forget what he felt for the beautiful boy in his English class. They danced to every slow song and at the end of the night, they politely said good-bye and see you on Monday.

"So you admit it," Sam attempted to steer the conversation into safe territory. "It's a date."

"We're going to Vito and Nick's. I'm buying." Jimmy smiled. "This belly hasn't had a real pizza in over a year."

The sports pennants and model airplanes taunted Sam. No, he didn't want to pretend to go on a date with Sandy's cousin. But a night out on Jimmy's dime would mean less time in his house. "Fine."

"Neato."

"With olives," Sam went on. His belly hadn't had a good pizza in a little while too.

Jimmy made a sound like he was about to throw up.

"Green and black."

Jimmy doubled over along with another sound effect. "On half," he said when he straightened up.

"Whatever, as long as I get my olives."

"Oh, you'll get your olives." Jimmy moved his eyebrows up and down as he left Sam's bedroom.

That didn't even make sense. Sam stood up, pacing around his room. He put his suitcase on the bed, opened it, closed it, and put it on the floor. His eyes fell to the shelf with the model airplanes he'd never wanted to build in the first place, but it was what he'd gotten every year for his birthday for way too long. Jimmy liked the planes, so everyone thought Sam would too.

Sam opened his closet door. He loaded several model airplanes in his hands and set them on the floor, nudging them to the back of the closet with his foot. Sam surveyed the room and took the tacks out of the Chicago Bears and St. Louis Cardinals pennants and rolled them into a little tube. Those too went into the closet, where they unrolled over the model airplanes. The Chicago Cubs pennant met the same fate but Sam left up the White Sox pennant from their 1959 World Series run. His dad, Jimmy, and him would plant themselves in front of the TV during each game. If a game was on during dinner time, then Sam's mom made hot dogs, just like what they would have eaten if they were actually at the stadium.

It was one of the few times Sam could remember when being with his family came close to what he felt at the Stones concert. The only thing that compared was going to the demonstration with Suzy. And miles above that, was any time he spent with Anthony.

Two girls scurried out of the house and down the thin path that had been cleared in the snow. Sam recognized Sandy right away. Jimmy had been dating her ever since senior prom three years ago. Her dark hair spilled out over the fur collar of a red pea coat. The other girl was shorter with hair just below her ears. She wore the same coat, only hers was the color of mustard. Jimmy hopped out of the car and opened the front and back door so the girls could get in.

Sam felt stupid riding in the backseat on the way over to Sandy's but Jimmy insisted it would look even weirder if he jumped in the back when he pulled up to the house. Patty climbed in and smiled shyly at Sam. She was pretty, with shy brown eyes and a kind smile. She was going to be a great grammar school teacher. Sam felt as bad for her as he did for himself for getting roped into this.

"Hi, Sam," Sandy flashed him a smile as Jimmy closed the passenger door. "This is Patty."

"Hi," Sam and Patty said at the same time and for some reason that made Sam even more uncomfortable.

"I knew this was a good idea." Sandy smiled at Jimmy.

"You're full of good ideas." Jimmy picked up Sandy's gloved hand and kissed it. "Isn't she Sammy?" He looked in the rearview mirror to meet Sam's eyes.

"Jimmy always said you were smart," Sam said to Sandy.

Sandy scooted over the bench seat to lay her head on Jimmy's shoulder. Patty stayed on her side of the car. "I heard this pizza place is really good."

Sam nodded. "The best on this side of the city." At least something good was going to come out of this evening. Jimmy better not flake on the olives.

Sam sat back as the waitress brought a large pizza to the table, half of which had black and green olives. The other half had Italian sausage and mushrooms.

"Oh my goodness," Patty inhaled the steam coming off the pizza. "This looks outta sight." She laid her napkin on the lap of her dark blue skirt which looked nice with the light blue sweater she wore.

When she had taken her coat off, all Sam could think about was how Anthony had a sweater in the same color except his had a stripe going around it.

As the steam from the pizza floated around the table, Sandy went on and on about how proud she was of Jimmy for being so brave and for helping so many people. When she said she was so happy he was safe and everything could go back to normal, Jimmy's smile became stiff and he glanced at Sam.

"Let's serve this up, huh?" Jimmy picked up the triangular server and lifted a piece of pizza high in the air in effort to break the long trail of cheese stuck to the pan.

"How do you like school?" Sam asked Patty after everyone was served and Sandy and Jimmy went back to being lovebirds by holding hands and sneaking little smiles at one another.

"I *love* it," Patty squealed. "Doesn't it feel good to get away and finally do things on your own? My parents were so worried since I'm from this little town and U of I is so big." She ducked her head and picked up her piece of sausage and mushroom pizza. "I'm sorry. I'm talking too much, right?"

"No, it's okay," Sam tried to assure her. He went somewhere else for a moment, thinking what it would be like if in some alternate world where he could go on a date with Anthony and put his head on Anthony's shoulder the way Sandy did to Jimmy in between bites of pizza and sips of Coke. "Big school, small town. That's far out. Do you like your roommate?" He took a big bite of pizza to have an excuse not to talk for a few minutes. If Patty wanted to talk the whole time, that was fine by him.

Patty nodded excitedly. "She's cool all right. She came to U of I from Madison. That's where you go to school, right?"

Sam could only nod because of his full mouth.

Patty waited a moment for him to talk but laughed when Sam made exaggerating chewing motions. "Maybe I should start eating before it's all gone."

Sam gulped the food in his mouth. "Dorm food's not bad, but it's not this." He took another big bite.

After the pizza was gone, and Sandy insisted they would all have to go out again the next time Patty was in town, Sam sat in the backseat of the station wagon with Patty, their breath coming out in thick puffs. Jimmy and Sandy walked up the narrow walkway to Sandy's porch. Sam knew enough to know Jimmy needed a few minutes so he would have to occupy Patty for a little while longer. Sam felt bad for her. She was a nice girl and a smart girl. Any guy would think she was keen and might even be devising a way to see her again.

"You're so interesting, Sam," Patty leaned over from her side of the car and studied his face.

The pizza churned in Sam's stomach and threatened to rise up into his throat. She didn't want to kiss him, right? And he shouldn't kiss her anyway. It was a blind first date, if you could even call it a date.

"I've been called a lot of things," Sam tried to joke, "but I don't think anyone has ever said *interesting* before."

Patty scooted over. "Yeah, you let me talk about myself and things

I like. You like to study and think hitting the books is a gas." She scooted over a little more so her thigh was about six inches away from Sam's. "Will you write to me?" She held out a napkin that had her school address scribbled on it. She looked at him with shy eyes and Sam could tell that asking was a big deal for her.

Sam looked at the napkin and took it. "Sure." He felt a plastic smile spread over his face as he put Patty's address in the pocket of his jacket with a pat. "I mean, I'll try to find the time. I'm thinking of taking an extra class this semester and try to get into graduate school early." He looked through the window to see if Jimmy would return to the car any time soon, but he was busy kissing Sandy. Patty caught Sam's eyes but quickly averted her gaze.

After a few seconds they broke apart, holding hands. Their mouths moved but there was no way Sam could tell what they were saying. Sandy wasn't smiling, her head cocked to the side. Jimmy kept talking.

"They really love each other," Patty commented.

"They've been going steady for a while," Sam said.

"I'm glad you're not going with anyone. I had a nice time."

"It was…nice." Sam couldn't think of anything else to say.

Patty continued to lean toward him, her big brown eyes gazing up. He took a deep breath and kissed her on the cheek. It could hardly even be considered a kiss since it was small and quick.

Sam had known Anthony for almost six months before they kissed for the first time. That kiss started out small, on the lips, but morphed into a kiss unlike anything else Sam had ever experienced. There wasn't a lot to compare it to, but Sam had no idea it could be like that.

The streetlights and Christmas lights in Sandy's yard brought a little light into the station wagon. Based on the color of her cheeks Patty was cold, embarrassed, or swooning.

Sam shouldn't have kissed her. What if she visited next Christmas and wanted to know why he never wrote? What if Jimmy and Sandy got married and Jimmy became cousins with Patty? He pressed his mouth into a tight smile at Patty as he glanced at Sandy's porch, willing Jimmy to come back to the car.

Jimmy pulled Sandy into him, wrapping her in a hug for a few moments before finally making his way down the little path in the snow.

"I guess the coast is clear." Sam got out of the car to open Patty's door.

"It was nice to meet you, Sam. I hope to see you again," Patty smiled, her red lips amplified by her white teeth. She stepped out of the car and stood in front of him. "Have a merry Christmas."

"You too." Sam stepped to the side so Patty could get by. "I mean, you too. Merry Christmas."

Jimmy approached the car. "You kids need another minute?"

Patty ducked her head like Jimmy had swung open the closet door during Seven Minutes in Heaven. "No, we're good."

"We're good," Sam repeated, having no idea what that meant.

Patty giggled and shuffled up to the porch where Sandy was waiting for her.

Jimmy got in the car and slapped Sam's knee with a grin. "She's *good?*"

"That's what she said," Sam shrugged.

"Way to go, Sammy." Jimmy put the station wagon in gear and pulled away from the curb.

"I kissed her on the cheek." Sam took the napkin out of his jacket pocket and crumpled it into a ball.

"You might as well have gone all the way, based on what Sandy told me about her." Jimmy raised his eyebrows.

"Are you two copacetic?" Sam changed the subject. "Sandy didn't look too happy when you left."

"Yeah, we will be." Jimmy focused on the road. "She's not stoked about the whole Missouri plan."

"Oh." Sam knew what it was like to have the person you love be so far away.

"I told her she could move down there and find a job. I think they might have some housing on base for married couples."

"Married couples? What?" Sam turned on the bench seat. "Did you ask her yet?"

"Not yet." Jimmy gave Sam a sly smile. "It's a lot to ask. She has to leave everything and follow me to a place where she doesn't know anyone." He elbowed Sam, keeping both hands on the wheel. "Plus, there's no Vito's there."

"Wow." Sam smiled, genuinely happy for his brother. Everything was falling into place for him. But then his smile faltered. He would never be able to follow Anthony around if he decided to pursue a career in the army. That was part of the reason he passed on officer school.

The happiness he felt for Jimmy and Sandy morphed into a ball of ice that lodged itself in his gut. Anthony could only be his lifelong best friend, nothing more. It wasn't fair.

Sam pressed the napkin with Patty's address into a tighter, smaller ball. He rolled down the window a few inches.

"What the hell, Sam? It's freezing."

Sam tossed the napkin out the window. "Patty's not really my type."

"You didn't think she was choice?"

"Not really."

"Huh," Jimmy shrugged. "If a smart girl like Patty's not your type, then I have no idea what chick is."

"Yeah, I don't know either." Sam settled into the seat, wishing he could somehow disappear into it.

DECEMBER 31, 1967

Anthony had been in Vietnam for a little over a month and so far, he'd walked what had to be hundreds of miles, waded through a million rice paddies, searched several empty villages, killed a thousand bugs that bit his neck and arms, and drank Cokes and smoked cigarettes with the guys outside of this café. Not even a cold Coke provided any relief on a blazing afternoon.

And now they were raiding another ville. Sometimes there were chickens. One time there were rats, but no VC. In fact, no one at all. Not even a little kid begging for a chocolate bar.

Another day, another ville to raid. They had to take a small convoy about fifteen clicks away from base and then walk a few clicks further. The order was to search and destroy but it was more often like *tiptoe* and *sneak around*. At least it wasn't raining like it had been last time. Their boots had slopped through the muddy rivers that were once roads. Picasso had gotten trench foot and a two-day vacation.

Jersey suddenly stopped walking and Anthony almost ran into the pack on his back. He turned to the guys and gave them a signal, indicating he had heard something. In the stillness of the afternoon, murmurs from distant voices met Anthony's ears. It sounded like a girl, a woman. And she was talking to someone. He tightened his grip on his gun as everyone resumed stalking toward the ville. The squish of his boots in the thick mud echoed through the afternoon that had suddenly gone still.

Anthony strained to hear what the woman was saying, not that he would have been able to understand any of it. He thought there might have been another voice but it was hard to tell. Women often worked with Charlie, hid Charlie, and helped Charlie carry out missions or gather information.

With the voices getting louder, Jersey gave orders on how they should position themselves as the huts came into view. Anthony was behind Jersey with Capper behind him and Lennox behind Capper. Picasso, Tim, QB, and Mikey would go around to the back of the hut. They headed toward the shack where the voices came from. All the villes looked the same, with little shacks with thick roofs that might have been made of straw or hay.

The group halted as a pile of dried grass crunched under Capper's boot. Everyone held their breath. The voices from inside one of the huts didn't stop.

Jersey signaled to continue. He slowly raised his gun into the firing position and kicked open the door.

The women froze and stopped talking. After a second, one of them wiped her hands on long black, baggy pants. "Hello, America," she said in tentative English, holding out the plate.

"Good morning, ladies," Capper nodded.

Jersey eyed the plate, piled high with rice and cocked his gun. "Lots of food there."

"Eat." The woman held the plate out further, smiling.

"You expecting company?" Capper stepped forward.

Anthony had his hand ready on his gun. He scanned the inside of the meager hut. A lopsided table, several chairs, a barrel. There were three or four more plates resting on a little shelf.

"Fish?" the other woman held out a second plate.

"Who else is here?" Anthony's fingers moved to the trigger as his eyes swept the cramped quarters. One of the chairs was at an angle.

"For you." The women continued smiling, obviously struggling for more words.

"Smoke?" The woman holding the rice mimed smoking a cigarette.

"What's in there?" Capper gestured to a covered barrel with his gun.

"Fish. Very much fish."

Anthony's heart beat in his ears and pulsed in his hands. "Why would you need very much—"

The lid flew off the barrel and a VC popped out. Two others came out of a cabinet-type thing that looked way too small to hold anything, let alone a person.

Instinctively, Anthony's finger found the trigger and pressed. He sprayed bullets at the guy in the barrel while Jersey, Capper, and Lennox took care of the cabinet.

The women screamed.

Anthony blinked and everything changed.

The women crouched on the floor, shrieking. Little shards of wood dusted their black clothes. Blood spattered over the walls and floors.

One body was folded over the top of the barrel. The blood pooling from it crept closer to Anthony's boots.

The other two VCs lay on the ground as if they tripped over one another. One of them had half of their face blown off. Clumps of rice and a broken plate mixed in with the blood coming from those bodies.

"Sarge!" Anthony yelled. "Sergeant Avery!" He couldn't take his eyes off the VC and the barrel. He had killed a man. A man he was supposed to kill. A man he was trained to kill. It was what he was supposed to do. He had done his job. Blood poured out of the man's body. Anthony had never seen anything like it. Blood was literally flowing out of the man's body, making little red rivers around him.

"Holy shit," Lennox muttered with his gun still at the ready.

Anthony opened his mouth to yell again but the sound of Avery's boots stomping into the hut interrupted him. Avery surveyed the scene.

"We don't know. We don't know," one of the women sobbed.

Anthony pointed his gun at the women. They lied once, they would do it again. His eyes swept over their bodies, looking for evidence of a weapon, a knife, a wooden spoon, but they only held on to each other.

Sergeant Avery had Mikey radio in the results of the raid. Chances are, the women would be taken prisoner and a helicopter would be sent in to retrieve them. They would have to stand guard over them until the bird arrived.

"That was some good quick thinking, Capone," Capper nodded with approval.

"You too." Anthony gestured to the VC on the floor with his head since his gun was still pointing at the women whose cries had turned to whimpers.

"One kill doesn't mean shit out here," Jersey grunted. "You think we won the war because of a couple dead VCs. Fuck no."

"Calm down, man," Capper said. "No one's saying anything like that." He and Anthony followed Jersey out of the hut. There was no need to stay inside with the dead bodies, and it wasn't like the women were going to try to make a run for it in a ville full of soldiers. "Besides, I didn't come all this way to play poker and take your money." Capper elbowed Anthony with a chuckle.

"Yeah, me either." Anthony forced his mouth into a tight smile. He tried to be as cool and calm as Capper, who was nowhere near as cool and calm as Jersey. Anthony eyed Jersey, who stood in the center of the ville as if ready to take it over.

After the huey came and took the women somewhere, the sun was beginning to set, which meant they had to find a place to stop for the night. Everything and everyone had to be set up and secure before night fell. On cloudy, rainy nights, you couldn't see anything, and sleeping under your poncho was like sleeping in a coffin being pelted with rain. On the rare cloudless night, the moon shone so bright, it was possible to think, just for a second, that you were on a camping trip with your buddies. The problem was, you shared your campsite with bugs that could find any speck of exposed skin. Guys constantly slapped at their necks and arms, but still always woke up with bites from the little bastards.

As Anthony dug his foxhole for the night, he did his best to hurry. There would be no time to write a letter tonight. Clouds covered the moon and light would soon be gone. Anthony wanted to write a letter that was about more than sitting and waiting. No more telling Ma not to worry because there was nothing going on and no more letters from his dad saying he didn't remember hearing that the Army turned into an all-expense-paid vacation. Even though Anthony's dad had fought on an actual beach, there hadn't been any time for any R&R.

"I was beginning to think LBJ played a big joke on us, telling us there was this war going on he needed us to fight in." Capper started to dig his own hole a few yards away.

Anthony shook the grime off his poncho. "That mine Tim almost stepped on would have been a really bad joke."

"We already know Charlie's a rat. Maybe he and LBJ were in it together." Capper took a photo of Lorraine out of his helmet and put it on the ground next to him.

Anthony eyed the clouds and the moon. He had a couple minutes. There wasn't a picture of Sam tucked into his helmet but he did have his letters. Anthony found the most recent one and dug it out of the envelope. It was delivered the day before they'd packed up for this latest mission.

December 25, 1967

Anthony,

Merry Christmas. I know they don't have Christmas trees and wreaths where you are, but getting to see Bob Hope must have been a good substitute. The news said he was doing another tour. Jimmy's jealous because no one that keen ever came to visit him.

He asked Sandy to marry him yesterday when he went over to her place for Christmas Eve. She said yes so I guess that means I'm getting a sister. Jimmy has some job with the Air Force at a base in Missouri so he's heading there soon and Sandy will join him after they get married some time next summer.

Of course, this makes Mom ask me if I met any girls at school and will I bring one home next Christmas to meet her and Dad. I told them I need to find someone who loves ketchup as much as me. Mom had no idea what to do with my response so she said, "I'm sure you'll find someone perfect for you one day, Samuel."

I already have found someone and she has no idea.

It kind of sucks being at home. I want to get back to school. That's a stupid thing to say to you because I know you wouldn't mind being home.

Anthony stopped reading and closed his eyes, remembering being with Sam in his bedroom the day before he left for Basic. His smirk as he allowed Anthony to take a photograph of him with his mind. He could see everything so clearly. The blue eyes. The part in his brown hair.

The guys liked Sam's letters and talked about him as if they knew him. "Oooo," Capper had teased. "College boy found himself a college girl. Who is she?"

Anthony had shrugged. "I don't know. He's never mentioned this girl before."

More than their secret code encased in ketchup, that was probably the most open Sam could be in a letter without completely saying everything. He was so smart and so good with words. Anthony wished he could think of something like that for Sam.

The clouds covered the moon and within seconds the drops started to fall. Dammit. Anthony quickly folded Sam's letter and tucked it in the pocket of his pack where he kept them. He scrambled to set up his poncho to make some sort of tent that might prevent him from getting totally soaked.

Anthony settled under his makeshift home for the night, sensing sleep would somehow soon find him. But, the rain began to fall harder and the bugs filled their bellies by making a midnight snack out of his forearm. Instead of Sam's face or his bedroom at home, Anthony saw the face of the VC popping out of the barrel. Determined eyes zeroed in on him. A weapon about to be raised but Anthony used his first. The flowing rivers of blood on the side of the barrel.

It was just a VC. One of thousands of VCs who had been killed and would be killed. It was their fault they were getting killed in the first place. Anthony curled up in his hole, trying to get his boots under his poncho. He didn't know what was worse. Getting wet or hearing each drop of rain as it bounced off his poncho. The *tap tap tap* made sleep impossible.

Anthony tried composing a letter to Sam in his head. He had to assure Sam he was still alive. Whatever he read in the newspaper or heard from Suzy or Gloria, he was alive and okay. At any other point in his life, Anthony hardly would have thought that *okay* meant sleeping in the middle of a downpour in a foreign country where the enemy might be a few yards away, ready to kill him.

JANUARY 18, 1968

Suzy tossed her notecards on the library table with a sigh. She crossed her arms inside of her dark blue and purple poncho and sighed again.

Sam glanced up from his biology book. He and Suzy still had two pages of vocab to go through. "What?"

"There's a million vocabulary words. I'm never going to remember them."

Sam reached over the table and patted Suzy's arm. "First of all, there's only about three hundred words."

"Well it might as well be a million." Suzy twisted the fringe of thread around the edge of her poncho.

"And, that's what happens when you study with Gloria. Miss Academic Probation herself."

"Oh, come on," Suzy gathered up the notecards. "She's off academic probation."

Sam turned a page in his notebook and scribbled something about the parts of a cell. "I hear she's eligible for sainthood too." Suzy threw a balled-up piece of paper at him. Sam threw it back with a smile. This was the way it was ever since returning from Christmas break. He and Suzy studied, ate lunch together sometimes, and cut up a cat in biology last week. That was it. Anthony was crazy. There was no way Suzy was scheming on him.

"You know what you need?" Suzy put all of her books and materials into a pile. "A study break."

Sam glanced at his watch. It was almost five and he had been studying nonstop for the past day and a half. His history final was in two days and the rumor was it was one hundred and fifty multiple choice questions and then seventy-five true/false questions. Biology was his last one and then his first semester of college would be over. "Yeah, maybe. I'll do some more studying after dinner tonight."

"I was thinking more about a party. Want to come?"

"A party? Seriously? Exams start tomorrow."

"When did you become a bookbuster? I'm not telling you to skip a test, Mr. Salutatorian. Just take a break. It'll be good for you."

"Remember how well it went last time I went to a party with you? No, thank you." Suzy had apologized a hundred times, feeling responsible for Anthony running off. She wasn't mad at him, but at the war. Sam understood. He was mad at the war too, but probably for different reasons.

"You're making up excuses. I know you had a good time until... well, until you didn't." Suzy leaned over the table, whispering loudly. "Come on, please."

Sam hunched over his books, his body getting ready to go back to work but his eyes wandered all over the page. "Why does it seem like you're always trying to convince me to do something?"

Suzy's mouth dropped. "Because you never just say yes! No to the protest, which you ended up loving. No to SDS. No to parties. You don't make this easy, Sam."

It was hard to make out the chicken scratch in his notebook and Sam didn't know if it was because his eyes needed a break or if his handwriting was really that bad. "I'll think about it."

You would have thought Sam said he'd pick Suzy up in a Thunderbird. She giggled and clapped her hands.

"Don't get too excited." Sam stacked up his books. "I said I'll think about it. I'm not gonna have time to go to parties next semester, so I may as well try to get it in now."

"You're serious about the six classes?"

"Completely."

"I'm gonna head over around seven if you want to go," Suzy said. "I can't stay too long if I don't want to get locked out."

"Where is it?"

"Mifflin Street. And it's going to be outta sight." Suzy gave Sam a wide grin before weaving through the maze of tables and heading out of the library.

Sam saw a package tucked under Mike's arm when he entered Sullivan. The mail. He hadn't heard anything from Anthony in over two weeks. Sam was still trying to figure out how long it took letters to get to Vietnam, and he had no idea how and when Anthony would be able to write.

Mike waved the small box at Sam when they passed one another. "A little 'good luck package' from my girl back home."

"Cool." Sam wandered over to the mailboxes, trying his best not to get his hopes up. Anthony was fighting in a war, not playing around at sleepaway camp. Sam reached into his mailbox and felt something poke his finger.

Sam saw FREE printed in big block letters in the corner of an envelope. He carried the letter to the couch in the common area and tore into it.

Sam,

I killed a guy for the first time two days ago. That's a hell of a way to start a letter but it took me a while to write that down so there it is. It wasn't anything like the shooting range at Basic or the hand to hand shit Dalton taught us. You don't know what it feels like until you do it. I know my pops killed guys and you know Jimmy did even if he doesn't tell you about it. I knew it was going to happen and I knew it wouldn't be anything like what we see at the movies, but it was still different than what I expected.

My pops said he felt proud. Of course we all know killing is wrong but Pops said when you do it in a uniform and the bad guys are running toward you, you know you did the right thing. I know I did the right thing too. It's the main reason I'm here. Plus, if I didn't kill him, he would have killed me or Capper or Jersey or anyone else over here with me. Sarge says our VC body count is going up and now I'm a part of that. It makes me feel like I'm doing my part over here. Maybe I can help end this. Is this how you felt at that Dow thing?

The thing is, this guy wasn't running toward me on a beach with his gun pointed at me. He jumped out of a barrel. It was like some fucked up Looney Tunes cartoon. Fighting Charlie is like being in a goddamn cartoon sometimes. I'll have to watch out for anvils falling from the sky.

But there's one less of them and I'm still here. That's the goal, right?

We're back at base camp for a couple days and then we're heading out in the bush again. Standing guard is the worst part of the day. It's dark and you're alone and Charlie could be ten feet away from you but you have no idea.

It sounds scary and I guess it is, but you don't need to be afraid or worry about me. I obviously know what I'm doing. So, if I'm alive, and everyone else in my platoon is alive, and a package from some church just arrived with a few bottles of ketchup, I guess it's a good day.

Anthony

P.S. Oh yeah, so there's someone perfect for you, huh? Who is it? It better not be Gloria!

The last line of the letter made a smile fill Sam's chest. He could read in between the words and decipher everything Anthony didn't write but was clearly there.

But then his eyes drifted to the beginning of the letter. It was going to happen. That was what Anthony trained to do, and as he had written, if he didn't kill the VC, the VC probably would have killed him. Sam tried to separate the feelings swirling together in his belly. He had tried to talk to Jimmy about what went on over there but never got anything.

Sam's feet took him up the stairs and to his dorm. He wished Paul would be on one of his marathon calls with Debra, tucked into the little alcove with the pay phone. Sam had a stash of dimes in a sock he would gladly give him if it meant he could have the room to himself for forever or for at least the next couple hours.

But nope, Paul sat at his desk, bent over a book. "How were your study sessions today?" he asked without looking up.

"Fun."

"I'm going to ace econ tomorrow."

"Probably." It was already hard to concentrate on what Paul was saying without a million thoughts spinning around in Sam's head.

"What's up?" Paul asked, with an annoyed edge in his voice.

"Huh?"

"You're just standing there. What's up? Did your girl call it quits?" He nodded to the letter dangling from Sam's hand.

"My girl?"

"I thought you made her up." Paul went back to his book. "You never talk about her or anything."

The feeling of the sun bursting from his chest on move-in day seemed far away. "Oh, yeah. My girl," Sam said. "We called it quits a while ago." If by "his girl," Sam was referring to sophomore year when he went steady with this girl named Linda for about three months then it was the truth. They called it quits quite a while ago.

"Oh." Paul wrote something in a notebook.

Sam was about to thank Paul for his sympathy during this difficult time but went to his desk and turned on the radio instead. He heard Paul grunt a little when the chorus for "Don't Worry Baby" by The Beach Boys came on. It was the perfect song for the moment. Maybe Brian Wilson was Sam talking to Anthony or vice versa. But some some crooning falsetto wasn't doing anything to settle Sam's mind.

He grabbed his bio stuff and decided what he needed to do was study. That would take his mind off Anthony's letter and how easily the situation could have been reversed. Sam pushed the thought away into a far corner of his brain and opened his textbook to a chapter. It wasn't reading, it was looking. No information from the page made it to Sam's brain. He fought to keep an image of Anthony, bloodied and injured, from creeping into his mind.

"What's this song?" Paul cut into Sam's trance.

"Huh?" Sam turned. "It's 'Don't Worry Baby.' It's a Beach Boys song."

Paul furrowed his eyebrows for a few seconds, listening to the singer's plea to his worried girlfriend. "I don't think it's going to do anything to make you feel better about your girl. Can you turn it off?"

"I didn't know you were an expert on the subject." Sam exhaled loudly as he cranked the dial to turn the radio off. He should have gone back to the library after dinner.

With the only sound in the room coming from Paul's pencil scratching his paper, Sam drummed his thumb on his leg. He glanced at the clock. 6:43. If he was going to meet Suzy outside her dorm, he'd have to hurry.

Sam ignored the cold air blasting him in the face as he walked as fast as he could to Suzy's dorm. She was right. He needed to go to a party. Sitting in his room pretending to study was going to make for a long night. As Sam approached Suzy's dorm, he saw her already about a half a block away. He immediately recognized her long brown suede coat that she hugged around herself and the long blonde hair spilling out from under a striped knit hat.

He grinned and walked right by Suzy, stopping suddenly as if just noticing her. "Oh, good evening, Miss. I was wondering if you were aware of any festivities occurring on this frigid night?"

"I knew you would come." She looped her arm around his elbow.

Sam glanced at their interlocked arms. "Are we getting married or something?"

Suzy practically skipped down the sidewalk, oblivious to the cold. "No. It's warmer this way."

They walked for a while, finally stopping when they got to a house with a large front porch wrapped around it and a small balcony at a second-story window. Faint lights shone behind bed sheets hanging in the upper window. Sam thought he could make out peace signs scrawled on them.

"Over here." Suzy gestured to Sam from the side of the big porch and walked around the house to the back.

Sam stepped in the footprints that made a trail along the side of the house. "Do we have to sneak in or something?"

"We're not climbing in through a window," Suzy giggled. "The door to the upstairs apartment is in the back."

Tiptoeing through the trail of prints, Suzy stopped at three rickety stairs that led to a door. It looked red, but it was hard to tell in the dark. The porch was so small, there was barely enough room for Sam to stand on it with Suzy. He crammed his hands into his pockets and watched his breath make little puffs in the night air as he heard music coming from inside. This was exactly what he needed to get-

"Hey!" A voice came up behind Sam and Suzy.

They turned to see Gloria shuffling toward them in the same willowy skirt she wore to the Dow demonstration. She had to be freezing. Sam pressed his lips into a thin line at the sight of her. Standing outside of a house with Gloria and Suzy brought him back to the only other party he'd been to. The only thing missing was Anthony.

When Sam was in his dorm room at night, with one hand in his pillow on the collar of the Snoopy shirt, he sometimes allowed himself to think that might have been the last time he'd ever see Anthony alive. With Paul grinding his teeth in the bed a few feet away in the shoebox of a room, Sam would take the shirt out of the pillowcase, unfold it, and lay it on top of him.

Sometimes, if the room was especially dark, Sam would feel something rise up in his chest and throat and then his eyes would get wet and warm. He would hug the shirt draped over him and wait for the feeling to pass.

"Oh," Gloria glanced at Sam as she stepped on the bottom stair. "I see you convinced your boyfriend to come."

Suzy swatted at Gloria. "Sam's not my boyfriend."

"Well, I'm a boy," Sam said. "And I'm your friend, so if you're going to be technical about it…"

"Okay, fine. You're my boyfriend," Suzy laughed.

Gloria raised an eyebrow at Sam. "Well, I guess that makes me the third wheel. Too bad your friend has to be all the way in Vietnam. We could have had another double date."

"You're not his type." Sam turned toward the red door, wondering if it would magically open or if they needed some kind of secret password to get inside.

"Oh, I know," Gloria laughed.

Sam narrowed his eyes at Gloria as Suzy pounded on the door

three times. Maybe there was a secret knock.

As Suzy was about to pound on the door again, it opened, reveal-
ing a tall, skinny guy with hair down to his shoulders and a full beard.
There was a dark flight of stairs behind him and Sam couldn't see
where it led.

"Suzy, you made it," the guy grinned.

"I told you I would." Suzy stepped into the small entryway. "This is
Danny."

Danny wiped his hand on his The Who T-shirt and extended his
hand to Sam.

"And this is Sam," Suzy said.

"The more the merrier, Sam." Danny turned to Gloria. "Who
invited you, huh?"

Gloria looked shocked for a half second and then broke into a
grin. "I was in the neighborhood."

Danny chuckled and gestured to the stairs. "Welcome to my
palace." He led everyone upstairs.

Once inside, the music was louder. Sam breathed in the sweet smell
of grass hanging in the air from the people on the couch passing around
a joint. "Satisfaction" by The Rolling Stones was playing. Of course. It
was the song they played at the end of their show where Sam screamed
himself hoarse. It was the song Sam thought of while screaming along
with Suzy at the Dow demonstration. And now it was on at this house
full of hippies. Instead of feeling out of place in his blue, green, and white
plaid shirt and the shorter haircut he got while home for Christmas, Sam
felt completely at ease. No one here was going to yell about the music,
the mess, nothing. Skipping a night of studying was a good idea. Not
thinking about Anthony for a few hours was a good idea. He'd spent
too much time imagining Anthony lying somewhere in the middle of
the jungle all by himself, bleeding to death while bullets whizzed all
around him. He was here to have fun, right?

"Satisfaction" had ended and "Cry to Me" started up. It must be a
record. Sam smiled. He wished he could have brought his record player
and a few from his collection to school, but there wasn't any room
and it would have been a waste anyway. Paul probably would have

scratched each one taking the needle off when he felt the music got too loud, which would have been all the time. Maybe Sam could just sit on the armrest of the couch and pretend everything was right with the world. Pretending was something he was very good at.

Since Suzy and Gloria had followed Danny into the little kitchen, Sam settled on the armrest of a blue couch with some kind of diamond pattern all over it. The group on the couch —two guys and one girl, huddled together in a cloud of smoke—ignored Sam. For being at a party, they looked completely serious. He saw Suzy and Gloria join a cluster of girls standing around in the crowded kitchen. There weren't a lot of people at the party, maybe twelve, but the place seemed packed.

"You want one?" Danny held out a can of Blatz to Sam.

"Yeah, man. Thanks."

"No sweat." Danny took a long pull from his own can. "Stones are boss, you dig?"

Sam nodded. "I saw them in concert last summer." He was about to tell Danny about the set list when a yell came from the trio on the couch. It was so loud it made the record skip.

"What am I supposed to do?" one of the guys jumped off the couch. "Run away to Canada?"

The girl grabbed the boy's hand. "It's an idea. And I can go with you."

The guy shook the girl's hand away. "Sounds like a real fucked up happily ever after." He ran a hand through his shaggy hair and reached the door in a few big steps. "I gotta book."

"Robbie, wait." The girl grabbed a big poncho sweater off the other armrest and scurried after him.

The remaining guy on the couch went to the outside balcony with only his T-shirt and suede vest on. Sam could see him hug himself as puffs of air swirled around his head. The whole party froze for a second longer before the conversations started to buzz again.

"Robbie got his draft notice." Danny looked as if he were telling Sam that a childhood friend had passed away.

Sam slowly nodded. "I had a feeling."

"He failed a couple classes last year and doesn't have the deferment anymore."

"Hmmm." Sam let that sink in as another song started up. It had this long weird name he could never remember. A few assignments, a failed test, and he would be in the same position as Robbie. He was always so pompous and confident about his grades. Hell, he was at a party the day before a big final exam. Sam hadn't gotten drafted yet, but he'd always assumed that he'd still be in school, doing his graduate work, and the war would be way over by then. "What's he going to do?"

"He's got some options."

Sam let out a breath. He had come to this party to get away from the war but it followed him everywhere.

"There's too many guys in his position." Danny shook his head with his mouth pressed into a thin line. "I keep hearing shit about how the guys in Washington say this thing's almost over. Westmoreland goes on TV and tells everyone we're winning. We're not winning shit. I don't think anyone counts a ride home in a body bag as a prize."

"My brother was over there. He came back a few months ago." Sam didn't know what else to say.

Danny looked like he had cursed in church and the priest might have heard him. "I'm glad he made it home safe."

"He seems okay." Sam imagined Jimmy, a little skinnier, a little quieter, but still the big brother he had grown up with. "I have another friend over there now. He joined the Army."

The music stopped and Danny walked over to the record player and took the needle off the spinning record. "I guess joining is better than being drafted. If you're going over there, it should be your choice, not some guy in a suit who sits behind a desk all day."

"I don't like it." Sam heard himself say the words out loud. "I don't like that he's there, even if it was his choice. I don't like that this kid I don't even know has to go because he failed a test or something." All the times Suzy tried to get him to do something more than hang up posters and he couldn't bring himself to do it, feeling like it was wrong or a betrayal to Anthony and Jimmy. Maybe because Danny didn't tell him what to think, Sam let these thoughts hiding in his brain to tumble right out of his mouth.

"You're not the only one, Sam. Not even close." Danny knelt and pulled a plastic milk crate full of records from behind the little table the record player sat on. "Guys are burning their draft cards, running to Canada, risking jail time. For what? Huh?"

"Something about communism? Protecting democracy?" Sam wasn't sure if Danny was looking for an answer or not.

"That's what they say. Maybe it's how it started out. But now?" Danny shook his head so his longish hair hit him in the face a little. He believed every word coming out of his mouth and was willing to do something more than staple a few signs in the student union to get his point across. "I finish school at the end of this semester, and I don't know what I'm gonna do if I get drafted."

Sam thought about his plan to graduate early and dive into graduate school. He had a few more years. Danny only had a few more months. "What are you going to be when you grow up?" Sam asked.

The tension in Danny's face morphed into a grin. "I'm hoping to go to Egypt to dig up some mummies. I double majored in anthropology and archeology."

"Wow. That's boss. I just want to be a history professor."

"Don't sell yourself short," Danny said. "That's badass too. You get to stand in a lecture hall in front of all those kids and tell them what actually happened. Not some watered-down version Uncle Sam wants us to tell everyone."

"Well, when you put it that way," Sam chuckled.

Danny gestured to the milk crate of records. "You got a preference?"

Sam felt a smile in his chest. "You got any Beach Boys?"

"You serious, man? The Beach Boys?"

"Worth a try," Sam shrugged. "Maybe The Doors?"

Danny flipped through the records. "That I can do." He took out their self-titled album and in no time the opening guitar notes exploded throughout the room. A few moments later, Jim Morrison began to sing.

"Break on through to the other side!" A group of five people shouted together and laughed. Suzy and Gloria stood in the middle of them. Suzy caught Sam's eye at the end of the refrain. She danced her way over.

"I'm glad to see you finally looking like you're having fun." Suzy elbowed him. "Thanks for keeping him company, Danny."

"He's a cool cat." Danny nodded at Sam.

"He's getting there." Suzy looked at Sam with a grin.

"Sam, you're welcome at my palace any time." He raised his beer. "No invitation needed. Or draft card."

"Thanks, man." Sam hoped the next time Suzy was planning to go to a party here, she'd tell him about it.

Danny wandered over to the group continuing their singalong. Gloria swayed to the music as if a slow love song came from the record player.

"Danny's a real gone cat," Sam said.

"He's really smart," Suzy nodded. "He's a good person to know. If you need something, he's the guy to go to."

Sam glanced around the apartment. Behind the group of singers, he spotted a ripped-open case of Blatz. "Right now, I need a beer."

"Grab one for me too," Suzy said.

"Sure thing." After dodging the group trying to pull him into another refrain, Sam discovered the case was empty, but there was a full one on the floor in the back of the cramped kitchen. There were only four other people wedged between the stove and the opposite counter, but it was like navigating the high school halls seconds before the bell rang. Sam was wrestling with the flaps to get them open when he felt something brush his arm. He looked up and saw Gloria smiling down on him.

"What do you want?" he asked, ripping off one of the flaps.

Gloria shook her head, the smile still covering her face. Tangles of dark hair hung in her eyes. She was probably high. "Me? I don't want anything. Except maybe a beer."

"Uh, okay." Sam put a can in Gloria's hand.

Gloria shrugged a shoulder. "Suzy, on the other hand. Maybe see if she wants something."

"Light My Fire" was starting up and the couch was clear. Danny had given Sam a lot to think about and Gloria didn't fit into his thoughts right now. Beer and good music was all he was in the mood for. "I know," Sam held up another can. "I'm on it."

"Oh, Sammy. Do you think I'm talking about beer?" Gloria gave Sam a little smirk before joining a small circle passing around a joint.

Sam cracked open the can of beer meant for Suzy and gulped half it in one breath. The next time Suzy dragged him out to a party he would need to specify Gloria needed to stay home.

JANUARY 30, 1968

Even with the tan that darkened his face, Capper was blushing as he read the latest letter from Lorraine. Mail call was exactly what everyone needed to take their minds off the fact Tim had stepped on a mine yesterday. He died instantly but they had to wait two hours for the bird to come get the body. It was even harder because they were in a field of tall grass up to Anthony's chest. When it happened, everyone heard the noise and hit the ground. When it was clear they weren't under attack, no one even knew it was a mine or that it was Tim who stepped on it.

Picasso had stumbled upon the body. Now, he lay on his rack, sketching something with big pencil strokes, just just as he always did whenever they weren't in the bush. Anthony didn't see the body up close, just a bloody heap on the ground from a few yards away.

"You gotta share, Capper, come on," the guys urged Capper, who was no longer reading aloud. His eyes scanned the rest of the letter, the pink becoming more apparent on his dark face.

"I told her not to write anything about that."

"About what?" Mikey stood behind Capper to get a look at Lorraine's swirly handwriting on pink stationery.

Capper held the letter to his chest and pushed Mikey in the shoulder. "She's just remembering prom night, that's all."

"Prom night?" Mikey asked. "You gotta give us more than that."

"Nope," Capper folded the letter. "I am a gentleman."

"Fuck you are. I've heard you talking in your sleep," QB piped up. "You're really not gonna tell us the rest?"

Capper nodded at Anthony. "Capone's got a letter. Bother him about his."

A chorus of boos came from the circle gathered around Capper. "Until next time." Capper presented Anthony with a swoop of his arm.

"It's from Sam." No matter how many times Anthony read a letter from Sam, he still felt nervous something in it or in his voice would give everything away.

"Bitchin'," Mikey looked up from his bunk. "What's he have to say about college life?"

Anthony glanced at the letter that wasn't very long.

Anthony,

As of next week, I'm officially done with my first semester of college. I think I'll end up with all A's and B's. Maybe I shouldn't have gone to a party the night before finals started, but there wasn't going to be much studying going on in my room anyway. Paul hates all music, even The Beach Boys. That probably makes you hate him as much as I do.

"The Beach Boys, Capone?" Capper asked. "Are you kidding me?"

"Are you kidding *me*?" Anthony laughed at Capper. "You sing 'It's My Party' in your sleep."

"Hey, Lesley Gore is a talented lady," Capper looked shocked. "And it was the first song Lorraine and I ever danced to."

"On prom night?" Picasso said from his rack a few feet away, his eyes on his drawing.

"Shut up and let Capone keep going." Capper gave Anthony a smile as if doing him a favor.

I went to this party with Suzy and met some cool cats. They had bitchin' music and warm beer. Not a bad combination.

I register for classes next week and am going to go for the six classes. Two history classes, some pre-calc shit, intro to political science, English 102, and some phys ed class I have to take. It's going to be tough but nothing compared to what you have going on over there. I got your last letter and I've been thinking about it a lot. I don't know how you do it. I hope you're doing okay, but I guess I don't know what OKAY means in the middle of a war. So, maybe I should say keep doing what you're doing. It's working so far.

But it does sound like you need some ketchup and maybe an umbrella too. Take care of yourself. Tell Charlie and his pals they're not allowed to hurt you or any of your friends.

Sam.

"Again with the ketchup?" QB said.

"You heard the letter." Anthony focused on folding the letter in the same place Sam did. "Everyone thinks he's a little crazy." Sam went for the six classes. He was going to push through school and Anthony was going to finish out his year and save some money when he got back. Everything was falling into place.

"Maybe stop the party for now," Jersey spoke up. He always claimed to be uninterested in the mail but still listened to each word read. "It's been real quiet out there the last couple days. That means Charlie's up to something."

Anthony, Capper, and everyone else eyed each other. "He's always up to something," Lennox said. "That's why we're here."

"You have a private conversation with him you need to tell us about?" Capper asked.

"There was talk of no fighting over Tet but I don't believe it for a second," Jersey said.

"Tet?" Mikey looked at everyone for an answer.

"Some holiday," Jersey explained. "They all celebrate it. North and South. Maybe Charlie will surprise us but I wouldn't bet my mother's life on it." He picked up his helmet and covered his face with it.

Everyone stood completely still. A little boom came from some-where outside, far enough away but that didn't mean it wasn't going to get closer. Anthony followed Capper, QB, and Mikey outside. Another boom almost made them all hit the ground but the color in the distance stopped them.

Fireworks. It was just fireworks.

Charlie wasn't going to attack, he was putting on a little show.

Somehow Anthony knew it was a dream even while he was in it. He knew he really wasn't in the empty gymnasium at Bowen High School. He knew Sam really wasn't there with him, jumping from riser to riser on the bleachers dressed in jeans and a button-up collared shirt with stripes on either side of the buttons. Anthony wore a set of fresh fatigues as if just arriving at Basic.

Sam jumped off the bleachers, skipping the last two steps, and landed on the wooden floor with a sound that echoed in the empty gym. Sam looked from his feet to Anthony, confused how he made such a sound.

Anthony took a tentative step toward Sam, as if walking across a frozen pond.

Something rattled the doors to the gymnasium. Anthony tried to run to the other side but his feet remained glued to the floor. He grabbed his leg, trying to move it manually.

The doors shook harder this time, as if the Incredible Hulk was on the other side, seconds away from ripping the door right off its hinges. "We know you're in there!" A booming yell came from the other side of the door.

Anthony and Sam looked at each other, terror spreading to every limb. "Run!" Anthony cried, still pulling at his legs. "Run!"

"Get your asses out here now!" The door shook again. "I said get the fuck out here!"

Anthony reached for Sam, certain this was it. But, if this was how everything ended then he would die with the person he loved most. Something grabbed his shoulder and when Anthony turned around—

He woke up.

It was dark and so loud.

Capper stood over him, shaking his shoulder. "Shit, Capone, we gotta move out."

Anthony had to shake off the dream quickly as he fumbled for his helmet, and laced up his boots with numb fingers.

"What did I say? Huh? What did I say?" Jersey centered his helmet on his head. "Fucking Charlie." He made it out of the barracks in a few long strides.

When Anthony made it out, he saw pockets of the dark jungle sky explode with balls of fire that weren't far away. It was fireworks only a couple hours before. No one thought about avoiding mines or booby traps as they hopped into the convoy of jeeps and sped off toward the explosions.

Jersey stood up in the front seat with his gun at the ready position. With orange streaks lighting up the night sky behind him, he looked like some hero out of a movie.

Anthony had to crane his body around to see where they were going. Capper sat next to him, clutching his gun and straining to see what might be hidden on the side of the road. A scattering of huts lined the way. Suddenly, the sound of gunfire came from one of them and bullets hit the side of the jeep. Anthony sprayed a round of ammunition into the huts. Something heavy fell on top of Anthony and he almost fell out of the jeep.

"Oh shit," Capper said.

"What? What?" Anthony yelled. He tried to untangle himself from whatever was on top of him but felt something wet on his back. He was hit. He was bleeding. Anthony didn't feel any pain, except for his legs beginning to cramp from the weird angle his body was bent at.

"Jersey's hit! Jersey's hit!" Someone yelled as the weight was pulled off of Anthony and he was able to sit up.

Anthony looked behind him to see Jersey sprawled over the front seat. The orange explosions, getting closer and bigger, lit up the blood spreading across Jersey's chest, soaking his shirt. He was hit in the arm too, and it made a pool of blood in the backseat at Capper's feet.

The bullets kept coming from the shanties on the side of the road. Another jeep pulled up alongside Anthony's. Sergeant Avery barked, "Lorenzo! Capstone! Get in here!"

Anthony jumped out of his jeep and into the backseat of the Sergeant's. His brain didn't register any thought of getting hit by a bullet, it just reacted to the order. "Lennox!" Avery yelled. "Turn around and get him back to base."

Lennox jerked the steering wheel and the jeep did a sharp U-turn.

"Merry Fucking Tet," Sergeant Avery yelled. "It's happening all over the goddamn country."

Anthony adjusted the helmet on his hand and gripped his gun as the explosions revealed a meager skyline in the distance. From the jeep, he could see the walls that had been blown out and fires burning in the streets. They were going right into the thick of it. Jersey said it was going to happen. Leave it to Charlie to attack in the middle of a holiday.

No, this wasn't an attack. It was an ambush on a scale so large and no one saw it coming. Charlie had so many tricks up his sleeve, it was impossible to keep track of them. To protect yourself from them. With his dad, there was this beach he stormed while the enemy ran toward him and his dad killed them. It was clear what you were supposed to do.

They passed a burning jeep, turned over on its side as the ground shook with another explosion coming from somewhere.

Anthony breathed in the smoky air and blinked in an attempt to stop his eyes from stinging.

His dad fought in a war. What the hell was this?

FEBRUARY 1, 1968

If there was a letter from Anthony in the mailbox, it meant he was okay. It didn't matter that the letter was sent before Vietnam imploded, it just needed to be in Sam's mailbox. He turned on the radio to get some work done and couldn't find any music, only reports of a bunch of explosions happening all over Vietnam.

It took Sam two tries to get his key into the mailbox keyhole. He dropped it the first time and picked it up with shaking hands. He opened the door and crouched to look inside.

Empty.

Sam reached into the little steel rectangle and searched every corner. He stretched his arm all the way inside, past his elbow.

Nothing.

Sam slammed the little door. The force made the door bounce off the latch so he slammed it again. It was stupid. He knew it was stupid. The state of Anthony's safety didn't depend on the contents of his mailbox but that didn't stop Sam from sprinting to the door and racing up the stairs. At the top of the stairwell, he ran right into Mike.

"Watch where you're going, McGuern." Mike looked like Sam had squirted mustard on his new shirt.

Sam ignored him, flinging open the door leading to his floor.

"Shit, man. What are you on right now?" Mike called after him.

Sam had to get to a radio. If he could find a Beach Boys song *then* everything would be fine. He lunged at the radio perched on his desk and twisted the dial to turn it on. The chorus to "Groovy Kind of Love" assailed his ears.

What a stupid song. He turned the dial past the snow and static to find the next station.

A newscaster's voice emerged through the crackle. "...multiple coordinated attacks on a number of South Vietnamese targets..."

"Come on, come on," Sam pleaded with the radio as the little needle went through more static. "We Can Work it Out" emerged from the white noise. "Just let me find some fucking Beach Boys!"

"What are you doing?"

Sam turned to see Paul standing in the doorway.

"I'm looking for a song," Sam almost screamed. "What does it look like I'm doing?" He turned the dial. Maybe one of the songs was over and a new one would start soon.

"Look, man," Paul stepped into the room. "Maybe you should turn it off."

"God dammit," Sam raked his hands through his hair. "What do you have against music? Everyone likes music."

"I like it to be quiet sometimes," Paul's voice rose.

"No, you like it to be quiet all the time." He went back to the dial and the chorus to "God Only Knows" materialized. Yes. It was a miracle. Sam felt his whole body relax. He held his head in his hands as the chorus finished and the next verse started up. Anthony was fine and he wasn't shot or killed or—

Abruptly, the music cut off. Right in the middle of the last song he'd heard with Anthony. "What the fuck," Sam exhaled. He turned the dial to the left and then the right. Nothing. He moved the antennae around. Nothing. Where did his song go?

He picked up the radio. The chord dangled from it, unplugged from the wall. Paul stood at his desk, arms crossed. "Why did you do that?" Sam pushed Paul so he fell into his desk, knocking over his pencil cup.

"Because I said to turn it off and you never listen." Paul quickly recovered and pushed Sam, sending him backwards into his desk and knocking the radio on its side.

"I never listen?" Sam shouted. "*I* never listen? Fuck you."

"Stop cussing around me." Paul took a step toward Sam. They stood a few inches apart in the small aisle between the desks.

"And I told you all I wanted to do was listen to a song."

Paul drew his arm back and cold-cocked Sam in the face. Thankfully, it wasn't a direct hit but it still connected with Sam's cheek. He felt blood on the inside of his mouth where he had bitten down. Ignoring the throb in his face, Sam crouched and tackled Paul by the waist. They crashed into Paul's desk, sending books and binders to the floor.

"What's going on in here?"

Paul and Sam leapt away from each other as much as they could in the small space between their desks and saw their RA, Jerry, looking like a Beatles reject. He stood in the doorway along with half the residents of the floor.

"Looks like they're fighting, sir," Mike giggled from somewhere in the crowd.

"Cool it, Mike," Jerry said without turning around.

Paul straightened like a drill sergeant just walked in. "This man is rude and inconsiderate with no respect for what it means to share a common space." He jutted his index finger at Sam.

"Yeah?" Sam smirked. "Well, Jerry, this guy is a fucking asshole."

Jerry held his hands up as if that would diffuse the situation. "Both of you need to cool your chops. You could get kicked out for this."

Sam narrowed his eyes at Paul, who was huffing and puffing. There was no way he was getting kicked out of school because of Paul or anything else. He could get drafted while Paul had a free pass thanks to the tree he fell out of. Sam needed to stay in school, ace his classes, graduate early, and find a graduate school he and Anthony could run away to.

"You guys take the night to let this blow over and I won't tell anyone about it," Jerry said. "You dig?"

"You expect us to stay in the same room together?" Paul asked.

Jerry crossed his arms, trying to look authoritative with his mop top. "Yes, I do. Unless you have another idea."

Everything boiling over inside of Sam continued to rage. "I'll cut out. Wouldn't want you to be further inconvenienced."

"Thank you, Sam." Jerry nodded at him. The crowd behind him began to disperse upon realizing this was the extent of the night's entertainment.

Paul stood off to the side, holding on to his desk chair like it was a shield. "Good."

Sam did a brief sweep of his room. He wanted to take his pillow with him so he could have Anthony's Snoopy shirt when he got to wherever he was going. He also wanted to take Anthony's letters but knew it would look weird if he dug into his bottom desk drawer. Instead, Sam raised the collar of the winter coat he was still wearing and walked out of the room. The remaining spectators parted as he approached.

"We'll talk about this tomorrow. Okay, Sam?" Jerry called after him.

"Sure thing." Sam was already down the hall. He pushed open the door to the stairwell and ran down the stairs as fast as could, swinging himself to the lower floor by holding on to the railing. When he got outside, he took a deep breath of the frigid night air and exhaled. His breath came out in a thick cloud that swirled around his head. Something in Sam's chest seized as he remembered he still had no idea if Anthony was okay and there was no way for him to find out. He had found the song and heard part of it. That had to count for something, right? Or maybe since he only heard part of the song, it meant Anthony was injured but alive or stuck somewhere but okay.

Sam wiped away the tears at the corner of his eyes. Why couldn't Paul let him listen to the damn song? All he needed was to finish the song.

Sam marched down the sidewalk, mainly for something to do because it was too cold to stand still. He had no idea where he was going to spend the night. He didn't know anyone in his new classes well enough to ask if he could crash on their floor. He wasn't even allowed in Suzy's building, let alone her dorm room. Although, she probably would have found a way to sneak him in if she didn't have to worry about her roommate. But with the new semester schedule, he hadn't seen much of her anyway.

He kept walking, right off campus and toward downtown Madison, where he'd only ventured a few times when he went to those parties. Sam stopped as if he'd tripped over something in the sidewalk. Danny did say he was welcome at his place. He did say if he ever needed anything, just ask. Sam slowly picked up his pace again, trying to remember the streets he and Suzy took to Mifflin.

They had walked east. Sam looked to where Lake Mendota was to center himself, figured out which way was east, and started walking. His anger at Paul escalated with each step. Not only didn't Sam finish his song but now he was also kicked out of the dorms for the night.

Sam kept walking and came across a guy in an ROTC uniform and a flat top. It could have been Paul in another life, one without trees that people fell out of. Someone probably pushed him.

"Hey, man," Sam waved to the guy. "Do you know how to get to Mifflin?"

The guy stopped and furrowed his eyebrows at Sam. "Why do you want to go there?"

"Do you know how to get there?"

The guy turned and pointed to a distance further east. "Keep walking on Campus Drive and make a right at Bassett. You'll run right into it."

"Thanks."

"No sweat."

Sam kept walking, wishing he could have managed to grab Anthony's letters, the Snoopy shirt, something for him to hold on to while he wondered if he was okay or not. Even if a letter came tomorrow or the day after, it wouldn't mean Anthony was alive.

Sam stopped, sucking in a mouthful of frozen air. It was a morbid thought, reading a letter from someone who was alive when they wrote it but was dead by the time it was received.

He picked up the pace and resumed the game he played with the mailbox and the radio. If he could make it to Mifflin street, Anthony would be okay. If he could find the house where he and Suzy had partied, that meant he was more than okay. He wasn't injured. Maybe scared, curled up in some foxhole, but totally fine.

And if he could convince Danny to let him stay the night, maybe Anthony would be in some news footage so he could see for himself.

Sam stopped in front of a house, studying the windows and roof. It looked like the one he and Suzy had gone to, but then again, most of the houses on the street looked the same. Many of them had large porches consuming the front of the house. He wanted to sneak around the back to see if there was a staircase but that wasn't the best choice. This house had a bed sheet hanging in the window but no peace sign like the night of the party. But, the blinds in the other window hung at an angle just like the ones in the window by the record player.

Sam took in a breath of winter air. Was this seriously his only option? Crashing at the pad of some guy he met once? There was no way he'd remember him. But there were no other options besides the bench outside the library.

Sam maneuvered through the footprints that led to the back of the house. This was definitely it. He climbed the three rickety steps and pounded on the red door.

He knocked again, pretending it was Paul's face. As Sam drew his hand back for another pound the door opened and he had to stop his hand in mid-punch. The wind burned his skinned knuckles.

A guy with long blonde hair pulled into a low ponytail stood in the doorway. Baggy jeans hung off his thin frame. Sam remembered him from the party. "Hey, man. No need to break the door down."

"Sorry." Sam shoved his hands into his pockets. "Hey, I, uh, I was here a couple weeks ago for a party…" He trailed off, not knowing what else to say. Now that he was here, the request and the belief he would be able to stay seemed ridiculous.

The guy squinted his eyes as if trying to remember Sam.

"I came here with Suzy. We had class together."

"I know Suzy." The guy smiled a little as if Suzy were standing right in front of him.

"Yeah, me too." It was getting colder by the second and Sam couldn't believe the guy stood in the open doorway in bare feet and an open denim jacket with nothing underneath. "I talked to Danny for a little while—"

The guy's smile widened as he nodded. "You're the professor right? The one who's going to get history *right* when he bestows it upon the impressionable collegiate minds?"

"Yeah, that's me. I mean not yet." Sam grinned. "And Danny's going to head to the desert to dig up mummies."

The guy laughed. "That sounds right. Come on in."

Sam stepped inside and puffed some warm air into his tingling hands. He followed the guy up the stairs that led to the apartment. When he opened the door, the guy extended his arms and proclaimed, "Good sirs, we have an intellectual among us. Proper behavior is encouraged."

A loud and long burp came from the kitchen, followed by a laugh and someone clapping. But all Sam could hear was the music. It wasn't The Beach Boys, but rather Jefferson Airplane. It was such a relief to be in a place where the music flowed from the speakers like water from a faucet.

"Oh hey, Sam," Danny waved from his spot on the couch, wearing an army green coat with a brown T-shirt underneath. "We're getting ready to pass around a joint. You want in?"

"Uh, no." Sam ran a hand through his hair, suddenly self-conscious around the people he didn't know. But, he did just remember that Nick was the name of the guy who answered the door. "I was actually wondering if I could crash here tonight."

Danny and Nick eyed one another, having some sort of silent conversation.

"My roommate went ape and almost broke my radio and we got into a fight and then the RA said—"

Danny held up a hand. "As long as the couch is fine, you got a place for the night."

Sam exhaled. "Thank you. Seriously. I'll stay out of everyone's way." He sat on the armrest of the couch, just like at the party. Sam rubbed his hands on his thighs as Danny passed the joint to Nick. Maybe Sam should take a hit.

Jefferson Airplane faded and the DJ announced the time and temperature before beginning the next song. Sam sat up, recognizing it immediately. He inhaled the sweet and stale air as the opening notes to "Satisfaction" floated into his ears and filled his head. First the guitar and then the drums joined in. Memories of screaming at the concert and then screaming at the Dow demonstration came flooding back.

"You okay?" Danny asked.

"Yeah," Sam slid off the armrest to wedge himself in the corner of the faded blue couch covered in embroidered diamonds. "I'm okay."

Nick took a hit, humming along to the song.

The smoke swirled around Sam's head along with Mick Jagger's voice. He didn't know if Anthony was okay, but the song had to mean something. Some Beach Boys would have been too much to ask for, anyway. Danny had told him at the party there weren't any Beach Boys records in the house.

The next morning, Sam jogged to his dorm in the same clothes he wore the night before. All he could think about on the couch on Mifflin Street was what if Paul had dug into Sam's bottom desk drawer or his pillowcase and found all of his treasures from Anthony. Lying on the blue couch, hearing the faint snores from Nick, Sam imagined Paul going ape and trashing his side of the room, destroying his stuff or throwing it away. In his mind, Paul had torn up each of the letters into little pieces and left them in a pile of confetti on Sam's desk.

Sam picked up the pace a little. Because Paul was so damn predictable and scheduled every minute of his life, Sam knew he was already in Kronshage Hall, grabbing some breakfast and going over the registration guide. Paul was supposed to register for next semester in about an hour. Sam had two hours before his appointment.

When he got to his dorm, it looked exactly the same as he had left it. Sam sat on his bed and immediately went for his pillow. The shirt was there, just like he had left it. He went for the drawer next and exhaled in relief when he discovered the address book was also untouched. Sitting on his bed and holding the Snoopy shirt, Sam remembered that Vietnam combusted a couple days ago. In between songs on the radio last night, the news cut in to talk about the mass casualties to civilians and some military personnel.

With the shirt on his lap, Sam traced the faded red collar with his finger and then moved on to the cuffs on the sleeves. Finally, he ran his finger along the lines of Snoopy's doghouse. His stomach churned, and not because he hadn't eaten dinner last night or breakfast this morning.

Sam scanned his shoebox of a room. Paul had put his desk back together last night, with everything in its place. The pencil cup stood exactly two inches from the edge of the desk. The binders and books lined up in the order of his schedule for the week.

Then Sam's eyes fell on his radio, still turned on its side with the antennae bent at a weird angle. The rage from the night before attacked Sam in his chest. If Paul were to walk through the door right now, he would slug him and then Sam would get kicked out of the dorms for real.

Sam froze for a moment as an idea sprang into his head, more screwed up than walking out of the dorms with no place to go. They couldn't kick him out if he didn't live here anymore.

He quickly folded the Snoopy shirt and tucked it into his pillow. His body felt like it had to do a dozen things at once. He gathered his books and notebooks and dropped them in a laundry basket. He took his suitcase out from under his bed and stuffed as much clothes as he could into it. The address book with the letters from Anthony went into the pillow which went on top of the books.

Outside, Sam walked as quickly as he could, making sure the open end of the pillowcase was tucked into the basket so nothing would fall out. It was hard to walk fast carrying a basket of books and a poorly packed suitcase.

"Sam! Hey, Sam!"

Sam did his best to pivot and see Suzy trotting up behind him.

"What are you doing?" Suzy hugged her big poncho sweater around herself.

"I'm moving out of the dorms." Sam turned to resume his trek to Danny's.

"Why?" Suzy started up her trot again.

"My roommate's a dip."

"Where are you going?"

"Danny's," Sam said, eyes forward. "He said I could crash at his pad." That wasn't exactly true. He said Sam could crash there for one night.

"You're going to *live* there?" Suzy's eyes widened. "That's so boss."

"Yep."

"Let me help you." Suzy reached to take the pillow out of the laundry basket.

"No," Sam yelled louder than he had intended. "I mean, no. I'm okay."

"Are you okay?"

"Just peachy."

"Come on, Sam." Suzy picked up her pace. "What's going on?"

Sam stopped walking and paused to take a breath. Suzy would understand. "I'm worried about Anthony."

Suzy placed a hand on Sam's arm. "I dig that."

"No, I don't think you do." Sam adjusted his grip on the suitcase handle and started up again.

"He's your best friend. Of course you're worried about him."

Sam stopped again. "The whole country is exploding and I have no idea if he's okay. All I know is that there were a bunch of attacks, all at the same time and it's a big fucking mess." Saying it out loud was too much. Sam loudly inhaled through his nose. He had to put down his suitcase to wipe his eyes.

"Hey," Suzy said softly. "He's okay. I know it."

"Yeah, sure."

"You're a good friend, Sam, to care so much for someone." There was something wistful in Suzy's tone. "Anthony's lucky to have you care about him so much." She shuffled to the side a bit. "I was going to compare my class list with Gloria but I can ditch her if you want. I can walk with you."

"No, that's okay." Just saying it made Sam feel a little bit better. Everything he'd been feeling for the past sixteen hours had been so bottled up inside of him.

"Okay. But I'm here if you need anything. You know that, right?"

"I do," Sam nodded. He glanced at his watch. He couldn't miss his registration appointment. "I gotta split if I'm going to make it there and back."

"Okay. See you later." Suzy smiled before bouncing down the direction they came from.

There was no way Suzy had a crush on him. Gloria was stupid. Suzy was just a good friend who came along at the right time.

Sam walked as quickly as he could to Mifflin, knowing the way this time. Once on the porch, he set the basket on the ground to pound on the door. After a few seconds, no one came and Sam wondered if everyone was at class or passed out. The apartment was silent when he left.

The knob turned when Sam tried it. He pushed the door open with his back as he tried to balance everything. When he got to the top of the stairs, Danny was coming out carrying a yellow coffee mug and a few books tucked under an arm.

"Sam," Danny exclaimed. "You're an early riser, huh?"

Sam didn't have time for small talk. "Is the couch still available for tonight?"

Danny glanced in the apartment. "There's room at the inn, my friend."

FEBRUARY 2, 1968

Anthony gingerly lifted his T-shirt over his head. Even though he was already covered in layers of dirt and ash, he didn't want to touch any of Jersey's blood that had been caked onto his shirt for the past two days. Whenever Anthony turned a certain way, he could feel the stiffness of the shirt where the blood had dried.

He rolled his shirt into a ball around the blood stain and stuffed it into his laundry bag.

"That's sick, Capone," Capper commented as Anthony flopped onto his rack.

Anthony let his helmet fall to the side of his bed. When he turned to face Capper, he left a smear of grime on his pillow. "The line for the shower is too long," he murmured. It felt like his body was melting into the bed.

"So you're going to stink up the place?" Capper took off his shirt and tossed it under his rack. "I know your meatball-making mama taught you better."

"She told me not to get killed." Anthony closed his eyes. A shower did sound good but after being awake for the past thirty-six hours, sleep sounded better. He heard the sounds of the guys grunting and sighing as they tugged off their boots.

By some miracle, he followed his mom's orders. It was nonstop for two days. Two days of bullets and fires and civilians crying in the street and fellow soldiers being dragged to makeshift bases.

Everyone had made it through. QB had to make an early exit after taking some debris to the face and Mikey had gotten shot in the arm. QB was already waiting for them when they got back to base, gauze covering his cheeks and ear. Mikey would rejoin them in a few days because most injuries were not an automatic ticket home.

"You heard about Jersey?" Capper asked quietly, as if not wanting to be caught talking in a library.

"I did."

"That sucks, man," Capper said.

"Yep, it does." There wasn't anything else to say. If Anthony could get a couple hours of sleep then he'd be able to write a letter to his mom and Sam. Who knew what they were showing on the news. His mom was probably sleeping at the church, convinced her extra devotion would guarantee her son's safety. Maria definitely spent the evening in the kitchen or maybe she just went to her room, knowing the news wasn't going to get any better. Hopefully she had a stockpile of Trixie Belden.

And Sam. Anthony wasn't sure what Sam would hear on the radio or if he had access to a TV. News about what happened had to make its way around campus. And if college was anything like high school, no one would have any idea what was really going on. Everyone would come up with their own version. The truth was, Anthony was okay.

There was that word again. *Okay.* It was weird how much the definition had changed.

FEBRUARY 10, 1968

Sam saw FREE written in block letters and tore open the envelope.

Sam,

I'm fine. I made it through whatever the fuck that was without a scratch. Well, that's not completely true. I did get a couple scratches because there was so much shit flying all over the place. But I'm still here. Here in Vietnam, in one piece.

Dinner should have been served with extra ketchup to celebrate the fact so many of us made it back to base. A couple guys got hurt but they're back and okay. This guy in my squad, Jersey, didn't make it. He was kind of an asshole but one hell of a soldier.

I wanted to let you know as soon as I could.

Anthony

Sam let out a breath. He blinked to prevent the words in front of him from blurring.

Thank God.

He was sorry about that Jersey guy, he really was. But, thank God.

Sam read the letter three more times before putting it in the envelope and tucking it into his Early Civilizations textbook. Feeling like it was the first day of spring with the birds chirping and the sun shining, he practically skipped down the sidewalks of campus on the cold and gray day. Sam was going to meet Suzy at Kronshage Hall for lunch and there was a good chance he was going to fly all the way there. Ever since running into each other on the way back to Mifflin, they had eaten together a couple times.

"I don't think I've ever seen you look this happy." Suzy waved at Sam from outside the dining hall doors. The fringe from her coat waved too.

Sam hustled to Suzy and grabbed her by the shoulders for a hug. "It's a great day, isn't it?" He let her go and felt the smile on his face spread even wider. He pulled her in again.

"What has you so excited?" Suzy said into Sam's shoulder.

He pulled the letter out of his textbook. "Anthony's fine. He's okay."

Suzy jumped up and down a little and went in for another hug. "Outta sight, Sam!"

Sam squeezed Suzy a little harder. "I know. I can't believe it." Sam laughed like a kid running through the sprinkler on a summer day. Suzy smiled up at him. When Sam went back in to continue the celebratory hug, his face smashed into Suzy's and somehow, their mouths connected.

The thrill of the physical contact coursed through Sam and even though his brain told him to disconnect, something kept him glued to Suzy. She threw her arms around him and began kissing him. Sam wrapped his arms around her waist. He wasn't thinking about Anthony or Suzy or the feelings he had or didn't have. He was lost in the feeling of a kiss and being so incredibly happy.

"Get a room!"

Sam jerked away from Suzy.

Suzy smiled at the ground, her hair concealing part of her sparkling face. "They must think we're going steady or something."

"I have no idea where they got that idea." Sam tried to make a joke but his smile fell. "I'm sorry."

"Don't be."

"But I am," Sam insisted. "We're friends."

Suzy tossed her hair out of her face. "I've never kissed any of my friends like that."

"Me either. Until now, I guess." He'd just lied to Suzy. He'd kissed Anthony when they were just friends, before they were whatever they were now.

THE WAR ON ALL FRONTS

"You know," Suzy smiled at the ground. "Gloria told me she thought you were a fairy or something because you never kissed me or asked me on a date."

Despite the brisk day, Sam's cheeks felt hot as he noticed how Suzy hesitated when she said *fairy*. She had no problem cussing at police officers but that word was too much for her to say, huh? "Gloria knows everything, that's for sure." He hadn't thought about that weird conversation with Gloria at the Mifflin party in a while. Classes, the war, and Anthony took up too much space for him to think about her.

Everything told Sam to run away but instead he stayed. "I'm sorry, Suzy," Sam finally said. "I'm not the kind of guy who kisses a bunch of chicks."

"I know, Sam. I've known you for a while and you've never tried anything. You're not like a lot of other guys."

"I guess you're right." Sam laughed. "But we're copacetic, right?"

"Copacetic," Suzy nodded.

"Okay, cool." He backed up a few steps. "I have to jam. Sorry about lunch. I forgot about this calc study group I have later today. I need to jet over to Mifflin to get my books."

"*You* need a study group, Mr. Salutatorian?"

"When you're the best at everything else, it's okay if math isn't your best subject." Sam hoped the joke would let him off with a clean getaway.

"Oh, okay." Suzy paused.

Sam started to hurry away. "Another time, okay?"

"Yeah, sure."

Sam clutched the letter from Anthony in his hand as his steps got faster and faster, recalling the elation he felt upon reading his words. This was how he showed Anthony how much he cared? How relieved he was? How grateful? By kissing the girl that Anthony was convinced was scheming on him?

FEBRUARY 19, 1968

Since Tet, five of Anthony's fellow soldiers were KIA and over a dozen had been injured. The ones killed weren't part of his squad but it didn't make the pill easier to swallow. It was best not to think about how any of the casualties could have been him if he were the one to take the path with the mine or had gotten assigned the hut where the VC sprayed bullets through the door as soldiers approached. They might have struck first but they didn't make it out of the hut alive.

And now it was summer camp again. Lounging on cots, drinking Cokes and beers, playing cards and volleyball. But mail call was still the most exciting part of the day. Capper was in the middle of a letter from Lorraine when the door to the barracks swung open.

"No welcome back party, boys?" Mikey belted out.

Everyone immediately forgot about the letter from Lorraine, filled with suggestions for jobs Capper might find when he got back to Kentucky. He hated all of them.

"What? You're back?" QB swung his legs over to the side of his rack.

"No ticket home, huh?" Anthony said, opening a letter that had arrived from Sam.

Mike gestured to the gauze wrapped around his bicep. The bandage was so thick, his T-shirt sleeve was cuffed above it. "Not for a little graze."

A graze? Blood had reportedly been squirting out of Mikey's arm while he waited for a jeep to find him. By the time it got to Mikey, he had lost a serious amount of blood.

"Get back to that letter, Capper." Mikey took a seat on his footlocker. "We all know I'm not getting anything from Kathy any time soon." Right before Tet, Mikey had gotten a "Dear John" letter from his girl. She had met someone at the drugstore where she worked. It wouldn't have been fair to continue the relationship with Mikey. She had insisted it was the right thing to do.

"You don't want to hear about this shit," Capper waved the letter around.

"Lorraine knows someone who can get Capper a job at the new Piggly Wiggly," Lennox explained. "Maybe work his way up to assistant manager."

"I believe she said it was for shift *managers*. I'm not going to be anyone's assistant." Capper put the letter in the envelope. "What'd you get, Picasso?"

Picasso sat with a blue envelope on his lap. He held up a card with balloons on it. "A birthday card from my folks."

"It's your birthday?" Capper asked.

"Two days ago. The big 2-2."

"You didn't tell us?" Capper looked shocked.

Picasso shrugged.

"Come on guys," QB said, raising his hands like a conductor. "A one and a two and a three…"

Anthony grinned and put his arm around Capper on one side and Lennox on the other. They swayed from side to side in a loud and off- key rendition of "Happy Birthday."

Picasso rolled his eyes and endured the performance, half-heartedly clapping as everyone took a bow at the end. "Thanks guys but that was terrible."

As the laughing subsided and Picasso set up his birthday card on his footlocker, Anthony unfolded Sam's letter, ready to inhale every word. Rarely did he get a private reading of a letter before sharing it with everyone.

Anthony,

Six classes aren't as hard to get through as this letter is to write. When you left, I told you I'd tell you everything and we wouldn't keep secrets. Well, I kissed Suzy. Not a friendly little peck on the cheek but a real kiss. A big kiss. I didn't plan on it. I got your letter about being okay after that Tet thing and I was so damn happy and relieved. I couldn't think about anything else after I found out. They made it sound like the whole country exploded and I had no idea if you were okay. So when I got your letter, I can't explain what I felt. And then I saw Suzy and it happened. I don't know how, but it did. It was nothing. It meant nothing. I don't feel anything for her. It was a one-time thing, you dig? I only did because I was so happy. Does that make sense? Do you believe me? Kissing Suzy was nothing like kissing you. Nothing compares to kissing you.

I'd send you a box of ketchup if I could, but there's no grocery store in walking distance and everyone would probably think it would be weird if I bought a dozen bottles of ketchup and nothing else. I don't know if they would understand if I said it was for a very good reason.

Don't hate me. Please understand.

Anthony stared at the letter without seeing the words on it. A jumble of emotion swirled inside of him. Jealous that Sam kissed Suzy. Relieved that Sam said it was nothing. Scared it could turn into something. Regret if he didn't—

"All right, Capone, you're up." Capper called from his rack.

"Not this time, guys, sorry." Anthony tried to sound casual as he folded Sam's letter.

"Aww come on, that's not how it works," Mikey said. Anthony didn't expect for Mikey to sound so hurt.

"I'll read the next one, I promise." Anthony held up the "Scout's honor" sign and tried not to wince. Sam had held up that sign the last he saw him when he said there was nothing going on between him and Suzy and there would be no secrets between them.

"We're not Boy Scouts, Capone," Capper laughed. "We're soldiers. Now read your damn letter."

Anthony had to think fast. There was no way out of this, unless Sergeant Avery barged in to say they needed to go out, but that wasn't likely since they'd just been out there for four days. For almost a whole second, Anthony actually thought enduring another attack would be worth getting out of reading Sam's letter.

There was no way he could explain it. The truth could get him kicked out of the army or worse. And there wasn't time to think of a good lie. He had no idea how to pretend his way out of this one.

"I can't this time, guys. Sorry." Anthony tightened a fist around the letter. He was genuinely sorry. They had shared all their letters during their time over here. Everything from Lorraine's ideas for Capper's life after the war, to Lennox's grandma being in the hospital, to QB finding out a friend had been KIA a month ago. They needed each other's letters and they needed to share them with each other.

"I haven't gotten any mail in two weeks." Lennox leaned against a wall. "And there's nothing in there we haven't heard or can't handle. You think Mikey wanted to read us the letter from that skirt who dumped him? Fuck no."

"I was happy to let you guys share in my misery," Mikey said.

"And what about all that lovey-dovey shit Capper's girl writes about," Lennox continued. "He shares it all. We all do."

Capper smirked. "All of you are jealous of that lovey-dovey shit."

"I'll read the next one, I promise," Anthony said. "And the next time my mom sends cookies, you guys get 'em all. I won't take one." He stuffed Sam's letter into his back pocket.

"Read it for Eddie Bear," Capper pretended to plead. "What could be in there that none of us ain't heard, huh? And we shared it anyway because that's what we do. Mikey's girl–"

"Ex-girl," Mikey interrupted.

"Ex-girl," Capper nodded. "And Lorraine made me promise I wouldn't tell anyone we went all the way before I shipped out." He gave all the guys a look. "Shut it if you ever see her. Not one word." He turned to Anthony. "So, come on, Capone. Whatever's in there is no big deal to us. We just want to hear it."

Anthony didn't have time to think. "It's from Sam and he wrote about some stuff I don't think he'd want me to tell all of you about." That was true but for different reasons than the guys would think.

All eyes were on him, pleading to let them take part in a letter because nothing came for them today or because they had walked through rice paddies, seen one another's blood, and watched too many of their own carried away in a chopper. All those things should have made Anthony able to tell them anything, but there were some things dark nights in the jungle and birthdays spent far from home weren't going to change.

"We're never gonna see him," QB offered. "Right?"

With his stomach churning and his legs feeling like they were about to give out, Anthony slowly unfolded the letter. "Okay, fine. But only because you guys asked so nicely." He held the letter even with his eyes but didn't see any of the words. "Hey Anthony, these six classes are kicking my ass. I was a real dummy for thinking I could handle them. I think I might be scheming on my friend, Suzy. I kissed her a little while ago. And I know she likes me but I don't know if I like her. Kick some VC ass. Write soon. Sam." With his heart pounding more than it ever did when raiding a ville, Anthony folded the letter and put it in the envelope.

Lennox broke the silence in the barracks with a low whistle. "That was heavy, Capone," he inhaled through his teeth. "I can see why you wanted to keep that one close."

"Come on, buddy, you know that was bullshit," Capper said. "If you don't want to read it, I'll do it for you." He sounded like a friend wanting to help out a friend.

"You asked me to read it, I did." Anthony stuffed the envelope in his back pocket.

A grin passed between Lennox and Mikey. "Let's see what it really says."

Before Anthony could blink, Lennox tackled him and reached for his pocket with a grin.

Anthony squirmed under Lennox's weight. "Get your hands off of me," he yelled. His mind raced with the limited options he had with his arms pinned and the letter a couple inches from Lennox's hand.

His pointer finger got closer and closer.

"Are you some sort of faggot or something?" The word tasted like vomit in Anthony's mouth.

Lennox sprang up off the ground, glaring at Anthony.

It worked. He knew it would.

"What did you call me?"

Anthony spit the remnants of the word on the floor. "Some dude reaches for another guy's ass, what else am I supposed to think?"

"Fuck you." Lennox lunged at Anthony again. This time, it wasn't about the letter. Lennox got him around the waist and they both fell to the ground. He punched Anthony across the face.

It was like being back on the sidewalk when he should have fought George for messing up Maria's ice cream cone. Or when he should have fought Tommy Maloney and pushed him into the Slurpee machine.

With his whole face pulsating, Anthony dodged the next swing from Lennox and rolled out of the way.

"Cool it, guys." Capper's voice came from off to the side, but Anthony was only focused on Lennox.

"Lay off each other," Picasso said from somewhere.

"Call me that again," Lennox growled. "I dare you."

QB stood near Lennox and Anthony as if wanting to break them apart.

The two circled each other like angry wild animals. Anthony clenched his fists. He wasn't going to get hit again. "You like the way it sounds? You want to hear it again?"

"Maybe you're the fag," Lennox jerked his body at Anthony. "Your mom and that dude are the only ones who write you."

Anthony managed not to flinch.

"Shut up, Lennox," Capper said. "There aren't any fags here."

"There's no girl waiting for you. Just some fairy waiting for his fairy boyfriend." Lennox lunged at Anthony. They fell over a cot and got tangled up in each other.

"What's going on here?" Sergeant Avery stood in the doorway, his short stature filling it.

Everyone stood at attention, still and eyes forward.

Anthony scrambled to his feet, staring ahead as if Sarge wouldn't notice his puffy face or Lennox's bloody nose.

Sergeant Avery took off his sunglasses so everyone could see his eyeballs give each soldier an extra-long look. He settled on Anthony and Lennox, his eyes going between the two of them.

A million thoughts flooded Anthony's brain. He couldn't get kicked out for fighting, right? Or court-martialed? Or put in some sort of military jail? What would his dad say? What if—

"Lorenzo. Lennox," Avery barked.

In one smooth move, Anthony parked himself in front of the sergeant. He looked past Sergeant Avery's head, at a palm tree by the gate that led into the base.

Avery took a step forward, only a couple inches from Anthony, reminding him of Dalton puffing coffee breath in his face.

"If it didn't mean a ton of paperwork I don't have time to do, you two would be facing some serious restrictions."

Anthony stifled an exhale of relief.

"You just made squad leader." Sergeant Avery turned to Lennox who was promoted after Jersey was killed. "It could be gone like that." Sarge snapped his fingers. He remained stoic and pressed his lips into a tighter line.

"Instead, I'm going to figure out how to win this war and you two are going to make sure nothing like this ever happens again. Am I clear?"

"Yes, Sergeant Avery," Anthony and Lennox shouted.

"You get to clean the latrines. Two weeks. And this never happens again." Sergeant Avery made every syllable count.

Cleaning the shitter and stinking for two weeks was a small price to pay to keep Sam's letter a secret. It was the worst duty but one Anthony would gladly do.

"Don't get too used to this vacation, gents. We move out tomorrow." Sergeant Avery put his sunglasses on and walked out of the barracks.

Lennox wiped a smear of blood on the back of his hand and lay on his rack with his hands tucked behind his head. It was like he was back at home and hanging out in his bedroom at home, listening to music.

Everyone else stood, eyes darting between Lennox and Anthony.

Anthony felt the stare of everyone burn a hole in his standard issue T-shirt. He gingerly pressed his cheek. It was swollen and it felt weird to open and close his eye. With his head down, Anthony took a few strides and walked out the flimsy door. He squatted outside, his back against the wall, fists rubbing his eyes.

A pair of boots came out and stood next to Anthony. "You shoulda just read it, Capone, and none of this woulda happened." Capper gazed into the distance like he was taking in a breathtaking view. "We don't care what they say. We like hearing about life back home."

"I know," Anthony said to the dry, dusty ground. "But couldn't one thing be just mine?"

Capper shook his head. "Not in the Army. There's not a whole lot here that's just for you. You dig?"

FEBRUARY 28, 1968

Sam,

You can't write a letter like that ever again. I told you, we have to read them out loud. We all do, no matter what it's about. All the guys were bothering me about it and said I had to read it. I didn't know what to say so I called Lennox a fag and we got into a fight. It was probably my worst day here and I've seen some pretty messed up shit. Sarge was pissed but we didn't get into too much trouble because I guess writing up a report and following through with it is a pain in the ass. Lucky for me, I guess. I know it won't be the same story if it happens again.

Please don't stop writing, but be careful. Leave the ketchup stuff. The guys think it's weird and you're weird and I don't care. That's ours and probably the only thing in this world that is.

Does Suzy really know there's nothing going on between you guys? She knows the kiss meant nothing? Please find a way to answer that in your next letter.

My mom would kill you if she found out you were eating pasta from the cafeteria. And that would suck for so many reasons. Go for something that goes well with ketchup.

Anthony

Sam lowered his head when he was done reading. What an idiot. Why didn't he remember? Anthony had told him they all read their letters. Sam could've gotten him kicked out of the Army or worse. Much worse. He revised the letter about Suzy in his head, figuring out how he could have gotten his point across. Sam clenched his fists. Goddammit. He had written about *kissing* Anthony.

What if one of them *had* managed to read it? What if it was discovered somehow? What would have happened to Anthony?

"That from your friend?" Danny took a rolled-up newspaper out of his back pocket before sitting next to Sam.

"Yeah." Sam rested his head on the back of the dingy couch he had slept on for the past month. It was more comfortable than it looked.

"How's the war going?" Danny shook out the paper.

"It sucks." And Sam almost made it a lot worse.

"Holy shit." Danny sat up, intently scanned the front page. "What?"

"Cronkite said what all of us have been thinking for a long time." Danny angled the paper so Sam could get a look.

Sam did his best to scan the article. Every night, Walter Cronkite gave America a recap of the war and Sam's parents never missed it. Since being away, Sam hadn't kept up with Cronkite's recaps and mainly got his news from radio snippets and the newspapers in the student union, or the ones Danny left lying around. Danny followed the news more than a lot of guys Sam knew.

Sam found phrases on the article like *mired in stalemate*, *last gasp before negotiations*, and *did the best they could* but he couldn't make sense of any of it because his brain was going too fast. Apparently, Cronkite gave some address to the nation on CBS the night before and it was big news today. "It's going to end soon? Everyone's coming home?" He already had an image of Anthony on an airplane, headed home.

Danny folded the paper and tossed it on the floor. "It's not going to happen tomorrow, Sam. And probably not the day after either."

"So, when?" Sam asked like a little kid who wanted to know when it was time to open up his birthday presents.

"Who knows? But if Cronkite is talking, maybe people will actually listen. The people who *need* to listen and haven't been."

Sam couldn't stop the bubble of excitement ready to burst inside of him. If the nation's most respected reporter put aside his usual routine of only giving the facts and stats and gave his own opinion, somebody had to take note.

And then Anthony would be home and Sam wouldn't have to worry about sending a letter that said the wrong thing ever again. He settled into the grimy blue couch with the fading diamond pattern. It held the stench of pot and a semester's worth of dust, but right now it felt like a king-sized bed at some fancy hotel.

A few days later, the war was still going on. Sam felt so stupid for believing everyone would simply pack up and go home because some newscaster said what Danny and a bunch of others had been saying for a while. He flopped on the couch he'd been sleeping on, eating on, studying on, getting high on for the past month and flipped through the pages of his calc book. He had to get through the night's assignment before Danny, Nick, and Jack came home from their classes. As much as he liked living on Mifflin, it was hard to get any work done when all of them were around.

Attempting to make sense of the mixture of letters and numbers in the first problem, Sam balanced his notebook on his knee. Before he got through the second problem, someone came bounding up the stairs and flew into the apartment. Sam dropped his notebook and saw Danny rush into the kitchen when he went to pick it up.

"Hey," Sam said. "Did your class get out early?"

Danny didn't look at Sam. "I had to take care of something." He picked up a binder that must have been hiding somewhere in the kitchen and flipped through some pages. He scanned a page and took out a small rectangular piece of paper.

"Are you okay? Can I help you with anything?" Sam asked.

"Nope. Everything's copacetic." Danny glanced at the clock, his body visibly relaxing a little bit. He ducked into the kitchen and emerged a few minutes later with a sandwich.

Sam waited for Danny to explain why he came in like a tornado but he just stood by the card table that doubled as a kitchen table, tucking a piece of turkey back into his sandwich. Danny's behavior was about as confusing as the swirls and symbols in his calc textbook. Sam was about to finish the assignment when someone knocked on the door.

Danny double checked that he had a rectangular piece of paper in his shirt pocket and opened the door. "Hey, Alan. I got it right here."

Sam couldn't see Alan but could hear his low voice. "Thanks, man. Thanks a lot."

"No sweat." Danny leaned forward. "Now listen. When you get off the bus in Duluth, Father Mathews is going to be waiting for you. He'll have the whole collar get-up on, but he'll also have a sign that says YMCA."

"A priest?" Alan's surprised voice came from the other side of the door. "I thought those dudes took a vow not to lie and shit. You sure about him?"

"Absolutely."

"Okay." Alan sounded unsure.

Sam didn't even try to pretend he was writing in his notebook. He craned an ear to the door. He thought about Robbie from the party when he first met Danny and how he stormed out with his girlfriend crying after him. Now Alan was here, getting a bus ticket to Duluth. The pieces of information moved around in Sam's head, trying to fit together.

"It's all worked out, I promise," Danny said.

The floor by the door creaked. "Okay."

"Good luck, Alan. What you're doing takes guts."

Another floor creak. "Not according to a lot of people."

"A lot of people don't have your decision to make," Danny insisted.

Something churned in the depths of Sam's stomach. Everything clicked into place.

"Well, see you later, I guess." The floor creaked again followed by the sound of steps hurrying down the stairs.

"Bye, Alan," Danny softly called after him. He shut the door and stared at it for a moment. His eyes met Sam's.

A few moments of silence passed between them. Sam's pen fell from his hand, making a little squiggle on the page.

"I think it takes guts too." Sam pried the words from his throat. It was a strong admission. He didn't think Alan was a coward, or unpatriotic, or a traitor.

"You're damn right it does," Danny said. "Just so you know, that doesn't happen too often. Maybe a few more times than usual with the semester ending and people graduating or failing classes."

"Okay."

"If you're not okay with it, you can go."

Sam straightened. Was Danny going to kick him out? Did he have to go back to the dorms? Where could he stay?

"No, no," Danny held up his hands, reading Sam's mind. "I'm not saying that in a 'bug out' kind of way. I'm saying, know that it's what happens here and it needs to stay here."

Sam nodded.

"It's no secret guys dodge, and when they decide it's what they need to do, they know where to go."

"And you're that guy."

"I'm that guy. Jack and Nick too," Danny added.

Sam remembered Nick opening the door with his blonde ponytail and loose jeans. He had no idea Nick was coordinating bus schedules and secret meetings. "I thought Cronkite said they needed to call off this whole thing and bring our guys home."

Danny shook his head. "No one in charge is listening."

"Well that sucks." He picked up his pen to finish his homework. A student deferment wasn't going to do him any good if he failed a bunch of his classes.

MARCH 15, 1968

It was another search and destroy mission. Sergeant Avery had gotten some intel that Charlie and his pals were using a ville about forty clicks away as a hideout. They walked the last five clicks so Charlie wouldn't know they were coming. If he was in the ville, then the road in would be peppered with mines and traps. Everyone took tentative steps on the compacted dirt road. Tire treads made little trenches so it was hard to step firmly on the ground and detect anything that might have been out of place.

Even before the fight, part of Anthony was jealous when Lennox was promoted to Jersey's role of Squad Leader. The two of them completed their latrine duty for two weeks, hating every minute, and then it was like nothing had ever happened. When it came time to read the mail, everyone shared, everyone listened, everyone gave Capper a hard time for the little hearts Lorraine dotted her i's with.

So Lennox was up front, followed by Capper and Anthony was in the middle, with Mikey behind him. The middle seemed like the safest place to be on most missions. Anthony was ready for the day when he would get some sort of promotion, but not if it meant someone had to die in order for him to get it.

The huts ahead of them looked like little dots under the dome of a brilliant blue sky. But the sky was dark in the greater distance. It was like someone had painted a line and filled in one side with dark clouds. It was either hot and sticky or raining buckets, nothing in between.

The group halted as Lennox held up a hand. Anthony cocked his head. Was that a howl? A wail? Everyone glanced at one another as they resumed their trek forward, but with more caution.

"Sounds like a dying dog. I bet it has rabies," Capper muttered to Anthony. "I did not come all the way here to end up like Old Yeller."

"Shut up," Anthony whispered through clenched teeth.

"Maybe that's what the VC are doing now. Bombing the shit out of us didn't work so they created mad dogs-"

"Shut up, Capper," QB hissed from behind Mikey. "It's not a dog."

"Everyone, shut up," Lennox said from the front.

Without anyone saying anything, their pace slowed to a halt. Everyone stood, listening to the wail. "It's coming from the ville," Anthony said.

"It's definitely coming from the ville," Capper agreed. "Charlie's got these dogs working for him now. He's trained them to sic anything that comes within ten feet-"

"Shut it, Capper," Lennox demanded.

Everyone stood still again as the mysterious wail continued. "I don't think it's an animal." Anthony cocked his ear at the sound. "Do you think...do you think it's a person?"

"Maybe it's a kid?" Picasso suggested from behind Lennox. "Is Charlie messing with a kid?"

"It's not a dog he's training," Capper jumped in. "It's kids. And this kid didn't complete his mission, so Charlie-"

"Shut the fuck up, Capper. Now." Lennox turned to look at Capper. "Our job is to search and destroy. Let's do this."

Search and destroy. That meant *someone* would be destroyed. They had gone on several other S&D missions in the past and each time came up empty. The only thing they managed to accomplish was burning the huts to the ground.

"Kids like candy, cake, soda. All that stuff," Picasso said. "Maybe we can bribe him with something. Anybody have anything?"

"I got half my chocolate bar left," QB offered.

"I have one of those cakes in the can," Mikey said.

If they could get through this mission and only lose some c-rations *and* annihilate Charlie, it would be a successful day. The dark line in the sky crept closer and closer to Anthony and his friends. By the time they made it to the ville, the wail hadn't quieted.

"Radio back to Sarge," Lennox called to Mikey. "Let him know the ville's not empty and that there might be a kid there."

They continued their slow trek down the road. Grass almost as tall as Anthony lined each side, but the little clearing where the ville sat got closer with each step. A small cluster of huts came into clearer view. It looked like the dozens of other villes they'd swept. It even had two chickens strutting around as if they owned the place. The wail that was so loud a few minutes before had quieted to a whimper. It was clear which hut it was coming from.

Aside from the sound, everything seemed to be in place. Doors were latched shut, the huts looked maintained. Anthony scanned the ground, looking for an oddly placed clump of grass or a barrel that shouldn't have been where it was. The sight of a barrel sent him back to the moment a VC popped out of one. That was the only other time they went into a ville that wasn't empty.

Lennox led the way toward the hut where the whimpering came from. Anthony strained to hear any other sounds: someone whispering, someone crawling, someone loading a gun. Nothing, just the little cry Maria used to make when she was small and starting to get tired. Lennox would open the door and Capper and Anthony would sweep the hut. Mikey, Picasso, and QB would stay on the stairs in case someone jumped out of one of the other huts.

As Lennox prepared to knock down the door with his elbow, Anthony and Capper slowly climbed up the dingy porch. Once they were on top and the whimper was that much louder, Anthony could tell it wasn't a kid crying, but rather a baby. How small? He had no idea. But it was definitely the cry of a person who didn't know any words.

Just as Anthony was about to imagine a little baby in a diaper surrounded by VC, Lennox threw himself against the door and

Anthony's feet automatically responded. He took a big step into the hut with his gun at the ready. Capper squeezed in next to him.

A baby with a round face and a hearty head of black hair stopped whimpering and stared at them with wet, red eyes. The little lip quivered as drool fell on its chin. Tears clung to its eyelashes. It sat in the middle of the floor, clutching the leg of a small table.

Anthony's eyes darted around the hut. Under the table. In each corner. He settled on a barrel in the corner and sharply inhaled through his teeth. The lid on the barrel was lopsided. A VC must have jumped in there seconds before they came in. He knew it. Anthony and Capper locked eyes, silently communicating that the barrel and the little cabinet structure by the door were their next targets.

"Shush," Capper encouraged the baby who watched their every move in the small space.

Anthony pointed his gun at the barrel, trying to steady his shaking hand on the trigger. Lennox stood in front of the cabinet, ready to open one of the small doors to a space Charlie would have no problem folding himself into.

On a silent count of three, Anthony shot at the barrel and Lennox flung open the door to the cabinet. The baby screamed. Little splinters of wood flew into the air.

"What the fuck?" Capper said.

"What?" Anthony asked without taking his eyes off the barrel. Sure it was full of holes and appeared to be empty but that did nothing to put him at ease.

With the baby screaming and screaming, Anthony turned and saw a pair of legs in the cabinet. Lennox opened the door to reveal the full body of a woman. Despite the baby crying and the shots that annihilated the barrel, the woman didn't move. Lennox slightly bent to get a better look.

"Is she dead?" Capper yelled over the screaming baby. "She looks dead."

"What's going on in there?" Mikey called from outside.

"We're not sure," Lennox replied. "What's going on out there?"

"Nothing yet," Mikey replied.

The baby wailed louder than it did when they first heard it coming up the road. Anthony wanted to cry his head off too. Gunfire in a little hut was loud and the fact that the only people in the ville appeared to be the baby and this woman was scarier than a ville full of VC. Charlie *had* to have been here and not long ago.

Lennox knelt next to the woman. "QB! Get in here."

In a few short bounds, QB was next to Lennox. He felt for a pulse in the woman's wrist and then in her neck. He turned to Lennox, Capper, and Anthony with a shake of his head. "She's dead."

"How?" Capper asked. He shot the crying baby a glare. "Can someone shut that kid up?"

"You got a baby bottle in your pack?" Lennox asked. "Or maybe see if it wants some of Picasso's C-ration cake."

"Should we radio Sergeant? Let him know?" Capper suggested

"No," Lennox quickly said. "We can handle this."

"Pick it up." QB rummaged through his medic pack. "Give him a damn hug."

"Are you shitting me?" Capper swung his gun around to his back. "How do you know the kid's not a booby trap?"

For a second everyone was silent, contemplating that distinct possibility, as the baby's cries grew louder. Anthony's eyes darted all over the kid. Cloth diaper. Wet face. Dirty feet. If the baby was in fact a booby trap, Anthony had no idea where something might be hiding. With the red in the baby's face spreading to its neck and shoulders, Anthony bent over in an attempt to look under the diaper.

"God, just shut up, kid," Anthony muttered. "I'm trying to help you." He grabbed onto the table, looking on it, under it, off to the sides. Capper looked like he wanted to run right out of the hut.

Lennox held up his hands. "Careful, Capone," he said as Anthony rattled the table and lifted a leg off the floor.

The wail sounded like a siren going off in a locked bathroom. "I don't think he's rigged up with anything. I think it's safe."

"I don't know Capone. Don't do it." Capper took a small step forward.

Lennox took a step too.

The baby looked up at Anthony and let out a scream that was somehow louder than any noise made so far. Before he could think, Anthony snatched up the kid, held him to his chest, and squeezed his eyes shut, waiting for the consequence of his actions.

Nothing.

No explosion. No Charlie lurking somewhere.

Anthony squeezed the kid harder, letting out a deep breath.

Capper looked at Anthony with his mouth open in disbelief. Lennox looked relieved.

"Thank you," QB exhaled as he got to work examining the woman who had been stuffed in the cabinet.

Anthony then realized he had a baby in his arms and had no idea what to do with it. The baby looked at him with wet eyes, seemingly in shock that it was finally picked up after crying for all this time. It looked at the floor around him and kicked his feet a little. But as quickly as the kid quieted, it started up again.

"Get that kid to shut up," QB yelled.

"How?" Anthony juggled the kid in his arms the way he saw his nonna do with all of his younger cousins.

Capper went to the door in two strides. "Anyone know what to do with a baby?"

In the doorframe, Anthony saw Picasso and Mikey eye each other and shrug. "No clue," Mikey said.

Anthony's arms and shoulders tensed. He couldn't put the kid down. He couldn't hand it off to someone else. The first thing that popped into his head was a children's song his nonna sang when he was really small. He started humming, trying to remember the words.

"What are you singing?" Lennox asked. He glanced at the baby as if it might try to jump into his arms and then quieting it would be his responsibility.

"Some song in Italian about going fishing." Anthony continued humming. There was another lyric about a dog. He racked his brain trying to remember it. He continued to jiggle the baby and hum and remember a word or two. Just when he was about to attempt some Beach Boys, the kid's little hand landed on his forehead with a little slap and a giggle.

Lennox laughed.

"Hey," Anthony pretended to be mad. "What's that all about?"

"Maybe he's a Beatles fan," Capper said.

QB stood up with his medic pack, looking at the woman slumped in the cabinet. Her long black hair hung over her face.

The smile vanished from Anthony's face. In his moment of joy, he'd forgotten about the woman. He squeezed the baby in his arms. "What happened?"

"I'm not sure," QB said. "No sign of injury. No sign of a struggle. It's hard to believe she put herself in there. I don't know."

"Mikey," Lennox called. "Radio Sarge. Tell him we have a dead civilian and an abandoned baby. We're gonna need a dust off."

Capper let out a laugh. "That was some of the bravest, badass shit I've seen over here, Capone."

"What?" Anthony asked.

"I heard from someone in another squad that this VC mom had a bomb on her kid and when she handed him off to an American soldier, they both blew up."

"No way." Lennox shook his head.

"I don't know if it was brave. All I did was pick up a crying baby." Anthony angled his neck to look at the baby who had relaxed in his arms and now rested on his shoulder.

"I wouldn't have done it," Capper said.

"Yes, you would."

Capper shrugged. "I don't know."

Anthony carried the baby outside, feeling like he had to shield the kid from the fact it was alone in this world. When he thought about all the things he'd done so far—the shots he'd fired, the villes he'd raided, ambushes he'd been a part of— holding this baby until the chopper arrived was the most important one yet.

MARCH 25, 1968

Sam sat on a bench outside Kronshage Hall. His lunch of tomato soup and a sandwich made him feel tired, like he'd consumed triple helpings at Thanksgiving dinner. A pile of books sat next to him. Sam's advisor was right. It was crazy to take six classes and today's calc quiz proved that. So many squiggles and lines and so few numbers. Sam could make corrections by the next class to improve his grade. There was also an English 102 paper due by the end of the week.

But all of that could wait a few minutes. Sam took an envelope out of his jacket pocket and tore open the flap.

Sam,

I think I finally feel like I'm making a difference over here. It only took about four months but at least I get it now. It's not about annihilating Charlie. It's about helping the people he's hurting. Last week there was a baby that was all alone in a hut with a woman who I think was his mom. QB thinks either Charlie poisoned her or she did the job herself. If we didn't get assigned the mission, who knows what would have happened to the baby. A few days ago we came across this old lady with another mom and a baby. I think the kid was about a year old and by the way the kid was screaming you knew something was wrong. The poor ladies looked like they'd walked a million miles in their sandals.

It always takes the civilians a little while to figure out we want to help and we're not here to hurt them. They relaxed a little when QB came up with his medic stuff. The kid had a high fever and we were able to get them to a hospital.

It's not shooting a gun or anything, but it's easier and it feels better.

How are the classes going? Any more ideas about what comes next after you barrel through all these classes? I don't know how you're making it through calc. Trig was hard enough for me back in high school. It's crazy, but sometimes I think about being back at Bowen and it seems like it was years ago instead of less than one.

Keep studying hard and I'll keep doing what I'm doing over here. That includes getting to the ketchup care packages before the other guys.

Anthony

The calc quiz and English paper didn't matter. The only thing that did was Anthony not only being okay, but *feeling* okay. He felt good. And if Anthony could feel good about what he was doing over there, then Sam could do his part here. First, he would give himself a couple minutes to feel the sun on his face. Spring was coming.

"Hi, Sam." Suzy approached him wearing a long flowing dark blue skirt and suede coat.

"Hey." The kiss was nothing. Sam knew Suzy knew it was nothing. But that didn't stop him from avoiding her the past month.

"Are you getting some lunch?" She stopped at the bench.

"Nope." Sam stood and gathered up his books. "I already ate."

"Oh."

"I gotta jet to Mifflin to do some calc. This class is kicking my ass." He picked up his books and hugged them to his chest.

"Okay. Some other time."

"Some other time," Sam repeated, quickly walking down the sidewalk path with his armload of books.

Danny was the only one home, sitting on the couch that had become Sam's bed over the past few months. He hunched over a binder.

"Looks like you're hitting the books too." Sam set his books on the kitchen counter.

"Huh?" Danny looked up. "Oh, hey, Sam." He went back to

whatever was in front of him, scanning one page with a finger and then flipping to another.

"You got a big test coming up? I don't think I've ever seen you study so hard before." Sam took his calc stuff out from the pile of books and sat at the other end of the couch. Maybe the thing about osmosis and textbooks could work.

"I'm trying to have a plan in place before the next guy needs it."

Sam stretched his eyeballs all the way to the side, trying to catch a glimpse of what had Danny's complete attention.

"I need a little more time to figure out the details. Alan met up with the priest so I have to give him a break. Robbie headed west first and then went into Vancouver." Danny recited the list like it was ingredients in a recipe he needed from the store.

"Robbie from the party?" Sam clearly remembered Robbie storming out of the party and his girlfriend crying after him.

"Yeah, Robbie from the party."

"Wow." Sam sat on the opposite side of the couch, doing his best not to disturb Danny. *Medical Deferments* was written at the top of the page. Sam couldn't make out the whole list but he was able to read *psychosis, arthritis, bone spurs,* and *homosexual.* He glanced again at Danny after reading the word but he was too busy clutching a bus schedule in one hand and turning a page in the binder with the other. This one had a list of towns and cities in Minnesota and Canada.

Anthony didn't wait to get drafted but jumped at the chance to go over there even though he had a ready-made deferment. But, it would have meant the end of him if he used it. Even though he thought of the war often, being drafted wasn't something that occupied much space in Sam's brain. He knew he was in the clear for the next three and half years and that the war would be over way before then. Besides, the latest letter from Anthony sounded good. Maybe this thing really would be over sooner than everyone thought.

Sam stared at the jumble of symbols, trying to imagine what it would be like if he had to make the choice. Would Alan and Robbie ever see their families again? Their friends? Was America no longer their home for the rest of their lives?

"It works better if you pick up a pencil."

"Huh?" Sam looked at Danny who nodded to the blunt pencil ready to fall from Sam's hand. Sam closed his fist around it. "Oh, yeah. I'm having a hard time getting into it."

"Are you having a hard time with this?" Danny nodded at the binder and held it a couple inches off his lap.

"No, not at all." Sam tried to act surprised Danny would even ask him such a question. "I know guys dodge and I get why. I just didn't know so much went into it."

"It's not like planning a family camping trip," Danny said. "Some of these guys have no other choice. And to be told you have to go get yourself killed is fucked up." Danny's voice rose at the end. This was something he was passionate about. Something he was willing to go to jail for. Something he might even be willing to die for. "They're not over there fighting Nazis or trying to put an end to slavery, Sam. I don't even know what they're doing over there except getting maimed or killed, and annihilating innocent people."

"I don't think those VC's are exactly innocent," Sam began.

"I'm not talking about Charlie. I'm talking about civilians. Civilians caught in the middle of it who just want to grow some rice or catch some fish."

"Oh. Yeah." Sam looked down, feeling like a little kid who didn't get a dirty joke and was then embarrassed when someone had to explain the punchline. Anthony just told him how he'd helped civilians and how he and his fellow soldiers had gotten the little baby to a doctor. "My friend's over there because his dad fought in World War Two. He actually did fight Nazis."

Danny nodded. "And that's admirable. If there's some crazy shit going on, someone needs to do something to put an end to it."

"And that's what you're doing." Sam jutted his chin at the binder.

"It's definitely some crazy shit." Danny's posture changed, as if an actual light bulb went on over his head. "Maybe Superior is the way to go." He flipped a page.

The weight of the book on Sam's lap reminded him he also needed to get back to the task at hand, but he had one more question. "Have you thought about what you would do if you got drafted?"

Danny looked up. "I haven't given it much thought. I'm too busy thinking about the people who got called up now. You dig?"

Sam nodded.

Danny took a pencil out of his pocket and wrote something in the margin of the paper with a list of cities and towns on it.

Sam knew he needed to get his mind on his work but it seemed like an impossible feat, considering it all made about as much sense as forcing someone to go halfway around the world to fight in a war they'd do anything to run away from.

MARCH 29, 1968

Two days of humping through the jungle without any sight of Charlie. The only kills Anthony and his squad accumulated were the bugs that gnawed at their faces and any centimeter of exposed skin. They had come across an abandoned ville yesterday. Everything was in order, like the people who lived there had left with every intention of returning. When Anthony had heard movement behind him, he raised his gun and Mikey laughed at him for being spooked by a chicken.

There was so much *walking* in this war. His dad hopped off the boat, strolled up to the beach and the bad guys were already there, waiting to be killed. And now it was night two of trying to find a place to stop before it would be too late to secure a position.

Nights were the worst. Guys bitched because they couldn't smoke. The little orange glow from the cigarettes gave Charlie a bullseye to hit. The silence amplified gunfire coming from somewhere that always seemed too close. Or, the drone of the bugs was so loud, Anthony wondered if Charlie had somehow trained them to provide cover for their movements.

With the bugs already doing a number on their faces and hands, Anthony and his fellow soldiers felt their way through the thick jungle leaves that finally gave way to a clearing. Sergeant Avery had said it was just up ahead and Anthony was having a hard time believing him even

OCION

though the Sergeant had never lied before. Well, when he radioed the body count from the last ambush, the number was ten more than the actual dead, but Sarge had never lied about anything when it came to his men.

When they stepped into the clearing, it was like someone had turned on a light. The moon shone, full, bright, and low in the sky as various shades of orange and pink faded into the horizon. Anthony squinted at it and could make out the Man in the Moon staring down on them. Maybe one of those rocket ships from NASA was orbiting the moon at that exact moment.

"We made it," Capper breathed.

"Made it where?" Picasso asked, taking off his pack.

Capper shrugged. "Through the jungle." He gestured to the clearing. "And it looks like we have a nice place to call home for the night."

Anthony set down his pack, trying to judge how much time he had before complete darkness enveloped their little clearing. The bottom of his pants were still wet from the walk through the rice paddy that afternoon. It would be great if they could dry by morning and if he could write a letter. Anthony hadn't written to Sam or his parents in over a week. His mom had told him in her last letter she wanted to hear from him more often.

"It's like having a picnic in the park, but instead of ants we have man-eating blood suckers," Capper went on as he dug through his pack. "I've been saving this all day." He held up a C-ration can with cake in it. Back across the pond, a lot of food came in cans, but not cake. It was pretty good, especially if you poured syrup from the fruit over it. Capper had been looking forward to it all day.

QB slapped at his neck. "Little fuckers."

Capper opened the can and dug into the cake with his fingers. "We have a symbolic relationship. I don't swat at 'em and they leave me alone after doing their thing."

"Symbiotic, idiot," QB said. "And it sounds like the bugs are getting more out of the deal than you."

"Whatever, man. But you don't see me hitting myself in the face."

Anthony's eyes swept over the jungle they'd just emerged from. He looked for any hint of a leaf swaying in the extremely still night.

A small cluster of tents had sprung up in the few minutes since they'd arrived at the clearing. Anthony set his up in between Picasso and Lennox while Capper wandered a few feet away with his can of cake.

"Don't go too far," Anthony advised.

"We've been humping for two days with no sign of him. He's fast asleep right now, just like my bug pals," Capper smiled, spreading out his arms as if reaching a mountain summit. He turned in a circle, grinning at the stars in the sky.

A soft click echoed in the quiet night.

Capper turned to Anthony.

Somehow it all happened in slow motion even though it happened in less than a blink.

Capper's mouth dropped as he looked at his feet. An explosion sent him flying back, his arms flailing like he'd jumped off a swing at recess. The can of cake flew through the air.

Anthony reached for Picasso and Lennox on either side of him and pulled them down.

QB covered his head with his pack.

Mikey hit the ground, flat on his stomach.

Anthony scanned the perimeter of the jungle again checking to see if the detonation of the mine alerted any VC hiding in the leaves.

Nothing.

He sprang to his feet, running toward his friend.

"Capper!" Anthony slid next to him.

"I'm okay, man. I think I'm okay." Capper's breath came in short bursts, unaware of the dirt and blood covering his face.

"QB!" Anthony yelled even though he was already on his way.

"My legs hurt a little, Capone." Capper pointed to his legs with his eyes. "Are they okay?"

Anthony didn't want to look, but he had to. His friend asked him to.

With his chin to his chest and his face toward Capper, Anthony only moved his eyes. He didn't see Capper's feet. He didn't see Capper's legs. Anthony swallowed the C-rations he'd drowned in ketchup that had crept out of his stomach and into his throat.

Don't cry.

"Oh fuck," Capper's voice cracked. "What about Lorraine?"

Anthony gripped Capper's hand as QB gave him several doses of morphine. "You're going to see her again."

"Radio for a dustoff!" QB yelled.

Capper struggled to return the grip. "My letter…" He looked up at Anthony.

"I got it. It's in my pack."

Capper's tears came out in waterfalls. "I don't think I put everything in there."

Anthony thought he saw something move behind the curtain of leaves. "Don't worry about that goddamn letter."

Capper craned his neck as if trying to sit up. "No, I didn't tell them how I'd lie about going to church and really went to play ball."

"Well, you'll have to tell them yourself," Anthony tried to smile. "Tell them about all the trouble Eddie Bear got into that they don't know about."

"Fuck you, man. Eddie Bear." Capper tried to return the smile. He glanced at QB. "Hey, can I have some more of that stuff? I think it's working. My legs don't hurt as much."

QB gave Anthony a look before giving Capper another dose.

"There's more where that came from," Anthony said to Capper as his eyes fluttered shut. "Hey, tell me about those ball games—"

Little orange bursts came from behind the leaves. Tiny craters formed in the dirt around Anthony and Capper.

Anthony threw himself on top of Capper.

"We gotta take cover." QB started to backtrack. "Come on, take an arm!"

Anthony felt totally exposed without his helmet on. Dirt flew up all around him as he sprang up and grabbed one of Capper's arms. Maybe if they got him to safety fast enough there would be a way to help him. But would the chopper be able to find a landing zone once it found them?

With bullets whizzing past his body, Anthony and QB pulled Capper to where everyone had set up a little barricade. They managed to get him over the top while the rest of the guys provided cover.

Anthony put a poncho under Capper's head, keeping himself as low to the ground as possible. "You okay, man?" What a stupid, stupid question.

"Doing all right now. Think I'll crash here for a little bit and let you guys take care of this." Capper gave Anthony some sort of wink before nodding off as if on a couch.

God dammit.

Don't cry.

"He's gone, Capone," QB yelled. "Get your ass up here!"

Anthony unstrapped his weapon from his back and blindly fired into the depths of the jungle. He couldn't see the targets but they were out there somewhere.

APRIL 5, 1968

For the first time since moving into the house on Mifflin, Sam didn't carry books across campus with him as he headed to Sullivan Hall. Classes were cancelled at the University of Wisconsin. Dr. Martin Luther King Junior was assassinated the day before. Sam only carried the latest issue of *The Daily Cardinal*, its headline shouting out what he already knew. He remembered when Dr. King moved into a shabby flat in Chicago to prove a point about how terrible the living conditions were. While Sam had complained how the radiator made too much noise, Dr. King dealt with rats and roaches scurrying all over the place.

He pulled a letter from Anthony out of his mailbox, hoping it might offer some solace on this day. It was ridiculous, wishing a letter from the front lines would be able to accomplish that, but Anthony's last letter was hopeful. Maybe there was more where that came from, and maybe it would do something to cancel out what Sam had been reading in the paper and hearing on the radio all day. With nowhere to go and no desire to do any work, Sam sat on a couch in the common area of his old dorm and opened the letter.

Sam,

Capper is gone. I know you didn't know him but I wish you did. I want to write his name so there's more proof that he existed. He was KIA yesterday. I was proud to train with him and serve our country alongside him. Lorraine, his girlfriend, wanted him to go home and work at the post office. Slinging stamps never would have cut it for Capper.

   I sent his letter to his parents. They're going to know what it is before they even open it. Why else would some guy their son went through Basic with send them a letter, huh? Capper had my letter so I had to give it to QB. Charlie doesn't play by the rules and we have no idea what we're walking into sometimes. You go to an abandoned ville crawling with hidden VC. Or you stop for the night after a day of humping your ass through rice paddies without any commotion and Charlie's there waiting for you. We were stupid for thinking it was going to be a quiet night.

   I don't know what to tell my dad about what's going on over here. He wants to hear about strategy and attacks and I don't have that for him. I just tell him I follow orders and the sergeant likes what I do. It's true for the most part. Sarge is okay. And I'm doing okay too. They still send ketchup over here so as long as I have that I'll be fine. I don't know when I'll get your letters but it helps to have mail waiting for me when I get back to base. Don't forget I have an audience when I read them. Keep them coming, okay?

   Anthony

Sam's hands shook as he refolded the letter and put it in the envelope. He wished he would have waited until he had gotten to Mifflin to read it. In an attempt to erase the news in the letter, Sam tried to reseal the envelope, but the glue had already worn off.

Lorraine. Anthony never mentioned Capper had a girlfriend. It made it sadder, to know one more person was going to cry and miss him. Sam didn't even know Capper. He only knew the scraps of information Anthony put in his letters and was familiar with the name he threw around a couple times when they last saw each other. So why did it hit him so hard? Why did he feel like he was about to completely lose it, right here in Sullivan Hall?

Sam balled up a fist and put it to his mouth. What he actually felt was relief, relief that it wasn't Anthony. He was sorry for Capper's parents and Lorraine and all the other people who would never see him again. But if Anthony was still alive, Sam was grateful. Did that make him a terrible person?

He tucked the letter into the pocket of his windbreaker and sat with his head in his hands for a moment. He just needed a second to breathe and—

"I thought you dropped out of school."

Sam knew the voice. Every limb of his body bristled at the sound. Paul stood off to his side, his hair freshly buzzed, his books in front of him like a shield. Of course, he would be carrying around his books on a day when no one went to class.

"Fuck off," Sam said.

Paul tried to remain stoic but his arms twitched. "Nice greeting."

"Nice world we live in, huh? People dying all over the place. Getting killed here, getting killed over there." Sam held up Anthony's letter and waved it in the air. "You go to war, you die. You try to do some good in the world, you die."

"Dr. King knew what he was doing was dangerous." Paul spoke like someone delivering a lecture.

"Spoken like a candyass who knows everything," Sam scoffed.

Paul narrowed his eyes. "Yeah? This coming from the guy who doesn't know anything."

He threw his books on the couch and crouched like he was going to tackle Sam when Jerry the RA approached the two of them. "Again, you guys? Come on, I thought this thing had blown over."

"I guess it didn't." Sam glared at Paul.

"Are we gonna have to kick you out of the dorms for another night?" Jerry's eyes darted between the two.

Sam smirked and shrugged. "Sure. Go for it. Kick me out for the rest of the semester." He pushed his way past Paul and out the doors. He was going straight to Mifflin and forget about everything that was wrong with the world. Maybe he'd just sit on the stained, stinky couch, smoke some grass, and pray the radio had something on besides the shitshow in Vietnam and the shitshow at home. He stormed out of Sullivan Hall and stomped down the sidewalk.

But as Sam approached Bascom Hall, a massive gathering of people blocked his path. There had to be thousands and thousands of people, way more than when Dow came to campus.

"If you want to do something about the problem, go home and start there!" A deep and commanding voice boomed from the entrance to Bascom Hall. The sounds of applause rippled through the huge crowd.

Sam looked around. Was the guy talking directly to him? Everyone else had their eyes forward as they clapped.

Then a girl started to speak. Sam stood on his toes and squinted. She looked too young to be a politician or some sort of community leader. She had to be a student. That struck him. Someone his age was speaking in front of a crowd of thousands, pouring out her pain and anger.

"Where am I? The black student on campus," she said as tears filled her voice. "There's a cry from the black people that will be heard and we don't care how you hear it!"

Sam stood up straight, staring at the girl speaking, giving her his full attention. There was no way she could know, but he heard her. He was listening to her.

"I'm wondering, what type of people are you? You never get upset about anything!" The tears in the girl's voice grew louder.

Her anger hit Sam in the gut. That was exactly what Paul told him on the day before the Dow demonstration, that nothing bothered Sam, that nothing upset him. And now, this girl was calling him out too. She had a right to call him out.

"I, too, have a dream," the girl continued. "Every durn one of you are gonna pay!"

Sam ducked his head in guilt. It was a cool day but he felt his face get warm.

"There's something wrong with this whole durn world!" the girl cried out before stepping back into the small group of people who stood facing the crowd. They started to descend the stairs. Everyone started moving as if one large entity. It seemed like everyone already knew what was going on while Sam stood still in the sea of people, waiting for directions.

People began to sing. It was soft at first, but then more voices joined in. *Ain't gonna let nobody turn me around.*

Sam didn't know the song. Some of the people around him sang along with confidence, clearly knowing every word. A few individual voices distinguished themselves as they passed. Their voices were loud, strong, and determined.

Turn me around.

Like that day in October, in this exact spot, so many people came together for a common purpose. But there was no yelling, no swearing, no cheering now.

Ain't gonna let nobody turn me around.

The group of people standing at the top of Bascom Hill walked past Sam, singing with remnants of tears streaking their faces and their eyes fixed on a destination beyond the edge of the crowd.

Sam felt himself get pulled along. He tried to ignore the feeling that he didn't belong as the massive group made their way off campus. Sam had no idea where they were headed, but he was going there with them.

Ain't gonna let nobody turn me around.

Nothing was going to turn this crowd around. Just like Danny, when someone came to him, seeking a way out. Anthony didn't turn around from the war. He volunteered to go in. Dr. King didn't turn around when people threw bricks at him, because all he wanted was for everyone to be treated the same.

Was Sam an imposter for marching through the streets of Madison to honor a man who gave his life to make the world better while he sat back, complaining about noisy radiators?

With the Capitol building getting closer with each step, the song changed. Different words made their way through the crowd to Sam's ears.

We shall overcome.

He knew this one.

We shall overcome.

Sam's lips moved. There were so many people, so many voices. He might not have known all the words to this song but he was going to learn them.

APRIL 9, 1968

Anthony lay on the couch in his family's home, his head nestling into the indent he made on the armrest many years ago. Instinctively, he knew he shouldn't be there in Chicago, watching a *Beverly Hillbillies* rerun, he should be out in the jungles on the other side of the world.

A familiar scent floated to the couch and Anthony took a deep breath and smiled. Mixed with the ever-present aroma of garlic and sautéing meats, was the flowery fragrance of tè alla camomilla– chamomile tea to his non-Italian friends who didn't understand the magical healing powers of the dried flowers and leaves. Most tea came in bags or boxes. Anthony didn't know where his mom's came from because she always spooned it out of an old jar with no label on it. Whenever it got low, it got filled up again somehow.

Whether it was a bad cold, the flu, or simply an upset stomach, the tea was a cure for everything. Anthony touched his forehead and cheeks, checking for a fever, but they felt fine. He lay still for a moment, attempting to detect any sign of sickness.

Anthony closed his eyes. No doubt his tea would be ready in no time and right now, he had no problem letting his mom treat him like he was her little boy again.

Anthony opened his eyes at the sound of water boiling. He furrowed his eyebrows, confused at how he could hear the water boiling from the couch and above Jed Clampett's twang. He sat up, eyes darting to every corner of the living room as the sound of bubbles popping got louder and louder.

And then something kicked him.

Anthony's eyes popped open to see Mikey squatting outside of the tent he managed to make out of his poncho. Raindrops fell from Mikey's helmet like it was part of the dark clouds that rolled in as they were setting up camp for the night.

"You're up, Capone." Mikey stood and made his way to his own makeshift tent.

At least he got a couple good hours in.

Anthony reached for his helmet and gun and walked straight into the rain that pelted everyone sleeping under their poncho tents. He braced himself against a tree, scanning the perimeter of the camp, looking for any sign of movement, any sign of life that existed outside of his fellow soldiers and the millions of bugs swarming over his hands and face.

Charlie had gotten Capper because Anthony and the others had let their guard down for a second. Less than a second. It would not happen again. At least not while he was on guard. With his finger on the trigger, and the rain pouring down in buckets, Anthony strained to see between the curtains of leaves. What he really wanted to do was go back into that dreamland and so he could have a sip of his mom's magic tea.

Returning to base after days out in the bush meant mail would be waiting for them when they returned. And their beds. Both were more than welcome to Anthony and his soggy, sore body.

Almost everyone had at least one letter waiting for them. Mikey's brother was graduating high school soon. Lennox's mom wanted to know if he was getting enough to eat and getting enough sleep. The boys on the news didn't look like they were getting much of either. QB's girlfriend got a job for the summer at some soda shop where she had to roller skate to the cars. He worried that a car full of stupid kids were going to harass his girl, a crime for which he would fly a plane home himself.

"Where do you think I met her?" QB asked. "I was cruising with some friends. She was cruising with some friends. It's what we did. It's what we still do." He scoffed, scanning the barracks and the guys scattered about it. "It's what I *used* to do."

Anthony tuned out everyone's attempts to convince QB his girl was at the soda shop strictly for financial reasons and nothing more. He was too busy looking at each letter of the familiar handwriting on the outside of the envelope in his hands. No matter how messed up everything over here seemed, everything was a little more bearable if a letter from Sam arrived.

"What do you got, Capone?" Mikey asked.

"Who else?" Anthony waved an envelope at the guys. "Sam."

"College can't be that hard," Mikey commented. "He finds time to write a bunch of letters."

"It's a breeze compared to what we have going on over here," Picasso said. He didn't have a letter waiting so he had started sketching the New York City skyline.

"Let's find out." Anthony opened Sam's letter.

Anthony,

So I'm guessing no one's going to listen to what Cronkite said on TV a few months ago and you and your friends are going to have to finish this thing out on your own. You're about halfway, right? If you get home in time for Thanksgiving maybe my mom will make extra mashed potatoes and she can talk your ear off about Jimmy's wedding. I told you he asked Sandy to marry him, right?

Spring Break is coming up and everyone's talking about catching busses or trains home for the week and I think I'm going to hang here. My dad and I aren't getting along. But, hey, what's new, right? He still thinks sales is where it's at. And Mom is lost in wedding plans. She's excited to get the daughter she never had. I'll spare you the details even though she doesn't do me the same courtesy. I'm already not looking forward to spending the whole summer there, so if I can put it off for a couple months, then I will. My parents will probably come up and spend a day in Madison. I'm sure it will be outta sight.

I don't know if you guys get anything about the news back home over there, but did you hear Dr. Martin Luther King Junior was killed?

"Killed?" Picasso put down his sketchpad.

"Are you serious?" Lennox said.

Anthony reread the sentence. It didn't say *died*, it said *killed*. "Yeah." He looked up at everyone staring at him. "I guess so."

"That's heavy," Mikey exhaled. "What else did he say?"

They cancelled classes for the day because of it and there was this huge demonstration on campus. The news said there might have been 15,000 people there. It was nothing like the other demonstration I told you about. It was different. I'm not sure how to describe it. I walked with everyone to the Capitol Building. It's not going to bring anyone back to life or make anything easier for anyone over there but it got me thinking a lot. There's a lot that's messed up in the world and right here at home and I need to figure out what I'm going to do about it. I'm still studying my ass off and planning on graduate school, but there's more on my mind than that.

Anthony paused. There was so much Sam wasn't saying and he couldn't figure out what was left out. What was clear was how messed up things were all over the world.

Anyway, don't tell your mom but they had meatball sandwiches in the cafeteria the other day and I had two. I was hungry. Of course, nowhere near as good as hers but nothing a little (or a lot) of ketchup can't fix. I used almost a whole bottle.

Take care of yourself,

Sam

Anthony folded the letter, imagining the stack of mail in his footlocker growing by one. He got the usual little stomach drop when Sam mentioned ketchup, like he usually did, but it was overshadowed by the image of all those people in one spot mourning the death of Dr. King. He was a man trying to do some good, trying to make some real changes, and he got killed for it. It sounded like he died in a war.

Everyone sat for a moment, absorbing the news in Sam's letter. Picasso's pencil scratched his pad of paper while Mikey stowed the stash of candy bars his mom sent over. They would all get a chance to partake in one later on.

The rattle of a bus and its squeak to a stop caught everyone's attention. They eyed one another and got up off their cots and foot lockers.

"Welcome home, Privates!" A voice came in through the door to the barracks. They heard some new guys were supposed to be arriving any day. Bad news from home was forgotten as everyone eyed one another and jumped up to crowd around the door.

Anthony recognized the looks on the FNGs' faces when they disembarked the bus and walked onto the base. One had the same expression he knew he did when arriving just a few months ago. But it seemed like years. It was clear the skinny blonde guy was scared shitless. It looked like he had never spent much time in the sun and might have been twenty years old, maybe less. The guy coming off the bus behind him might have been a little older. It was hard to tell. Everyone seemed to be the same age in Vietnam, making it hard to believe that high school was less than a year ago for some of them.

The guy stepping off the bus with the skinny, pale guy had the same expression as Capper did from their first day at Basic. He already owned the base without even stepping a foot in it yet.

Capper.

Anthony had to look away from the confident swagger of the guy who had reminded him of his dead friend. This guy might remind him of Capper but no one could replace him.

Anthony shook his head and focused on the guys lining up in front of the bus. The more time he spent thinking about what happened to Capper, the harder it was to stop. Especially at night when the bed next to his was empty.

QB sauntered out without a shirt on and a cigarette in his hand. He took a long drag. "Welcome to paradise, gentlemen!"

Mikey snickered. "Paradise, my ass. If you like mud and rain."

The scared guy and the confident guy exchanged a glance, clearly trying to decide if they should also snicker or remain as stoic as possible.

"Paradise?" the confident one scoffed. "I don't see no sandy beaches. Lots of dirt. Lots of grass. No beach, though."

QB took another drag. "Can't you smell the salt of the ocean? Feel the breeze?" He took a deep breath with his eyes closed as if being sprayed with the fine mist of an ocean wave instead of baking in the thick heat.

"Well damn," Mr. Confident shrugged. "No one told me to pack my swim trunks."

He even sounded like Capper.

"You're not going to need any swim trunks," Lennox cut in.

"Well good, then I came prepared." The confident guy strode past everyone and into the barracks, surveying it. "This bed taken?" He might as well have been arriving at summer camp, claiming a certain bunk.

Of course he would claim Capper's bed. "Nope, man," Anthony said as if the FNG had asked him if he had any smokes. "All yours."

"Righteous." He put his poncho and rucksack on the bed. "I'm Theodore Robbins from Minneapolis. Everyone calls me Teddy."

Teddy. Teddy Bear. Eddie Bear.

Emotion swirled in Anthony's stomach, rose into his throat, and threatened to come out of his tear ducts. He had to stop this. He had to stop thinking about Capper flying through the air and how easy it was to drag his legless body to the barricade. Imagining the memory as a piece of paper, Anthony mentally folded it, twice, three times, four times, until it was a tiny square that could barely be seen.

"You okay, man?" Teddy gave Anthony a sideways glance.

"Yeah, Teddy," Anthony quickly said. "I'm Anthony, but not a lot of people call me that." He smiled as he tucked the imaginary tiny paper of Capper somewhere in his brain. It was the same place where he put the memory of being bent over under Jersey on the night of Tet, the memory of the VC jumping out of the barrel, and whatever else needed to be safely stowed away. Anthony didn't know where the memories ended up but he was fine with that. It meant they would be hard to find.

APRIL 11, 1968

Sam stared at the Salisbury steak on his tray. It was covered in some sort of gravy, reminiscent of a meal served on an aluminum tray his mom had pulled from the oven many times. This Salisbury steak had the same brownish gravy but it was thicker than what Sam's mom tried to pass off as dinner. He reached for a bottle of ketchup and smacked the bottom of it as the ketchup oozed its way out of the bottle and on to the steak.

A blob landed off to the side. Another smack and a blob landed almost in the center. Sam gave the bottle one more hit for good measure. It was almost closing time and he was glad to have made it. With the cafeteria closing for spring break in a couple days, most of Sam's meals during would be cans of soup and cereal.

"Hi, stranger."

Suzy.

Sam looked up and smiled. "Hi." It had been two months since the kiss that meant nothing and Sam always found an excuse to make a quick getaway. It wasn't easy with a letter in his hand and a tray of half-eaten food in front of him.

"Can I sit down?" Suzy asked.

"Sure."

Suzy sat with a tray of mashed potatoes and a pile of mixed

vegetables. "I have to read *The Odyssey* over break. Have you ever heard of that one, Mr. Salutatorian?"

"Some guy's trying to find his way home. It takes a while. End of story," Sam smirked.

Suzy sat back with a smile. "Groovy. I'll write up that summary before I head home."

"Tell him you heard it from an expert." Sam spread the ketchup over every morsel of Salisbury steak.

"Seriously, though. We never see each other."

"I've been really busy."

"I know."

"Six classes," Sam recited his list. "Trekking back and forth to campus every day. So much studying. It doesn't leave a lot of time to do much else."

"I can't imagine taking six classes," Suzy said.

"I don't recommend it."

After eating a bite of mashed potatoes, Suzy stirred some vegetables into them. "Tell me all about what it's like to live on Mifflin. Those guys are famous at SDS even though they haven't been to a meeting in months." She might as well have been asking Sam what it was like to be backstage at a Rolling Stones concert.

Sam shrugged. "It's pretty quiet."

"Liar. Between the parties and getting high all the time, I bet it's pretty quiet."

"No, it is pretty quiet." Quiet, yes. Uneventful, no. "Everyone mostly does stuff for school." Kind of.

"And smoke grass," Suzy said slyly.

Sam shrugged. "There might be grass. I cannot deny or confirm."

"I think you just confirmed." Suzy ate some of her potato and vegetable mixture.

"Maybe," Sam shrugged. It felt good hanging out with Suzy again. She was fun to be around. He felt bad for trying so hard to avoid her, but being around her required a lot of effort. Sam already knew Suzy was enthralled with everything about Danny and his apartment. He could joke about smoking grass, or not, but he couldn't say anything about how Danny's stance against the war went beyond the SDS meetings he stopped going to and yelling at cops.

"It would be cool to come by some time," Suzy said, almost like a question, talking to her plate of food.

"Uh, yeah." Sam took a bite of his ketchup slathered Salisbury steak. "But I already feel like I'm in the way. I don't know if I should start bringing all these people over."

"Not *all these people*. I'm not saying have a party or something."

"Oh, I know," Sam nodded. "But you'll tell Gloria and then she'll tell a bunch of people and then it's sleeping on the library bench for Sam for the rest of the semester."

Suzy laughed and Sam knew he had found a way to move the conversation in another direction.

"Still giving Gloria a hard time, huh?"

"She makes it easy," Sam said.

"Well, maybe after spring break," Suzy suggested.

"Maybe," Sam grunted.

Suzy crumpled up her napkin and tossed it on what was left of her dinner. "Are you headed to Chicago for the week?"

"Nah. I'm gonna stick around here and try to get ahead on some studying."

"You are such a square!"

Sam threw up his hands. "What can I say? You found me out."

"But it would be boss. Living on your own for the whole week, on Mifflin. Meanwhile, I'll be home, helping my mom cross stitch these flowers for the church bazaar."

Sam laughed so hard, he thought some ketchup might come out of his nose.

"What?" Suzy crossed her arms, pretending to be offended.

"Cross stitching? Are you serious?" Sam made a sewing motion.

"Yes, cross stitching. My mom has been making these stupid things for about fifteen years and now she has me doing it too." Suzy smiled despite sulking in her chair. "Groovy spring break, huh? I wish I could stay with you on Mifflin."

Sam sharply inhaled and a small chunk of ketchup-slathered

Salisbury steak got lodged in his windpipe. He smacked himself in the chest and let out a loud hacking cough. The next one dislodged the meat and Sam coughed a couple more times.

Suzy stood and leaned over to Sam's side of the table. "Are you okay? Do you want me to get someone?"

"No," Sam choked out the word. "I'm fine." Yeah, totally fine. Suzy's suggestion might have sounded like it was rooted in her desire to not spend her break sewing with her mom, but there were so many other ways to take it.

The University of Wisconsin was a huge school, and the only people he had connected with were a flower child from New York whom he hadn't meant to kiss and an apartment of draft dodgers.

On Sunday, Sam met his parents at Mickie's Dairy Bar. He had to take a bus to get there and almost missed it because he forgot the schedule was different on the weekends. Sam's parents left Chicago early in the morning and planned to spend most of the day before heading back home. The plate of fried potatoes, eggs over hard, and rye toast occupied Sam's dad for most of the meal. He said a little bit about how Jimmy was doing well in Missouri while his mom went on about his wedding plans. But by the time the station wagon parked at campus and Sam began showing them around, his dad had a full belly and a lot to say.

"Everyone else went home for the week, huh? Seems like you're the only one here," he said as Sam led his parents toward the heart of campus.

"I'm not the only one today," Sam responded. Maybe it was a compliment his dad wanted him home.

"It's a shame we can't see the dormitory." Sam's mom cut in. She wanted to see everything she missed when she left Sam at school in the fall because his dad had shooed them off campus so quickly. "I wanted to see what the room looks like with you *living* in it."

"We can walk to the other side of campus to see it, but we can't go inside. They're locked up for break, Mom," Sam was glad he didn't have to come up with some lie to keep his parents out of the room he hadn't slept in for almost three months. He was used to the stiff neck he woke up with every morning along with the need to untangle his legs when getting up.

"They're locked up because kids are supposed to go home, not stay up here and sleep in some stranger's apartment," Sam's dad spoke up from a few steps behind.

"He's not a stranger," Sam sighed. "I had a couple classes with Danny and when I told him I needed to spend my spring break studying he said I could stay at his place. He was actually glad someone could keep an eye on it." That was close to something Danny actually did say.

As they walked past one of the libraries, Sam gestured to it grandly. "Speaking of studying, here's where I spend most of my time. I promise." They stopped in front of Memorial Library. "There's another one closer to my dorm but this one's bigger."

Sam's mom smiled. "We saw your grades from last semester."

"They were good," his dad had to agree.

"Paul seemed like he took his studying seriously. How was his semester?" Sam's mom asked, slipping a coat over her shoulders as the morning sun disappeared into afternoon clouds.

Sam shrugged. "I'm sure he did very well." That wasn't a lie. Paul and his detailed calendar of slash marks were probably fine in their little musicless world.

"I was worried you were going to get paired up with some hippie freak," Sam's dad piped up. "Good thing you got that Paul kid. Seems like someone who might rub off on you. Kind of like your dago friend, Anthony. He's a good kid."

Sam stifled a snort. As much as it was good to know his dad thought Anthony was a good guy, it was laughable to think he and Paul were anything alike. "Paul isn't shipping out any time soon. That's for sure."

Sam's mom walked up to the library doors and peeked inside with her hands cupped around her eyes. "It's huge."

Sam looked through the window next to his mom. It was weird to see the empty library only lit up with slivers of natural light.

"Do you think you'll take more English courses?" his mom asked. "I would love to hear about some of the Shakespeare plays you'd be reading."

"I don't think there's any Shakespeare in my future. I might be done with English requirements after this semester." Sam continued down the sidewalk path and his parents followed.

"She even went to the library to check out…what was the name of that?" Sam's dad looked at his mom. "A summer dream? A dream in the summer?"

"*A Midsummer Night's Dream*," she smiled.

Sam's dad looked as if he was trying to remember ever hearing that title before. "Huh."

"Over there's Memorial Union. I eat there if I'm at the library kind of late." Sam pointed. "You can't sample its delicacies, but it does have a window to look through."

As Sam led the way, he thought how campus had never been so quiet before, especially with the weather being warmer. Usually there were groups of students walking to class or just hanging out. It was weird being on a campus of empty buildings and locked doors.

Sam peeked into the lobby of Memorial Union. It looked different with little slants of daylight seeping into its dark corners. The bulletin board by the doors was still visible, though. Among the signs for on-campus jobs and students looking for roommates or rides home, was a scattering of signs declaring *End the war in Vietnam*, *Bring our troops home*, or *Tell Uncle Sam hell no, we won't go*.

Sam's dad laughed a little as he straightened. His mom had her hands curled around her eyes to get a better view of the dining hall.

"They let them hang up stuff like that?" Sam's dad pointed in the bulletin board's direction.

"People are always looking for jobs or a ride home," Sam said.

Sam's dad shot him a look. "That's not what I'm talking about."

Sam remembered how Suzy got him to staple signs to posts all over campus after the Dow demonstration. Some scraps of them were still up but most had disintegrated from being in the rain, wind, and snow.

"Remember when you were caught up in all of this?" He gestured through the window.

"In all what?" Sam asked.

"All of this." His dad jutted a finger in the direction of the signs.

"What do you mean by caught up?" If *caught up* involved living in a house with someone who helped guys dodge the draft, then yes, he was very much still caught up in all of this.

"Don't get smart with me, Sam." His dad turned away from the window.

"I'm not getting smart with you, I just want to know what you mean by that." Sam felt something boil over. "Am I throwing bricks at police officers? No. Am I paying more attention to what's going on? Yes."

"Why don't we walk over there?" Sam's mom pointed in the direction of Bascom Hill. "That looks like a nice place to sit for a little while."

"Paying more attention?" Sam's dad narrowed his eyes at him. "That's what you're doing?"

"Yep. That's exactly what I'm doing."

Sam's dad glanced at his mom. His mom had a look of apology on her face. "It seems like all the kids do here is ditch class so they can walk around campus yelling about things they don't like." He had that tone in his voice that let Sam know his dad had been holding this in for a while and was ready to let it all out.

Sam threw his hands out. "Are you serious? What's your bag, Dad?"

His dad's mouth dropped. "*What's my bag?* Who talks to their father that way? You sound like one of those freaks I see on the news. They don't go to class. They don't study. They parade around complaining about the world."

"There's a lot to complain about, don't you think?"

"James, Sam, please," Sam's mom looked around as if she expected to see a crowd of people witnessing their outburst. "Let's go sit over—"

"Don't pretend like you don't feel the same way, Betty."

Sam's mom looked like she'd been caught in a lie. "We're not sure if this is the best place for you." She spoke like she'd rehearsed these words before. "We saw the big crowd on the day after Martin Luther King was killed and—"

"And what?" Sam interrupted. "People were walking. They were singing and talking. And he was murdered. Don't you think people should be mad about that?" Sam knew this visit wouldn't go well but he didn't expect it to be a complete disaster. "Would you rather I be back home? From what I heard there's more going on in Chicago than just singing and talking."

Sam's mom and dad exchanged a glance. "What we're saying," his mom said, " is maybe this isn't the right place for you. There are so many colleges where you can study history. Have you thought about finding another place to go next year?"

"No," Sam said flatly. He started walking, unsure where, but he needed to move.

"Jimmy told us about Sandy's cousin, Patty, at the University of Illinois." Sam's mom did a quick shuffle to catch up with him. "Maybe that would be a good school?"

"You're trying to find a girl for me? Jimmy's getting married, so you want me to start thinking about it?" Sam shook his head in disbelief as he stopped walking and glared at his parents. "I'm not leaving. I like it here."

Sam's dad grumbled something and was about to talk but his mom cut him off. "Is it because of that girl, Suzy?" Her tone was gentle, like she was trying to soothe a little boy who fell off his bike and got scraped up.

Sam grabbed the tips of his growing hair and stifled a yell. "Suzy? No. It's not about a girl. It's about being someplace where I feel like I belong." He stomped over to a bench and threw himself on it.

"You belong here?" Sam's dad stood in front of Sam with his arms crossed, demanding an explanation.

Sam sprang off the bench so his dad wouldn't be looking down on him. "Yes. I'm not transferring. I'm staying here."

His mom stood off to the side. "It was just a suggestion. Something you father and I talked about a couple times."

Sam looked from his mom to his dad. He tried to imagine those conversations, wondering if they rehearsed this scene in the car on the ride up from Chicago. If there had been more traffic, perhaps they would have had more time to prepare an argument.

"I'm not sure what you think goes on here." Sam struggled to keep his tone even. "But it is pretty much what is happening on most campuses across the country. Probably even around the world."

Sam's dad grunted with a shake of his head.

"I've never gotten into a fight or been disrespectful to a police officer or someone in charge," Sam continued. "I've never done anything illegal." He left out the fact that on several occasions he'd witnessed something illegal, but that was besides the point.

Sam's mom looked like she was ready for this to pass while his dad stood with his lips pressed together. The argument was over, for now.

"How about I show you where my history classes are?" Sam started walking. "If you want to know what I'm doing here, you should probably see the building where I spend most of my time."

As he heard his mom come up behind him and his dad say something about only staying for a little while longer, Sam thought about how this visit would only be a few hours long. A whole summer at home was going to be painful.

APRIL 26, 1968

The tall, skinny, scared FNG that arrived with Teddy didn't last long. His name was Tommy but everybody called him Skinny. And now, Skinny didn't look like Skinny anymore. Blood and dirt covered most of his face and hair. Anthony was ordered to wait with QB for the dustoff.

It was a routine walk through a ville that everyone was pretty sure was abandoned. No cows, no chickens, no Charlie. But a row of mines were hidden by the door of the hut Skinny was assigned to check out. After a sweep of the village, the rest of it came up clean. Only that hut had been booby trapped.

"The chopper would have an easier time getting to us if we moved him closer to the road," QB admitted while sucking in some air through his teeth.

"Probably." Anthony looked from his grimy hands to Skinny's bloody body. He'd moved bodies before. He'd had to lug Lennox across the ground when he got a graze to a leg that earned him a few days of vacation. When they'd come upon a ville on fire about a month ago and discovered at least a dozen dead villagers, he helped move them out of the huts. He'd dragged Capper's body behind the barricade his fellow soldiers put together in a matter of seconds. With Skinny's blood soaking his uniform and the ground under him, Anthony cursed himself. *Now* was not the time to think about Capper. *Never* was the time to think about Capper.

Anthony strained for any sound of helicopter blades slicing through the thick heat.

"Come on." QB stood up and grabbed Skinny's boots, only worn for a couple weeks and still looked almost brand new.

With a nod, Anthony got Skinny under the arms. All he could focus on were his fingers curled under Skinny's armpits. Blood covered his hands, getting stuck under his mud-stained fingers. He started walking backward, grateful they had done a thorough sweep of the ville. It was definitely empty. No Charlies were going to jump out from somewhere.

As he and QB carried Skinny to the road so the chopper might have an easier chance at finding them, Anthony wondered who Skinny gave his letter to. Did he even have a chance to write a letter? He had to. All guys wrote a letter. Nobody mentioned them, but they all had one.

Skinny was twenty-three years old. Four years older than Anthony even though he looked younger. When he first learned Skinny's age, Anthony thought it was weird how old he felt at nineteen in comparison to the new arrivals.

He raised an eye to look at QB, grimacing under the heavy sun as sweat dripped down his face. QB was twenty-two. If they had met back in the world, Anthony and QB never would have talked. QB the football star and Anthony, the back-up second basemen. He would have seen QB as the cool guy—way too cool to talk to him.

But over here, there was no such thing as being too cool. It didn't get you anywhere and it definitely didn't save you. Anthony had thought Jersey was such a badass, and look what happened to him.

Dammit. Thinking about Jersey would lead to thinking about others and Anthony couldn't do that now. He adjusted his grip, which caused Skinny's head to shake from side to side.

They only had to make it to the road and then they could put Skinny back on the ground. It looked close, but was taking so long to get there.

"You know," QB said as they shuffled through the dirt, "one of those fuckers could jump out from the other side of the road right now and we'd never have a chance."

There was no point in saying something to agree. It was true.

"Here's good." QB veered off the road a bit so they could huddle against some grass that stood as tall as Anthony's chest. They set Skinny on the ground as carefully as possible even though they both knew he was already gone.

Anthony and QB sat at the edge of the road with their legs outstretched as if they were two kids hanging out on their front lawn. And they waited. There was so much waiting over here. QB leaned back a little and immediately jumped up. "What the—"

Anthony jumped up too. "What? What happened?"

QB bent to examine an area of tall grass. It looked different. Anthony wouldn't have been able to explain it. The grass just looked *different*. As if his eyes were a pair of binoculars, Anthony zeroed in on something in between the grass. It was all same color, so it was almost impossible to see.

Sticks. Long sticks with handmade, pointed spikes on the end.

Anthony carefully pushed away some grass to either side and felt his hand come across something solid. He sucked in a breath as he revealed rows upon rows ofof razor-sharp sticks hidden among the infinite blades of grass.

Anthony touched his back, even though he knew he didn't walk into the patch of homemade spikes. He was just wearing his T-shirt. Who knows what backing into that patch would have done to him and QB.

"Fuckin' Charlie," QB muttered.

"Fuckin' Charlie," Anthony agreed.

The sound of helicopter blades slicing the air got louder with each passing second. QB and Anthony looked towards the sound's direction as the little dot in the distance morphed into a chopper. With the last of Skinny's blood draining from his body and QB waving his hands at the nearing helicopter, Anthony tore at the grass around the spikes. They were so close to one another, he could only get a couple out of the way at a time. With the chopper blades blowing the grass so the spikes came more into view, Anthony realized how deep they stretched into the grassy space between the road and empty ville.

As the chopper landed and QB stood to meet it, Anthony tried to yank a few more grass blades out of the ground. Those few might make a difference to the next squad that came down this road or to the next group of civilians trying to find safety. He managed a couple more handfuls before QB signaled that it was time to load Skinny into the medevac.

MAY 11, 1968

Suzy was being quiet, especially for Suzy. Almost always, it was something about SDS, a demonstration she'd just attended or wanted to attend, or at least something about Danny and Mifflin. For a week after spring break it was nothing but the dread of being home for summer with a family who didn't understand her and thought cross stitching was a way to contribute to the war effort.

Sam could dig that.

The two of them started hanging again after spring break, having lunch when their schedules allowed. Now, they sat out on Bascom Hill, studying in the sun rather than the stuffy library where they would spend their fair share when final exams started in a few weeks. Sam decided he would spend more time studying outside next year.

He looked through the syllabus for English 102 and then at the one for Early Civilizations, making sure he had the right page count for the final papers. "Why do teachers wait until the last few weeks of the semester to pile it on? They had months to get it all in."

Suzy nodded, twirling her hair around her finger.

"My 102 professor is making us walk on our hands when we hand in our paper." Sam cocked his head, trying to get a good look at Suzy's face.

Suzy went to work on another lock of hair. "Really?"

Sam narrowed his eyes. "Yeah. If we fall, he takes off ten percent."

"That sucks." Suzy turned to Sam. Something was up, something more than *The Canterbury Tales* and how to synthetize one of the tales with a poem she studied earlier in the semester. "I was talking to Gloria the other day—"

"Wow. What a bummer," Sam laughed a little but the look she gave him cut him off.

"Did you like kissing me?"

"Huh?" Sam said.

Suzy ducked her head, reminding Sam of Sandy when Jimmy brought her over for the first time to meet everyone, or when Patty asked him to write to her at school. It was the little nervous smile and uncertain eyes. It made Suzy look less like an anti-war flower child and more like a girl who should be wearing a sweater set.

"I know you heard what I said."

In less than a second, Sam realized how much harder this year would have been if it weren't for Suzy. He never would have met Danny and lived on Mifflin. Who knew where Sam would have gone if they had never became bio partners.

Sam felt like each limb wanted to run in a different direction but were too heavy to move. "Because we're friends, right? We're friends."

"And that's why you never asked me to go on a date?"

"Yeah."

Suzy nodded.

Sam set aside his syllabi and notebook. "Where's all this coming from?"

"I waited all semester and nothing. And I thought that after we kissed, that maybe..." She trailed off. "I mean, we talk, we hang—"

"We protest against Dow Chemical," Sam interrupted with a smile, but Suzy's look wiped the smile off his face. Sometimes he just needed to keep his mouth shut.

"Exactly. So, why?"

Sam searched for an answer. His heart beat in each fingertip. He had so much practice keeping himself together. He was so good at it. Why was he having such a hard time now?

"If you're scheming on someone else, tell me."

"It's Gloria," Sam quipped with a smile. He stretched his arms as if getting ready to exercise. "Whew. It felt good to get that out. Really thought I was going to take that one to the grave."

"That's funny," Suzy said, completely serious. "And also total bullshit."

She was the flower child again. Sam couldn't imagine Patty even thinking a curse word, let alone saying it. "You don't think Gloria would want to go steady with me? That hits me right here." Sam put a hand to his heart, knowing the jokes weren't going to get him out of this.

Suzy narrowed her eyes at him. A few moments of silence passed and Sam couldn't take it any longer. "What?"

"Are you...queer?" her voice dropped to a whisper on the last word.

Sam froze, the answer, any answer, stuck in his throat. He swallowed. "No," he laughed a little.

"Are you?"

"No, Suzy, come on." Sam struggled to regain the composure he had to have whenever he and Anthony were out in public when they were nothing more than good friends to the rest of the world.

"Is that why we never...?"

Sam felt the expression on his face change. His eyes widened in a plea for understanding. Maybe he couldn't pull himself together because he didn't want to lie to Suzy. By not answering, he was giving her an answer. It was scary, a lot scarier than when he was trying to figure out if Anthony felt the same way as him.

"Shit." Suzy gathered up her books in one quick motion and stood. "For real?"

"Are you going to tell anyone?" Sam jumped to his feet, hoping they wouldn't have to finish this conversation walking through campus.

"And have Gloria make fun of me for chasing a fairy all year?" She scoffed and shook her head. Tears balanced on the edge of her eyelids. "I wish you would have just told me from the beginning so I didn't..." She wiped her eyes.

"Tell you?" Sam glanced around at the clumps of students studying on Bascom Hill. He lowered his voice. "Seriously? Do you think it's common knowledge? Something everyone knows and I chose to keep from you?"

Suzy folded her arms.

"You are one of two people in this whole entire world of billions who know. Two." Sam held up two fingers, feeling his face get warm.

Suzy cocked her head. "Who's the other person?"

"Anthony."

Suzy's head nodded slowly. "Oh."

Sam left it at that. Anthony and Suzy would never see each other again and it wasn't like Suzy was going to call the head of the United States Army and make Anthony's life a living hell. If anything, she'd try to find a way to help him get out of the Army.

"I think I'm going to study in my dorm." Suzy took a step back. "I have a lot of work to do. We just got this paper to write about 'The Wife of Bath' on top of the final paper." She bent her head and her long hair fell over her face.

An invisible weight pushed down on Sam, crushing his shoulders. "Hey, Suzy," he said in a hoarse whisper. "You're not…you're not going to tell anyone, right?"

"No, Sam, I'm not going to tell anyone." She turned and walked away.

Sam exhaled, his eyes fixed on Suzy's swinging hair and the fringe on the vest she wore since the weather was warmer. After a few seconds, students crossed behind her and Sam could no longer see her. The magnitude of what he had done hit Sam. He began to sweat, jeans sticking to his calves and his shirt sticking to his back. He was outside but felt like he was trapped in an elevator.

Sam's eyes darted in each direction, to the boy and girl holding hands, to the kid with his nose in a book, to the group of guys coming right toward him. All of his senses felt heightened as if he had suddenly developed superpowers.

Sam started walking to his dorm, as quickly as he could. He needed some time before heading to Mifflin and needed to check the mail. Every person he passed seemed to be looking at him differently.

Did those kids move on to the grass to get away from him? Were those whispers? How could he even hear whispers in an open area full of people?

Sam couldn't keep track of all the thoughts flooding his brain. If Suzy did tell someone, what would happen? Would Danny kick him out? Would he get kicked out of school? What about his parents? And Jimmy?

Sam felt like he was going to throw up. He should have kissed her again. He should have made up some dumb story about how a girlfriend from high school wanted to get back together.

Sam opened the door to his old dorm and his feet carried him to the mailboxes.

He immediately saw FREE written in the corner and instead of feeling elation he felt deflated. He wanted to tell Anthony what happened with Suzy but he couldn't. There was no way he could put it into a letter and there was no way to write it in some kind of code that would get the point across.

Instead of tearing into the letter like he usually did, Sam carefully picked at the flap of the envelope as if trying to save the wrapping paper covering a birthday gift. If he could spend some more time opening the letter, it would be like spending more time with Anthony. He would do anything to be with him right now, even board an airplane to Vietnam and try to find him.

He leaned against the wall by the mailboxes to read his letter, the closest he and Anthony would ever be for at least the next six months.

Sam,

I am determined to find my reason for being here, because right now, I don't have any fucking idea. I see all these people who need help. They're hurt or hungry or homeless. Or all of the above. But we spend our days chasing Charlie through fields, in jungles, into villes that he already left, and he's almost always one step ahead. Some days, I swear this whole thing is something someone made up and we're chasing no one. And other days, I know he's real and we're here to annihilate the bastard. If we could just find him.

I don't want to tell you about today or yesterday. I'm fine, but I don't see the point in telling you all this shit you can't do anything about. I want you to tell me more about college. Not the classes or anything like that. I want to know what it's like to walk around the campus. I didn't get to see much of it or get a feel for what it's like because Gloria was being a ditz. And it was dark.

Tell me about walking to class and walking by that big lake right by campus. I forget the name. I keep thinking Lake Michigan but that's not right.

Don't worry about me. I'm okay. Even more okay when I realize I'm about halfway done. I thought I would come here and really make a difference. I thought I would be a part of something that was helping the world be better and safer. I guess there's still time to try but who knows how. Sarge tells us we're doing our job and doing it well. Maybe I should ask him what that job is. I think it's to not get hurt or killed. I'm doing good in that department so far.

Feel free to tell me about the ketchup in the cafeteria. While it's better than nothing, I'm sure ketchup back home is better than the stuff that's been sitting in a box for two weeks. But I'll still take that over anything else.

Take care of yourself,

Anthony

Sam hung his head, feeling like a complete dipstick. Whatever he had going on, it was nothing compared to Anthony. Who was Suzy going to tell anyway? The football team? She barely knew what a football was. Her SDS buddies? They were too busy trying to organize the next protest to give him a thought. If he had to tell someone, Suzy was probably the safest person.

Sam scanned the letter again, feeling the weight of every word and how heavy they were in comparison to whatever he thought he had to endure.

MAY 23, 1968

After raining for three days straight, the sun came out. A clear blue sky and almost a hundred degrees but feeling much hotter with the humidity. Sarge kept reminding everyone to drink water like he was a coach putting his team through a grueling practice.

Every time he breathed in, Anthony felt like he was inhaling the heat. It was thick and wet and got caught in his lungs. Even as dusk settled in, the heat showed no signs of mercy.

"God damn," Mikey took off his shirt. "You get soaked when it rains and soaked when it doesn't."

Anthony wiped his forehead on his shoulder, accomplishing nothing. He put his helmet on his head. It kept some of the sun out of his eyes but also made his head feel like it was in a broiler. Heat permeated off the small brim of the helmet and enveloped Anthony's face. At least it would prevent someone from having to tell his dad that he got shot in the head because it was *really* hot. There were a whole bunch of ways to die over here and it would have been stupid to give Charlie a clear target.

It was hard to survey the land in the extreme heat because of the little lines the sun made when it wavered off the rice paddies. Plus the grass seemed to get taller with each step. Anthony swore that only a few minutes ago, the grass was up to his knees and now it was at his waist. It was the perfect place for Charlie to hide. Five dead Charlies today would equal at least fifteen in Sarge's book. Last week, when they wasted ten hiding out in a ville about fifty clicks from base, Sarge radioed the number at thirty two.

Anthony didn't want to question Sergeant Avery or get on his bad side but he did make sure he heard Sarge correctly when he gave the number. "Thirty-two," Sarge had confidently repeated. "Numbers like that help with the effort at home. It lets everyone know the job is getting done and we're going to win this thing."

Anthony didn't know what it was going to take to *win this thing*. All he knew was that it was impossible to tell one day from another. Even the images burned into his mind blended together. He kept finding little places in his brain to hide everything. He put Skinny there after he was loaded onto the huey. He and Capper could keep each other company.

Sweat ran down Anthony's face in rivers, stinging his eyes. He shook his head in an attempt to clear his vision. What was up ahead? Dusk made it even harder to distinguish a tree from a person.

He squinted through the relentless heat, looking deep into the distance. There were buffalo out there. Real goddamn buffalo. Wait. Real buffalo in Vietnam? He stopped walking and squinted harder to get a better look. Black figures dotted the darkening horizon and Anthony swore they were actual buffalo, just like the pictures in the Encyclopedia Britannica he'd seen in fourth grade.

"Anyone else seeing this?" Anthony asked.

"What do you got, Capone?" Lennox dropped back to walk next to him.

"There's something out there." Anthony pointed his gun in the distance.

Lennox squinted. "I got nothing."

Teddy came up next to them. "I can't tell from here. Maybe wild dogs?"

"Maybe cows?" Picasso joined the conversation. Cows roamed the roads of Vietnam like stray cats and dogs.

"I don't think so," Anthony murmured as the figures in the distance gradually got larger. In less than a second, the buffalo morphed into a different shape. "What the—"

"It's an ambush!"

Lennox and Anthony locked eyes for a second before hitting the ground. He crawled on his elbows as fast as he could. Mud caked his elbows and knees. Murky water filled his boots.

Teddy grunted and crawled a few meters behind.

Bullets came from every direction.

"Come on, Capone!"

Mikey's voice came from behind him as a bullet lodged in the mud to Anthony's left. Another grazed his helmet. He actually heard the buzz it made as it skimmed past him. Mikey waved him on like he was a Little League coach who wanted Anthony to stretch the hit into a double.

Anthony flung his body into a trench, landing on QB, but quickly rolling off of him. Teddy and Picasso tumbled in right after. Anthony swung his gun around to his front and aimed at what he thought were a herd of buffalo seconds before. It was Charlie and all his friends, but Anthony was with his friends and they were going to annihilate them all.

He stood to fire and felt a piercing pain in his back. With a yell, he turned and saw himself face to face with Charlie. At the end of Charlie's gun was a bloody bayonet. Anthony looked down and saw dark red spreading over the side of his shirt.

Picasso pivoted and shot another VC running toward them.

"You fucking stabbed me?" Anthony yelled, raising his weapon. Dalton would have been proud. He handled the gun like a drum major with a baton, seeing Tommy Maloney and then the faceless VC who set the mine that blasted Capper. Anthony yelled, striking Charlie in the face, the ear, the back. Charlie fell, but swung his gun, knocking Anthony down at the ankles. He landed right on his injured side and goddamn, it hurt.

Picasso fired somewhere behind their trench while Lennox fired to the front.

A round of gunfire came from somewhere close. Anthony rolled over and tried to stand up.

"Fuck!" He yelled to the sky. It felt like someone had lit his leg on fire. He glanced down, expecting it to be engulfed in flames, but there were only two small holes in the thigh of his pant leg.

Anthony sucked air in through his teeth. A flash of black caught his eye. It wasn't just any VC. It was *the* VC. The one who shot him. With the fire in his leg burning, Anthony tried to stand up but it was impossible. He fumbled with his gun, trying to point and shoot but none of his limbs listened to his brain. He had to kill this guy before he got away.

"Come back here, you fucker!" Anthony yelled, his voice cracking. Tears spilled out of his eyes, making rivers through the dirt caked on his cheeks.

A barrage of bullets came from somewhere close. Anthony covered his head with his hands as if that would offer any protection.

"I got him!" Teddy yelled.

Anthony brought his hand to his side and felt how wet his shirt was. It was a different kind of wet. Different from the rain and the sweat that had soaked him for seven months. Through a wall of tears, he saw his red hand. And the fire in his leg still raged on.

Who had his letter? He had given it to QB.

"Medic! We need a medic over here!" Lennox yelled from somewhere far away.

Someone ran toward him and Anthony screamed.

"I'm here to help you, Capone." It was QB. QB was going to help him.

Anthony looked up at the sky. Only a hint of the ocean blue color remained as it got darker by the second. He and Sam were going to the ocean. He felt QB touch his leg and the fire burned even hotter.

"What did you get yourself into?" QB tore something from a package and took a syringe out of his medical pack.

"I need help, QB."

"I know, man." He stuck the syringe in Anthony's leg. "I'm gonna help you."

Anthony tried to widen his eyes. Maybe that would make them stay open. Everything around QB was getting darker. Maybe a storm was rolling in. There was always so much goddamn rain. He reached out, trying to find QB's arm. "Can you find Sam? I need to talk to him."

"Sam?" QB's voice sounded far away. "The college boy?"

"I need to talk to him. Please." Anthony couldn't keep his eyes open anymore. Or maybe the sun had already set.

"You'll talk to him soon enough."

"Where is he? Is he here?" Anthony felt himself being moved as the fire in his leg shot flames through his whole body. He only hoped it was QB getting him to the chopper and not his soul leaving the earth.

JUNE 1, 1968

The mailbox was empty, again. Sam knew it was sometimes impossible for Anthony to write if he was spending days away from base in the pouring rain, but he had never gone this long without a letter.

The first day of final exams was today. He had just finished up his history final, which was as painful as the one from first semester with one hundred true/false questions and five questions that required a written responses. Sam's brain hurt as he thought about the series of Ts and Fs he'd written into all the little blank spaces.

He had already written Anthony twice about the end date of the school year and making sure all letters would go to his parents' house for the summer. Despite the reliability of the United States Postal Service and the US Army mail service thus far, Sam wondered if Anthony got those letters. Maybe he'd been in the jungle this whole time and wouldn't know where to write. It was too easy to imagine a pile of envelopes stacking up in the empty mailroom that would be closed for the summer.

Sam's insides twisted as he latched the lock on his little mailbox. This wasn't like that Tet thing where he knew something terrible was going on. The news had been the same: nothing good, but nothing indicating there was anything more than usual to be worried about.

He patted his pockets, feeling for change. Two nickels, three dimes, and a quarter. His focus zeroed in on the payphone by the stairs. He dug into his pocket and pulled out two dimes. That had to be enough. It would take less than a minute to call Mrs. Lorenzo and ask her if she'd heard from Anthony. But, what if she hadn't heard from him either and freaked out? Or, she could say, yes, she got a letter yesterday. Sam rubbed the dimes together between his finger and thumb. He slid the dimes into the slot before he got the chance to linger too long on the possibility Anthony's mom had gotten other news, news that was delivered with a knock on the door by someone in uniform at an odd time of day.

Sam's fingers knew which buttons to press without any direction from his brain. With the phone to his ear and the ringing sound coming from the receiver, Sam tried to calm the tornado in his stomach.

"Hello?"

"Hey, uh, Maria?"

There was a pause. "Yeah?"

"It's Sam." The swirling sensation increased as Sam began to feel a little lightheaded.

"Oh. Hi."

"So, uh, is your mom around? I had a question I wanted to ask her." The hand gripping the phone began to sweat.

"She's not here right now. She's at church, praying," Maria said quietly. "That's all she does now."

Sam felt like an electric mixer spun inside his stomach. "Why? Why has she been praying so much?"

A noise came from the other end of the phone. "It's Anthony," Maria finally said with a big crack in her voice. "He got hurt."

The ground dropped out from under Sam. He struggled to stay standing. "What?"

"They told us he's in some military hospital over there."

"Is he okay? What happened?"

"I don't know. They don't tell me anything." Maria started to cry.

"Nothing?" Sam pressed. "Can you think of anything they said? Something you heard?" He tried to push the worst images out of his brain: Anthony wrapped in bloody bandages, Anthony in some field by himself screaming for help, Anthony by himself in some hospital screaming for help. They played in his mind like the reels shown every night on the news.

"They say I don't need to worry and that I should pray for him, but what's that gonna do? Praying didn't stop him from getting hurt, right?" Sam could hear the tears rolling down Maria's cheeks.

"I'm sorry for calling, Maria. I—"

Suddenly some shuffling and muffled sounds came from Maria's end. Sam could make out the words *nothing, fine,* and *it's Sam.* After another second, the noise on the other end cleared.

"Sam?" It was Anthony's mom.

Sam's heart felt like it was going to beat out of his chest as he began to sweat. "I'm sorry for calling, Mrs. Lorenzo."

"I'm glad you did. We—"

"No, I'm sorry. I gotta go." The entryway to the dorms started to spin and Sam tried to grab the wall but there was nothing to hold on to. He couldn't get the phone on the hook no matter how many times he tried. His eyes and hands wouldn't work together.

"What's going on, McGuern?" Mike came up to Sam. "Haven't seen you in a while."

"I, uh, I needed to make a call." He leaned against the wall. If he moved, he'd fall over.

Mike smirked. "Let me help you." He made a show of getting the phone in place on the first try. "You're welcome."

As Mike sauntered off, Sam tried to figure out how to make his head stop spinning and slow his breath. No matter what, it came out in short bursts.

Anthony was hurt, really hurt.

Sam opened up a spiral notebook and fumbled to uncap a pen.

Anthony,

Please don't die. I told you not to die and you told me to wait for you and I am. I am waiting for you. We're going to California, remember? Or do you want to go somewhere else? We can go anywhere you want. Anywhere. Don't die, okay? Ketchup, ketchup, ketchup. All the ketchup in the whole goddamn world.

Sam could barely make out the words he'd just scribbled, wondering how much trouble Anthony would be in for not reading his letter aloud or what would happen if he did.

It didn't matter. He didn't know where to send it.

Sam dragged his feet to Mifflin with a steady drizzle swirling around him. During the time it took to walk there, the drizzle progressed into rain. Standing for a moment, letting the drops pummel his hair and face, Sam wondered about the rains that fell in Vietnam. Jimmy mentioned them a couple times. Anthony seemed to be perpetually soaked. This rain was nothing in comparison. Anything Sam was dealing with in Madison, Wisconsin was nothing in comparison.

He was drenched by the time he got to Danny's and walked around to the door at the back of the house. On the porch, Sam shook his hair out as best as he could, feeling the added length slap his cheeks and the back of his neck. He needed to get up the stairs and into the shower to wash everything away.

Sam walked in to see Danny sitting on the couch next to a guy who had his head in his hands. His wavy hair shook along with his shoulders. Nick and Jack each sat on an armrest. Nobody looked up at Sam when he opened the door.

"I can't go there. I'll do anything not to go there." The guy was *sobbing*. Sam had never seen a guy *sob* before. His dad had shed tears when Sam's grandma died but he didn't sob. Jimmy had cried when he was eleven and ran his bike into a lamppost, breaking his wrist. But he didn't sob. Sam cried at night sometimes when he clutched the Snoopy T-shirt and reminisced about Anthony's visit to his dorm and the few precious minutes they had together. But he didn't sob.

"If you're sure, we can make it happen," Danny said calmly. "We can get you in touch with the right people."

Of course the Army needed more guys. Sam almost smirked. With Anthony hurt and other soldiers getting killed, the Army needed replacements. Danny would be busy for a long time, planning ways for guys to avoid going over there.

The guy kind of nodded, not in agreement but understanding, as his sobs quieted but racked his breathing. "What's gonna happen to a guy like me in Basic, let alone over there? Someone's gonna find out about me and I'm done."

Sam stepped forward and closed the door behind him. Everyone's head snapped toward Sam. The sobbing guy looked like he was caught doing something illegal. He jumped up, his red, wet eyes darting to every corner of the small apartment. Danny stood to put a hand on the guy's shoulder. "Relax, Ricky. Sam's cool. He wouldn't be allowed to step foot in here if he wasn't."

"He is?" Ricky eyed Sam.

Sam took a step back, feeling like Ricky could see right through him.

"He's going to have to be." Danny gave Sam a look. It wasn't mean but the message was clear.

"I'm cool." Sam held up his hands as if offering peace.

"We're trying to figure out a way to get Ricky out of here," Danny explained. "He got his draft notice."

Sam was surprised Danny found it necessary to explain anything. "I dig that. I wouldn't want to go either."

"It's not just that. There's more." Ricky's voice wavered as he glanced at Danny. "You sure he's cool?"

"One of the coolest cats on campus. I don't let just anyone stay here." Danny assured Ricky. "You can say anything."

"I'm…I'm gay."

"What?" Sam said, more sharply than he intended. Out of all the words in the world Ricky could have said, that was the last one Sam was expecting.

"I know, I know," Ricky went on, his voice getting thick again. "You think I'm some sick fuck who needs to be locked up or something."

"No, I don't." Sam's voice shook. "I don't think that at all."

"And they're going to kill me," Ricky's face reddened. "I don't have to worry about some VC doing it. Do you think they'll kill me?" He looked at Danny.

"You're not going to have to find out the answer to that. Not if you don't want to."

Ricky eyed Sam standing frozen by the door. "You don't have to worry about catching it or anything. I'm not staying."

"I'm not worried," Sam said, his voice hoarse. "It's okay."

"The Army won't think it's okay." Ricky inhaled loudly through his nose and wiped it with his hand. "Well, you're right, Danny. This is either one of the coolest cats on campus or he's a damn good liar. Anybody else would have fallen over themselves going down the stairs as soon as they heard."

"I told you." Danny gave Sam a look of thanks.

Sam nodded and then stepped to the door. "I just remembered I had to go to the library for something." He felt something rise from the depth of his stomach and rise into his throat.

"You're going back out in this?" Danny gestured to the rain still coming down.

"Yeah." Sam's breath started to come in short bursts and he felt like he wasn't getting enough air.

Danny rose, a serious look on his face. "This stays here, Sam. No one can know."

"No one can know," Sam repeated. He tripped over the uneven floor at the threshold of the apartment. "No one can know. Got it."

Sam raced down the stairs, tripping on the last three and landing on his knees. A tingling pain shot through his body. He blindly reached for the doorknob through a wall of tears. Now he was the one sobbing. *No one can know.*

On the porch, Sam hugged his knees on the top step. It was covered just enough so only his sneakers got soaked. He cried for Ricky. He cried for Anthony. He cried for himself. He cried because there were others besides him and Anthony. He knew there were more. And the more there were, the more it meant they weren't as messed up as everyone else thought.

Sam didn't know how long he sat on the porch. But by the time he stood up, the rain had pummeled his sneakers, socks, and the bottom of his jeans. His wet toes struggled to curl inside his shoes when Sam tried to bring some life back into his body.

He didn't even know what he had been thinking about the whole time he was outside. It was like his mind and body jumped ahead to whatever time it was right now. Sam stood, his muscles sore from sitting in the rain for so long.

The door to the house opened and Sam glanced at the noise.

Ricky came out and froze when he saw Sam. "You've been sitting out here the whole time?"

"Yeah," Sam said, feeling embarrassed.

"Well, no need to hide out in the rain anymore." Ricky shoved past Sam.

"I wasn't hiding. I was thinking."

"Thinking about how I'm a sick fuck? Or a coward?" Ricky took a step toward Sam as if ready to fight.

"Hardly. You're one of the bravest guys I know." The memory of Anthony's grin flashed before Sam's mind as the weight of worry pressed down on him. "And I know a couple of really brave guys."

"God bless America," Ricky scoffed, stepping out into the rain that had slowed to a drizzle. "Home of the brave." He hurried down the steps and ran off as if already trying to escape everything.

Sam headed up the stairs and inside. If Danny needed any help getting Ricky out of the war, Sam was willing to do pretty much anything.

JUNE 2, 1968

Anthony was under water with no idea how to get to the surface. He didn't feel like he was drowning, but he couldn't do anything to clear his vision and get closer to the figures floating above him. He thought he was opening and closing his eyes and it felt like his eyelids were going up and down, but nothing changed. Fuzzy images passed overhead. He could make out hair color and where a face should be but nothing else.

And he was so hot. It was like he was on some grill spit, being held over flames. His back hurt, his leg hurt, everything hurt.

Anthony tried to move his head, but it was so heavy.

Sounds drifted into his ears but they were just syllables. He thought he heard his name a few times and wanted to yell *Yes, that's me, help me* but his mouth wouldn't work. No sounds came out.

After he'd been drifting through this hazy sea for what felt like ages, Anthony heard a clear voice.

Capone, I'm gonna go play ball and I need another guy.

Despite the oppressive heat coming from somewhere and the fog that prevented him from seeing anything, something inside of Anthony smiled. He knew who the voice belonged to.

You want in?

Capper sounded so happy.

I need your dago ass, man.

Anthony tried to form words, but failed. Somehow, he knew that simply thinking the words would be enough. *I'm coming, Capper.*

He felt his eyes close as the muffled voices and blurry faces disappeared.

JUNE 8, 1968

Freshman year was over.

Sam took his calculus final that morning and that was it. All he had to do was check his mailbox and then leave campus for the summer.

The mailbox area in Sullivan Hall was busy since everyone else was checking the mail one more time. This was Sam's last chance to hear from Anthony before heading home. He still had no idea if he was okay or what exactly had happened. Fearing the worst, Sam slowly turned the key to the little metal slot and opened it, trying to peek inside. There was something wedged inside, and even though Sam's gut told him it wasn't from Anthony, he tore it from the mailbox.

Sam's whole body sank. It was just a postcard reminding him of the end-of-year checklist.

The common area of Sullivan Hall was teeming with guys lugging boxes and suitcases, ready to pack up their family cars and head home for the summer. Sam's half of his dorm had been empty for almost six months already. It had been hard to think of an excuse as to why his parents should pick him up on Mifflin instead of the dorm. Nothing sounded plausible. In the end, he had come up with some story about Paul wanting to give his sixteen-year-old brother a taste of college life and had asked Sam if he would mind moving all his stuff out a couple days early so he and his brother could hang loose in the dorm. He didn't even know if Paul had a brother.

"How thoughtful of him to give his brother that experience!" Sam's mom had beamed over the phone when he told her. "And how thoughtful of you, Sam, to give up your bed for a few nights."

"It's no big deal." The lie had Sam's mom getting him in line for consideration for sainthood. That was an unexpected bonus. He'd have to add it to the list of lies and secrets he'd already told and kept.

"Seems a little inconsiderate," Sam's dad had grunted when he heard the plans. "I would have expected more from that young man."

Now, as Sam walked through campus, he wondered what his sophomore year at UW would be like, where he would live, who he would live with. He couldn't imagine living in the dorms. Besides, what if he got stuck with someone like Paul again?

Just as Sam passed by Bascom Hall, he almost tripped over his feet. About fifteen feet in front of him he saw a girl with straight blonde hair that hung to the middle of her back and a purple bandana knotted around it. The fringe on her vest swung with each step. He hesitated before calling out. "Suzy! Hey, Suzy!"

The girl turned around with a confused look on her face. It wasn't her. She saw Sam looking at her and half smiled. "Not me."

"Sorry. My mistake."

"No sweat." She waved and continued on her way.

Sam slowed for a minute. He hadn't seen Suzy since she found out about him and as far as he knew she hadn't told anyone. His first year at UW would have been a lot different if it hadn't been for her. Bascom Hill and the Commerce Building held extra meaning because of her. But, there was little time to reflect and remember. Sam's dad was probably heading into town at this exact moment. The plan was to pack up the car and head out as quickly as possible. The summer at home was going to be hard enough. It would get off to a bad start if Sam's dad got stuck in a traffic snarl on the way home.

A horn blared from outside, just like it did on the morning Sam left for Madison. He made his way downstairs and onto the back porch with a box of books and school supplies. The pillow with the Snoopy shirt was tucked under his arm.

Danny was out front, talking to Sam's parents, his hair pulled into a low ponytail, dressed in a pair of jeans and an unbuttoned army green shirt. "Anthropology and archeology, sir," he was saying.

"Hmm," Sam's dad looked Danny up and down. "Where is it you hope to work?"

Danny gave Sam a grin as he came out from around the back of the house. "Eventually, I'd like to work with an excavation team in Egypt. But until then, I hope to get a job at a lab."

Sam's dad nodded at him. "Sam's going to be a professor."

"Yup," Danny said. "We know all about it. And from what I can tell, he's going to be better than most of the ones I had."

"We know he's worked hard this year." Sam's mom smiled.

Danny grinned at Sam as he joined everyone gathered by the station wagon.

"You'll have to come back from the desert to sit in on a lecture," Sam suggested, setting the box and pillow on the grass next to the suitcase and laundry bag he'd already brought down.

"How were your exams?" Sam's mom asked.

Sam shrugged. "I studied nonstop for a week, so we'll see if it paid off."

"I'm glad you found time in between all of the extra curricular activities we talked about when we were last here," Sam's dad said.

Sam pressed his lips into a smile. "I'm here to study, Dad. You know that."

"It will be so nice to have the house feel a little full again," Sam's mom changed the subject.

"It's going to be a blast," Sam said.

Sam's dad opened his mouth, but squinted at Danny. More accurately, he squinted at Danny's chest. Sam followed his gaze and saw the dark green button with swirly light green letters on it. "RFK?"

Danny looked at the button. "Yeah. RFK for the USA."

Sam's dad still squinted at the button, nodding. "Hmmm."

"I know it might seem in poor taste," Danny explained, "but I'm not ready to retire it yet."

Sam's mom sniffled. "It's horrible, isn't it? He was so young."

While taking his last final, checking the mail, and making sure everything was packed up, Sam managed not to think about how Robert F. Kennedy was assassinated just two days before at a campaign event in Los Angeles. The same news reports played over and over on the radio. Danny stayed in his room for the whole night. RFK was going to be the one who set the country on the right path. Why did anyone who tried to do something good get hurt or killed?

"You would have voted for him?" Sam's dad gave Danny a stern eye.

"Yes, sir." Danny nodded. "I was definitely planning on it."

Sam's dad looked to Sam as if asking him the same question silently. After a few seconds he said, "Let's hit the road."

"Thank you so much, Danny, for accommodating our son the past couple of nights," Sam's mom smiled at Danny with a nod of thanks.

"No problem, ma'am. A couple of nights is no sweat." Danny sneaked a smirk in Sam's direction. "Sam knows where to go if he needs a place to stay."

"Give me a minute to make sure I didn't leave anything here," Sam called, already on his way to the back of the house.

Sam's dad looked as if Sam had said there was a five car pile-up on the road out of Madison. "Make it quick. I'll gas up down the street and then we're leaving."

"10-4." Sam waved a hand as his mom and dad got into the car and pulled away from the curb.

"Got everything?" Danny asked at the top of the stairs.

"It's all in the car. I know it is. I just wanted to say thanks again without my mom listening in. As you can tell, she had no idea."

"It's cool. No problem." Danny waved a hand. "And, my dad was stoked about my career plans too when he found out what I wanted to do. He'd be thrilled if I wanted to be a professor instead of someone who wanted to dig up sand for a living."

"Thrilled. That's my dad." Sam stuck out his hand. "Well, congratulations on graduating. Officially done, huh?"

Danny grinned. "Officially done. But remember, Nick and Jack said you can crash here whenever you need to."

"That's good to know." Sam's eyes roamed each corner of the apartment and settled on the blue couch. It wasn't too bad sleeping on it. He drifted over to the tiny kitchen where he had eaten many sandwiches while leaning against the counter. Tucked into the corner by the fridge stood the binder full of bus schedules, names of towns, and people it was safe to ask for help. "I learned a lot this year."

Danny nodded. "More than you thought you would."

"For sure." He scanned the apartment again, remembering the first time he came here with Suzy. "Hey, do you ever see Suzy anymore?"

"I haven't seen her in a while. SDS took too much time away from classes and the work I did here."

"Yeah, I haven't seen too much of her either. I was just asking," Sam said, sad the year was ending without a chance to see Suzy again. "My dad's going to be back any second. I should wait for him out front."

"Did you ever hear anything from your friend?" Danny followed Sam down the stairs.

Sam shrugged and shook his head.

"I know he chose to go," Danny went on. "And I respect that."

Sam heard the sound of the car pulling up. Now that it really was time to leave, he wanted a few more minutes and then a few minutes more. His dad was already starting up and they weren't even on their way home yet.

"So, I'll see you in August, right?" Danny asked. "The DNC?"

"Definitely." It was hard to think about the Democratic National Convention knowing RFK wouldn't be on the stage to accept the nomination for president. Sam had been planning to go ever since he heard the convention was going to be in Chicago. But the tone and motivation had changed in the last two days.

"I can't even think of who's going to be nominated now…" Danny shook his head, lips pressed tight together. "I don't know how it's going to work yet, but you're already in the neighborhood. Come by so we can let the nominee know what the *people* want in a president."

As a honk sounded from the front of the house, Sam imagined a space full of people, all rallying for a big change the country needed. Just like Dow and the walk to the capitol building in honor of Dr. King. He had to go. "I'm there. Let me know where and when, and I'm there."

"Yeah you are," Danny grinned.

As his dad was about to lay a hand on the horn, Sam trotted out to the car and climbed into the backseat. As his mom smiled at him from the rearview mirror, Sam rolled down the window. He couldn't take his eyes off the house he called home for the last five months, seeing it differently than he did that night of the party or when he pounded on the door, begging for a place to stay for the night. The red door of the downstairs apartment stood out against the gray house. Sam had seen it for the first time that morning he left early to get his stuff from the dorm. The blinds in the window still hung at an angle. The peace sign sheet still covered one of the windows.

"Bye, Professor! See you next year!"

Sam stuck his head out the window to see Jack and Nick walking in the opposite direction, waving like they were at a parade. Nick swung a long strand of love beads in the air while Jack took a red bandana out of his back pocket and waved it around.

"Bye, guys!" Sam waved. "Next year!"

Sam's dad looked in the rearview mirror, past Sam, and out the window at Jack and Nick's shrinking figures. "Freaks," Sam's dad muttered.

JUNE 10, 1968

After an eternity of blurry faces, muffled voices, and soaking sweats, Anthony's head cleared and he found himself in Danang Hospital. The thick wrapping around his side and back had a blotch of dark red in the middle. Every time he craned his neck to get a look at it, a shot of pain coursed through his body. A thicker bandage covered the bottom half of his left leg and another encased his thigh. Only his knee was visible.

Everything hurt. Even the parts of him that weren't injured. Even his hair.

Anthony blinked, making sure he was taking in the scene before him correctly and that this wasn't all a dream. There were beds in a row on either side of him, half of which were full, and another row across from him, also about half full. The space was longer than the gymnasium at school, but not as wide.

Injuries of every degree lay in the beds. Arm injuries. Legs. Burns. Whole bodies wrapped in bandages or gauze like mummies. A couple guys looked like they were taking a snooze without any visible signs of an injury.

Anthony didn't get sick out in the bush, but being in the hub of all of this made him feel like he was going to throw up. He looked around his bed for something to vomit into and saw a bedpan within his reach.

He reached off to the side but the shooting pain made him yelp and leave the bedpan where it was.

"Bitchin'. You're awake."

"Huh?" Anthony looked in the direction of the voice and saw a guy who looked younger than him sitting upright in the bed next to him. He seemed perfectly fine except for the gauze wrapped around his head covering his eyes.

"The docs said you would pull through. It was just a matter of time."

"Hmm." Anthony had no idea how long he'd been out and didn't remember anything except for some fuzzy faces and muffled sounds. The last clear thing he remembered was QB being with him after that ambush. He wondered if all the guys were in the field or at the base.

"I heard the Yankees are doing better this year."

"Oh yeah?" Anthony scanned the full beds, trying to gauge the extent of everyone else's injuries. A couple guys at the far end propped themselves up on their elbows talking to each other while others read a book.

"One of the nurses," the guy next to Anthony went on, "I think her name is Sharon. She fills me in on the scores every day. Yankees might break five hundred this year."

Anthony wondered how long the guy had been here. He acted like it was completely normal to not be able to see anything.

"I can't say I care much about the Yankees unless they're playing the Sox," Anthony said.

"White or Red?"

"White."

The guy nodded as if he and Anthony were having lunch together in the mess hall shooting the breeze. "They're not looking too good this year."

"Figures." Anthony tried to adjust his position in the bed but the slightest movement sent daggers through his leg. "How long have you been here?"

The guy shrugged. "Almost a month. They keep thinking I'm gonna see again and I keep telling them they're full of shit."

Anthony didn't know what day it was so the time frame meant nothing. When did he get hurt? What day was it?

"Do you know when I got here?" he asked.

The guy cocked his head in thought and shrugged again. "About a week. Maybe more."

A week? What the hell happened?

"You got a fever because of an infection," the guy said, reading Anthony's mind.

That explained why everything hurt like hell.

"I'm not a spy or anything," the guy explained. "I just don't have anything to do except sit and listen. I can tell you what's going on with anyone in a ten-bed radius. It's not a whole lot when the beds are empty."

A week. Damn. Anthony slowly turned his head to the other side and saw the three beds next to him were empty. The next full one contained a guy with bandages wound around his head and it looked like he wasn't going to wake up for a while. "What's your name?" Anthony asked the baseball fan.

"Private First Class Billy Klise from Topeka, Kansas."

"Anthony Lorenzo. Chicago." Anthony was going to give his rank but it didn't feel right given everyone else was fighting Charlie and he had to go get shot and end up in some hospital. They sent Mikey back after that bullet to the arm. It would only be a matter of time until he was back with the guys too.

"Who's Sam?"

"Huh?" Anthony asked.

"Sam," Billy repeated. His head turned further toward Anthony as if he could actually see him. "You said his name a lot when you were in no man's land."

"I did?" Anthony's brain quickly went through possible explanations: Sam was a brother, a fellow soldier, a childhood friend.

"Yeah. You kept asking if anyone knew where he was." Anthony felt terrible for feeling grateful for the gauze and bandages covering Billy's eyes. He couldn't see Anthony begin to sweat and his eyes dart around to the other guys who might have heard him cry out. "There was a nurse here named Samantha for a while. The doc tracked her down thinking you were talking about her but you still went ape."

"Poor Nurse Samantha." Anthony tried diverting attention away from the real Sam.

"Don't worry about Nurse Samantha," Billy smiled. "She's a pretty one."

Anthony narrowed his eyes. "Pretty? How do—"

"How do I know? You mean if I can't see her?"

"Yeah."

Billy sat up a little straighter as if preparing to say something important. "Instinct. I could tell."

"Oh yeah?"

"Oh yeah," he nodded. "Soft hands. She smelled like roses and had the cutest little laugh. I bet she's a knockout."

Anthony relaxed, feeling like the conversation had drifted into safer territory. "I'm sorry I never got a good look at her."

"She got transferred to another hospital somewhere near Saigon. I think you missed your chance."

Anthony gingerly sat back. Despite having gathered he was now much better than when he first arrived, he couldn't make any motion without thinking about how it might affect his leg and back. Even if he was just reaching up to scratch his nose.

Since Billy seemed to be taking a break from talking, Anthony decided to close his eyes. A five minute conversation had him ready to crash.

"We knew you'd come around, Private." Anthony forced himself to lift his eyebrows. A man in an army uniform approached him with a kind smile. Despite the sprinkle of silver in his hair, he couldn't be *that* much older than Anthony.

The man stopped at the foot of his bed. "I'm Captain Martin."

"I'm Anthony. Private Lorenzo," Anthony said. "But you already know that."

"When you first came in, we thought we'd be able to patch you up without a problem. But you developed this fever and we just had to wait for you to decide when to come back."

Anthony focused on the bandage wrapped around his leg. The big breath he took hurt his back. "How long did I make you wait?"

Captain Martin thought for a second. "About a week."

Billy was right.

"I didn't peg you for a Beach Boys fan," Captain Martin smiled.

"Huh?"

"'Sloop John B.' Not my personal favorite but it's grown on me over the past few months."

Anthony guessed he talked or sang while he was delirious with a fever. Billy said he was talking about Sam and now the doc claimed he was singing. What else did he say while he was out of it?

"When do I go back out?" Anthony asked. He thought about the welcome Mikey got after that bullet got him in the arm and how Lennox got grazed and was back in no time. It might take a while but when Captain Martin said he was ready, he would go back to his brothers.

"You work on building up your strength. We'll keep an eye on that wound," Captain Martin motioned to Anthony's side. "Soon we'll get you up so you can practice using some crutches. And then Private, you get to go home." Captain Martin patted Anthony's good leg as if telling him he'd earned all As on his report card.

"Home?" Billy piped up. "You got the needle in a haystack!"

"Don't get too excited. You've still got some time," Captain Martin said.

Anthony moved quickly to sit up and had to suck air in through his teeth. "I'm not going back out?"

The Captain shook his head. "That infection took a toll on you, Private. It will be a while before you fully regain your strength."

Tears sprang into Anthony's eyes, having nothing to do with the pulsating pain in his back and leg. "I can't leave them out there."

"You're not," Captain Martin insisted. "You absolutely are not. The best thing you can do right now is take it easy and we'll have you on some crutches in no time." He moved along to a bed across the room occupied by someone who was missing an arm.

Anthony gingerly sat back on his pillow. He wasn't going back out.

It's what every soldier wanted, what they talked about the most. Here he was, almost on his way home, and instead of being excited, he felt guilty. Guilty, tired, and sore. At least Billy had bandages over his eyes, so he couldn't see Anthony raise a hand to wipe his own.

JUNE 20, 1968

Sam was grateful his dad's station wagon wasn't in the garage when he got home from work. The last thing he needed after a day of cramming old geezer feet into loafers and crying kids not wanting saddle shoes was to hear his dad remind him how he could have been working with him all summer. The $1.60 an hour was better than the $1.40 he was paid last summer, but it was still a dumb job. Working with his dad would have been even worse. His dad believed a few sales calls would turn Sam into the second son he'd always hoped for. Jimmy was training new Air Force recruits. Sam was an expert with a shoehorn.

He hated the slacks he had to wear and the long sleeve button-up shirt that would already be soaked with sweat during his morning bus ride to work. After the ride home, the shirt stuck to his back and arms. All he wanted to do was take a shower and change when he got home.

"Hi, Mom," Sam called to the empty kitchen.

"Hello, Sam," his mom's voice came from somewhere upstairs. "You've got some mail on the table."

Sam spun to see a small stack of envelopes on the edge of the small circular kitchen table. He flipped through the electric bill, an advertisement for lawn care, and something from an insurance company. And then there it was: FREE written in block letters in place of a stamp.

Anthony.

Forgetting about the way the slacks clung to his calves, Sam raced up the stairs and headed for his bedroom. He stopped when he saw his mom standing next to his bed, folding T-shirts.

"I can finish folding those," Sam offered, his way of telling his mom to leave.

Sam's mom looked at the basket of underwear and socks and then at Sam, as if he'd offered to do the laundry for a week.

"You will?"

"Sure. No sweat."

"Thanks, Sam. I guess I can get started on dinner now." Sam's mom started to leave, but stopped at the threshold. "Or, I have some time. I might try to read a few pages before putting the chicken Kiev in the oven." She smiled like a kid who got the last cookie in the jar. She'd started visiting the library more often and was about a third of the way through *Mrs. Dalloway.*

"Sounds fun." Sam inched to the door, hoping his mom would get the hint to leave. As soon as her foot was on the top step, he shut the door and tore into Anthony's letter. Sam tried to read the whole thing at once instead of taking it one word at a time.

Sam,

I'm going to skip all the stuff about the hospital and getting hurt because none of that matters right now. I'm coming home. I don't know the exact date yet. My leg is still all messed up but I don't need to use crutches all the time anymore. For a while I couldn't do much of anything but then they made me get up and I would do laps around the hospital ward. It was pathetic. I couldn't even make it one time around without getting winded and needing one of the nurses to help me back to bed. Captain says there's a chance I could get another bad infection, but once I'm strong enough, they're saying I can go home. It isn't exactly how I planned it, but it's happening. I told you I'd be back.

I don't like thinking about leaving all the guys over here and how I get to go home and they don't. I know they don't think I'm some candyass that's skipping out on my duties, but I feel like I need to finish this with them. I should be out there until it's time for all of us to go home. I'm glad to be going home, don't get me wrong. I've just had a lot of time to think lately. I know what I hoped to do over here and I think I did some of it but I don't know when I think too much. That's pretty much all there is to do.

Billy is the guy who has the bed next to me. He's going home tomorrow after being here for a while. He can't see anymore because of some accident. I guess when it comes down to it, I'd rather have a bum leg for a little while than not knowing if I'll ever see again. He seems to be okay about it, but I wonder what it'll be like for him when he gets home. I'm trying to figure out what I'm going to do when I'm back. Besides eating, because we know Ma won't let my first meal home be a ketchup sandwich. One thing about the hospital, the food is better. And there are more movies to watch. It kind of reminds me of the common area of your dorm, except everyone has bandages or something and are shuffling around. And there's no Gloria.

I'll see you soon. It feels good to write that and know it's true.

Anthony

Sam read those four words over and over again. *I'll see you soon. I'll see you soon. I'll see you soon.*

He reached into his pillow, the one that still housed the Snoopy shirt, folded and tucked into a corner. After shaking it out, as smooth as possible, Sam put the shirt over his front, as if he were in a store and wanted to see how the shirt looked on him. Then, he folded over the sleeves so they wrapped around his shoulders a little. With the letter clenched in his hand, Sam wrapped his arms around himself and closed his eyes.

He saw a filmstrip of Anthony in his head: seeing him for the first time in high school, being next to him in his room before Basic, seeing him at the bus station in Madison. He tried to switch to another filmstrip, one he'd never seen before. What would Anthony look like when he got home? He would no longer have the close buzzcut. But would he still be bruised up? Would he still use crutches? He said his leg was getting better, but what had happened to begin with? As Sam tried to put the pieces in his head together into an image, he squeezed himself harder, wrapping Snoopy in a hug.

Anthony was alive. He was coming home. And soon, whenever

that might be, he wouldn't need to cry into the shoulder of some old shirt.

Sam wasn't sure what his dream was about, but the noise coming from somewhere didn't belong in it. He blinked a few times and found himself on his bed, with the Snoopy shirt covering him like a small blanket.

"Let's go, Sam. Dinner." His dad rapped on the doorframe a couple times.

It took Sam a second to put everything together as a million thoughts barreled through his mind: the Snoopy shirt was out of the pillowcase and on top of him, Anthony was coming home, his dad could see the shirt, Anthony was coming home, it was too late to hide the shirt, Anthony was coming home.

In one motion, Sam swung his legs over the side of the bed and balled up the shirt. He tossed it and it landed in between the bed and the wall.

"Hi, Dad." Sam quickly stood up.

His dad narrowed his eyes at Sam, looking from him to the head of the bed where the shirt was wedged. "What's going on?"

Sam looked around. "Nothing. Just taking an after-work snooze."

"Tough day at work, huh?" his dad asked with a slight hint of sarcasm.

Sam shrugged. "It was a little busy."

Sam's dad nodded. "Welcome to the real world."

"What a place, huh?" Sam eyed the shirt as if it would get up by itself and tell his dad all his secrets.

"We all get there sooner or later." Sam's dad smirked. "I wanted to go to college to study business but I had to wise up fast."

Sam's eyes broke from the Snoopy shirt. "I didn't know that. What happened?"

"Your grandfather died when I was in high school. I was the only one at home to take care of my mom." His dad shrugged.

Sam knew the part about his grandfather dying but not how it affected his dad's future plans. He had no idea he even considered college.

"A friend of my dad's helped me get a job at his company," Sam's dad went on. "I started from the bottom and worked my way all the way up."

Sam wasn't sure what *all the way up* meant, but his dad did seem good at his job. His family was pretty well off compared to others. "I'm glad it worked out." He didn't know what else to say. Were he and his dad having a *real* conversation like the ones he saw at the end of every episode of *Leave it to Beaver*?

"I didn't have much of a choice. I couldn't spend a whole summer in a shoe store I never intended to manage."

And like that, the moment was over and things were back to normal.

"Only a couple of summers left so I better soak up all the fun now." Sam knew sometimes the best way to deal with his dad was to ignore the stinging thing he had said. "Once I start graduate school, I might get to teach a summer school class to the undergrads."

Sam's dad raised his eyebrows with a little nod. Was he impressed? Probably not. "Well, let's get through dinner first. Your mom's been cooking a lot. She never made any of this stuff when it was just her and me."

After his dad was on the stairs, Sam reached for the shirt and shook it out as if crumpling it up so carelessly would have somehow insulted it. As he refolded it into its small square that could be tucked into his pillowcase, Sam was again struck with the reminder Anthony would be home soon. Securing the shirt in its hiding place was also a reminder that just because all this time had gone by with him at college and Anthony in Vietnam, a lot of things hadn't changed.

PART III
THE WAR WITHIN

JULY 11, 1968

The plane descending made Anthony's stomach drop. He had
fallen asleep during the last couple hours of the flight. Even though
he was cleared to go home and could hobble without the crutches a
little bit, Anthony still got really tired. Sitting on a Freedom Bird and
rapping with a group of fellow soldiers proved to be too much.

The conversation had centered around firsts. The first thing they
were going to eat or drink. The first bar they would go to. The first
person they would see.

Anthony knew his first meal: veal cutlets. The exact same ones his
mom made before he left for Basic. He hadn't had them in almost a
year. His first drink: cream soda. They got cold Coke across the pond
but no cream soda. Then a beer. An ice cold one with his dad. He
made it home. That had to earn him at least one beer. Then maybe
a game at Comiskey if he could navigate the stairs with the stupid
crutches he still had to use if walking a long distance.

And of course, Sam. Anthony wished there was a way for Sam to
be the first person to greet him.

Anthony looked out the window at the city of San Francisco
getting bigger and bigger as the plane got closer to the ground. The
stretch of ocean gave way to the city. Amid the buildings were these
clumps of gigantic green trees. There were even areas where the city

seemed to disappear and Anthony could only see the monster trees, like they were trying to reclaim land.

He was home. Well, almost home.

Anthony felt his insides smile. He and Sam had talked about California. San Francisco looked like a pretty boss city. If he ever made it back to this city, maybe it would be with Sam.

The plane touched down with a noise louder than Anthony was expecting and a slight shake went through the whole cabin. One more plane ride and then he'd be home.

Anthony was the last one off. He had to use the crutches in the narrow aisle because he'd sat for so long, which made his leg stiff and sore. From the top of the stairs, Anthony's eyes zeroed in on the pavement, seeing every little stone that worked together to create the sprawling runway. Tears formed at the corner of his eyes. How long had it been since he'd seen pavement? What a stupid thing to make him feel so happy. If it didn't mean tossing his crutches and bags aside and throwing himself down the stairs, Anthony would have bent to kiss every little stone he could.

He eventually dragged himself into the airport and leaned against the wall to take a break. The added weight of his bags, combined with his stiff, sore leg, made even walking much more difficult. He swallowed whatever was rising in his throat and willed the tears to stay in his eyes. Don't cry. Not now. He had made it home, mostly in one piece. There was nothing to cry about. As he adjusted his balance on the crutches, Anthony wondered what Lennox, Mikey, QB, Teddy, Picasso, and all the others were doing at this exact moment. A feeling of guilt filled the depths of his gut. He should be out in the jungles and rice paddies with them. It was night over there now. Were they in the fields or snoozing in the barracks?

"Hey, Lorenzo." A soldier from the plane came up to Anthony. "You're headed to Chicago, right?"

"Yep," Anthony replied.

"Yeah, me too. One more stop before I make it back to New Jersey."

Anthony stopped the wince from showing on his face. Jersey. He would never be going home. "So close, man."

"I know." The guy lowered his head. "Me and a couple other guys were talking about changing into civvies before getting on the next plane. They said it might be a good idea."

"Huh?"

He shrugged. "Some of us heard it would be better if everyone didn't see you in a uniform. A lot of guys aren't getting a warm welcome."

"That's a load of horseshit."

"Tell me about it, but I figured I'd let you know." He flung his bag over his shoulder and ducked into a nearby bathroom.

Anthony leaned on his crutches, calculating how long it would take him to get to the next gate, and how long it would take him to get to the bathroom and change into different clothes. He couldn't believe he even had to think about it and had no idea what that guy was talking about. No one was going to give a soldier returning home from war a hard time, right?

As Anthony hobbled through the airport to the next gate, gingerly putting more weight on his leg with each step, he caught several people looking at him but they quickly looked away when he made eye contact. A woman actually buried her small child's face into the hem of her skirt. Or maybe it just looked that way. Maybe the kid was afraid of flying.

After finding a seat by the gate, Anthony took the last letter he got from Sam out of a pocket in his duffle bag. It arrived at the hospital four days before he was scheduled to head home. There would be no more letters after this. Only talking in person or over the phone, at least until the fall, but that was still far away.

Anthony,

I can't tell you how good it felt to hear from you. It's rough going right now, but you'll be home before you know it. Your mom's probably already planning your first meal back. Sans ketchup, but that's okay. More for us!

I was so worried after I didn't hear from you for a while I actually called your house. I think Maria might have freaked out after my call. I'm sorry if I scared her. I'll have to tell your mom I'm sorry for hanging up on her.

But you're coming home! Outta sight. We can hang loose all summer.

Well, not ALL summer. I'm back at Kinney's and it's such a drag. It's either crying kids who don't let me measure their feet or old guys with feet that smell so bad who think I measured them wrong. I'm stuffing one of these geezers in a box and sending him over there. One whiff and I know the VC will hightail it to North Vietnam. I am sure Uncle Sam will personally write me a thank you card for my contribution to the war effort.

It was either Kinney's or go on the road with my dad as his apprentice or assistant or whatever. It might have meant more dough, but it would also mean spending hours a day in the car with my dad and I think I'll take the crying kids over that.

Do you know exactly when you'll —

Anthony felt like someone was looking at him, so he looked up from the letter and into the eyes of a kid, maybe about seven. It could have been him a decade ago. Parted black hair, navy blue trousers, and matching vest. All dressed up for his plane ride.

"Hi," Anthony said.

The kid cocked his head. "Did you kill anyone?"

Anthony coughed. "What?"

"Did you —"

"Alexander. Get over here!" A woman in her Sunday best grabbed the boy's wrist and dragged him to a row of chairs on the other side of the waiting area. The woman looked at Anthony as if he was the one who had asked the question to her kid. She plopped Alexander in a chair, turning his head around.

Anthony scanned the waiting area. Most of the chairs were taken, except for the three seats on either side of him. Suddenly self-conscious of his travel attire, Anthony slouched, trying to blend in with the chair the same color as his uniform.

The plane was empty, with the exception of the stewardess who was going through each row collecting garbage. Anthony heaved his bag onto his back, putting his arms through the straps. It was going to be harder to get down this aisle with the crutches and pack than it was to wade through a rice paddy with all of his gear and gun over his head. A day of flying and sitting did a number on him.

He wondered who would be there to greet him when he got off the plane. Everyone knew that picture of the sailor kissing the girl draped over his arm. Smiling people looked like they were cheering in the background. It looked like there might have been some kind of parade going on. Anthony's dad had told Maria and him his homecoming story many times, and it sounded exactly how the picture looked, with so many people happy to welcome the boys home.

As he made his way into O'Hare airport, he strained for a glimpse of his parents. It turned out they were easy to find. The airport was full of people rushing to get somewhere and his parents were the only ones in the sea of bodies not moving. Anthony stopped to breathe at the sight of them. His mom stood on her tiptoes since she was just over five feet tall. She wrung a handkerchief in her hands and tugged at the hem of her blue and white floral dress. Anthony's dad stood almost a foot taller in a brown plaid short-sleeve shirt and brown pants. A White Sox baseball cap covered his head as it turned in every direction. When he spotted Anthony, he froze for a second before pulling Anthony's mom's elbow with a nod.

Everything stopped moving around Anthony as he focused on making it to his parents. It took everything he had inside of him not to break down right there. His mom was already crying. She brought the handkerchief to her mouth, her eyes lingering on the crutches. Anthony did his best to put weight on his left leg so it didn't look like he needed them.

Anthony's mom rushed up to him and squeezed him so hard he almost lost his balance. Her arm stretched right across where Charlie's knife had got him and Anthony stifled a sharp inhale.

"You're home, you're home," she cried into his shoulder. "Thank God you're home."

Anthony's dad stayed a few feet away, like he was picking up a relative at the airport he had never met and wasn't sure what the right greeting was. He took off his baseball cap and held it in his hands as if that were a sign of respect. More silver hair, a lot less black.

Anthony nodded a hello at his dad from over his mom's head.

His dad nodded back.

Anthony's mom finally released him, leaving him with a wet splotch on his shoulder.

"You did your best, son," Anthony's dad put a hand on his soggy shoulder. "I know you did."

Anthony's nose started to tingle and he didn't even breathe for fear he would start to cry in the middle of the airport. Instead he nodded, having no idea what to say. He had given it his all. More than his all. And it wasn't enough. Not enough for his country or his fellow soldiers that were still there. But he had tried. Tried what? To win? To beat the bad guys?

Anthony's dad took the duffle bag from him and slung it over his shoulder. "Come on. Let's get you home."

As he walked away and his mom wiped away her tears, Anthony struggled to keep his inside. What had he come home to?

It was a quiet car ride home. The streets looked familiar, but Anthony felt like a stranger. His mom kept looking in the rearview mirror with a little smile and a tear resting on her eyelid. It was like she had to assure herself Anthony was still there. It was hard being comfortable on the plane. It was harder getting comfortable in the backseat of his dad's Vista Cruiser.

Once they got home, Anthony's mom went right into the kitchen, going from cabinet to cabinet. She insisted that nothing would come out of a can and she was going to make some real food.

Anthony cocked his ear to the kitchen, straining to make out every sound he had longed to hear during his nights out in the bush. He wanted to go to his room, but didn't want to make a show of going up the stairs and further prove how he came back a gimp. Anthony's dad sat on the chair by the couch, staring at the blank TV.

"I'm sorry I got hurt, Pops." Anthony felt something in his throat catch. He tried to swallow it.

Anthony's dad leaned forward to put a hand on his shoulder. "It's not like you went and got hurt on purpose, right? Plenty of soldiers get hurt in war."

Anthony dropped his head, unable to hold his dad's gaze. He thought everything would feel right once he got home, but he had no idea what came next.

"You did what you could over there," his dad said.

"Leave him alone, Antonio. Let him rest." Anthony's mom swept into the room carrying a tray.

"I've been resting for the past month, Ma," Anthony tried to joke. The last thing he wanted to do was rest but it was also the only thing he could do at the moment.

"Here." Anthony's mom presented him with a saucer with little gold leaves around the rim.

Anthony inhaled the steam coming from it. So many rainy nights he dreamed his mom's tè alla camomilla would fix everything. But with the tea in front of him, with the sweet smell of flowers inviting him to take a sip, Anthony knew there was so little this tea could fix.

"Thanks, Ma." Anthony's voice felt thick. "Keep it warm for me. I'm going to my room for a little bit, okay?"

"Do you want something else?"

"I'll drink it later, I promise." He heaved himself off the couch and fumbled with his crutches before making his way to the stairs. His dress shirt was damp with sweat. Maybe he'd feel better after changing into a T-shirt.

"Do you need some help?" his mom asked.

"Nope. I got this. Before I left, Captain Martin told me to keep practicing the stairs." Anthony couldn't look back. If he did, he would completely fall apart. He braced himself against the wall and labored up the stairs, putting a little weight on his leg with each step. When he stopped at the top for a break, Anthony found himself face to face with Maria's closed bedroom door. Gone were the signs calling for boys and brothers to stay away. In its place were cut outs of flowers. They seemed so juvenile in comparison to her Rosie the Riveter poster. Anthony would have to ask her about the door remodel when she came home later. Apparently, she had some sort of steady babysitting gig for one of the women his mom met while packing boxes at the church.

Once in his room, Anthony leaned the crutches next to the door and shuffled over to his bed. He sat in the stillness, straining to hear sounds of traffic or people talking on the street below. It was too quiet. Anthony hobbled over to his record player. His leg was sore but it wasn't as stiff as it had been before. He set the needle on the last record he'd played in this room before his time on leave was up. It was the same record over and over again for the entire ten days he was home.

It started up in the middle of "Sloop John B" and Anthony smirked. He had made it home. The warm air coming in through the window had the slightest hint of a cool breeze. The two didn't go together. The wind had only blown heavy rains or stifling heat for so long.

Anthony settled himself on his bed and closed his eyes. "Sloop John B" faded and before he knew it the opening notes to "God Only Knows" started up.

"Dammit. Goddammit," Anthony whispered as the tears he held in at the airport, on the ride home, and in the family room forced their way out. "Oh, shit." He sobbed, clutching the blue and white striped bedspread his mom had bought the summer he turned thirteen.

JULY 13, 1968

Sam balanced a small tower of shoeboxes on his way out of the backroom and put them on a bench next to an old man with spots all over his hands and hair protruding out of his ears.

"Are those wide?" the man asked Sam, eyeing the boxes suspiciously.

"No, sir." Sam took a box off the top of the tower. "You are *not* a wide, right?"

"That's correct." The man didn't sound convinced.

Sam dug the plastic and paper out of a casual, brown loafer and knelt at the man's feet. This was the worst part of the job. Actually, the absolute worst was having to touch some old guy's feet. As the man stuck his toes into the shoe and attempted to cram in the rest of his foot, Sam did his best to hold the shoe in place.

The man grunted a little with each shove.

"Maybe a shoehorn will help." Knowing it wouldn't, Sam dug a shoehorn out of his pocket anyway and placed it by the man's heel. He glanced at the clock. Thirty-five more minutes and then he would be on the bus. It was a whole day of grumpy geezers and all Sam wanted to do was get to Anthony. He was so close. After waiting and hoping for months and months, these last couple hours were the longest of his life.

"Would you like to try the next size up?" Sam asked after a few futile tries.

The man grunted. "I am an eleven. Not an eleven and a half. Not a
ten and a half. An eleven."

"Eleven. Got it." Sam eyed the clock again. The second hand
hadn't even completed another rotation.

"Are you even listening to me, young man?"

"Yep. I mean, yes. I'm paying attention."

"When I was your age, we didn't question what our elders told
us. We took what they said and held it to be true. It was a thing called
respect." The old guy glared at Sam.

Everything inside of Sam had to stop him from throwing the
loafer at the guy's head. He forced his mouth into the politest smile he
could manage. "Would you like to try the gray on instead?"

"Yes. Yes, I would." The man stuck his stocking foot out.

By the time Sam arranged the brown loafer in the box and dug out
the gray one, the second hand had made another rotation around the
clock. Thirty-three rotations to go.

With "Jumpin' Jack Flash" coming from his radio, Sam tried to
guess if Anthony's hair would still be buzzed or if it had grown out,
if he would be able to walk or if he would need help getting around.
The biggest question, and the one that weighed the most, was if and
how they could be alone. As Sam went through the shirts in his closet,
he wondered if some miracle would get Anthony's parents out of the
house and keep Maria locked in her room. Sam smirked to himself.
Did he actually expect anything about their situation to change just
because they had waited so long to be together?

Sam's fingers fumbled on the buttons of his red short-sleeve shirt
and he realized he had buttoned it wrong. As he straightened out his
shirt to make sure the holes lined up this time, "Hello, I Love You" by
The Doors started up and Sam couldn't suppress the laugh that came
out of his mouth. It was like the radio knew exactly what he was going
to say to Anthony in a few short minutes. The length of his hair didn't
matter. Whether he limped, crawled, or was missing a leg didn't matter.
The only thing that did was that the moment they had been waiting
almost eight months for was finally here.

If it wasn't so hot, he would have run the six blocks to Anthony's house, but since it was Chicago in the middle of the summer, Sam had to settle for walking as fast as he could. He didn't want to be all sweaty when he saw Anthony.

Forget butterflies. Giant prehistoric dinosaur moths flapped in Sam's stomach. Each step closer made the dinosaur moths flap their wings harder and faster.

If he craned his neck, Sam could see the white awning jutting out over the porch of Anthony's house. More details came into view: the thin sidewalk leading to the porch, the red flowers Mrs. Lorenzo planted around the lamppost, the railing Mr. Lorenzo repaired last summer. After turning to go up the front walk, Sam stopped. Everything around him froze, except for the figure sitting on one of the two chairs on the tiny porch.

Everything Sam had felt on the walk over flooded into his throat and he swore he was going to cry right there.

Anthony looked up and saw him. A smile spread across his face. The smile got bigger as he ran a hand through his black hair. It was longer than when he'd left but still shorter than before he'd shaved it all off. The definition underneath Anthony's T-shirt was evident but he still looked thinner than when he last saw him. His face looked tired but the life in his eyes was unmistakable.

Sam paused by the lamppost, expecting Anthony to leap off the porch as soon as they saw each other. But Anthony took his time getting up, gripping the armrest of the wooden lawn chair and pulling himself up. He took a tentative step forward and then another.

"It's still a little sore," Anthony explained, sounding apologetic.

Sam swallowed the emotion that continued to clench his throat and turned his attention to Anthony's face. He should have been ready for this. Anthony was shot twice in the leg and stabbed for Christ's sake. He focused on the fact that Anthony was here, in front of him, in a blue shirt with little stripes at the collar and sleeves. He didn't have to wonder anymore where Anthony was and if he was safe.

Sam had so much practice holding everything in. There were so many times he had to pretend. All Sam wanted to do was race up the three wooden stairs, straight into Anthony's arms, and kiss him again and again so he could know how happy he was that they were finally together. But Sam couldn't. Instead, he took a step forward, and then another, keeping his eyes fixed on Anthony, not even allowing himself to blink.

****

Anthony felt self-conscious as he tensed and relaxed his leg in an attempt to stretch it out. He didn't want to limp to the edge of the porch as Sam neared the stairs. The little sidewalk leading to his house seemed as if it were a mile long. With their gaze fixed on each other, Anthony believed each step closer allowed Sam to notice something else about him. Like Sam would be able to see through his pant leg where the two pink and white gouges stood out against his skin.

Sam paused before going up the steps. With wet eyes, he leaned back with his hands in his pockets. "Well," he said softly, "that's a fucking improvement, if you ask me." He chuckled and wiped his eyes.

Anthony ducked his head and laughed. "Asshole."

When they finally stood across from one another, Sam inhaled, his smile spreading even more. It was so different from his usual smirky grin. There was so much in it: relief, joy, restraint.

"I knew you'd come back," Sam said.

"I knew you'd wait for me." Anthony's eyes traveled over Sam's dark hair hanging over his forehead, the ocean eyes holding his gaze, the freckle on his ear lobe, each button of his shirt. Every nerve in Anthony's body told him to spring forward.

Sam leaned forward at the exact same time. Anthony swore he heard Sam's thought. *It'll be okay. It'll be really fast.*

And they hugged each other. In the brief second they were connected, Anthony felt the damp cotton of Sam's shirt and breathed in a mixture of Dial soap and Right Guard. Sam's hair brushed his cheek as they broke a part. It wasn't nearly long enough.

The familiar smirk curled Sam's lips. "So, did you get enough ketchup over there?"

Anthony laughed. "I had my share."

"Where can we go?"

Anthony imagined his mom getting the large baking dish from the high shelf. She would have to get the stool from the broom closet to reach it. She was planning on lasagna for tonight. Maria could be home from her babysitting gig at any time. Anthony's dad had said he would try to catch the early bus home from work. "Nowhere good."

Sam nodded, already knowing the answer before Anthony said it.

"We can hang in the back," Anthony offered. It wasn't the confines of his room in the empty house but at least they could be alone.

Sam opened the screen door and pushed open the front door. "Lead the way."

Anthony took stiff steps past Sam. Getting to the back door meant going through the kitchen.

"Anthony?" his mom called. "Did Sam—"

"Hi, Mrs. Lorenzo," Sam grinned when Anthony's mom's head came into the doorway of the kitchen.

She brought her hands to her face and shrieked a little. "Samuel! So good to see you." She rushed up and embraced him as if he were the one who had returned from war. It was the greeting Anthony wished Sam could have given him.

"It's good to be seen," Sam said.

She wiped her hands on her apron and turned to the counter full of sheets of pasta. "It's going to be just like before," she gushed. "All of us having dinner together." Anthony's mom beamed at the boys before returning to her baking dish that could hold a lasagna big enough to feed everyone in Anthony's platoon.

He ignored his crutches leaning against the wall, trying his best not to drag his leg behind him as he led Sam to the back door. With his eyes fixed on the lacy white curtain draped over the top of the door, Anthony was determined to make it down the three steps that led to the tiny patio. If everything was going to be the way it was before, like his mom had said, Anthony's leg was going to have to cooperate.

"Here." Sam pulled out the chair closest to the door.

Anthony eased himself into the lawn chair. He winced as the

chair's plastic slats pinched his legs through his jeans.

"Are you okay?" Sam asked from behind.

Anthony turned and saw the creases of worry on Sam's forehead. "I'm good." It was the first time in a while that he meant it when he said it.

"Me too." Sam bent and put his hands on the back of Anthony's chair. "Let me help you push this in." Ever so quickly, he kissed the top of Anthony's head.

He felt the slight pressure of Sam's lips through his hair radiate from his head, to his chest, and all the way to his belt buckle. Even after Sam had sat down across from him, the spot on his head still tingled.

It was like when they first started hanging together and just liked being together. There wasn't a lot of talking or anything. Being together was enough.

"How are you?" Anthony finally asked. "How's your summer?"

"It's great."

"Dealing with your dad? Being at Kinney's?" Anthony said. "Sounds like a real bitchin' summer."

"Oh yeah, for sure." Sam nodded with a little smile. "What about you? How are you doing?"

Anthony had no idea how to answer the question honestly but right now, in this moment, he was okay. "You know, I think I'd be better if you helped me with my chair again." He made a show of trying to push in the chair a little more.

Sam grinned. "Happy to help." He went to Anthony's side of the table and gripped the back of the chair.

Anthony closed his eyes as he sensed Sam leaning over him. This time, the kiss was a little longer and a little heavier but the effects were still the same.

The door to the house opened and Sam quickly stood and jumped off to the side and flew into his chair. Anthony craned his neck to see his mom coming out of the house, balancing two cans of Coke and a couple of glasses. "I thought you two might like something to drink while you catch up."

As his mom set everything on the table, Anthony looked at Sam's hand dangling over his armrest. Anthony imagined taking that hand, holding it, and never ever letting go again.

As much as Anthony enjoyed simply being with Sam, he was looking forward to dinner and not just because his mom's lasagna was on the menu. Dinner meant saying grace. Saying grace meant holding hands. Holding hands meant he could touch Sam again. Anything was better than sitting out on the patio like they were simply two pals hanging on a summer afternoon.

"Shall we?" Anthony's mom smiled at everyone, about forty-five minutes later when they were seated around the table. She extended her hands to either side of her.

Anthony's hand slid into Sam's. It was warm, sweaty, and familiar. He closed his eyes, not in anticipation of the prayer, but because Billy told him your other senses were heightened when you couldn't see and Anthony wanted all of his attention to be on what it felt like to finally hold Sam's hand again.

As Anthony stretched out his other hand to hold Maria's, everyone closed their eyes. *Bless us, oh Lord for these thy gifts….* Anthony fought the swell rising in his chest and squeezed his eyes shut. He was thrust back in time, to almost a year ago, in this exact same place, with these exact same people. These people around this table were what he had clung to and prayed he would return to.

As the prayer came to an end, Anthony gave Sam's fingers a squeeze, hoping to hang on for a little longer. Maria tried to pull her fingers away but their mom started a postscript to the prayer.

"Dear God, thank you for the people around this table."

Anthony hoped his mom would pray for the next hour so he wouldn't have to let go. Under the table, he ran his thumb over Sam's knuckles.

"I prayed every day for this," her voice caught and she sniffled a little.

Anthony opened an eye to see his mom take a deep breath.

"Thank you," Anthony's mom said again, in a firmer, stronger voice. "Thank you. Amen."

"Amen," everyone chorused as their hands broke apart.

"I assume you'll be coming by more often for dinner now that Anthony's home and you're here for the summer?" Anthony's mom handed Sam a plate with a hearty slab of lasagna and broccoli.

"If the invitation is open and Maria doesn't mind." Sam glanced at her.

Maria shrugged as her mom handed her a plate. "I'm not home that much. I'm working now."

Anthony wasn't sure if she really was working a lot or avoiding him. If they were the type of brother and sister who didn't get along and whose primary mission was to annoy the crap out of each other, it would make sense. Still, he had a hard time recognizing the girl who sat next to him with the long straight hair that reached for the waist of her denim pedal pushers. It was just like Suzy's, Sam's friend, but black instead of blonde.

"Sounds like Maria approves," Sam grinned.

Instead of making a face or pouting at Sam, she moved some broccoli around on her plate.

"Maybe you can do some work around here in exchange, huh?" Anthony's dad chuckled to let everyone know he was joking. "Maybe we can work out some sort of trade."

Sam cut into his lasagna with the side of his fork. Cheese and sauce slid in every direction. "Believe me, I'd much rather spend time anywhere besides Kinney's and I wouldn't mind getting paid in food when it's like this. But, money seems to be the preferred form of currency."

Anthony's mom laughed. "I know Anthony must be so happy to be back with his best friend. I don't know if he made any friends in the Army. Maybe that one boy you mentioned...Eddie Cap...? What was it you called him?"

Anthony's smile turned to plaster and remained stuck to his face. He looked at his plate but the sauce and meat oozing out of the pile of pasta suddenly made him feel sick. Anthony forced out a laugh that sounded more like a cough. "It wasn't summer camp, Ma."

"Damn right it wasn't," Anthony's dad raised his beer at Anthony with a nod and clinked an imaginary glass before him. His dad's expression changed as if he'd just remembered something. He got up from the table, opened the fridge, and reached inside. With a proud grin, Anthony's dad pulled out a beer. "Boys who go off to summer camp don't get to have a cold one with their pops, right?"

"I'll take one of those." Sam raised his hand as if signaling a waiter.

"I'm sure you would." Anthony's dad raised an eyebrow at Sam. He popped the cap off the bottle and presented it to Anthony.

The condensation dripped down the bottle, instantly making a ring on the table. This is what Anthony had imagined and hoped for. He took a long swig, feeling the cold spread over his stomach. It was the coldest beer he'd ever had and it tasted so good. But, it didn't stop the lasagna sauce from seeping toward his broccoli, threatening to overtake his entire plate.

****

After dinner, Maria called her friend, Sheila, from the upstairs phone, Anthony's mom put leftovers in Tupperware, and his dad settled into his favorite chair. Sam held the back door open for Anthony so the two of them could spend a few minutes on the patio again before he had to get home. It was hard enough to get through a shift at Kinney's. It would be even harder now with Anthony home.

"The bugs will eat you alive," Anthony's mom called after them, waving a wooden spoon stained from stirring gallons of tomato sauce.

Anthony snorted as he leaned against the house. "If the bugs over there didn't eat me alive, a few Chicago mosquitos don't have a chance."

Sam swatted at a bug that landed on his forearm and forced a smile. He didn't know what to say when Anthony brought up the war. He wanted to ask him to say more so he could better understand what he endured and what those guys Danny helped were escaping from. And that thought made Sam wonder if he should tell Anthony about what he witnessed while living on Mifflin Street and how he dug why those guys made the choices they did. Should he ask or wait for Anthony to say more? Jimmy never directly answered the questions or avoided them all together.

Instead, Sam gazed up at the dark second-story window, visualizing

Anthony's bed, the White Sox pennants hanging on the walls, the record player sitting on the corner of the tall dresser. He would give anything for the house to be empty.

"There has to be a time when my mom's gone while Pops and Maria are away doing their thing." Anthony looked at the dark window as well. "She hasn't left me alone for five minutes yet, but I know she still does some stuff at St. Francis."

Sam thought about the schedule he had for the next couple weeks. It was mainly day shifts but a couple went until closing. "You let me know and I'll come over."

Anthony shook his leg out a little and adjusted his weight. A grimace crossed his face.

Sam stepped forward, putting his hands up as if Anthony was about to fall over. "Does it still hurt? Are you okay?" He had no idea what *okay* meant.

Anthony looked at his leg and shrugged as he pushed himself off the side of the house. "It just gets a little stiff. But I still get tired all the time." He looked like he was about to say something else.

"You can tell me if it's more than that."

After a couple seconds, Anthony offered Sam a small smile. "It's good to be home." He nodded a little.

A silence hung between them for a few moments as Sam waited for Anthony to say more. He had to think of something to close this gap between them. There was so much he didn't know about Anthony's time over there and so much Anthony didn't know about Sam's last semester at school. Sam stood on his tiptoes checking if he could see over the fence into the neighbor's yard. The top of the fence blocked most of his view. He leaned to the side to see into Anthony's house. Mrs. Lorenzo finished what was left in her wine glass and set about washing it. Anthony's dad had to be glued to the latest updates about the war. Sam glanced at the neighbor's fence again. It was dark and no one would be able to see them if they stayed close to the house.

"Come here." Sam stepped in front of Anthony and spread out his arms.

Anthony looked up and then from side to side and behind him.

"We'll be okay," Sam assured him. *We have to be okay.*

Anthony gave himself a little push forward and almost fell into Sam's arms. Sam caught him, feeling the muscles tense through the sleeve of Anthony's shirt. He wrapped his arms around Anthony, holding him as tight as he could. God, he'd waited so long for this, prayed for this, was so afraid it would never happen again. He focused on what was here in front of him, in his arms.

Anthony let out some sort of noise. A cry? A choke? Sam tightened his embrace. "I got you, okay? If anyone sees us, we'll just tell them you tripped and I had to catch you."

****

In his dream, Anthony was walking through a rice paddy with the water up to his thighs that crept closer to his crotch with each step. His gun pointed straight ahead. There wasn't anyone else with him, just the setting sun and a descending darkness that enveloped the pink and orange sky. Anthony gulped, keeping his eyes forward, struggling to make out the dangers that could be lurking a few feet ahead of him. He didn't want to be alone in the jungle at night. He wasn't even supposed to be here. That plane brought him back to the World a few days ago. What was he doing over here? And all by himself?

A VC appeared out of nowhere. He had his gun raised too, with a bloody bayonet on the end. Anthony looked all around, searching for the person the VC had just stabbed. It was starting to get dark and Anthony squinted in the distance. There was someone else out there. The VC spotted Anthony and adjusted his gun a little, so it was aiming straight at him. Anthony's finger curled over the trigger. It was getting dark fast. The VC was getting closer. Holy shit. It was the one that stabbed him and shot him. But Teddy killed him, right? Anthony was right there when it happened. The figure in the distance came into focus. Anthony almost dropped his gun. Capper. What was Capper doing out there?

"Capone!" Capper called. "I could use some help, buddy!"

The VC turned in Capper's direction and grinned as the darkness crept over the paddies like it was a living thing. Anthony screamed as Charlie fired.

His eyes snapped open and it took him a second to make sense of the soft surface he slept on, the lack of bugs flying in his face, and the stillness he found himself in.

He was home. Not alone in a jungle. Just alone in his room.

Anthony's heart beat in his ears as he stared at the ceiling, his breath came in short bursts like he'd just run the hill in Basic. He couldn't get the image of the smiling VC out of his head. The ceiling looked like it would press down and squash him at any second.

Anthony threw the covers off of him and sat up, being careful not to move too fast. Tightening his stomach muscles, Anthony rocked back and forth to give himself some momentum to stand up. He needed to get to the window. He needed to suck in a chest full of real Chicago air. Air that was filled with engine fumes, the neighbor's garbage, and a slight coolness never found in any breeze over there.

Anthony raised his window as much as he could and thrust his head outside. The night air felt cooler than he expected because of the sweat around his hairline. He gulped, willing the images of Capper and Charlie and to go back into the little folds in his brain where they belonged.

He'd thought that being home again would magically give him the life he wanted and dreamed of. He was sure seeing Sam would make all the bad things stay away. But, not even Sam was that powerful.

JULY 22, 1968

Sam plopped himself down in a bus seat next to the window. The open window let in fumes and stifling air, but it was better than an aisle seat. Those felt like being in a broiler even when it wasn't that hot outside. The starched button-up shirt and slacks only added to Sam's discomfort.

At least Sam had two letters to distract him from the old man breathing loudly behind him. His mom had commented how he was quite popular today, getting mail from all over the country. That was a slight exaggeration. The letters came from Indianapolis and Ithaca. Sam's mom beamed as if knowing a secret when Sam told her Suzy lived in Ithaca before settling in a chair on the porch to start reading *Howard's End*. She'd gotten it from the library a week ago and was excited to finally get a chance to begin.

The other letter was from Danny and Sam tore into that one first, feeling the need to delay finding out whatever Suzy had written.

Sam,

I hope the shoe store and THE MAN isn't sucking the life out of you. I've been looking for research jobs since graduation and wouldn't you know, there aren't many to choose from. For now, I'm in the mailroom at the bank where my dad works. He's so proud of his son, the archeologist who went off to school only to come home and dig through piles of mail.

So, the DNC is going to be BIG. I don't even know how big, but there are going to be hundreds, probably thousands of people coming to your little town to give Hubert Humphrey and all his pals the what for. Have you ever been to Grant Park? I don't know much about Chicago but a lot of what's happening is going to be there before the convention. A lot of people are planning to camp out until the fuzz kicks them out. But do you think they can kick out over a thousand people? We'll find out!

One thing the mailroom gives me is a lot of time to think. I spend a lot of time thinking about the way things are right now and how there has to be more we can do to change it. If enough people come to Chicago and let HH know this war is complete bullshit maybe someone will get the message this time.

Any word about your friend? Has he made it home yet?

I'll get you more information about what's going on in August soon. Keep working hard, Professor. Those shoes don't sell themselves.

Danny

Mailroom Archeologist

Sam chuckled at the idea of Danny in a tie, pushing a big bin of mail through the desks of the bigwigs at the bank. He imagined him tossing the letters and oversized envelopes like frisbees at the bald heads and mustaches as he plotted his trek to the DNC.

The news talked almost nonstop about how the mayor was ready for a fight, calling for added police to be ready for the droves of protestors he already knew were planning to descend upon the city. But, Danny talked about people camping out. Maybe it would be more like the Dr. Martin Luther King Jr. demonstration instead of the one with Dow.

The presidential candidates were coming to be officially nominated and things were all messed up since Johnson's decision not to run again and RFK's assassination. From what Sam gathered in the days following his death, a lot of people wanted RFK to be president, himself included. His mom never said she was one of them, but she leaned into the TV a little more whenever his name was mentioned. When his family watched the coverage of RFK's funeral procession, Sam thought his mom was going to cry. His dad remarked that it was like JFK's assassinatation all over again with the way Sam's mom was acting. However, Nixon was getting his vote.

As the bus puttered southbound, Sam realized he hadn't thought much about his stance against the war in a while, with him being away from school and with Anthony back home. It had consumed so much of his brain for the last few months of school. What would it feel like to be one of thousands? He'd seen footage of protestors marching in DC and the student protests organized at Columbia University. Danny had mentioned Grant Park. It was huge. Would enough people come to fill it? Sam leaned his head against the window and he felt the vibration of the bus shake his skull.

He wanted the war to end. He didn't want anyone else to have to go over there and come back hurt or broken. It had changed Jimmy in ways Sam still didn't fully understand because he was so far away. It made Anthony disappear and go somewhere else even though he sat right in front of him. He would jump at the trash cans being knocked over in the alley, would tense when they were simply sitting outside as the sun started to set, and would often look behind him as if to reassure himself that there was no one there. They'd been spending their time together on the patio, either sweating in the afternoon heat, or fighting off the mosquitos at dusk. But, Anthony's mom was *always* there just like how Sam's mom was *always* at his house, consumed with new recipes and Virginia Woolf.

Sam smirked. What did he expect? That he and Anthony would see each other every day to go on dates, hold hands, and make out? For some reason he thought that it would be different when Anthony returned home, everything would be *fine*, as if the world would allow them to be together the way they wanted to be.

As the bus heaved to a stop and the man who was breathing down Sam's neck got off, Sam composed a response to Danny in his head. If Danny could plan routes for guys to escape to Canada, Sam could make it to Grant Park.

It was appropriate that Suzy's letter arrived today. She was the one who got him thinking and questioning things. She only stopped giving him a hard time about not jumping in headfirst because she stopped talking to him.

Sam stared at the return address written on an envelope bordered

THE WAR ON ALL FRONTS

in tiny purple flowers. Suzy didn't seem like a purple flower kind of girl, but she also cross-stitched so maybe she was. The bubbly letters brought him back to their biology labs and Sam realized that he missed her.

A woman in a brown and yellow plaid dress sat next to Sam and put her purse on her lap. Sam tried to scoot closer to the window as he opened the letter from Suzy.

Dear Sam,

I started this letter so many times and each time I threw it away. I had to go out and buy more stationery and the store only had pink or purple flowers to choose from.

Sam grinned. He knew the purple flowers weren't Suzy's first choice.

I want you to know that I don't think you're gross or weird or anything like that. I wish you told me sooner, though. It would have been easier to hear in September before I decided I was falling for a book buster who was such a flake about all the things going on in the world. You're getting better about that last part.

I wish you knew you could trust me. A few years ago, there was a paralegal in the same office as my dad and they were friends, but then he got fired because of some rumors. My dad came home that day all hacked. He was saying stuff about people thinking things about him because he was friends with this guy. Mom asked him questions about the time they spent together and what they talked about and who saw them together. It went on all night. I get how you thought I would have automatically hated you, but I don't. I really don't care what people think of me or who I hang with. Being friends with Gloria should confirm that, right?

I don't think I have to take anymore science or math classes for this lit degree, so there's a good chance we won't have any more classes together, and I'm bummed because I don't want you to stop being my friend. So if I don't take a history class, are you never going to talk to me again? Because that'd be an even bigger bummer.

If there were a way to pull it off, I would go to Chicago for the DNC. You should go in my place. The more you learn, the harder it is to ignore what is actually going on. Your first (and only) demonstration didn't go that badly, right? Maybe it's time to try it again, on a bigger stage. From what I heard, it's going to be more like a big party. Bands are coming and people will be hanging out. GO!!

I mean it, Sam. I don't care about what you told me. Not in the way you think I might. The only thing that matters about a person is what they stand for and believe in. You're one of the good ones. I know you are.

Love,

Suzy

Instead of letting Suzy's words fill his chest, Sam turned his body so his knees jammed up against the seat in front of him. He attempted to shield the letter from the woman next to him who continued to look ahead as if the back of the passenger's head in front of her was a television. He quickly scanned the letter again, checking for any words someone might see if they casually glanced over at him. Sam folded the letter and stuck it in the envelope. He let out a breath and looked out the window, focusing on his faint reflection rather than the cars and buildings.

Suzy didn't hate him. Suzy didn't think there was something wrong with him. Suzy knew there were others. Just like Danny, who didn't hate Ricky. He wanted to help him.

There was himself, Anthony, Ricky, that guy Suzy's dad knew, that teacher from Bowen who got fired. Sam counted out the names on his fingers. He searched for other names to add to the list, knowing there had to be more.

A few days later, Sam was on one knee, but instead of proposing marriage to Suzy, like his mom thought her letter was surely an indicator of, he was at the feet of another old man in need of a new pair of sandals. He insisted Sam measure his feet without socks on. The man didn't slide his foot all the way back to the end of the foot measuring device and the last thing Sam wanted to do was touch the man's crusty heel.

"I'm always a perfect eleven and a half." The man's words came from under a silver mustache. When he adjusted his foot, Sam exhaled in relief as the heel fit snugly against the designated spot.

Sam did his best to grin. "You were right, sir. Eleven and a half on the nose."

"Young man, I'd like to try that one, that one, and that one." The man pointed to several styles of huaraches sandals. "Size eleven and a half."

Sam took the three shoes off the display and nodded. "Eleven and a half. I'll be right back." As soon as he turned his back and headed for the back room full of towers of shoeboxes, the grin fell from Sam's face.

In the days since receiving the letters from Danny and Suzy, he found himself thinking that everything he was doing at home this summer had no point. Anthony was the only thing that was worthwhile. Sam took some extra time in the back room, which contained mountains of shoeboxes. What was he doing here? The simple answer was making money. As his dad had pointed out, Sam had no plans to advance in the shoe business. Was there something else he should be doing? Was there something else he *could* be doing? Being home made him so far removed from all the people and ideas that made him come alive at school. But being at school meant being away from Anthony, who had just come back to him.

Sam checked the picture and color on a tower of boxes and found one of the pairs of sandals. He moved on to the next tower looking for the dark brown pair. How was this accomplishing anything or helping anyone except for the man with the size eleven and a half foot?

While on the hunt for the light brown pair, Sam thought of Danny navigating the mailroom at the bank, waiting for the day he could be in a lab or out in the desert, or at least in the wilds of Grant Park in a month. How did he do it? How did he plan escapes for guys who had gotten their draft notices and then tolerate sifting through a bin of envelopes for men in suits and ties?

One thing was for sure: if he dragged his feet in the backroom any longer, the old guy was going to tell Mr. Purcell that Sam wasn't doing his job. Sam stacked the three boxes on top of one another, and pasted the grin on his face that said the greatest pleasure in life was helping this man find the perfect pair of sandals. "Let's start with these, all right?" He took a leather huarache sandal out of the box and the paper out of the toe. The man slid his foot into it, wiggling his yellowing toenails.

The man raised his eyebrows at Sam and nodded at the box on the floor.

"What?" Sam asked.

"I need to try them both on."

"Oh yeah. I'm sorry." Sam unwrapped the other sandal.

The man stood up, walked down the short aisle, turned around and walked to Sam. He looked as if he were chewing on something and couldn't decide if it tasted good or not.

Sam glanced at the clock. There was still an hour before closing, followed by all the vacuuming and straightening that came with the end of the day.

With a dissatisfied furrow in his eyebrows, the man slipped off the dark brown pair and asked for the light brown ones. As Sam unpacked the next pair, he realized how unnecessary his job was. Taking shoes out of a box was something anyone could have done on their own. The man knew his shoe size. He didn't need anyone to measure his foot. As the man walked down the aisle, still chewing on that invisible something, Sam started to feel really small. He thought about how he was the only one in that particular aisle at Kinney's, and then how the store was on one block in the whole city of Chicago, and how Chicago was one city in Illinois, which was one state in America, which was one country of the hundreds in the world.

As the man nodded at the dark brown pair, Sam repackaged them in the box. Maybe he was being too hard on himself. He was only nineteen years old, not even a sophomore in college. But there were guys younger than him who had to make the choice of running away or fighting in a war they didn't believe was worth fighting. Anthony had already been to that war.

With the man with the silver mustache a step behind him, Sam set the box of sandals by the cash register and then packed up the shoes destined for the backroom. As he found the designated towers for the light brown and gray sandals, Sam decided this would be his last summer at Kinney's. Next summer wouldn't involve sales with his dad, or being a lifeguard at the pool like Jimmy did for a few years. It would be something worthwhile, and not here at this store that made him feel so small.

JULY 31, 1968

The days started blending together. His dad would leave the house as Anthony would make his way down the stairs. Maria would grab two pieces of toast slathered with jelly on her way out the door, always running late to her babysitting job. She took the responsibility very seriously, and Anthony was proud of his little sister for growing up so much this past year. But, he rarely saw her, let alone talked to her. After dinner, she'd spend a lot of time on the phone, and every Saturday night, she'd sleep at Sheila's.

His mom was a constant. Always there. Always standing a little too close. Always wanting to make sure her son was okay, hoping that a hearty lunch or cup of tea would fix whatever was bothering him. "Can I get you anything?" she'd ask Anthony at least ten times before it was even nine o'clock in the morning.

Anthony didn't even know what was bothering him. It was something he couldn't put into words. For almost a year he'd been on his own on the other side of the world, taking part in dozens of missions, in charge of himself. Now that he was home though, he was back to being a kid. Only now, he was a kid with nightmares that came at all hours of the day.

"Who do you know in Kentucky?" Anthony's mom came into the front room holding a small pink envelope. He saw his name and address written in swirls of black ink. In the return address corner was written *L. Anderson* along with an address in Lexington, Kentucky. Anthony only knew one person from Kentucky, but he wasn't alive anymore.

"I'm not sure." He took the envelope from his mom and turned it over to tear open the flap. She went outside to water her tomato plants while Anthony unfolded a piece of pale pink paper.

Dear Anthony,

It feels weird to write to you as Anthony. Eddie always referred to his good friend from the Army as Capone. But I guess it must be weird for you to see me call him Eddie. I know everyone in the army called him Capper. But I didn't know Capper. I only knew Eddie.

Anthony was grateful for the garden his mom and dad planted in the corner of the backyard. Watering usually took at least fifteen minutes, and the last thing he needed was his mom coming in the middle of him freaking out. He tried to ignore the rising emotion in his belly and the wetness in his eyes.

Would you be able to tell me anything about Capper? Who he was? What he did? I can tell you about Eddie. I want to tell someone about him who didn't know him the way I did. If I can introduce more people to Edward Capstone then it will be like he didn't die. I miss him. I miss him so much. You know the worst thing that people tell me? That Eddie wouldn't want me to be sad. But, I don't know how to stop being so sad.

Here's some things you might not have known about Eddie. He won a spelling bee his first year of high school. He visited his grandma every Thursday on his walk home from school. He hated carrots. He loved butternut squash. He always got a mint chocolate chip cone when we went to Graeter's, this ice cream place nearby. We had our first date there. I got a strawberry cone. He played basketball every Saturday and sometimes on Sunday when he'd play hooky from church. He didn't think anyone knew about that but I did. I never told his mom. Our song was "It's My Party." Eddie really dug rock and roll but loved that song.

Did he tell you about all the plans I had for us after he was done with the Army? I know he probably wasn't keen on any of them but I thought we'd settle in Lexington after I got done with school. But now I don't know. In his last letter, Eddie said he thought about going to California. Did you know that? He never mentioned it before and at first I didn't like the idea of going far away to a place I didn't know but it doesn't sound too bad now. I'm looking forward to going back to school and maybe getting out of this place for a while.

I'm glad Eddie had a friend like you over there. I miss him and love him so much. I don't think I'll ever stop.

Warmest Regards,

Lorraine Anderson

With the walls closing in and his breath struggling to find its way into his lungs, Anthony stood up. It must have been too fast because he felt dizzy. He took several shaky strides to the back door and yelled out to his mom. "Ma, I'm going for a walk."

"Are you sure?" Anthony's mom called from the corner of the yard. "Is that a good idea?"

"It's a good idea," he assured her as he fought with his brain to put the image of Capper flying through the air back wherever it usually hid. "Captain Martin said it was the best thing I could do."

"Do you want me to go with you?" Anthony's mom set down her watering can.

"It's around the block once or twice. If I'm gone longer than an hour, send out a posse." Anthony closed the back door and exhaled. He'd gone around the world and fought in a war, and his mom wanted to chaperone him on a walk around the block.

Anthony stepped outside, still expecting a wave of wet, hot air to smack him in the face. The air was warm and a little humid, but he could make it across the porch and to the sidewalk without being soaked in sweat.

Simply walking wasn't much of a problem anymore. The crutches still rested on the wall by the stairs in case he needed them, but Anthony preferred to shuffle around instead. The real problem was how physically exhausted he felt when he hadn't done anything. Maybe *that* was the problem. If you counted the time in the hospital, Anthony had been lying around for two months. Everyone else was still over there, humping through the fields. Anthony could at least make it around the block.

He took slow but purposeful steps down the sidewalk, the same sidewalk he took to get Slurpees at 7-11 and to catch the bus to Bowen. The same sidewalk that took him to Politti's Garage every day last summer before Basic.

Last summer.

Anthony had to stop and take that in, only a few houses away from his own. If his mom were spying on him from the bay window, she would have rushed out to see if he needed help.

He started up again, allowing himself to remember pieces of Lorraine's letter: Capper the spelling bee champ, the grandma's boy. Anthony already knew all about his love for Lesley Gore. But he didn't know about California. Capper never told Anthony about that. It seemed like a pretty good idea. Anthony's city block was so small in comparison to the rest of the world. Even with his sore leg, he'd be around the whole thing in less than twenty minutes. The world was so much bigger than these four blocks.

He headed east on 87th Street, toward Politti's. Maybe Giovanni would be wrenching on a stellar car and they could rap for a while. He was about fifteen years older than Anthony, married right out of high school, and had three kids. They didn't have a lot in common, but spent many hours together bent over the hood of a car. Anthony hadn't been to Politti's since coming home, but maybe going there would help things feel more normal.

The sign with blue letters looked the same. Anthony thought the blue station wagon parked in the corner of the tiny parking lot was the same one that had been there for most of last summer. A Lincoln Continental sat on the lift. Anthony didn't recognize the guy lying underneath it.

"Is Giovanni around?" Anthony asked.

The guy rolled himself out from under the car, grease and oil covering his hands. "No, he's off—"

"Anthony? That you?"

Anthony recognized the voice immediately and turned in the direction it came from. "Hi, Mr. Politti."

A short, older man walked toward Anthony. He had a full head of thick white hair and grinned as he got closer. "Anthony. Look at you! When you get back?"

Anthony shrugged, suddenly self-conscious. "A few weeks ago."

"A few weeks ago? And you coming by now?" Mr. Politti furrowed his eyebrows and wagged a finger at Anthony. "What you doing with yourself?" He put an elbow on a shelf of various car parts.

Anthony stuffed his hands into the pocket of his jeans. He wanted to wear shorts but didn't want to answer any questions about the white gouge on his calf that stood out against his olive skin. "Just hanging loose for now."

Mr. Politti nodded. "Hang loose? You deserve to hang loose for a little while, eh?" He smiled. "But not too long. You come back and I give you your old job, okay?"

"My old job?" Anthony had to make sure he heard right. He didn't wander over here looking for a job. He was looking for some evidence of his life before the Army. And he had found it. Everything about Mr. Politti was so familiar. The wave of white hair. The gold bottom tooth that was a little less shiny than a year ago. The mischievous dark eyes. Maybe this is what he needed. "I can start tomorrow."

Mr. Politti looked surprised. "Tomorrow? You sure?"

"Yeah." Anthony looked at his leg. He suddenly felt like the high school kid who had begged Mr. Politti for a job at his garage over a year ago. "I mean, I don't know if I can crawl under cars or anything. But I can help with oil changes or fluid changes? Clean up the shop and organize stuff."

The old man looked Anthony up and down, nodding. "You sound like the kid who beg and beg me for a job last summer." He smiled, holding his hands in a praying position. "Please give me a job. Please."

Anthony remembered. His dad was the one that saw the hiring sign in the window and said Anthony needed to march right over there and convince Mr. Politti he was the right guy. "I guess I'm back to being an apprentice."

Mr. Politti looked as if Anthony swore in his presence. "Apprentice? You no apprentice. You going in slowly. That's okay."

Anthony inhaled the scent of gasoline and grease. It smelled almost as good as the manicotti his mom made for dinner last night. "So, tomorrow?"

"Tomorrow." Mr. Politti nodded as a smile spread across his face. "You start tomorrow."

That evening, after dinner, Anthony and his dad sat silently watching Walter Cronkite come on the television screen for his daily recap. Maria sat on the chair on the opposite side of the room, twisting her hair into a wreath that she wound around her head. Anthony had no idea why she chose that chair. It was stiff and everyone thought it was uncomfortable. For some reason Anthony was nervous to tell his parents about going back to work. His mom was full of questions when he returned from his journey around the block, asking for details as if he'd been gone for a year instead of an hour.

As Walter Cronkite wished everyone a good evening, Maria sighed and stood up with a huff.

Anthony's dad looked at the TV and then at Maria. "You don't have to leave. He's not even talking about anything bad."

"It's all bad." She ran up the stairs, her long hair slapping her on the back with each step.

Anthony eyed his Dad.

"She used to beg us to let her stay so she could watch everything and now she runs away at any mention of it," Anthony's dad explained with a shrug.

Anthony's mom came in and sat next to him on the couch. "You don't need to watch this anymore anyway." She gestured to the TV. "Anthony's home. He's safe. We don't need to know every little thing and he doesn't either."

Sensing this could turn into something bigger that he wanted to avoid, Anthony took a breath. "I walked over to Politti's today."

"All the way there?" his mom asked

"Oh yeah?" His dad shifted as if Anthony had told him he'd gone to a White Sox game. "I haven't seen Luigi in a while. How's he doing?"

"I'm going to start working there tomorrow."

"You are?" Anthony's dad nodded in approval. "Getting back into the swing of things. That's good, real good." He leaned to the side to give Anthony a pat on the knee.

"Are you sure?" his mom asked.

"Yeah, I figured it was time. I can't sit around here forever."

"You can sit around as long as you want," Anthony's mom said.

"I guess I could, but I really don't want to."

Anthony's mom stood. "I wish I would have known to prepare for this. I don't know if I have enough to make two lunches for the week." She stalked into the kitchen and opened the refrigerator.

Anthony leaned forward to see his mom scan the contents of a shelf. "She's not happy about this."

Anthony's dad turned to see the same scene. "I think it's good." After a few seconds of Cronkite's update, he got up to turn off the television, and sat back down. "When I got back...after it was over..."

Anthony glanced at the doorway to the kitchen, wishing his mom would walk in or Maria would come down from her room and interrupt this.

"What I'm trying to say is that even though we might have gotten a parade, none of us wanted one. We were just happy to be home," Anthony's dad started again.

"I got it, Pops. I'm fine." Anthony stifled a sigh.

"I'm sure you are. I know you are. But I remember being over there with all the guys—"

The memory of Capper's death threatened to escape from its hiding spot in Anthony's brain. "Yeah, Pops, I get it." He pushed himself off the couch. "I'm going to bed soon, I think. I haven't had an early day in a long time."

"Early days, late nights. It was a tough schedule." Anthony's dad nodded in understanding. "Sometimes it was the middle of the night, right?"

"Yep," Anthony said tightly, staying focused on the metal bracket that held the railing in place. If he broke his line of vision from it, he might have to relive the night when Jersey died and everything around him exploded. "'Night, Pops."

After he climbed the stairs, Anthony lay in bed without bothering to take off his jeans. For a moment, he listened to the silence, barely making out the sounds of the television his dad must have turned back on. After a few seconds, he swung his legs over the side of the bed and went to his record player. He needed some noise. Something to drown out all the sounds coming from somewhere in his head. With the opening guitar notes to "Turn! Turn! Turn!" starting up, Anthony went to his bed. Maybe after a day at the garage, everything would feel like it was going back to the way it was supposed to be.

A siren woke Anthony up. At the sound, he rolled over to hit the floor. His leg throbbed when he landed but Anthony ignored it, surprised to find that the ground was soft. The siren sounded again and he realized that it was the phone ringing. He ran his hand along the blue carpeting that had covered his bedroom floor for over ten years.

"I'm sorry, Sam," Anthony heard his mom say. She must have picked up the phone on the little table in the hallway. "I think he's already gone to bed."

Anthony picked himself up off the floor and scrambled to open his bedroom door as quickly as he could.

"I know it's only a bit past eight, but—" Anthony's mom started.

"I'm awake, Ma." Anthony held out his hand for the phone. She turned to look at him, a flowing pink robe hung off her body. "I was just listening to some music."

"Sam's calling for you." Anthony's mom handed him the receiver and padded into the bathroom.

"Hi." Anthony held the powder blue receiver up to his ear.

"Hi. Are you okay? Sleeping before the sun?"

"I'm fine. My dad was watching something lame on TV, so I listened to some music instead."

Sam chuckled. "Something rocking, like The Beach Boys?"

"The Byrds."

"Not much better."

Anthony smiled. "Your opinion."

"So, the geezers are gonna have to get someone else to find their loafers since I'm off tomorrow. Do you want to get a slice?"

"Yes, definitely." Anthony leaned against the wall, facing Maria's closed door of flower stickers. "But I'm working tomorrow. Can we hang later?"

"You're working?"

"Yeah, back at Politti's."

"Are you ready for that?"

"I'm done sitting around," Anthony said. "I know that."

"Later is fine, especially if I can be gone before my dad gets home from work. James McGuern and I work best when we're not in the same room together."

"Some things never change."

"That," Sam said, "is something that will never change."

"I'm glad I can help." Anthony imagined him and Sam sitting across from one another at Vito and Nick's. It was going to be outta sight. "I start at seven. I'm guessing I'll be done by three thirty, like my old shift."

"Cool. Call me when you're done."

"I will."

Silence hung between them for a moment, with Anthony wishing he could leave Sam with the same words as the guys and girls going steady did.

"Good night, Anthony."

Anthony heard each word individually. *Good night.* He thought about the meaning of the phrase. "Good night, Sam." Anthony hung up thinking tomorrow was already shaping up to be a normal day. Politti's during the day, hanging with Sam at night. It was the same schedule he had many times the summer before.

Anthony ignored the stiffness in his leg as he stood in front of a set of shelves in the corner of the garage. His first task was to sort smaller parts and tools into designated boxes and bins. It was a job he regularly did when he first started. But Anthony welcomed the small pieces of steel in his hand, his eyes and hands needing little input from his brain to find where everything went. It was like he never left. Sure, he was jealous of Mario, who lay under a 1963 Chevelle, but being at the garage felt good. Great, even.

With a thin layer of grime under his nails and feeling slightly winded, Anthony sat with Mario during his lunch break. A few months before, he could hump through the jungle for days, going only on a few hours of sleep. Now, a few hours of work wiped him out.

Anthony opened the metal green lunchbox his mom shoved into his hands as he was about to leave. It was the same color as the canteen he drank out of when out in the bush, but the lunch was nothing like what came out of the cans. Anthony's mom had packed him a pepper and egg sandwich, apple, orange, and two chocolate spice cookies. It was like being in high school when many of his classmates would ask if Anthony would be willing to trade the day's hot lunch option for the sandwich in his lunchbox. The answer was always no.

"Mr. Politti said you just got back." Mario took a huge bite out of his salami and cheese sandwich. "What's it like?"

"Hot. Rainy." Anthony tucked a piece of stray egg into his sandwich. "Really hot, actually. And really rainy."

Mario looked Anthony over for a second. "How old are you anyway? Were you even old enough to go over there?"

It was funny to think about what people were *old enough* to do. "I turned nineteen in April. I joined up right after high school."

"Seriously? After high school, the only thing I wanted to do was work on cars."

"How long have you worked here?" Anthony asked, grateful to turn the conversation toward something else.

Mario shrugged. "It'll be a year in September. I like it. Mr. Politti's good to work for. And this garage is a lot closer to home than the last one I was at."

Anthony nodded. "I like it too."

Mario leaned forward with a grin. "The other day, this old lady comes with her Bonneville. The car's so huge—"

A loud popping sound came from somewhere and filled Anthony's ears. His whole body tensed as he reached across the table and grabbed Mario by the shoulders. "Get down! Get down!" He pushed Mario off his chair as he hit the ground, landing hard on the concrete floor. Anthony lay on his belly, waiting for another sound, his breath coming in short spurts, soreness radiating through his body.

"Take it easy man," Mario said with an uneasy smile. "A car out there backfired. That's all."

Anthony lay on the ground for a second, gingerly getting up because he had moved too quickly and his body definitely let him know. He knew what Mario said was true, but his brain and body still braced for another explosion to follow.

After managing to stay on his feet when another car backfired later on in the day, Anthony needed some pizza. More specifically, pizza with Sam. When they got to Vito and Nick's Pizzeria, it smelled like heaven. Anthony followed Sam to a table, and inhaled the aroma of cheese and tomato sauce as if it were oxygen. He ran his hand over the red and white checkered tablecloth. He had dreamed of red and white checkered tablecloths, pizza, and of course Sam, who sat across from him stirring his RC Cola with a straw. Everything was perfect. A grin covered Anthony's face.

"What?" Sam stopped stirring.

"Nothing." Anthony unwrapped his straw. He glanced around the restaurant at families gathered around tables, couples holding hands in a booth. One shared a root beer float. He tried to push away the fact that he couldn't reach over and touch Sam, and relish that they were at least together. "I'm feeling pretty good right now." It was true. He was tired and sore as hell, but he put in a good day's work at the garage and was now hanging with Sam. It was a good day.

Anthony stirred his Orange Crush, watching Sam scan everyone as well, probably thinking the same thing as him. The waitress dropped off large slices of pepperoni pizza for Sam and plain cheese for Anthony. She looked familiar but Anthony, but he couldn't remember how he knew her.

"Can I get you anything else?" she asked.

Sam shook his head. "Nope. I think we're good."

The waitress was about to turn away but paused. "Anthony, right?" She smiled.

"Yeah?"

"It's Wendy. We had a few classes together."

"Oh yeah," Anthony forced a smile. He remembered Wendy from algebra and a history class.

Wendy leaned on the table. "What have you been up to since graduation?"

Anthony shrugged. "Not much. You?"

Wendy shrugged. "Just this, but I'm thinking about applying for college in the spring."

"Cool."

Wendy hung out for another moment before flashing another smile and heading to another table.

Sam looked from Wendy to Anthony and picked up his pizza. "If I could change something about the world, I would make it so you could get any toppings you wanted on single slices instead of just the standard."

"I'm guessing you still like olives," Anthony said.

"Does Mick Jagger know how to dance?"

"Uh, I think so?"

"So, back at Politti's," Sam said. "How was it?"

Anthony looked Sam over. Something was up but couldn't put his finger on it. "It was good." After his first day back, the simple movement of picking up his slice made Anthony's shoulders ache.

"Yeah? Do you think you're going to stick around there for a while?"

Sam didn't mean for the question to be so big, but that was how Anthony thought about it. He had no idea how long he'd be at Politti's or how long he wanted to be at Politti's. As much as he wanted everything to go back to normal, and loved the familiar scents and sights of being in the garage, it seemed stupid to go off to war and live in the same house, in the same neighborhood, working at the same place as if nothing happened. "I'm not sure."

"All I know, this will be my last summer at Kinney's. I'm not looking to be my dad's apprentice, but I'm done with shoehorns." Sam tied his straw wrapper into a little knot, and then another, and then another until there was no more room left and the wrapper ripped.

It was like being in Sam's dorm room when he told Anthony about going to the Dow demonstration. Sam wasn't telling him something. Anthony didn't know if he could handle something big after a full day but he had to know. "What are you thinking about? How you're going to give Kinney's a big middle finger on your last day?"

Sam took a bite of pizza and half smiled. "Yeah."

Anthony eyed him. "What are you really thinking about? Tell me."

Sam sighed. "I'm thinking about Danny. He's one of the guys who lived at the apartment I crashed at last semester."

Anthony nodded. "I remember you talking about him." Was there a chance Sam and Danny—

"He got his draft notice."

Wendy came back to the table. "How's your pizza?"

Anthony looked at his plate with a full slice of pizza on it. "It's good."

She noticed Anthony's plate with a full slice on it. "Are you sure?"

"Yep." Anthony kept his eyes on Sam, waiting for Wendy to get the hint that he wasn't going to stroll down Memory Lane with her. After a few seconds, she was finally on her way.

So, Danny got his draft notice. "When does he report?" Anthony asked.

Sam leaned forward and lowered his head a little. "I don't know if he's going to."

Anthony let that sink in. "Oh." One time, while they were on guard together, Picasso had talked about how after he got his draft notice, he thought about somehow making it to Canada through Niagara Falls somehow. But when he woke up the next morning, he knew it would never work.

With the pizza untouched and the ice melting in their glasses, they sat across from each other just like they did in English class before that research project brought them together.

"I dig that," Anthony finally said. "Kind of. I chose to go. No one forced me. Plus, it wasn't much fun over there."

"I can imagine."

"I don't think you can."

Sam's head bent.

Anthony took a bite of pizza and rubbed his eyes while he

chewed. "God, I'm beat. I think I want to go someplace else, you dig?" Someplace else. He wasn't sure what he meant by that.

"You want to leave?" Sam asked.

"I think I do." Anthony loved being here with Sam. He loved being anywhere with Sam, but having Wendy for a waitress reminded Anthony how small this world of home actually was.

They got a box for their leftover pizza, which was most of it, and wandered outside to wait for the bus. "So where do you want to go?" Sam sat on the bench by the bus stop, the pizza box balanced on his knees. "You want to just head home?"

Anthony lowered himself next to Sam. "I'm not sure. I was thinking of maybe California." The three-walled bus stop trapped the heat from the day, which was a hot one. He closed his eyes and leaned his head back.

"California?" Sam laughed. "It might be hard to find a bus there right now."

Anthony shrugged. "Remember when we talked about maybe going there?"

"Yeah. By the ocean."

"I got a letter from Lorraine, Capper's girlfriend. She said how Capper talked about taking her to California when he got back."

"I think the only place you want to go right now is to bed." Sam elbowed him.

"I know. I'm sorry." Despite sitting on a hard bench and his head against the bus stop enclosure, Anthony felt his body begin to drift into sleep. If he could crash in the middle of a storm with Charlie less than a click away, he could doze off anywhere.

"We're copacetic. It just means we'll have to do this again."

The bus pulled up, expelling a puff of exhaust. Rather than take Anthony's hand to help him up, Sam braced himself against Anthony and tucked his hand under his armpit.

"Thanks." Any other time, Anthony would have refused the help but he was so damn tired.

On the bus ride home, Anthony lay back on the little headrest and closed his eyes, not quite asleep but not quite awake either. He felt Sam sitting next to him and thought how he was so sure everything would go back to the way it was. What exactly *was* that? Holing up in his room with Sam when the house was finally empty? Sitting across from one another at a pizza joint so no one would ever guess for a second this was a date?

As the bus took him closer to his house, Anthony thought about how Sam would go back to school in a few weeks. What would happen then? Say he did go to Madison with Sam. Would he be able to fit into all of the parties, studying, and hanging with Suzy, Danny, and whoever else was part of Sam's life up there? If Anthony stayed in Chicago, would he be able to come up to visit? Would they call each other and shoot the breeze about homework and rebuilding engines? Would they have to wait until breaks where they would resume their routine of praying for empty houses and non-dates?

Anthony tensed when a hand grabbed his shoulder but it was only Sam telling him the bus had pulled up to their stop.

AUGUST 23, 1968

It was a miracle Sam didn't have to work the day Danny arrived in town and asked to meet him at this soda shop on Michigan Avenue, across from Grant Park. When Sam arrived, he noticed the park was filled with more than the usual tourists. From his seat by the window, Sam could see the love beads and tie dye. The DNC didn't start for another few days but the news had been showing footage of people already gathering in Grant Park.

"Professor!"

Sam turned and saw Danny coming in through the door. He looked the same as he did a couple months ago, dressed in worn jeans and a faded red T-shirt, his brown hair falling to his chin.

"Hey!" Sam slid off the stool and gave Danny a hug, clapping him on the back.

"It's already getting wild over there." Danny grinned, jerking his head across the street.

"Yeah, it seems that way. Is everyone staying out there the whole time?"

"The whole time or until they kick us out. There's this curfew in place. Everyone out by eleven, but I'm sure some of us will see if that's actually enforced or not." Danny nodded at the waitress who had walked up to them. "Can I get a cream soda?"

"RC," Sam said.

The waitress left with a smile.

Sam glanced across Michigan Avenue. The Dow Demonstration was a few angry kids in comparison.

"Pretty bitchin', right? I bet by the time the DNC gets underway, there'll be a few thousand more people out there."

"Wow." Sam wondered if any of the candidates cared about the growing crowd outside or if they would focus on the one gathered at the International Amphitheater. Even from inside the soda shop, he felt the energy of the crowd. "You can add at least one more." He wasn't sure how yet, but Sam knew he had to get himself over there.

Danny looked Sam up and down with a grin of approval. "All right, then."

The waitress brought them their drinks and two straws.

Danny raised his glass to Sam. "To changing the course of history."

"I'll drink to that." Sam clinked his glass against Danny's. "So, how long are you staying?"

"I'm crashing at a place on Division until the twenty-seventh and then I ship out." Danny said it as if telling his mom when he'd be home from work. "I'm going to miss the big show on the twenty-ninth but them's the breaks, I guess."

Sam glanced around, checking to see if anyone could overhear them. "Shipping out to…" He wanted to say the name of a Canadian town or some place along the Boundary Waters but didn't know what people could hear or what they could decipher.

"Basic," Danny said as if it were obvious. "At Fort Knox."

Sam froze, his hand glued to his glass of RC. Danny finished his cream soda and tossed a few coins on the counter.

"Come on." Danny slid off his stool. "Let's check out how things are going." He nodded his head toward Grant Park.

It took Sam a second to respond and unglue his hand from the glass. He left it half full and followed Danny out the door. They waited at a crosswalk in silence. Drumbeats came from somewhere in the crowd as the buzz of a thousand voices wafted from the other side of Michigan Avenue.

"I didn't think you were going…I mean it seemed like…" Sam searched for the words.

The signal changed and they jogged across Michigan Avenue to avoid getting hit by an impatient car wanting to turn right. "I didn't think so either," Danny said as they stepped onto the sidewalk. Without the shade of the buildings blocking the sun, the rays blasted Sam through his T-shirt. "But I learned a lot by helping those guys get to where they wanted. Some guys asked for help but didn't take it when offered. Some guys would have gotten on a bus that second if they had the chance."

Sam followed Danny down a sidewalk path leading into Grant Park. The noise and crowd that he could make out from the soda shop multiplied. It was Dow times a thousand.

"And you're not getting on that bus?"

"I am getting on a bus to Fort Knox." Danny snaked through the long-haired, love bead-wearing, peace sign-waving crowd as if he had a destination in mind.

"Oh."

Danny stopped to face Sam. "If you would have asked me six months ago what I would have done, the answer might have been different. But right now, I don't want to leave knowing that I might not see anyone ever again. My parents, my little brother and sister. Even my dog." A wistful smile crossed his face. "You don't get how big the decision is until you have to decide. You dig?" Danny turned around without waiting for an answer.

It took Sam a second to start walking. Of course he'd asked himself what he would do if he got his notice. It was easy to say he'd blow it off in some sort of grand gesture of protest and run away to a far-off place he'd never been to. But would he?

As groups of people crossed between him and Danny, Sam wondered if he would be able to leave his mom. And what about his brother or his dad? Sam's dad was a pain in the ass most of the time, more so now than ever, but would he be willing to possibly never see him again? The idea of having to make such a decision made his stomach churn.

A drum beat came from somewhere and pulsed with Sam's heartbeat as he followed Danny to a statue with people climbing all over it. There were so many signs with the familiar slogans of calling for an end to the war in Vietnam and bringing everyone home. All over the park were police officers in their blue helmets, batons out. Clumps of National Guard Officers filtered around the park with their rifles at the ready. Sam had never been so close to a gun before and he glanced at Danny for guidance on how to react. But, Danny might as well have been strolling through the park like a tourist on a typical summer day.

Sam caught up with Danny and muttered under his breath. "Are they causing any trouble?"

"Not yet." Danny nodded at one of the guards, grinning. "Howdy, Officer." He tipped an imaginary cowboy hat.

None of the guards acknowledged Danny's greeting as he and Sam walked by. Sam glanced back at them. The guards appeared ready to march into battle instead of standing in the middle of a crowd chanting, singing, and hanging around.

"Look who I found," Danny announced when they came to a stop. He grandly gestured to Sam. "The Professor's gonna join us."

Sam spotted Jack and Nick at the base of the statue. They hopped off and trotted over. "Couldn't stay away, huh?" Jack shook Sam's hand.

"I guess not." Sam grinned. Despite the police officers and National Guard that could turn any second, he felt relief upon seeing Nick and Jack. They were all together again and that feeling was more powerful than some guys with guns.

"Are we gonna see you on Mifflin this fall?" Nick asked. "We got an open bedroom now."

Sam glanced at Danny. The room would have been empty anyway since Danny graduated and wasn't going back to Madison. "I don't know," Sam said. Even without Danny there, the thought of being in the house on Mifflin made him yearn for the start of the school year. "I like the idea of it, though."

"We'll take that as a yes, Professor." Nick bowed.

A snort sounded somewhere behind Sam, distinct from the buzz of conversation. Everyone turned in the direction of the sound and saw someone walking through the crowd, leading a pig on a leash made of rope.

"What is that?" Jack laughed.

"Come to the Civic Center," the guy leading the pig yelled, "where we will officially nominate Pigasus for president!"

"Pigasus for president!" someone in the crowd yelled. Soon more joined in and there was a steady chant calling for the pig's nomination.

Danny grinned as the pig snorted again and the guy led him deeper into the crowd. "Maybe I'll give Pigasus my vote. He might be better than the other options we have."

"You voting for the pig, Professor?" Jack asked.

Sam laughed. "I'm not voting for Nixon, that's for sure."

"Good start," Nick said.

Jack pulled on Nick's arm. "Let's see if we can catch up to them. Maybe I can get my picture taken with our future president."

"Bye, Professor!" Nick called as he was dragged away.

Danny turned to Sam. "They don't know yet." He jerked his head in the direction Jack and Nick had gone. "I'll tell them before the end of the week when the time is right."

Sam nodded a little. In the moment, he had forgotten.

"I'll be okay, man," Danny shook Sam's shoulder a little. "We mess up the system in our own way. None of them will see me coming."

Sam didn't know a lot about the Army, but doubted Danny was going to be able to do much of anything from the inside.

"This is what I want to do. I mean it. In the mailroom, the only thing to do is think, and I've thought about this a lot." Danny sat on the grass. "Maybe I'll learn something. Maybe I'll change something. What I've been doing so far doesn't seem to make much of a difference. Maybe this will."

"Then why are you here?" Sam asked.

Danny shrugged. "Because we got to get someone in office who knows how to end this thing. If I'm going over there, there better be a president who's on my side."

Sam raced home from the bus stop, knowing he was going to

catch hell from his dad. Sweat made his T-shirt stick to his back as he ran down the sidewalk, seeing his house get closer and closer. Traffic going south was worse than usual, probably from preparations for the DNC. It was already 6:17 as the bus had pulled up to the curb and 6:23 by the time Sam opened the door to his house and stumbled inside.

His parents sat on either side of the small kitchen table with their plates in front of them, the food getting cold. His mom had gone all out for her special birthday dinner: beef bourguignon. The tunnel of fudge cake she made for everyone's birthday sat on the counter.

"I thought you'd be home by six," Sam's mom said.

"I know. I'm sorry." Sam did feel bad. Since he had to work yesterday evening, they were doing a special birthday dinner tonight. His mom tried her best not to look hurt, resting her napkin in her lap and taking a sip of her martini. His dad narrowed his eyes at him with a look that said *see what you did*. "The bus was late and traffic was bad—"

"Where were you?"

"I told you, James," Sam's mom answered for him. "He was visiting a friend from school. It's okay, Sam. I'll have other birthdays."

"What friend?" Sam's dad asked.

It took Sam a second to answer his dad's question. When his mom said there would be other birthdays, the first thought he had was how Danny wouldn't be home for his mom's next birthday. Anthony was gone when his mom celebrated her day in January. "Danny. He lived in the apartment I crashed at." He slid in front of a plate of beef bourguignon.

"Is he visiting family?" Sam's mom asked.

"No, he's in town for the Convention."

"Is he with those idiots walking around on TV?" Sam's dad pointed at the TV in the family room with his knife.

"I don't know." It was true. There were various shots of people congregating around the city. Sam had no idea if Danny was a part of any of the other groups. What he was really thinking about was how his dad's birthday was in October. If he were Danny, he would miss that one as well.

"They're asking for trouble, getting all those people together,"

Sam's dad said. "And you know Daley's not going to stand for it."

"They're not doing anything, Dad. They're just hanging out."

The mayor had already been on television several times, insisting Chicago was going to be a great stage for the Convention and he was ready to take action against those that wanted to prove otherwise. Sam had seen it with his own eyes that afternoon.

"Why don't I heat these up?" Sam's mom made a show of taking the plates to the stove and putting the food back in the large pot.

"I'm sorry I was late, Mom," Sam said.

His mom turned with a smile. "It's okay, Sam. I'm glad you're here. It was an empty house with you *and* Jimmy gone."

Sam's dad stared at him, with the judgmental expression he'd seen many times. But it didn't bother him as much this time. Even though his dad gave him more stares than smiles and went out of his way to find something wrong with almost everything Sam said and did, he still didn't think he'd be able to make the decision that could result in him never coming home again.

With a belly full of beef and a head filled with questions, Sam couldn't sleep that night. It had nothing to do with his dad snoring like a bus needing a new muffler. He had learned to drown him out years ago.

Struggling to find a cool spot on his pillow, Sam turned it over and burrowed his head into it. Part of him felt guilty for knowing he would never be in Danny's position. He would be in school until 1971 and then go straight to grad school.

Sam kicked the sheets off and went over to the desk he hadn't touched in over a year. He pulled the chair over to the window and sat in it, looking down at the dark street, focusing on the pools of orange light the street lamps made. It seemed impossible that the city was so quiet when there was so much noise in other parts of the world. Sam wondered what Danny was doing in that house on Division. Was he sound asleep, at peace with his decision? Was he getting high as much as he could before heading to Fort Knox?

Sam had no idea if Anthony slept the night before Basic, but he did remember the day before he left and the memory filled his chest as he breathed it in. But then his breath began to come in quick bursts as Sam struggled to suck in enough air. It was like when he found out Anthony was injured and Maria couldn't tell him anything. He reached out to grip the window sill but his fingertips began to tingle and he couldn't hang on to anything.

Struggling to take in full gulps of air, Sam tried shaking the feeling back into his hands but it was impossible with it being so hard to breathe. Something in his brain told him to stand up, but when Sam stood, his legs wouldn't support him. He dropped to his knees, wringing out his hands, and gasping for breath as the tingling in his fingers intensified and the room began to spin.

AUGUST 24, 1968

Crammed in the backseat of the family Vista Cruiser, Anthony did his best to find a comfortable position. His leg felt fine most days, but working at the garage left him tired and sore. Plus, nobody would be comfortable with their kneecaps in their face. Maria, dressed in a light purple dress with white trim, looked out the window. She first came downstairs in pedal pushers and a blue shirt, but Anthony's mom had her march right back upstairs and put on something more appropriate for their nonna's seventy-fifth birthday party.

Being shorter, Maria should have been more comfortable, but she looked more on edge than Anthony. She pulled at the little sleeves of the dress every five seconds, still fuming from having to wear it.

Anthony sat back as much as he could and crossed his arms like a child. Hell, he was being treated like a child, so why not act like one? Anthony told his parents he didn't want to venture out to the suburbs and see everyone in his extended family. He tried playing into his mom's worries by saying he didn't think he was up for it. His dad was the one that stepped in, saying it would be the best birthday present for his nonna to see her oldest grandson on such a special birthday.

So he baked in the backseat of the car in a pair of gray slacks and a yellow and orange button-down shirt. He could have been home, calling Sam to see if he wanted to come over. The two of them had barely had any time alone since he'd gotten back. Most of it was spent on the patio. None of it had been spent in his room. The days going by constantly reminded Anthony how little time was left before Sam went back to school.

While his dad whistled along to a Dean Martin song on the radio and Anthony's mom looked out for their next turn, Anthony felt like the car was suffocating him. He could go around the world with a gun strapped to his back and rounds of ammunition hanging from his body but couldn't have a say in whether or not a family party was how he wanted to spend his Saturday.

If it was only going to be his nonna, Anthony would have been okay. But everyone? Since he only saw his aunts, uncles, and cousins a few times a year, it was always a slew of questions. How was school? What were his grades? Did he get a job? Did he have a girlfriend?

His dad glanced at him in the rearview mirror. "Are you okay back there?"

His mom's head snapped back as if she weren't the one who insisted he come to the party. A crease of worry deepened on her forehead.

"Just peachy," Anthony muttered.

Maria sat with her arms folded, slouching. If she tried hard enough, she might have been able to shoot lasers at the back of their mom's head. Sitting in the backseat was the closest he and Maria had been since he returned. This drive was nothing like the treks out to the suburbs when they were younger. The entire ride involved Anthony crossing the imaginary line in the backseat and Maria whining to their parents every time his hand crept toward her. Now, she turned her attention out the window where the houses began to spread out and more trees dotted the lawns and sidewalks.

They finally pulled into Anthony's aunt and uncle's driveway, where about a dozen cars lined the suburban street. A bunch of balloons hovered above the mailbox, tied in place with several ribbons. A huge homemade sign hung on the front door that read *Happy 75th Birthday, Nonna!* It was obviously made by Uncle Louie and Auntie Angela's kids, who were about ten years younger than Anthony.

Everyone was already gathered in the back, spread out on lawn chairs on the slab of concrete about three times the size of the one at Anthony's house. The group cheered a greeting when Anthony and his family made their entrance.

"There they are!" Uncle Louie got up from his wooden chair to shake hands with Anthony's dad. They went over to the patio door where three green metal coolers sat, all filled to the brim with beer and pop.

Anthony was wondering if he could somehow sneak a beer when a pair of arms threw themselves around him. "Anthony!" It was Auntie Angela, his dad's youngest sister. "We're all so grateful you're home safe." She held on for a bit longer before turning to Anthony's mom and taking a container of cookies from her. "Let's bring those inside. Maria, you look lovely. And your hair is beautiful."

In response, Maria ran a hand through her long, straight, black hair. "Thank you. I haven't gotten it cut since Thanksgiving."

"I told her that dress was pretty but she didn't believe me…" Anthony's mom's voice trailed off as she followed Auntie Angela.

"How's the leg treating you?" Uncle Louie asked Anthony, handing him a sweaty bottle of Coke.

"Uh, okay." Of course everyone in his family knew about his injuries and probably a little bit about his recovery. Anthony looked at the corner of the house he had just walked around and wondered how quickly he could retreat.

Anthony's aunts, uncles, and cousins lined up in some sort of receiving line. He once lined up in one for a funeral to offer condolences to a neighbor whose mom had died. He took a step back but the line moved with him. Anthony glanced around to see if Maria could rescue him but she was nowhere around.

Everyone needed an embrace and had an expression of joy and relief. After about four people had their turn, Anthony's nonna came out of the house and cut through everyone to get to him. She was shorter than Anthony by about eight inches, dressed in a black polka dot dress that went past her knees. Her tight curls were made by sleeping in pin curls. Upon seeing her, Anthony immediately went back to the nights he'd spent at her house when he was a kid and his nonna still lived in

Chicago. He'd wake up to the sound of her stirring a cup of coffee, her head a mass of little silver tufts of hair that hadn't been combed out yet. She held a wrinkled hand up to his cheek and looked into his eyes.

"My boy," she whispered. "My boy is home." She stood on her tiptoes and Anthony bent to accommodate her so she could kiss him. "I pray every day for you, my brave boy."

Something in the pit of Anthony's stomach cracked and threatened to break. "Happy birthday, Nonna," he choked out. He straightened, feeling like he did during the POW training when he had to turn himself off. She squeezed his hands and then went into the house. Even on her birthday, she would make sure everyone had enough to eat and drink.

Uncle Joseph, his dad's middle brother, came up to Anthony. "We're all so happy you could be here. That you *are* here." He embraced Anthony. "Do you remember Mr. Linetto, who used to live by Nonna's on eighty-sixth?"

Anthony searched his brain, grateful to have something to distract him. He pictured the old man with a head of thick white hair watering the small garden of tomatoes he had in his backyard. "Yeah. I think so."

"His grandson is heading over there in a couple weeks. He lives by you."

"Oh." The pit in Anthony's stomach cracked more.

"He's nervous about it. Maybe you can talk to him. Show him how you came back okay." Uncle Joseph smiled, waiting for a response.

Anthony's mouth tightened into a thin smile, like he was a little kid still learning how to smile for photographs. Talk to someone he didn't know about what he was going into?

Fuck no.

"I don't know. Maybe." Anthony tightened his stomach, hoping that would stop whatever was cracking inside of him. "I gotta find a bottle opener." He held up his bottle of Coke but instead of picking up the bottle opener by the cooler, he went into the house. The familiar smells of a family party greeted him and released some of the tension Anthony carried in his gut.

His mom bustled around the kitchen, helping Auntie Angela

organize a relish tray of a variety of pickles and olives. His cousin, Teresa, filled black olives with cream cheese while another cousin, Dora, cut up vegetables for a salad. They were about five years younger than Anthony and barely looked his way. Nonna stood at the stove, using a wooden spoon to stir her much-loved dish of potatoes, homemade tomato sauce, and peppers. "You remember this?" She waved her spoon over a pan so large, it almost covered two burners.

"I could never forget it," Anthony said.

"Go find your sister." His mom opened a plastic container of artichoke hearts. "She should be helping Dora with the salad."

If it gave him a reason to leave the kitchen and get away from everyone, Anthony was happy to help. He slipped out the front door, hoping to hide out for a few minutes but found Maria sitting on the porch swing. He was about to go inside, thinking she wouldn't even want him to sit with her. But, if Anthony had to choose between his little sister and a backyard full of relatives, he had to go with Maria. He put a real smile on his face. "Well, Maria, your dress is *lovely*."

She smirked at him and slid over a little. "You don't look that great either."

"This is a drag." Anthony sat next to her.

"It sure is." Maria rested her elbow on the armrest and put her chin in her hand.

It was quiet on the porch. Based on the number of cars lining the street, Anthony guessed no one else would be pulling up and maybe he and Maria could hide out until it was time to eat. He could think of an excuse as to why she never reported for salad duty later. They sat for a few moments, their feet moving the swing slightly. Anthony looked at the back of his sister's head, the lace of the sleeves of the purple dress, and the white shoes with a little strap and buckle going across her foot. "I never see you. Everything copacetic?"

Maria shrugged and turned to Anthony. "I'm busy. Babysitting. Reading. Hanging with friends."

"Redecorating your bedroom door?" Anthony said. "Nice flowers."

Maria's expression clouded.

Anthony held up his hands in apology. "I didn't mean I didn't like them. I just thought you would have moved on to George, Paul, John, and Ringo or something like that." He missed a year of his sister's life and felt like he didn't know how to talk to her and had no idea what she liked besides talking on the phone.

Maria picked at a piece of cracked plastic on the armrest, her hair hiding most of her face. "You don't see me that much because I don't know what to say to you." Her voice was quiet. If they were sitting on the porch at their house in Chicago, a bus might have drowned out her words.

"What?"

"Dad went ape when I put those stickers on my door. He said I ruined the finish and they would never come off. I told him I didn't care because I never wanted them to come off."

"Uh, okay. So you really like them, huh?" The sun hung in the sky directly behind Anthony and he felt the rays heat his neck. "I didn't mean to make fun of them."

Maria sniffled loudly. "It's the only way I can say what I feel. Dad doesn't know it's not about the finish on the door or some stupid girlie thing. I can't put a peace sign on my door. I can't be like Sheila. Her parents don't care that she puts buttons on her purse and wears jeans everywhere." Another sniffle. "I saw a picture of someone putting a flower in a gun and then I saw those stickers. Those stupid stickers and my *lovely* hair are the only ways I can say what I really feel."

The conversation went in too many directions. Anthony wished he would have left the bedroom door alone. "What do you feel?"

"I'm a pacifist." Maria said it as if in confession over at St. Francis.

"A pacifist?" Anthony asked. "Do you even know what that—"

"Yes, I know what it means," Maria snapped. Tears clung to her eyelashes. "I'm sorry. I didn't mean to talk to you like that."

"I'm sorry for forgetting you're not so little anymore." This wasn't the same girl who ran up to her room with Trixie Belden and a glass of milk on the day before Anthony left for Basic. It also wasn't the same girl who welcomed him home while on leave with a big hug, wearing her school uniform.

"I'm sorry you got hurt," Maria continued her confessional tone.

"I'm sorry you had to go over there. Dad says I should be proud of you and it's wrong for me to talk like this." She began to get choked up. "I am proud of you but I don't like what's going on. Nancy Franklin's cousin died over there last week. He was only twenty-one years old but that's older than you." The tears fell from Maria's eyelashes. "I don't like it at all and I want it to stop."

Anthony looked at his sister's knee, wondering if he should put a hand on the hated purple and white dress. A lot of guys died over there and he stopped his brain from thinking about them. At least he couldn't put a face to Nancy Franklin's cousin. "I want it to stop too." Anthony thought of Lennox, Picasso, Teddy, QB, and all the others still over there. He wished they could come home.

They sat in silence for a few moments, the creak of the swing and a car driving somewhere down the street being the only noise. Anthony wished there was a way for him and Maria to stay out on the porch for the rest of the party, even if it meant missing out on his nonna's signature potatoes.

Maria wiped her face. "I really hate this dress."

Anthony wiped the back of his neck, feeling the sweaty collar. "And I really hate this shirt."

The screen door opened and Maria and Anthony jumped a little at the sound. "There you are." Anthony's mom poked her head out. "Dora's done with the salad already." Her expression changed when she noticed Maria's red eyes. "Is everything okay?"

Anthony stood. "We're good, Ma. I started feeling a little dizzy being around everyone and Maria stuck around to keep me company."

"Everyone's so happy to see you," Anthony's mom explained. "Nonna's asking if you're all right."

"We're coming back in," Anthony said.

She didn't look like she believed him. "Well, we're setting out the food in a few minutes." She gave them another glance before going inside.

"Come on." Anthony patted Maria's knee. "At least we know the food will be good, right?"

One corner of Maria's mouth smiled as she stood up, smoothing the wrinkles of her dress.

Anthony was half asleep on the way home a few hours later, after "Happy Birthday" had been sung, and more hugs were given, and everyone had told Anthony *again* how happy they were that he was home safe. His dad pumped the brakes hard, and Anthony's head knocked against the window as he looked around in a daze.

"What's going on here?" his dad said.

The car was stopped on Lake Shore Drive in the middle of a traffic jam, which was unexpected for a Saturday evening. On the east side of the road, hundreds of people were gathered in Lincoln Park. With the windows open, it was possible to hear drumbeats and some sort of chant. Anthony could see people holding a variety of signs. From what he could tell, a lot of the people looked like some of those he encountered at that party in Madison before he shipped out.

"What are they doing?" Anthony's mom asked.

"You've seen it on the news all week, Eva," his dad responded. "They're going to yell and scream about how mad they are. They can shout all they want when they fight in a war." He grumbled as the car began to creep forward.

Maria slouched in her seat, arms crossed, her mouth in a thin line.

Anthony gazed out the window. He'd seen footage of the crowds in Grant Park on the news too. His dad glanced at him in the rearview mirror. It looked like he wanted Anthony to provide backup but he couldn't. All those people hanging out in the park wanted change. Sitting in a park was a safer way to bring about change rather than humping up hills and through rice paddies.

With the people in Lincoln Park and Grant Park miles away, Anthony lay in his bed replaying his conversation with Maria. He wasn't mad at his sister. He dug why she felt the way she did. He rolled over, and hugged his pillow, wishing it were Sam wrapped in his arms. Tomorrow evening it would be. They would finally have Anthony's house to themselves. His mom and dad were going over to their friends' house to play bridge, and Maria was going to the movies with Sheila and then sleeping over at her house.

Sam was coming over tomorrow and that knowledge managed
to drown out the noises in his head: Maria crying, the drums beating
across Lincoln Park and all the way to Lake Shore Drive, grenades
exploding, men screaming. There had to be a way to not just drown out
the noises but have them quiet down.

AUGUST 25, 1968

Sam hurried down the stairs after changing out of his church clothes and into a pair of jeans and a brown T-shirt. In the middle of the sermon, he had exchanged a glance with Anthony who sat three pews in front of him. He could read the message on Anthony's face clearly.

Tonight.

Yes. Tonight. Finally. Sam had been looking forward to tonight for a long time.

But before *tonight* there were things he needed to do.

"I thought you had to work today," Sam's mom told him when he came into the kitchen to make a sandwich to eat on his way to the bus stop.

"I switched shifts with Harold." Sam dug in the fridge for turkey and cheese.

"Why?" Sam's dad peered at him over the top of the newspaper. Sam couldn't make out the headline but the picture was large enough for him to see the National Guard and police officers surrounding groups of demonstrators.

"He's looking to make some extra money and Mr. Purcell didn't mind, so..." Sam shrugged, trailing off in an effort to stop a little lie from spreading into an even bigger one. After seeing Danny and hearing his dad grumble about the protestors occupying Grant Park, Sam couldn't let someone's need for new loafers prevent him from being a part of it. The only person who could was Anthony. He'd have to make sure he caught an earlier bus to the South Side so they could have as much time together as possible.

"For someone not going to work, you're sure in a hurry." Sam's dad folded the newspaper and set it on the table.

"I am in a hurry." Sam didn't look at his dad. He placed slices of cheese and turkey on the bread as if it were a delicate process. They had had a nice two-sentence conversation about dashed dreams and now everything was back to normal.

"I thought you were going over to Anthony's tonight." Sam's mom dried the breakfast dishes and put them away in the cabinets. "How's he doing?"

"I am. I'll probably be out all day."

"I told you, Betty. He's going off to be with those freaks causing a ruckus in the park." Sam's dad jutted his chin at him. "No respect for authority. No respect for your brother that came home."

It was supposed to be a good day, some spent with Danny, Jack, and Nick, fighting the fight he couldn't ignore. And then the night with Anthony, the reason why this fight was so important. Any time spent arguing with this dad would be wasted. "Yep. You got it right."

Sam's dad slammed the kitchen table and slid his chair across the vinyl tile with green diamonds. "You're not going."

"I am."

Sam's mom stepped forward with a frying pan and a dish towel in her hand. "It's dangerous. There's this curfew and if everyone doesn't follow it or things start to get rowdy—"

He had his hand on the doorknob but Sam sharply turned. "Dangerous? Do you know what's dangerous? Trying to avoid mines and clouds of napalm—"

"Don't talk to your mother like that." Sam's dad shook a finger at him.

"Like what?" Sam threw up his hands. "What am I saying that's wrong or rude? Sitting in a park with my friends isn't dangerous.

At least it shouldn't be." Sam flung open the door.

"Be careful, honey. Please." Sam's mom looked as if she were sending another son off to war.

"I will." Sam turned to his dad to get any parting words from him. He shook his head as if looking at a lost cause. "You're the professor, right? You know everything. More than everyone else."

"I know what I think." Sam jumped down the three porch steps, and jogged to the bus stop.

As Sam got off the bus and trotted into Lincoln Park, finding himself lost in a sea of what had to be well over a thousand people, he glanced at his watch. He attempted to calculate how long it would take to get back to the South Side and then over to Anthony's house. He had at least a few good hours and couldn't be late.

The statue of Ulysses S. Grant stood high above the crowd and it was swarming with people in fringe vests and love beads, waving the peace sign. A low *ooooom* came from somewhere and Sam had to do a double take. It was him. It was Allen Ginsberg, sitting under a tree, surrounded by over a dozen people with their eyes closed and joining him in his *ooooom*.

Far out.

Sam finally weaved his way to the base of the statue, wondering how he was going to find Danny among all these people.

"Sam! Over here!"

Sam turned to see Danny coming up behind him with Jack and Nick close by. The same feeling he had had while chanting at Dow and walking at the Dr. King demonstration filled his chest. He belonged here. He knew it.

Danny clapped Sam on the back in a quick hug. "Welcome to the Festival of Life." He gestured to the park as if unveiling the entrance to a magical world.

"The Festival of Life?" Sam asked. He heard drum beats, guitar strums, and the low murmur of a hundred conversations. Everyone looked happy. Everyone was having a good time. The name fit.

"That's what we're doing, right?" Nick spread out his arms.

"Celebrating life? Celebrating how everyone has the right to live and not be forced to go somewhere they're going to get blown up?"

The warm feeling inside of Sam turned icy as he glanced at Danny. Here he was at the Festival of Life when he was heading to the very place they wanted to stop people from going to. But Danny looked as calm as Allen Ginsberg under the tree, starting up another round of *ooooom*. Sam gulped, trying to push the icy feeling away. If Danny could forget about that for the day, or at least pretend to, then Sam could too. He was good at pretending.

But it was hard to pretend this was simply a celebration of life and feeling good with the lines of police officers in blue helmets, and the National Guard members with guns in their hands spread out in small groups throughout the park.

"Hello there, good sir." Danny lifted an imaginary hat off his head and tipped it to a police officer.

The officer tightened his grip on his baton with a smirk. "See you at eleven, kid."

"Eleven?" Danny responded in surprise. "I'll be home by then, counting sheep." He elbowed Sam with a smirk before heading to the other side of the Ulysses S. Grant statue where Sam got a better look at the amount of people in Lincoln Park. He'd never spent any time here before. The few times he'd driven past, it looked like an open field in a busy city. Today, it looked like it was about to burst.

"Eleven?" Sam asked Danny.

Danny shook his head. "Curfew. Rumor has it, it's going to get ugly tonight."

Sam couldn't help but think of the tear gas and bleeding heads from the Dow demonstration. This was on a completely different level.

"Are you going to stick around to see what happens?" Danny asked.

Sam glanced at his watch, shaking his head. "I don't think so. I should cut out by five." The turkey sandwich he wolfed down while waiting for the bus churned in Sam's stomach. Something big was about to happen. History in the making, just like Suzy had told him so many times. But there was also something waiting for him on the other side of the city that made this fight much more important. With the *oooom* chant starting up again and a band starting to play, Sam told himself he would leave by 4:45 to make sure he was at Anthony's in time.

"At least you're here now. Plenty of people were too scared to show up. Even some of the bands. But they got MC-5 to play." Danny pointed to a cluster of guys with guitars. They all had hair almost down to their shoulders except for one who had a mass of curly hair that stood a foot off his head.

"MC-5?" Sam asked.

"Yep. There's supposed to be other acts. We'll see if they show up." Danny scanned the park as if musicians would somehow materialize out of the crowds and begin playing a set.

A hand thrust a business card in Sam and Danny's face. "If you know of anyone who needs some help, have them call me." They turned away from the band to see a guy who looked a little older than them, wearing glasses, brown slacks, and a yellow button-up shirt.

Sam and Danny glanced at the card and learned that the guy worked for a Legal Aid office on the South Side. Legal Aid?

"Just in case," the guy said. "More guards were called in. Daley is going to enforce the curfew as soon as the clock strikes eleven."

Danny took the card. "Thanks, man."

"Anyone who needs some help," the guy started walking away. "Call me." He then walked up to a group of girls in long skirts and gave them a card too.

"See what I mean," Danny said. "Someone on the other side working for our side. We got Mr. Legal Aid over there. I'll be on the inside once I ship out." He gave Sam a confident smile. "We're gonna finally end this. Plus, my dad thinks it's a good career move since no one from the pyramids is knocking on my door yet."

"You bet." Sam tried to sound as confident as Danny.

"Come on, let's go check out the band." Danny led Sam through a sea of people. If this was the Festival of Life, Sam decided he better be a good participant and take part in all that the festival had to offer.

A couple hours later, Sam's feet were getting sore from standing around and walking so much. He glanced at his watch more in the last twenty minutes than he had all day. If he was going to catch the bus and get to Anthony's by six, he should have left three minutes ago.

"What's up, Professor?" Danny asked.

"Yeah," Nick said. "You and that watch going steady or something?"

"No," Sam tried to laugh. "But I need to get going. I have something I need to do at six."

Jack and Nick gave each other a look. "Already?" Jack said. "It hasn't even gotten started yet." He jerked his head at the band that had been playing all afternoon. Danny had said there were supposed to be more bands, but so far, none of the other acts showed up.

"I want to be here, I do." Sam sidestepped away from the guys. "I'm bummed because I feel like I haven't really contributed to the cause today, you know?"

"You haven't contributed?" Danny rolled his eyes. "Just by being here, you've done something. I bet there's a lot of people sitting at home right now, wishing they had the balls to come out and be a part of this and take a stand for something."

Sam half-smiled. "It seems like everyone else is doing so much more."

"Come on, Professor," Danny rolled his eyes. "Did you run out when you found out what the three of us had going on over on Mifflin?"

Sam thought about Danny's binder filled with notes, names, and places. "Nope."

"Did you go straight to the fuzz and tell them about it?"

"No."

"See? One of the coolest cats I know. Right, guys?" Danny nodded at Jack and Nick.

"Not too many people could stand more than a few days on that couch," Nick said. "That's impressive."

Sam glanced at his watch. He needed to go. As far as he could tell, the traffic on Lake Shore Drive didn't look too backed up. He scanned the crowded park. A girl with a flower wreath in her hair started tapping a tambourine against her leg in rhythm with the band. If her hair was lighter, it might have been Suzy. If he saw her at school in the fall, he'd have to tell her about the high praise bestowed upon him by the Kings of Mifflin.

"All right," Sam said with another sidestep. "I'm gonna cut out."

Danny, Jack, and Nick held up peace signs in response. Sam looked at his hand as if he didn't know it was capable of making the gesture. He held up his pointer and middle finger and waved at them as he weaved his way through the crowd.

Sam tried to anticipate the way the people in front of him would move as he made his way out of the park. Some were swaying, lost in a cloud of smoke with a distinct odor. Now that he was on his way home, he realized how much ground he had to cover in a short amount of time. Sam focused on a space far ahead of him, determined to reach it. But then someone crossed his line of vision and he almost tripped over his feet.

"Maria?"

A girl with a purple wreath of flowers resting on her long black hair turned around at the sound of her name. Her eyes widened and her mouth dropped.

"What are you doing here?" Sam forgot all about his mission to get out of the park as quickly as possible. "I thought you were spending the night at Sheila's."

Maria looked at Sam as if she had caught him doing something wrong. She crossed her arms over a white T-shirt with a peace sign drawn on it. One wrist had a yellow bandana tied around it. "How do you know that?"

"Anthony told me. I'm heading over to your house now." Dammit. He shouldn't have mentioned Sheila. Was there any way Maria could put all the pieces together?

"You're going to see Anthony?" A look of urgency filled her eyes as Maria gripped Sam's arms.

Sam glanced at the fingernails digging into his skin. "Yeah."

"Don't tell him I'm here. Don't tell my parents. Don't tell anyone." With each sentence her fingernails dug in a little more.

"No one knows you're here?" Sam asked, looking around for someone Maria might have come with.

"Just Sheila. Her parents think we went to another friend's house."

"Get out of here by eleven," Sam said. "I've heard from a few people that shit's going to hit the fan after curfew."

Maria laughed. "Eleven? We have to be back to Sheila's by ten. Her parents are cool but they're not *that* cool."

Sam looked at the seconds ticking by on his watch. "Listen, I need to go. But please be careful."

"I will," Maria said. "Please don't tell anyone."

"I won't," Sam promised. "I mean it."

"Does Anthony know you're here?" Maria asked. She blended in so well with all the other flower children, looking so much different than the girl he made faces at over the dinner table.

Sam inhaled a mouthful of air drenched with pot. "No."

"Well, I don't think he'll hate you for it," Maria said.

"Good to know." Sam looked beyond Maria and swore the park was filling up before his eyes. "I need to book. Be careful."

"I will. I'm going to catch up with Sheila." Maria gestured to someone in a sea of people. "Bye, Sam." She waved a peace sign at him with a smile before heading further into Lincoln Park.

Maria blended in with the crowd before Sam could give her a peace sign back. Passing by a pile of clothes by a sign that said *free store*, he pushed his way toward Lake Shore Drive. The bus stop got closer and closer. Even if traffic was completely clear there was no way he was going to make it on time.

AUGUST 25, 1968

Anthony sat at the kitchen table, literally twiddling his thumbs. First backward. Then forward. Then backward again. The last time he looked at the clock, it was 5:58. He had been crawling out of his skin ever since getting back from the party. Maybe it was being around so many familiar faces who didn't know anything about him anymore. His mom added to it, insisting that Anthony eat something before she and his dad left. But it was nice to have Maria smile at him on her way to Sheila's.

The clock caught his eye. It was 6:07. Anthony stood and paced into the family room and flopped on the green couch, as if being in a different location would somehow make Sam appear. He thought about turning on the TV but that would mean getting up to turn the knob and there wasn't much to watch on a Sunday evening anyway.

He picked up the issue of *Hot Rod* that came in the mail a few weeks ago but hadn't flipped through yet. Anthony opened it, ready to scan the table of contents, when he found the pink envelope from Lorraine tucked inside. He'd forgotten that he'd put it in there. Anthony wrote her back, telling her about Capper, the guy who wasn't fazed by Jersey's badass attitude, the guy who saved his cake in a can until it was time to camp out for the night, and the guy Anthony was most proud to serve with. That was the Capper he knew. He had asked Lorraine what Capper had said about California. Sometimes, when Anthony woke up in the middle of the night, forgetting that he was safe in his bed and not out in the fields, he'd remember flying into San Francisco and how the city went right up against the ocean and disappeared into the tall trees.

Was he wigging out for thinking of going to the ocean? For thinking that some place far away from the streets and people he knew would help him feel normal again? Anthony was sick of waiting around in general, not just waiting for Sam. Every soldier's goal was to come home, and he accomplished that goal. But now what? His job at Politti's gave him money but he could work at a garage anywhere. He even started crawling under cars last week instead of being stuck with apprentice-type duties. The soreness and stiffness was still there, but now it was from working hard all day. Anthony only thought about his leg on his walks home when it reminded him he wasn't quite at one hundred percent.

As the clock ticked to 6:21, Anthony got off the couch and headed to the big window at the front of his house, hoping to catch a glimpse of Sam. As he was about to lift the curtain to get a good view of the street, the front door opened and Sam stumbled inside. His dark hair was stuck to his forehead with sweat and dark sweat patches spotted the back of his T-shirt and armpits.

"I'm sorry I'm late. I ran all the way from the bus stop." Sam walked over to Anthony and swept him up in a tight hug. "I'm sorry."

"What happened?"

Sam shook his head, searching for words but not saying anything. Anthony studied Sam's face. "What's going on?"

"I was in Lincoln Park. Riding the bus from there took longer than I thought."

"Lincoln Park?" The image of the crowds swarming the east side of Lake Shore Drive sprang into Anthony's head. "You were up there?"

Sam grabbed Anthony's hand and dragged him towards the stairs. "Can you just put on some Beach Boys and we'll be together and everything will be okay?" When they got to Anthony's room, Sam went to the record player but didn't put on any music. He stood in front of it with his hands on either side of it, taking deep breaths.

"What's going on?" Anthony asked.

Sam turned. "Just come here. Please." He took off his shirt, threw it on the floor, and held out his arms.

Anthony ripped off his striped T-shirt and melted into Sam's warm body. He wrapped his arms around him, smelling the faint odor of Speed Stick through the layer of sweat. Sam held Anthony's face in his hands and kissed him again and again and again. Anthony tried to kiss him back but Sam moved his mouth to different parts of his face.

Anthony shuffled toward his bed, not breaking his embrace from Sam. They lay on their sides, staring at one another. Anthony inwardly smiled at the farmer tan that perfectly made the outline of a shirt on Sam's arms and chest. Sam grinned as he looked Anthony up and down, but the grin suddenly fell from his face.

"What?" Anthony asked.

Sam averted his gaze.

Anthony followed Sam's eyes and landed on his side, where a two-inch long scar ran under his rib cage. The stitches were long gone but it still looked like they were there. It was less red now, more of a pinkish white, which stood out even more against his olive skin.

"It doesn't hurt anymore," Anthony said. Every time he got out of the shower and toweled himself off, it was a fresh reminder of what he had endured and what he had seen, and each time he had to tell those images to go back where they belonged.

Sam half smiled. "That's good to hear." He sat up, propping himself up on an arm. "I need you to know something."

His expression grew serious and Anthony wished he would smirk at him the way he used to.

"I need you to know that I love you."

A warmth filled Anthony's chest. "I love you too."

"And I need you to know I think you are incredible for volunteering to go over there and fight," Sam rushed on.

Anthony wanted to sit with Sam's words and let them wash all over him but his expression told him there was more to say.

"I'm not against you. I'll never be against you," Sam went on. "I'm against people getting hurt and people being forced to do something they don't want to do."

"I know. You told me this already. I dig it."

Sam looked out Anthony's window. "There's some shit going down in Grant Park and I want to be there—"

"Not here?"

"No, that's not what I mean." Sam struggled to find words.

Anthony remembered the image of the crowd camped out in Lincoln Park and news footage of them waving peace signs at the camera and holding up signs asking LBJ how many kids he killed today. He didn't know the count, but the answer was many kids. Too many kids. As Anthony looked into Sam's desperate eyes, he thought about how a plane full of new recruits were probably headed over there at that moment. Some of them would never make it home.

"Come with me," Sam said.

"What?" Anthony pushed away the image of a mine exploding on a still, dark night. "Where?"

"On Wednesday. Come with me to Grant Park."

"Are you serious?" Anthony had heard of guys who came back and marched in the streets against the war. His dad had grunted upon hearing the story. But his dad didn't go over there. The war he had fought in had clear good guys and bad guys. A clear beginning and end. This one seemed endless. He wasn't betraying everyone he fought with by going, right? If the goal of the people in Grant Park and Lincoln Park was for the war to end, well, that was Anthony's goal too. "I don't know."

"It's the night of the nomination and our last chance to get the right candidate in office," Sam explained. "Please. Come be a part of it."

Anthony imagined himself standing in the park of hippies, flower children, love beads, and peace signs. "I still get tired after work sometimes. I don't know how late I'll be able to make it."

"You get tired or think it's boring? We'll cut out," Sam promised. "You've been around the world and survived a war. A walk in the park will be pretty tame in comparison."

It was a good point. If he could go around the world, he could definitely make it a few miles north. If Charlie couldn't take him out, a park full of Glorias didn't have a chance. Plus, it was time with Sam, and that was something he couldn't pass up. Especially with him going back to school in a few weeks. "I've driven by Grant Park so many times, but I don't think I've ever spent any time there before."

Sam smiled. "Well, I remember you saying you wanted to go somewhere new." He made a face that said *you're welcome.*

"Going someplace new with you is even better," Anthony said. He glanced at the clock by his bed. His parents would be home in an hour. "Anywhere with you is better. Even my room."

That beautiful smirk of a smile crossed Sam's face as he leaned in, touching his forehead to Anthony's for a few seconds before kissing him again.

Anthony felt himself getting swept in Sam, breathing in to take in as much of him as possible. For now, the noises in his head were quiet. There were no mines, no screams, no endless nights. If only he could get his parents to play bridge every night. Or live in a world where he didn't have to sneak around in empty houses and behind locked doors to be with the person he loved.

AUGUST 28, 1968

After two nights of news footage showing police officers waving nightsticks at demonstrators and demonstrators throwing bottles at police officers, Sam called Anthony and asked him if he still wanted to go. Based on what he saw on Saturday and Sunday, Sam knew the fuzz were waiting for the second the clock struck eleven, just like some people in the park purposely loitered after curfew.

"Are *you* still going tonight?" Anthony had called Sam as soon as he got home from work.

"Yep."

"Then I am too. Some angry hippies and stupid cops don't scare me," Anthony responded.

They headed for the bus stop together after Anthony got cleaned up. While sweating on the ride north to Grant Park, Anthony grumbled about having to lie to his parents about where he was going. "Ma told me to be careful and to stay away from where it's not safe. Don't you think I know a thing or two about going somewhere that's not safe?"

"I had to lie too," Sam said. He had told his parents he and Anthony were going to see *Hang 'Em High* and probably get a slice or a Coke afterwards. It was believable since they knew Anthony was a big Clint Eastwood fan. Sam's dad told him to stay clear of the freaks and their shenanigans.

When they arrived at Grant Park, Sam thought it resembled two very different scenes from his college campus. All the kids stretched out on the grass reminded him of study breaks on Bascom Hill. But with the groups of police officers in blue helmets clutching nightsticks and standing in formation throughout the park, it was the Dow Demonstration times a thousand. Only this time, members of the National Guard with their rifles out also lined the sidewalks.

With the sun beating down on them and heat coming from the thick crowd, Sam led Anthony to the bandshell. He had no idea how he was supposed to find Jack and Nick among the thousands of people in the park and the hundreds sitting in the benches that made a half moon around the stage.

Sam looked up and down the aisles and on the stage, hoping to spot Jack's mass of curls or Nick's tie-dye shirt, but there was a lot of curly hair and tie-dye to sift through.

"I had no idea there'd be so many people," Anthony said.

"There's more people here than there were in Lincoln Park." Sam checked the stairs by the stage again and then the front of the stage. No sign of Nick and Jack. Just as he was about to tell Anthony he had no idea how to find them, he squinted and grinned. At the side of the stage with a red bandana making his hair poof out on top of his head stood Jack. "Come on. Over here."

"Professor, you made it," Jack called out to him. "And you brought a friend."

"This is Anthony." Sam introduced him to Jack and Nick.

"The more the merrier. And as long as there's more of us than there are of them," Nick jutted his chin at the police officers and guards, "I'd say we're in good shape."

"First, we party in the park," Jack held up his pointer finger. "Then, we all march to the convention to give all those bozos one of these." He held up his middle finger with a grin.

"I don't think I've ever seen so many people in one spot." Anthony turned to get a look at the whole bandshell and the people filling practically every seat.

"We could have had one more, but Danny had to cut out a

day early," Jack said.

"He really went, huh?" Sam nodded to himself. He knew Danny wasn't going to be at Grant Park today, but that didn't stop him from feeling his absence.

"He *said* he was going to Fort Knox," Nick raised his eyebrows, "but he knows better than anyone that a notice is nothing more than an invitation from Uncle Sam. Attendance is not required."

"He's going," Jack said. "He'll write as soon as he can. If the return address says Kentucky then we have our answer."

Maybe it was the conversation, the thousands of people in one spot, or the perimeter of police lining the park, but Sam's shirt went from damp to wet. He glanced at Anthony, who looked like a college kid hanging out in the common area in between classes. If the talk about Danny and the draft bothered him, he didn't show it. He looked way more relaxed than back in Madison when they went to that party with Suzy and Gloria.

Sam was about to crack a joke about Gloria to Anthony but he suddenly seemed distracted. Anthony squinted at something over Sam's head. Sam turned, following Anthony's gaze and saw the flag-pole off to the side of the stage with Old Glory hanging limply in the summer heat.

"What's that kid doing?" Nick asked.

Someone about Sam's age was shimmying up the flagpole. The crowd caught sight of him in a matter of seconds. Shouts of encouragement and cheering erupted from some pockets while gasps came from others.

As the kid advanced upward, the line of police officers began to move. "Shit," Jack shook his head. "He's giving them exactly what they want."

By the time the kid cut down the flag and slid down the pole, the police surrounded the base, nightsticks in the air, pushing aside and striking anyone in their way. Screams and shouts filled the air.

The feeling of being at a big summer party immediately vanished. Sam had expected the day to turn, but thought it would happen closer to curfew. "We need to get out of here." He searched for a way out of the park. The path he and Anthony took into the park was now filled with a line of police officers advancing toward them.

A wave of blue helmets chased everyone spilling onto Michigan Avenue. Jack and Nick headed for the west side of the street and Sam ran to catch up with them. He felt Anthony behind him, matching his stride. Thank god for the red bandana wrapped around Jack's head. It made it easier to keep an eye on him. The sound of a baseball bat hitting a watermelon came from somewhere behind them. Someone with blood streaming from their forehead raced past him, clutching the wound.

"Where are we going?" Anthony yelled.

"I have no idea," Sam turned his head ever so slightly to yell back. If he turned all the way around, he might have lost sight of Jack. The red bandana angled a little to the right and Sam followed. He grabbed a hold of Anthony's arm and pulled him along. It was hard to break free from the swarm of people. It was a tangle of arms and legs, with each one trying to go in a different direction.

At first, the goal was to march to the convention. Now the goal was to not get arrested or killed.

Those on the other side of Michigan Avenue pumped their fists in the air, chanting, "The world is watching! The world is watching!"

The world *was* watching. The world was watching Sam and everyone else flooding the Chicago streets. He knew the words to the chant and wanted to join in but saw another wave of blue helmets slicing through the crowd.

"Damn right the world is watching!" Jack yelled as he weaved through the maze of people. It was as if he'd been in this exact situation several times and knew what to do.

As the blue helmets came from every direction, the amount of people swelled. It was hard to tell the safest place to go to. Should they run further west? North? Any flash of powder blue made Sam wince and brace for the impact of a club against his head.

He glanced back at Anthony, whose eyes were also locked on something in front of him. His expression was serious and focused as if strategizing how to win a long race.

With his eyes on Jack's bandana, Sam thought about how Danny would know what to do in this situation. He would have had an escape plan mapped out, anticipating that this was going to happen.

Two cops dragged someone by the arms to a paddy wagon parked nearby. They didn't give Sam or his friends a glance as they tossed the person inside. The fuzz broke through the crowd, dragging people across the street to throw them in. They had people by their arms, their legs, their hair, their clothes. A lady who appeared to be older than Sam's mom but about six inches shorter, tried to escape the paddy wagon and was shoved back inside. With hands and feet fighting for a spot near the open door, it was slammed shut.

"The world is watching! The world is watching!"

Standing in the middle of Michigan Avenue, a cloud of tear gas filled the air on one side of Sam. Jack ripped off his bandana and held it over his nose and mouth. Anthony tucked the bottom half of his face into his T-shirt. Wails and cries screamed above the chant as batons connected with heads, arms, and backs.

A couple bottles sailed over Sam's head and shattered upon hitting the ground. There were some people up ahead throwing rocks and Sam knew their goal was to hit the fuzz but a couple barely missed him.

"You okay?" Sam asked Anthony. With his face tucked into his T-shirt, Sam could only see his eyes.

"Run up ahead, Capper. I'll cover you." Anthony crouched slightly, focusing on the people running by.

"Capper? He's not—"

A collective scream interrupted Sam. Nightsticks swung through the air, striking anything in their way.

"Run! Run!" Jack found some speed from somewhere and took off, heading north on Michigan.

With no other option, Sam took off after Jack. "We gotta move," he yelled back to Anthony who was a couple steps behind.

A huge crash came from somewhere and Sam's hands flew to cover his head as if that would provide any protection from flying debris. When he looked off to the side, he saw that the huge window of the Hilton Hotel had been broken and bodies of demonstrators lay among the shards of glass. Several blue helmets stood in front of the destroyed window. He glanced back at Anthony whose eyes were focused and dark, seemingly oblivious to chaos going on around him.

The more they ran, the more they found room to move and the crowd thinned out ever so slightly. "Where are we going?" Nick yelled.

"I have no idea!" Jack responded. "Keep moving!" He waved his bandana in the air, motioning further down Michigan Avenue.

Suddenly, fireworks went off behind Sam's eyes and pain radiated from up his arm, to his shoulder, and down his back. It took everything in his power to not collapse right there on the street and get trampled. With his arm throbbing and limp at his side, Sam stumbled and regained his footing.

"Keep going, Professor!" Nick yelled.

Sam saw a blue helmet inches from him, raising his nightstick for another blow. He couldn't get his legs to move any faster. Wincing, Sam braced himself for what was coming. But a loud grunt followed by a dull thud sounded instead.

Sam turned to see the cop stumble back a few steps and Anthony standing right in front of him, rubbing his knuckles.

****

Anthony shook out his hand, bringing the feeling back into his fingers. He raised his fist again, ready to deliver another blow. It wasn't some Chicago cop in front of him. It was the VC who had stabbed him. That day, the VC got the better of him, but Anthony had the advantage now. He glanced at the group of soldiers to his side. QB held his arm. Picasso and Lennox stood a few feet ahead. Again, Anthony had let Capper down, and this time, Charlie was going to pay.

Charlie stood, his gun swinging at anything around him, the bayonet millimeters from Anthony's face. He weaved out of the way, just like how Dalton had taught him in Basic. Anthony focused on Charlie's face, the dark eyes, and black hair falling over his forehead. This was his chance. He needed to take it. Anthony pulled his fist back to his ear but before he could take a swing, someone pulled him back at the waist. He was being carried away. Shit. Charlie got him. He'd punched one of their buddies and now they were taking him away to who knew where. Anthony squirmed and thrashed, desperate to get out of their clutches.

"Anthony, come on."

It was Sam.

Anthony tried to break free from Sam's grasp. "No way. That fucker got Capper. I'm not gonna let him take you too."

"Capper's not here," Sam yelled, his eyes frantically looking further north. "And no one's going to get me."

"We gotta get out of here," Jack said.

Anthony felt the world closing in on him. Something in his chest tightened as he struggled to breathe. He didn't need to save Capper because he was already gone.

A guy ran by, clutching his head, his long hair matted down with blood. "Medic," Anthony called out. "We need a medic!" But QB wasn't going to come. This wasn't Vietnam. This was Chicago.

"Over here. Come on," Sam panted, starting to run again.

Anthony heard the order but couldn't move. It was like he was observing the scene through a screen that made everything hazy. He felt Sam pull him along, and felt his feet moving forward.

"You know where we're going?" Nick asked as they hurried down a flight of stairs that led to the 'L' station.

"Yup. Follow me." Sam pushed his way through a turnstile and onto the platform.

As a train approached, Anthony craned his neck to the wall of bricks that formed the tunnel of the station. He didn't remember the last time he rode the 'L.' Maybe it was when his class went on a field trip to the history museum. That was a long time ago. Maybe elementary school.

The doors to the train slid open and everyone piled inside, flopping on the first set of open seats. Anthony and Sam sat on one side of the doors, facing Jack and Nick.

Once the doors closed, Jack's face broke into a grin. "Outta sight, Professor. That was a badass plan."

Sam let out a big breath as the train departed and headed for the dark tunnel. "That wasn't a plan. It just popped into my head and it worked."

"That was superhero quality," Nick said. "Something Danny would have done."

While Sam beamed at the compliment, Anthony saw his reflection in the window behind Jack and Nick. He found himself reciting facts to himself: *I'm in Chicago. I'm on the 'L.' There are no VC on this train.*

"And you," Jack grinned and nodded at Anthony. "You just clocked that cop. That's a whole new level of badass."

It was similar to coming back to the barracks after spending time out in the field and recapping the victories. Anthony focused on his reflection, trying to understand what was going on in the head of the person staring back at him.

****

Anthony and Sam got off at the next stop to catch a train heading south, leaving Jack and Nick to continue onto Division and the place where they were crashing for another night. Anthony seemed tired, like he did after their pizza date that really wasn't a date. He alternated between closing his eyes in a really long blink and staring ahead. Sam couldn't tell if he was scared, sad, or angry. And he had no idea what to say. The plan wasn't to drag Anthony into another battle after he'd come home from being in an actual war. As they walked down the sidewalk, the night was still and quiet in comparison to the scene on Michigan Avenue.

"I think you saved me back there," Sam said. "I don't think that cop would have stopped swinging if you didn't hit him."

Anthony didn't respond. He kept walking with a determined stride, his eyes fixed on something ahead.

"I knew there might be a scuffle with the cops but nothing like that." Sam quickened his pace to keep up with Anthony.

Anthony gave a little nod and kept walking, slightly dragging his leg behind him.

"Hey, are you okay?" Sam asked.

Anthony responded with a quick noise that either meant yes or that he had heard Sam.

"I'm sorry for asking you to go with me. I didn't know it would be that bad." Sam saw tears falling from Anthony's eyes as he blinked again and again. Finally he doubled over and let out a loud sob.

Sam wanted to grab Anthony and hold him but they were in the middle of the sidewalk a block away from Anthony's house. "What can I do? Tell me what to do."

"It was bad, Sam. Really bad." Anthony choked out. "All of it."

****

Anthony lowered himself into one of the chairs on his patio. He could see his mom through the little window above the sink, smiling at Sam. If Sam made a comment about how the house smelled good from the chicken she had made for dinner, Anthony's mom wouldn't give a second thought to her son sitting outside.

Sam had led him home and to the backyard, telling him everything would be okay and that he'd take care of him. Anthony wanted to believe him, but how could Sam take care of him? Sam would go home soon. He would go back to school in a couple weeks. He couldn't hide under Anthony's bed every night and remind him he was home in Chicago whenever he woke up in the middle of the night.

Anthony couldn't shake the image of the VC going after Capper. But it wasn't Capper, it was Sam. And it wasn't a VC, it was a cop. It was a good thing Sam, Jack, and Nick dragged him away. He was ready to kill that cop with his bare hands.

The back door opened. The noise shook Anthony out of the mixed-up memory. Sam set down a Coke and sat across from him. "I told your mom the movie was good. Not as good as *The Good, the Bad, and the Ugly*, but still pretty good."

Anthony took a long drink. The bubbles and the cold stung his throat.

"I'm sorry—"

"Don't be," Anthony interrupted. "I knew it wasn't going to be a picnic in the park."

"But it wasn't supposed to be a battle for Michigan Avenue either." The porchlight by the door illuminated Sam from behind, making it difficult to see his face. "I thought after you came home, things would be different. The war would be closer to being over and we would figure out what to do next, together. But this war is fucking everything up."

Anthony picked up his Coke and ran his hand up and down the bottle, wiping off the condensation. Capper always joked that the soda was sweatier than they were. Anthony took another drink and set the bottle down. "I think I need to get away, Sam."

Sam sat up, knocking his knees on the table. "All right. Where do you want to go? Let's go."

"No, I mean *away*." Anthony raked a hand through his growing hair. "Totally away. Away from everything."

"Where do you want to go?"

"I was thinking California. San Francisco. Like we talked about."

Ever since getting Lorraine's letter, Anthony had been thinking about his bird's eye view of the city when he was on his way home just a couple months ago. Maybe the rush of excitement he felt when landing in San Francisco wasn't because he was back from across the pond but because he was supposed to be there. Anthony would love to tell Lorraine that he made it to California. "Come with me."

"How about Madison? Jack and Nick think you're a cool cat. There's an empty room with Danny gone—"

"What would we do? Wait for Nick and Jack to leave so we could have the place to ourselves and then just pretend the rest of the time like we always do?" Anthony wanted to scream but if his mom heard anything, she'd be out in a second. "I'm so sick of pretending. I pretend that I'm fine and that nothing hurts so Ma doesn't ask me a million questions. I pretend that I'm okay with whatever happened over there so my pops doesn't try to talk to me about it."

Sam reached across the table and grasped Anthony's hands. "You don't have to pretend with me."

Anthony felt a sob rise in chest. One that was on the same scale as the one on the sidewalk. "I've been pretending ever since I got back. Pretending that I could just go back to walking the same four blocks and working at the same garage, and if I pretended hard enough everything would be fine."

"What can I do?" Sam leaned over the table. Anthony heard the tears in his voice. "Tell me what I need to do. Should I drop out of school? Transfer? What?"

With Sam's hands gripping Anthony's, they looked into each other's eyes. Silence hung between them as stark realization slapped both of them in the face. Anthony turned, his chin digging into his shoulder. This was going to hurt way more than the two bullets that struck his leg. That was nothing. Send him back Vietnam. Let him come face to face with Charlie. That he could handle. Not this.

Sam breathed in sharply and stood. He walked over to the back part of the house, away from the kitchen window. The same place they hid after the lasagna dinner when Anthony first got back. Anthony scraped his chair against the concrete slab, and followed Sam. The fence was tall enough. This part of the yard was dark. Everyone in the house was busy.

Anthony wrapped his arms around Sam in a tight hug.

"I thought that if you came home we would be okay because we were together," Sam said into Anthony's hair. "I thought it would be easy."

"This…" Anthony whispered, pointing to Sam and then back to himself, "this was never easy. And even though it's what I want more than anything, I don't know how to do this right now." A messy sob choked him. "But I don't know what to do without you."

Sam straightened and put his hands on either side of Anthony's face. "You can do anything. You've done so many things without me. You survived a war without me."

"I got through it because of you." Anthony put his hand to his chest, like he was afraid his heart would somehow pour out of his body. He needed to take this next step. How could he do it without Sam?

"And you're going to get through everything else," Sam sounded way more confident than Anthony felt. "And when you're through with this part and figure out what comes next, let me know, okay? You know where I'll be."

They leaned their wet faces toward one another, foreheads touching, breathing deeply. Anthony inhaled, hoping to breathe in as much of

Sam as he could. Just like when he left for Basic last summer, this was what he would take with him.

SEPTEMBER 8, 1968

When Sam walked into the empty apartment on Mifflin, it smelled like his closet when he left a week's worth of laundry on the floor. On the counter, Sam could see the corner of the binder. He had no idea what he was doing. Hopefully the information in the binder would be enough to get him started, along with some tutoring from Jack and Nick. They had confidence in his ability to evade the fuzz in the middle of a riot. Maybe Sam could also figure out how to help guys evade the draft.

Sam set a box on the floor and put his pillow on the armrest of the couch. He could have had Danny's old room but he was drawn to the old blue couch. Sam reached inside the pillowcase and pulled out a letter that he had folded into a sleeve of the Snoopy T-shirt. It arrived three days ago and Sam already had it memorized.

Sam,

I want to let you know that I'm okay. I've been staying at the Army Navy YMCA for about a week now. It's right by the ocean. I mean RIGHT by it. I can see the waves from my window. Sometimes the traffic dies down at night and I think I can hear them. I got a job at this garage about five blocks away and I know what you're thinking. I had to go to San Francisco to still work at a garage? I guess so. It's what I know how to do. My boss there said he couldn't believe I was only nineteen and knew so much about cars. I saw a sign at this diner for a short order cook and then this supermarket was hiring. I know I can learn how to stock shelves, but I don't want to. I don't know what I want to learn and do with the rest of my life. I'm just taking it one day at a time. Sometimes one hour at a time. Ma doesn't get it. Pops doesn't get it. I don't know how to make them see that just because every other Italian boy stays home until they're married doesn't mean I have to. Maria gets it. She gets more than I give her credit for. Ma wants to know how long I'll be gone and I don't know. It's quieter here in a way that I can't explain. It's still a big city, but not as big as Chicago. Maybe I'll get around to seeing all of it.

There's some other guys staying here that were over there. We don't talk about it but it's something we know about each other. I think we're all trying to figure out what comes next. I'll let you know when I do. Living here is probably like being in college. I have my own room and there's a cafeteria downstairs with an ice cream freezer and a condiments counter. The ketchup is always well stocked.

If you have a chance between classes and your extracurricular activities, write me back. Tell Jack and Nick I say hi.

Anthony

When footsteps sounded on the stairs leading up to the apartment, Sam quickly folded the letter and tucked it into the Snoopy shirt and then put the shirt under his pillow.

"Bitchin'. You're already here." Jack grinned upon seeing Sam. "You ready for another year at ol' UW?"

"Ready." Sam scanned the apartment that would soon be energized as he, Nick, and Jack unpacked their stuff and opened the case of beer Jack held. The blue floral couch was still there. The binder was still there. Anthony's Snoopy shirt was still there. Some things didn't change.

"Can't get ready for another year without some music." Nick set his record player on the little table by the couch and combed through the milk crate of records he had kicked over to the corner. "Maybe something to remind us of summer? Mamas and the Papas? The Beach Boys?"

Jack pretended to throw up. "Seriously, dude, The Beach Boys?"

"Shut up." Nick turned to Sam. "You're the deciding vote. What do you say?" He held up the two records.

Sam recognized the album cover. "Nothing says summer like The Beach Boys. Am I right?"

Jack pretended to throw up again but louder this time. "I'm living with a couple of candyasses."

Nick put the record on and grinned. "Shut it. These candyasses want to listen to some music."

"Wouldn't It Be Nice" started up.

Yes, it would be nice…if he were older, if the war was over, if kids weren't getting hurt, killed, and broken. And one day he would be older and live in a world where the war was over, one where he was done with school and he could figure out what came next and where that would be.

"Anybody need a snack while we unpack?" Jack called from the kitchen. He set a bag of buns on the counter along with a package of Oscar Mayer hotdogs, a bottle of mustard, and a bottle of ketchup. "You want mustard or ketchup, Professor?"

"Ketchup."

"On a hot dog? Don't your people frown on that?" Jack pretended to be shocked. "Are you sure?"

"Absolutely," Sam grinned.

AUTHOR'S NOTE

Many resources and people were involved in making this book as accurate and authentic as possible. I am most indebted to the team at the University of Wisconsin Archives who answered many emails and provided me with documents and resources so I could get a taste of college life in the late 1960's. They even had a campus map from the time so I could trace Sam's trek to and from Mifflin from his dorm. Stu Levitan's Facebook page, "Madison in the 60's," is full of articles and personal accounts of the city and campus during the decade. The American Archive of Public Broadcasting's website has a recording of the speeches given at the University of Wisconsin after Dr. Martin Luther King Junior's assassination. *CharlieCompany.org* is full of personal accounts and facts about training and serving in the Vietnam War. I was fortunate to visit the National Veterans Art Museum in Chicago which has multiple exhibits created by veterans of the Vietnam War. YouTube provided me with videos of Basic Training during the 1960's along with news clips from the time period. Bill Fowler answered my questions about being in the army during this time through emails that were pages long. Susan Lefkow Piggot was at the DNC in 1968 and graciously read those chapters to verify that they rang true. Michael Robbins gave me little details that helped capture the life of a college student during the late 60's.

The following were also instrumental in the writing of this book:

Bingham, Clara. *Witness to the Revolution: Radicals, Resisters, Vets, Hippies, and the Year America Lost Its Mind and Found Its Soul.* New York, Random House, 2016.

Edelman, Bernard. *Dear America: Letters Home from Vietnam.* New York, W.W. Norton & Company, Inc. 1985.

Faderman, Lillian. *The Gay Revolution: The Story of the Struggle.* New York, Simon & Schuster, 2015.

Kurlansky, Mark. *1968: The Year That Rocked the World.* New York, Ballantine Books. 2004.

Maraniss, David. *They Marched Into Sunlight: War and Peace, Vietnam and America, October 1967.* New York City, Simon & Schuster, 2004.

Meyers, Walter Dean. *Fallen Angels.* New York, Scholastic Inc., 1988.

O'Brien, Tim. *If I Die in a Combat Zone Box Me Up and Ship Me Home.* New York, Broadway Books, 1975.

O'Brien, Tim. *The Things They Carried.* New York, Broadway Books, 1990.

Steinman, Ron. *The Soldier's Story: Vietnam in Their Own Words.* New York, Barnes & Noble Books, Inc. 1999.

ACKNOWLEDGEMENTS

In a high school creative writing class, we had to pick from several novels to complete a group project. I wanted to read *What's Eating Gilbert Grape* (because of the movie) but ended up reading *The Things They Carried*. It was the first time I read something and said to myself this is *good* writing. Thank you, Mark Maxwell, for making me believe that I could be a *good* writer too.

A huge hug and thank you to Tina Schwartz, my agent, and Sam Weisz at Trism Books. An even bigger hug to Erica Weisz, my editor, who called me out when I was avoiding writing the hard stuff. She was excited after reading the first few pages and that excitement never dwindled.

This story came to life in Story Studio's Novel in a Year class that was compassionately and awesomely led by Jim Klise. I owe the best snacks and so much more to my NIAY pals: Ines, Ryan, Mandy, Terri, Tanya, Elena, Vanessa, and Deanna. Thank you for loving Anthony and Sam and sticking with them. Our group is going strong after almost four years. Let's never stop.

Thank you, Michelle Silverthorn, for reading the Dr. King chapter several times and telling me that Sam had to "earn" his place at the demonstration.

I want to thank Bill Konigsberg for writing amazing books and for the encouraging feedback he gave me after reading the first ten pages. I need to mention Carl Hauck, who went over this manuscript with a fine tooth comb. Thank you for doing such a careful reading and for being my friend.

My SCBWI pals also deserve a shout-out: Nicole, Malcolm, Wiggy, Alex, Sarah, Leslie, Lesley, and everyone else who drops by our monthly meetings. I love spending time with you.

When my debut novel was released at the beginning of the pandemic, Kristine Campbell (another SCBWI godsend) stepped up and developed a marketing plan for me. Thank you, Kristine. I'm grateful we ran the registration table together at Marvelous Midwest 2019.

A number of people made writing this book possible by simply being a constant in my life. Thank you to Michael and Elda Robbins, Rena Oclon, Kathy Olson, Rachel Anderson, Jenn Leis, and Maureen Ritter.

And of course my three favorites: Matt, Virginia, and Wallace. I love you and want to be my best for you.

ABOUT THE AUTHOR

With a BA in screenwriting and MFA in Fiction, **Kim Oclon** taught high school for six years before becoming a mom to the best girl and boy in the world. While teaching, she was fortunate to teach creative writing and film classes in addition to trudging through the classics. She also co-founded the school's first gender-sexualities alliance. A reader all her life, Kim's first literary loves were a series of Care Bear Books and *Grover's Book of Resting Places*. Eventually she graduated on to *Sweet Valley Twins* and *The Babysitters Club*. Kim is also the author of the contemporary young adult novel, *Man Up*. She lives in East Dundee, Illinois with her husband and two kids. Connect with Kim online at www.kimoclon.com